Murder at Lambswool Farm

OTHER SEASIDE KNITTERS MYSTERIES
BY SALLY GOLDENBAUM

Death by Cashmere

Patterns in the Sand

Moon Spinners

A Holiday Yarn

The Wedding Shawl

A Fatal Fleece

Angora Alibi

Murder in Merino

A Finely Knit Murder

Trimmed with Murder

Murder at Lambswool Farm

A SEASIDE KNITTERS MYSTERY

Sally Goldenbaum

AN OBSIDIAN MYSTERY

OBSIDIAN
Published by New American Library,
an imprint of Penguin Random House LLC
375 Hudson Street, New York, New York 10014

This book is an original publication of New American Library.

First Printing, May 2016

For more information about Penguin Random House, visit penguin.com.

LIBRARY OF CONGRESS CATALOGING-IN-PUBLICATION DATA:

Names: Goldenbaum, Sally, author.
Title: Murder at Lambswool Farm: a Seaside knitters mystery/Sally Goldenbaum.
Description: New York City: NAL, 2016. | Series: Seaside knitters mystery; 11
Identifiers: LCCN 2015047821 (print) | LCCN 2016001088 (ebook) | ISBN 9780451471642 (hardcover) | ISBN 9780698172098 (ebook)
Subjects: LCSH: Knitters (Persons)—Fiction. | Murder—Investigation—Fiction. | City and town life—Massachusetts—Fiction. | BISAC: FICTION/Mystery & Detective/ Women Sleuths. | GSAFD: Mystery fiction.
Classification: LCC PS3557.O35937 M83 2016 (print) | LCC PS3557.O35937 (ebook) | DDC 813/.54—dc23
LC record available at http:/lccn.loc.gov/2015047821

Printed in the United States of America
10 9 8 7 6 5 4 3 2 1

PUBLISHER'S NOTE
This is a work of fiction. Names, characters, places, and incidents either are the product of the author's imagination or are used fictitiously, and any resemblance to actual persons, living or dead, business establishments, events, or locales is entirely coincidental.

The recipe contained in this book is to be followed exactly as written. The publisher is not responsible for your specific health or allergy needs that may require medical supervision. The publisher is not responsible for any adverse reactions to the recipe contained in this book.

This one's for you, Sandy Harding.
My thanks for everything.

Acknowledgments

My thanks to three loyal and cherished friends who have lived with the Seaside Knitters as long as I have: Nancy Pickard, Sr. Rosemary Flanigan, and Mary Bednarowski, who are always there on a couch or at the Tavern happy hour or at the end of an e-mail or phone to brainstorm, console, encourage, and engage in working out motivations and the murder of yet another unsuspecting character.

A special thanks to Cathy Hendricks, who created and managed a Sea Harbor knit-along for readers (who knew?!). And thanks also to Deborah Gray—the gifted designer of the felt bowl pattern found in the back of *Murder at Lambswool Farm*—who generously allowed the Seaside Knitters to claim it as their own.

My unending gratitude to the writing and publishing community:

- To bloggers such as DruAnn Love and Lori Cass and many, many others who introduce readers to new books, who write reviews, and who spread the word.
- To fellow author Kate Carlisle, who generously opens her own giveaways and contests and online presence to those of us not quite as adept at such things.

- To those many generous authors who retweet other authors' book news, helping to promote new book publications and new authors, and who are always there with encouragement and understanding and goodwill for one another.
- To the NAL family—especially Michelle Vega, Bethany Blair, and Danielle Dill (along with the managing and copy editors and all those other behind-the-scenes people) who have been beside me in the labor and delivery rooms, bringing the Seaside Knitters mysteries to life.
- And last but definitely not least, my thanks and gratitude to Christina Hogrebe, Andrea Cirillo, and every single person at the Jane Rotrosen Agency, without whom the Seaside Knitters Mysteries would be wallowing at the bottom of the sea, never to see the light of a bookstore or enjoy the pleasure of being cradled in a reader's hands. To all of you there who have touched the Seaside Knitters Mysteries (and me) in many ways for many years—I thank you.

As you can see, it's an amazing community to be part of, and I'm grateful for my small place in its fold.

Thanks to my wonderful family, always loving and always encouraging, even when I'm absolutely sure I'm falling down the rabbit hole. And to those six bright lights who bring us such great joy—Luke, Ruby, and Dax; Atti, Jules, and Bashers.

Finally, my forever thanks to my in-house proofreader and brainstormer, who is always ready to make [i.e., carry out] his own Thai dinner in those final days of meeting a deadline—and to offer hugs at just the right moment: my husband, Don.

Cast of Characters

THE SEASIDE KNITTERS

Endicott, Nell: Former Boston nonprofit director, lives in Sea Harbor with her husband, Ben

Favazza, Birdie (Bernadette): Sea Harbor's wealthy, wise, and generous silver-haired grande dame

Halloran, Cass (Catherine Mary Theresa): Co-owner of Halloran Lobster Company

Perry, Izzy (Isabel Chambers Perry): Boston attorney, now owner of the Seaside Knitting Studio; Nell and Ben Endicott's niece; married to Sam Perry; daughter—Abigail Kathleen Perry

THE MEN IN THEIR LIVES

Brandley, Danny: Mystery novelist and son of bookstore owners; Cass's fiancé

Endicott, Ben: Nell's husband; Izzy's uncle

Perry, Sam: Award-winning photographer; Izzy's husband

Sonny Favazza and Joseph Marietti: Two of Birdie's deceased husbands

CLOSE FRIENDS & FAMILY

Adams, Willow: Fiber artist, Fishtail Gallery; Pete Halloran's girlfriend

Brewster, Jane and Ham: The Endicotts' oldest friends and cofounders of the Canary Cove Art Colony

Chambers, Charlie: Izzy's younger brother

Charlotte: Lambswool Farm's favorite ewe

Halloran, Mary: Pete and Cass's mother; works at Our Lady of Safe Seas Church

Halloran, Pete: Cass's younger brother and lead guitarist of the Fractured Fish

Marietti, Gabrielle (Gabby): Birdie's granddaughter

Risso, Andy: son of the Gull Tavern owner; Pete Halloran's best friend

Sampson, Ella and Harold: Birdie's housekeeper and groundskeeper/driver

Schultz, Carly: Andy Risso's girlfriend; nurse practitioner at the Hamilton Family Clinic

TOWNSFOLK

Arcado, Agnes: Arlene's mother

Arcado, Arlene: Staff member at Hamilton Family Clinic; daughter of Agnes

Barros, Dorothy and Robert: Izzy's former neighbors

Barros, Garrett: Former neighbor of Izzy's; son of Dorothy and Robert

Danvers, Daisy: Laura and Elliot's eleven-year-old daughter; Gabby's friend

Danvers, Laura: Socialite, philanthropist, mother of three

Mackenzie, Glenn: Visitor to town from Arizona; parents are Ann and Maxwell Mackenzie

SHOP OWNERS, TOWN PROFESSIONALS, ETC.

Arcado, M. J.: Owner of hair salon; husband is Ralph

Anderson, Mae: Izzy's shop manager; twin teenage nieces, Jillian and Rose

Brandley, Archie and Harriet: Owners of the Sea Harbor Bookstore

The Fractured Fish: Andy Risso (drummer); Pete Halloran (lead guitarist, singer); Merry Jackson (keyboardist, singer)

Garozzo, Harry and Margaret: Owners of Garozzo's Deli

Garozzo, Angelo: Maintenance engineer at day school and farm-hand at Lambswool Farm; Harry's brother

Hamilton, Alan, MD: Family doctor

Jackson, Merry: Owner of the Artist's Palate Bar & Grill; keyboard-ist and singer for the Fractured Fish

McClucken, Gus: Owner of McClucken's Hardware and Dive Shop

Northcutt, Father Lawrence: Pastor of Our Lady of Safe Seas Church

Palazola, Annabelle: Owner of the Sweet Petunia Restaurant

Pickard, Shelby: Owner of Pickard's Auto Repair

Pisano, Mary: Newspaper columnist; owner of Ravenswood-by-the-Sea B&B

Porter, Tommy: Policeman

Risso, Jake: Owner of the Gull Tavern

Russell, Claire: Landscaper and manager of Lambswool Farm

Santos, Gracie: Owner of the Lazy Lobster & Soup Café

Scaglia, Beatrice: Mayor of Sea Harbor

Sorge, Brady: Arizona attorney and Glenn Mackenzie's godfather

Thompson, Jerry: Police chief

Virgilio, Lily: Ob-gyn

Wooten, Don and Rachel: Owner of the Ocean's Edge Restaurant (Don) and city attorney (Rachel)

Murder at Lambswool Farm

Chapter 1

Some weeks later, after cool nights had resumed their soothing silence and summer dawns morphed once again into sleepy seaside days, Birdie would wonder out loud to Nell, Izzy, and Cass about the power of animals.

Could a gentle lamb be a harbinger, a warning that this summer would not "go gentle" into fall, no matter how blue the sky or calm the ocean or smooth the sand? Should they have leaned in a bit closer, cleared their minds, and listened to the bleating that echoed in the sweet-smelling air at Lambswool Farm?

Perhaps they should have.

But, in the end, would it have made any difference?

She'd been there for him, as intimate as a lover, for the whole long week as he had wound his way across the country.

But today, under a cloudless blue sky, Siri had failed him.

Glenn Mackenzie leaned one elbow out the window, his forehead pulled tight as he drove along the bumpy road.

Somewhere, somehow, he had made a wrong turn. Maybe it was when he'd turned Siri off for a minute and pulled over to check a text message.

But she was good at righting wrongs, and he followed her as best he could once he tuned back in. Turn left. Turn right. Do this; do that.

The last turn, when he'd begun to doubt the directions, had been a rebellious decision all his own. With the window down, he could smell the ocean air. It filled his head. Lured him, like the Sirens on their rocky coast. He'd decided to head that way—toward the sounds of the sea—and find his way by following the coast. He knew he was close. He'd get there. As his dad once said, *"The nice thing about not knowing where you're going—you can't get lost."*

The salty air blew in with purpose now, sweeping away his frustration and confusion.

But it didn't last. A half mile down the road things took a turn for the worse, but this time it wasn't a directional error.

Later he wouldn't be able to decide whether it had been a good thing or a bad thing.

But at that precise moment, as his Mazda began to climb a rise in the winding road, it was a bad thing.

The lurching that shook the car was robust enough to jostle a camera bag and cell phone onto the floor. And through the windshield, there was no mistaking the steam that snaked out from the edges of the hood. His car was smoking.

He veered over to the shoulder and switched off the ignition, then fumbled for the hood release. He'd felt a delay miles back when he circled Boston. The familiar car didn't respond quite as smoothly when he shifted gears, but he had ignored it. He shouldn't have.

He lifted the hood and immediately stepped away from the hiss and steam pouring out.

Glenn whispered a curse. He shoved his hands into his jeans pockets and stared at his car. Even before the gray cloud began to evaporate, he knew he had a problem—one bigger than the toolbox in his trunk could fix.

Glenn turned away from the car and looked around for the first time, taking stock of his surroundings. For a moment his frustration over a nonfunctioning car was forgotten.

Everywhere he looked, wide grassy fields rolled endlessly against a background of blue sky, colors so bright they caused him to narrow his eyes, take his sunglasses from the top of his head, and put them on. Enormous granite boulders were tossed carelessly across a pasture, the work of an invisible giant playing croquet. A split-rail fence, broken only by an entrance gate not far from where he stood, followed the road's curves, rising and dipping gracefully as if it grew directly out of the soil.

He rotated his shoulders, turning his head from side to side as he forced out the kinks of a long day in a cramped car. Gradually his blood pressure lowered. He leaned against the side of the car, arms over his chest, and breathed in the air. It was better than drugs. He wanted to drink it in, savor its salty edge; he wanted to overdose on sea air.

Not far from where he stood a flock of magnificent sheep, their long and lustrous fleece catching the late-afternoon light, grazed in the field. And far beyond them wind turbines were just visible on the horizon, their wings sweeping the sky like giant white birds. He wondered if he'd made his way into a Wyeth painting.

On all sides of him the quiet was so deep he could hear his own heartbeat. Only an occasional bleating of a sheep or squeal of a gull imposed on his solitude.

He wondered, not for the first time in recent days, what he expected from his trip. His life was now running along a predictable, manageable course. After years of changing majors—history and philosophy, dabbling in photography courses—he'd admitted to himself what he was truly good at. His parents had known it from the time he was a boy, as he'd always found microscopes and science kits intriguing. Science. Medicine. *"My son, the fine doctor,"* his mother would say, ruffling his hair.

He had finally finished medical school, done a three-year residency. And then to his surprise a postdoctoral fellowship had been offered and his direction changed again.

"Take some time," his father had said to him as the residency came to an end. After the sweltering ceremony, the two of them had gone off fishing together up in Rose Canyon. Father and son, a cooler of beer, some bait, Glenn's camera. And lots of time to talk about the past. The future. His dad had been healthy and robust that weekend, with no signs that the heart just beneath the surface of his chest wasn't working up to par.

"You say there's no rush?" Glenn had kidded his dad, reminding him that he'd been in school forever. His dad laughed along with him, but pushed his point.

"Once you start on that roller coaster of a career," Max had opined that day, "you can't just jump off to see the world. So do it now. Go hike a trail—use that eye of yours to take some photos of nice things. Your mother would have loved that." He had paused then, and Glenn knew what was coming next. "And I won't ever mention it again, but I'd like it if you'd take that trip back east we've talked about." He had patted Glenn on the back, then gone on as if he hadn't said it at all. "And then work your tail off and make your old man proud."

Glenn needed little encouragement. He'd taken two months, gone off on a bicycle trip in Spain. The trip back east had been put out of mind, and he had come back to Arizona only when he'd gotten the word that awful gray day six weeks before.

A Friday. Like on every Friday for forty years, Max Mackenzie had gone back to his office to unwind after the week's packed docket. He'd taken off his robes and waited for his friend Brady to join him in his chambers for a glass of fine scotch.

But before Brady got there—just for a minute or two—Max put his head down on his polished judge's desk for a snooze.

He closed his wise gray eyes—and he died.

The call came from his father's longtime clerk, Mildred, who, when she reached Glenn, said succinctly that it was high time the judge's only child got back to Tucson and properly buried the best man any of them could ever in a lifetime hope to meet. There would never be another Judge Maxwell Mackenzie. Glenn was the only Mackenzie left, she had said with some unnecessary drama. It was all up to him now.

Whatever the "it" was, Mildred neglected to say. *Life,* was Glenn's thought. And he assured her he'd do his best.

Once memories of his father had started, they ran across his mind like a fast-moving train, one after another. His father had been a good man. One of the best, as the magnanimous tributes at the funeral testified. The man who had molded Glenn's life—his role model and friend and wise father—was celebrated in endless stories told over bottles of fine whiskey after the service.

Mildred was right, and he knew far better than she did how lucky he was. Max Mackenzie had loved his younger wife, Glenn's mother, Ann, deeply and profoundly. And he had been the finest father a man could have—a gift that Glenn Mackenzie would carry through his life.

It took Glenn one month to settle the estate, to sign papers, to close bank accounts. One month to sort through seventy-five years of a life well lived.

He'd met one final time with his dad's best friend and lawyer—his own godfather—Brady Sorge. He hadn't really needed to hear what Brady had to say—the private information that he'd offered—but he took it and filed it away with all the other documents that spoke to his father's life. He knew his father's opinions; he had heard his advice, his wishes.

Glenn held his face up to the sky, breathed in one more stabilizing breath, and tucked the memories away. He slapped the side of the car for no good reason and shifted into fix-it mode.

LAMBSWOOL FARM, the freshly painted sign at the entrance to the property beside him read. Glenn walked over to the gate and looked up the long gravel drive. In the distance were freshly painted barns, bright green awnings on a small shingled house. It was a scene straight out of a movie. Even the sheep were perfect, one ewe about to give birth and a ram not far away. He moved the gravel around with the tip of his boot as he considered his options. It would be dark soon. The farm was thriving, lush; someone had to be around to keep it that way. Maybe someone with a truck who could give him a ride to a garage.

He started up the drive, noticing several workmen ahead—a roofer nailing tiles onto a barn, a painter lugging large cans out of what looked like a barn from the outside, but through the wide-open doors, light bounced off stainless-steel surfaces, like those in the many science labs he'd spent time in.

A gravelly voice coming out of nowhere stopped him in his tracks.

"About time you got here, kid," the voice shouted from beyond the fence.

Glenn looked over at a squat round-faced man with bushy eyebrows waving his hands in the air as he moved toward him. He wore wide jeans, an incongruous Hawaiian shirt, and scruffy boots. A Red Sox hat sat atop his head. Danny DeVito in a cowboy flick.

"Hi," Glenn said, holding out one hand as the man got close.

"Hi yourself. So, you've had experience on farms? You know what you're doin'? You work hard?"

Glenn held back an irreverent comment and tried a smile instead. "My car broke down." He pointed back down the drive.

"So? No problem. We'll fix it. A flat?"

"Nope. More serious than that. Damn car computers. It needs a tow."

"That's no problem. We got a place in town, Pickard's Auto—Shelby can fix anything, even my heap. First things first—follow me." He tossed words over his shoulder as he lumbered toward another building near the pasture. "I'm Angelo. You got a name?"

"Glenn. Where are we going? Shouldn't I be calling this Pickard guy? I need to get moving, and it's getting dark."

Finally Angelo stopped. He turned around slowly, his bushy eyebrows pulling together. "You answered the ad, right?"

"What ad?"

Angelo spoke to him slowly, as if he were a child. "The tractor ad. We need someone to fix the tractor—and then to drive it, as in plowing fields. Pitching hay. As in *work*."

He pronounced the last word *woke*, and with an inflection that carried judgment.

Glenn shrugged. "Here's the thing. I don't know anything about an ad, Angelo. But I can probably fix your tractor if you'll help me out with a tow or ride into town to get some help. I've had experience with tractors."

"So you don't want a job?" Angelo asked. At first he registered dismay, and then gave in to a slow smile that relaxed his face.

"Nah," Glenn said, then laughed along with this unusual fellow with the odd sense of humor.

"Yah, I gotcha," Angelo said. "It's not my lucky day, that's for sure. My Sox lose big and then I get you instead of a farmhand." He flapped his hand in the air and motioned for Glenn to follow him into the nearby barn, muttering under his breath about some punk kid who just up and quit on him the day before.

They walked single file past several stalls, fresh hay stacked against a wall, water troughs filled and clean. Above the stalls, a loft ran the length of the building, filled with supplies, a ladder, tools. And in a wide space at the back of the barn, just before a door that opened onto the field, was a shiny green John Deere.

"Great tractor," Glenn said. He walked over and ran his hand along the smooth hood. It looked as if it had never been used.

"Yeah, it's a pissah. But it'd be a damn sight greater if it ran," Angelo said, scowling at the machine as if it had personally done him wrong. "You sure you know what you're doing? I know all about things like furnaces and air conditioners and school equipment—I fix things over at my school all the time. But I'm not about to touch this green monster, not with the price tag it came with. And we need to keep moving, fixing things up around here. The clock's ticking. We got deadlines, you know." A guffaw followed his words.

Glenn didn't know, but he laughed anyway, partly because Angelo had, but mostly because of the accent, the missing *r*s, the New England twang. And he liked the guy. "Yeah, I know a lot about John Deeres. My dad had one of these. It wasn't new like this one, but they're all pretty much alike. I was riding the beast before I could walk."

"Your dad a farmer?"

Glenn shook his head. "But he had land he escaped to every chance he got, taking my mom and me with him. A ranch. Horses. We all loved the outdoors."

Glenn checked the starter, frowned into the silence, then went around to the side and hunkered down, fiddling with the machinery. "I'll need some tools. Screwdriver, pliers."

"You can figure this thing out and not that little Mazda out there?" Angelo's eyebrows lifted. "What's that about?"

Glenn laughed. "You just got some loose plugs in here is all. This thing is brand-new. Easy. Not so true of that one sitting on the side of the road. Bugs in some computer gizmo. Too big a match for me."

While Glenn worked, Angelo handed him tools and talked,

mellowing as he described the farm, the sheep, the gourmet dinners that would be served at Lambswool Farm in just a few weeks.

"Everything grown out here's organic," he was saying. "Vegetables as big as puppies. Food from the land, fish from the sea. But no lamb on the menu, they tell me." He laughed, the now-familiar gravelly sound. "These sheep will give some wool, some milk, but not themselves, nosirree. My girl Gabby would have your head if you touched a one of them with that in mind."

Glenn reached a hand up for a screwdriver. As he worked, he listened carefully, trying to fit together his surroundings with this man. A farm. Gourmet dinners. The best chefs on the North Shore fighting for a chance to come and cook a meal at Lambswool Farm. Guests (*customers?* he wondered) seated outdoors at long harvest tables. The sunset sky turning flaming red and gold and deep blue as the first course was plated.

Images ran through Glenn's head so vividly that he wanted to grab his camera from the car and capture them. What was this place, anyway? And who was this funny little Italian, going on like a poet laureate?

"So," Glenn said finally, pushing himself upright, "I think we're back in business, Angelo. Try it."

Angelo turned the key and the tractor roared to life. He laughed, his head back and the robust sound reaching up to the sky. Then he reached over and clapped Glenn on the back. "You're good, whoever you are. You sure you don't want a job out here?"

"It's tempting—believe me." Glenn smiled. He wiped his hands off on a rag and set it aside. "So, you own this place?"

"Own it? You crazy in the head? Birdie Favazza owns it. You know her?"

Glenn shook his head. "I don't know anyone around here. I'm just passing through."

"Ahhh," Angelo said, as if it was all falling into place. "You must be a vacationer, because no one just 'passes through' here. Cape Ann is stuck right out in the ocean. No passing through unless you meant to do it. But no matter—I, for one, am glad you came. And you'll be glad, too. Late summer, early fall in Sea Harbor is mighty nice. The grandest place on God's green earth. You got yourself a little cottage, maybe on Long Beach?"

Glenn hesitated. "No, not exactly," he finally said. "I'm not on vacation, not really."

"So what, then?" Angelo had his hands on his hips now, his head back, staring into Glenn Mackenzie's eyes. "You have a relative in Sea Harbor? If you do, I probably know 'em. It's a small place. Good people."

Good people. Glenn tucked the thought away.

"Well?" Angelo persisted.

Glenn slid over the question. "I'd say this place is not only beautiful but good luck—my car chose to die right here, on this road, where I'd meet you. So, you'll give me a lift?"

The expression on Angelo's face relaxed some. He grabbed a set of keys from a hook, then pointed through the open door to a truck parked just across the gravel drive. "Sure. I'll take care of you. Old man Pickard can tow 'er in tomorrow. And we've got the best B and B on the North Shore—Mary will put you up for the night if I put in a word for you." He winked.

Glenn walked back to his car and grabbed his bags from the trunk, locked the doors, and rejoined Angelo, climbing into the cab of his truck. He looked over at a tiny statue of St. Christopher wobbling on the dash, a Red Sox sticker glued to the visor, a pack of cigars shoved into a door pocket. The mat below his feet was thick with sand.

Angelo watched him taking it all in. "A mess, you're thinking? Yeah. But I love this old heap. And that sand beneath your feet is a symbol of the good life we have here. You gonna live in Sea Harbor, you gonna have sand in your vehicle." He started up the engine, then paused at the end of the drive. "Can't recall what you said when I asked before. We get our share of bums around here when the weather's nice, but you don't look like one. You're not a vacationer. But you're somebody's relative? Or a friend maybe?"

Glenn looked out the side window at a passing car, his eyebrows pulling together as he considered the question. When he looked back at the amiable man in baggy jeans, his expression was friendly, his tone nonchalant. "Nah," he said. "I don't know a soul. I'm just passing through, like I said. Thought I'd get some good shots of the ocean. We don't see much water in Tucson."

Glenn Mackenzie surprised himself at the ease with which he lied.

And he knew with certainty that it wouldn't be the last time.

Chapter 2

"His name is Glenn something or other," Birdie said, scooting the plate of blueberry muffins across the patio table to Nell and Cass. "He's staying at Ravenswood-by-the-Sea, and Mary told me that he's a wonderful guest. You know how she is—anyone staying indefinitely gets sized up in the first few hours to see if they pass her adoption criteria. Apparently Glenn passed. She spotted camera equipment in his belongings, and after he went on and on about the amazing bed in his room—the best sleep he'd had in months—Mary suggested sweetly that maybe he'd like to take some photos of the B and B for her new brochure. He agreed, and is now considered a first-class guest." Birdie took a drink of water and looked at Izzy. "He should meet Sam. Maybe Sam could give him some tips."

"Sure." Izzy licked the caterpillar of latte foam coating her upper lip. "Sam likes to meet fellow photographers. I'll ask him if he's heard of this guy."

Nell laughed. "Izzy, most photographers' names aren't on book covers or in galleries like Sam Chambers'. Most just take photos, then turn them in to some editor or some customer at a studio and get paid for it—or, like this fellow maybe, put them in family albums and stick them on a shelf."

Izzy laughed and reached down to knead her aging golden

retriever's ears. "I sometimes forget I have a famous artist hanging out in my house. Is this Glenn around for a while?"

"I don't know. His car broke down, so he'll be here a couple of days until it's fixed. I need to track him down to thank him before he moves on. He was able to unplug something or wiggle something or whatever one does to get a belligerent John Deere tractor to start. Brand spanking new, and Angelo said it simply stopped. There's lots to do out there, so we needed it fixed fast." Birdie's voice lifted with excitement as the topic shifted to her latest project.

"Birdie, you are loving every single minute of this, aren't you?" Nell smiled at Birdie's enthusiasm.

"Of course I am. Who would have thought that at my age I would be a farmer?" She clapped her hands in glee as she talked. "Sonny Favazza is in seventh heaven looking down on what we've done with that once-deserted farm. He told me that the land and old barns were mostly used by kids looking for a place to make out, or so he said."

"So . . ." Cass looked at Birdie. "Do you know that from experience?"

Birdie took the teasing in stride and chuckled at thoughts of a bygone era. The mention of her first husband—a generous man who had died when he and Birdie were still in the honeymoon years of their marriage—sobered her, but only a bit, and only for an instant. In spite of having married three more times over the intervening decades, Birdie's great and forever love was her first love, Sonny Favazza. *Saudade* was the Portuguese word for it, her friend and neighbor Alphonso Santos had told her.

"Saudade. A profound love that remains forever," Alphonso had said. *"There's no word for it in English."* Birdie took the word as her own. Hers and Sonny's.

Close friends knew Sonny informed everything she did: her joys and sorrows, her adventures and her lonely moments—and suspected he was probably looking down with some amusement on the old Favazza farm, an almost-forgotten piece of the Favazza trust that his Birdie had turned into a working farm, an organic garden, and a culinary experiment.

"Friday we'll meet at the farm. Claire needs feedback on some things. The last bit of paint is going on and she said the second barn is an inch away from being ready. It's almost tempted me to learn how to cook—though Ella has already nixed that idea quite robustly."

They all laughed, knowing Birdie's housekeeper kept a stern watch on the kitchen in Birdie's home, allowing her employer in only for conversation or snacks or sometimes a bowl of cereal. They were quite sure Birdie had never turned on the stove.

The shadow that fell across the table was short, just like the woman who owned it. They looked up into Mary Pisano's twinkling eyes. "You're talking about me—I can tell."

The nearly five-foot-tall owner of Ravenswood-by-the-Sea B&B and self-appointed columnist for the *Sea Harbor Gazette* leaned low, placing both hands flat on the patio table, her eyes bright and smiling. "And if you aren't, you should be. Here is my question. When can I see Lambswool Farm? I can write about it in my column far more eloquently once I've seen it."

Instantly Mary had an invitation to meet them on Friday at the farm for her own private tour.

Then she moved quickly to her second topic.

"The man who fixed the farm's tractor is Glenn Mackenzie. He was passing through the area, apparently, but it'll be a day or two before his car is fixed. He's taking the delay nicely and is in good spirits. A pleasant man. The town looked like a good place for an amateur photographer to be stranded, he said." She looked at Izzy.

"Yes," Izzy said before Mary could speak. She nodded. "I'll see that he and Sam meet."

"Good." After delivering the little information she knew about the guest—which was that he was polite and, according to his driver's license, thirty-four—Mary pointed to a table beneath a leafy maple tree where her laptop and coffee were waiting. She excused herself, claiming a deadline for her column. "Busy busy," she said, her fingers wiggling in the air as she walked away to the table that had her name invisibly emblazoned above it.

Chapter 3

Their introduction to the man staying in Mary's bed-and-breakfast came that evening, and it happened the way things often did in Sea Harbor: informally and by happenstance.

Or serendipity, as Birdie sometimes called it.

Ben suggested going out for dinner—he'd be home late from a yacht club meeting. Since it was his night to cook, maybe the paella at Ocean's Edge would be a nice substitute?

Before Nell had a chance to make the reservations, the group had grown. Izzy and Sam already had a sitter lined up and nowhere to go. They'd be happy to tag along. Birdie had planned on going anyway—the Edge served paella only occasionally, and the staff was under instructions to let Birdie know when it was on the menu.

Ben parked the car in front of the restaurant and opened the door for Nell, then walked around and helped Birdie out of the backseat. "For someone who doesn't cook, Birdie, you have a heck of a discriminating appetite."

Birdie laughed and wrapped her shawl around her shoulders. She took Ben's arm and walked with him and Nell to the restaurant's front entrance.

Don Wooten stood in the entryway, welcoming diners to his award-winning restaurant. "So, when does my chef get a turn at dazzling diners at Lambswool Farm?" he asked Birdie, bending over to kiss her on the cheek.

"Claire Russell and her staff are in charge of all that happens out there. I simply get to enjoy it all. That being said, your chef is most certainly on the list of the finest chefs on Cape Ann, besides being one of my favorite people in all the land. I hear he's agreed to be one of the chefs providing morsels for our private Sunday dinner. But I'm sure you know that. You must have signed off on it—and you and Rachel will be there, of course. I need all my friends."

Don nodded. The "trial run" dinner, as Birdie called it, was a smart idea. Their friends would have an amazing time, and the word-of-mouth praise that would follow it would be great. An excellent marketing ploy before the restaurant began serving its farm-to-table dinners to the public.

"We're looking forward to being a part of it," Don said. "It's the talk of the town."

He turned to Ben and shook his hand warmly. "Hey, Ben. I'm sorry for the slight delay with your table, but we'll have it ready before you can down one of our signature cocktails." He turned and motioned toward the packed bar. "Izzy and Sam are already there. They have a head start on you."

Izzy sat alone at the end of the polished bar, a cell phone in one hand and a wineglass in the other. Halfway down the bar, Sam was wedged in between Ham and Jane Brewster and several other artists from the Canary Cove Art Colony that the Brewsters had founded many years before.

Jane looked up, spotted the trio, and waved them over.

"We need an update on Lambswool Farm," Jane said as Ham ordered drinks for them. "I hear there's going to be a baby."

Nell listened to Birdie filling them in, sharing the happy news that one of their Leicester ewes was expecting any time now. She had apparently defied the seasonal breeding pattern, Birdie explained, choosing late summer to give birth, much to Birdie's granddaughter's delight. "Gabby is in love with this sheep. She's named her Charlotte and bakes her blueberry muffins regularly."

Nell left Birdie to describe more wonders of Lambswool Farm and wandered down to where Izzy sat alone in the curve of the walnut bar.

"And how is our Abigail Kathleen?" Nell asked, nodding knowingly at the phone in Izzy's hand.

Izzy dropped it into her bag. "Caught in the act."

Nell laughed. "You're a great mom, Izzy, dear, that's all. It can't hurt to check in. I'd be doing the same thing."

"Yes, you would," Izzy said.

Nell slid onto the empty barstool next to Izzy. "So, what else are you doing, sitting down here all by yourself?" Nell asked.

Izzy put her elbows on the bar and spoke in a conspiratorial whisper. "It's the perfect people-watching spot." She nodded toward the line of people sitting on stools, gesturing, laughing, with animated talk traveling up and down the bar. "I can see everyone from this little niche—a couple of college kids down there, probably on a last emotional date before heading back to school." She nodded toward Sea Harbor's hair salon owner and fire chief. "Check out M. J. and Ralph Arcado. They must be celebrating an anniversary or something with those champagne flutes. You can even spot a few remaining vacationers with those telltale sunburned faces. Their cottage refrigerators are empty except for dry cheese and crusts of bread, so they're splurging on one final seaside meal before heading off to Podunk, USA."

Nell chuckled as she fell into Izzy's imagination. "It's like *Rear Window*."

"Better even. But I haven't figured out that guy down there."

Izzy pointed with one finger toward the man at the opposite far end of the bar. "He doesn't have the vacationer or tourist look, but I don't think I've seen him before. And he's alone, so probably he's not anyone's visiting relative."

The man had his eyes on the television set above the bar and was drinking a beer. A stubble of a beard shadowed a square chin and strong bones. His dark hair was slightly mussed and touched the collar of his cotton shirt. Occasionally he'd pull his attention away from the television and laugh at something the bartender said to him, answer in an amicable way, then lift his head back to the soundless ball game playing out above the bar. His shirtsleeves were rolled up and muscular forearms rested against the rounded edge of the bar.

"He looks comfortable in his shoes, as Birdie would say," Nell said. "But I've never seen him before either. Maybe Birdie knows."

"Knows what?" Birdie asked, coming up behind them, her face level with her friends' from her standing position. She set her wineglass on the bar and gave Izzy a hug.

"Do you know that man?" Izzy pointed down the bar.

Birdie followed the direction of her finger. "Well, let me see." She pulled her glasses from the top of her head, put them on, and leaned in for a better look. "There's something familiar about him." She wrinkled her forehead, concentrating.

At that moment, as if sensing her scrutiny, the man pulled his gaze away from the game and looked down the bar, his eyes zeroing in on Birdie's. He caught her look and smiled before she had a chance to look away. He lifted a beer bottle, nodded slightly in a silent greeting, and then forked back the hair that had flopped across his forehead.

"Oh, dear," Birdie said to Nell and Izzy, finally looking away. "And I'm always reminding Gabby not to stare at people."

Sensing her embarrassment, the man slid off the barstool and walked to the other end of the bar, his beer in his hand. "It looks like we were both people-watching," he said to Birdie, a half smile lifting a corner of his mouth. "It's what you're supposed to do in bars, right?"

"You're absolutely right." Birdie held out her hand. "I am Birdie Favazza. And who are you? I think I saw you earlier today, running along Ravenswood Road in the wee hours."

He laughed and took her hand, swallowing it up in his own. "I'm Glenn," he said. "Glenn Mackenzie. I think I recognize you, too. You were walking along the road, right? You live in that great granite estate across the street from the Ravenswood B and B. Mary Pisano pointed it out to me when I asked about the neighborhood. It's beautiful. And Mary says you also own Lambswool Farm—which was my introduction to this town. I feel an intimate connection to that place."

"Well, now, it's serendipity, then," Birdie said. "I've been wanting to thank the person who generously fixed the new tractor out there, and that person, it seems, would be you. Angelo Garozzo was impressed. He says you are marooned here while Shelby Pickard puts your car back together."

Glenn shrugged and swept the hair from his forehead again. "Angelo says my car's in good hands. And Sea Harbor seems as good a place as any to be without wheels for a couple of days."

"Of course it is," Birdie said, finally turning toward Izzy and Nell and handling introductions all around.

"Do you know anyone in town—other than Mary, Angelo, and Shelby?" Izzy asked.

"Well, those three are proving to be a mighty helpful trio. But nope, not really. I'm a stranger in paradise."

"Well, then," Birdie said, her chin lifting up to look into his face. "You'll join us for dinner—it will be my thank-you for helping Angelo out. Besides, one shouldn't eat the Ocean's Edge paella alone. There'd be no one to hear your cries of utter delight."

Glenn laughed. "The bartender tells me it's the best this side of Valencia. I was about to order a bowl at the bar to check out his claim, but food always tastes better with company. I'm not imposing?"

"Of course not," Nell, Izzy, and Birdie answered in unison.

"There are a couple of others joining us—you won't be the only guy," Izzy said, looking down the bar to a series of vacated barstools and wondering where Sam and Ben had gone.

A waitress appeared at Nell's elbow and whispered, "Those two are vultures, Nell. You'd better move fast if you want more than a handful of crumbs." She looked over Birdie's head and offered Glenn a smile. "Shall I set another place?"

"Glenn, this is Arlene," Birdie said, nodding to the waitress. "She's the person you want to know at the Ocean's Edge. Arlene has clout. She can pull strings."

Arlene tossed her head at the compliment and flapped menus at them to follow her. With practiced ease, she maneuvered her shapely body through the maze of white-clothed tables and high-backed leather booths. From nearly every spot, one could glimpse the sea, but Arlene was heading toward a table just inside the wide porch that circled the restaurant—a table with not just a glimpse but a whole magnificent panorama of the endless ocean.

"Wow," Glenn said, his eyes widening.

A series of sliding glass doors separated the back of the restaurant from a wide dining porch. The low glass railing kept the breeze at bay, the view intact. Beyond it, harbor lights were beginning to twinkle as small boats made their way toward the harbor slips. The evening breeze was crisp and gusty, rippling the striped awnings over the porch tables.

Glenn walked over to the sliding door and stared out at the view, his hands shoved into his pockets.

Nell came up beside him. "It's lovely, isn't it?" She pointed out a sailboat far away. It looked like it was held up by the narrow line of the horizon, its rudder anchoring it to the sea, its white sails stark against the darkening sky. "I never tire of it. It arouses the senses in a fundamental way—smell, touch, hearing, even taste."

Glenn nodded, his eyes still on the rolling tide. "I love Arizona—the wide-open spaces, the crisp air, the mountains. It's in my blood. But this . . ." He shook his head and finally pulled away from the view, focusing on Nell. "I've traveled a lot, seen a lot of nice things, but there's something about all this—the sea, the town—that gets to me. I don't know what I expected, but it wasn't this."

Nell was quiet, wondering how she had envisioned Sea Harbor the first time Ben had brought her up to Cape Ann to meet his parents. It was the summer between their sophomore and junior years at Harvard. What she remembered most was that she had fallen in love with it, in an instant, just like she had fallen in love with Ben. A slight rearranging of her heart, in a way that changed it forever.

"I wish I had my camera," Glenn went on. "I was trying not to be conspicuous, not be pegged as a tourist with a Nikon hanging around my neck."

Nell smiled. "We have nothing against tourists. Besides, most of them use cell phones when snapping pictures. But hopefully you'll have time to take some photos before you leave us. For now, simply tuck the images away inside yourself—that's what I do. Sometimes they're the best kind—always readily accessible."

Ben and Sam stood as they turned and walked toward the table. The men showed no surprise that the number in their party had grown. It was one reason Nell always asked for the round table—the one that more easily accommodated extras. Don Wooten had once told Nell that he'd engraved her name on the bottom of the table, though she'd yet to crawl beneath to test the veracity of this.

Izzy had already explained that they'd picked Glenn up in the bar. She introduced him to her uncle and husband.

Glenn shook Ben's hand, then looked over at Sam, his eyes widening as Izzy said her husband's name. "Sam Perry?" he said, having some difficulty getting the words out. "*The* Sam Perry?"

Sam laughed. "Probably not. I'm sure there are dozens more. Have we met?"

They hadn't, Glenn assured him, at least not in person. Glenn's voice took on a certain awe as he spoke, and he explained his surprise. He was a fan, plain and simple. He had attended a talk Sam gave at a museum a while back, but they hadn't actually been introduced. But he owned several books of Sam's photographs, as well as two prints from an early collection that he'd purchased from a gallery in Arizona. His mother had been an amateur photographer and had loved Sam's prints.

"Arizona?" Sam said, brushing off the attention and switching the subject. "So that's where you're from?"

Arlene interrupted before Glenn could answer, encouraging everyone to please sit down so she could take drink orders. She wedged herself in between Sam and Glenn, her attention on Glenn. A lock of reddish blond hair fell over her cheek.

"Better do what Arlene says." Ben laughed. "She runs a tight ship."

Arlene took the teasing in stride, brushing the wavy lock of hair behind her ear. But none of them missed the appraising glance and tilt of her head that she gave Glenn Mackenzie as he pulled out his chair. It rolled over his body like a wave, head to toe. In the next instant she was back to business, recording their drink orders in her head without taking a single note.

When she was gone, Ben brought the attention back to Glenn. "So you're a photographer, too?"

"Just an amateur," Glenn said. "But I love it, all the parts. I like fiddling with the equipment, the science of it. I liked developing when I was a teenager and people still did that. Maybe what I like the most is the unique view of the world you get when you're looking at it through a lens. My mom gave me one of her cameras—an old Nikon—when I was ten. It was love at first sight. I always have my camera close by. But I'm not an artist, not by any stretch of the imagination. It's not my profession."

"And what is that?" Izzy asked. She pulled the basket of calamari away from Sam and piled some onto her own plate, then passed around the tray of sauces—a spicy chimichurri, a rich marinara, and a pot of homemade anchovy mayonnaise. "Your profession, I mean."

Glenn considered Izzy's question as if he were sorting through several choices. Then he said, "A doctor. It took me a while to settle into anything, hence the fact that I still haven't been out in the trenches. My dad was a lawyer—and pretty much an icon to me—a really amazing human being. And for a while I thought I should follow in his footsteps, kind of like a tribute, you know?"

Nell glanced over at Izzy. She'd been the same way with her dad, a respected Kansas City lawyer. Izzy had known from early on that her father's greatest pleasure would have been to see his daughter follow in his footsteps. Law school. Law partner. And so she had. For a while.

When Glenn continued with his own story, the difference in the two scenarios was clear.

"The problem was," Glenn said, "I just didn't think the way a lawyer thinks, whatever that means. I found law texts really boring. Fortunately my dad was a wise man—a judge, actually. And he knew it even before I did. 'Don't follow me,' he said. 'It's not in your genes. Be yourself. That's where and when you'll shine.' He made me feel great. He was good at that. So he guided me toward something I *did* excel at. Science. Biology—my mother's genes, I guess. I knew he was right. I loved medicine. Ate it up. So that's where I ended up. Went to medical school and got my MD."

"A specialty?" Ben asked

"I did a couple of internships—internal medicine, pediatrics. Liked those a lot, but it was hard to decide. I got offered a postdoc in medical research. I like that a lot, too."

"Did you go to school around here?" Izzy asked.

"No. Back home. Arizona."

Nell listened with interest. He and Izzy looked about the same age, but Izzy had already been a litigator in a prestigious law firm, tried cases, then cast it all aside, moved to Sea Harbor, and opened up the Seaside Knitting Studio. It was as if she'd lived two professional lives while Glenn hadn't yet begun his first.

Glenn looked over and seemed to read her thoughts. He laughed lightly. "It took me a while to get through college. I wasn't very decisive and changed majors every time the weather changed. But man, I am one fully formed liberal arts graduate. You'd be hard-pressed to find a major I haven't tried." He stopped talking and took the platter of escargot that Nell handed him. He put a few on his plate and began to fork out the succulent snails from inside the shells.

But Birdie still had questions. "So, what brings you to this part of our great land? Are you looking at research institutions in Boston? We have the finest in the world."

Arlene was back with their drinks and a basket of French bread to soak up the garlicky butter sauce. She fussed a little, gently scraping some calamari crumbs from the table near Glenn's place.

Nell noticed the look of relief on Glenn's face at the interruption. She could see that he had talked more about himself than he was comfortable with. Escargot and Arlene offered a gracious way to slip into the shadows. Nell understood. They sometimes forgot that there were people who found baring their souls to strangers uncomfortable.

As Arlene moved off to another table, Glenn wisely took the offensive and started in with questions of his own.

"So, what are you working on now, Sam?" he asked.

Sam glanced at Ben, laughed a little as if it were a private joke, and then said, "It's something Izzy's uncle Ben, here, talked me into doing. Ben and Nell have their hands—and their friends' hands—in all sorts of good projects going on in Sea Harbor. This particular project is a photographic series of Sea Harbor that will benefit the museum."

Glenn leaned in with interest. "Is there an angle to it? Or simply photos of the beauty around here? You could probably stand in one single spot and shoot a whole album."

"True. But this shoot does have an angle," Ben said. "It's sort of a Norman Rockwell thing, life in a small town, with text to run along with the photos that we'll put in a book, and the museum will put the originals on display and then sell the books. Ben has also recruited our friend Danny Brandley to do the text—"

"The mystery writer," Glenn said, impressed again.

"Yep, that's the one."

"For such a little place, this town is a literary and art haven," Glenn said with a smile.

Sam laughed. "Anyway, that's a warning that Ben's a dangerous man to be friends with. We'll focus on things here that make Sea Harbor different from, say, Boston, or even a smaller place like Danvers."

"Like what?" Glenn asked.

"Well, for starters, if you walk down Harbor Road you won't see a single Starbucks or Target or Home Depot. No big-box stores. Not that they're bad, but this place has a ton of family traditions—businesses that have been here a long time, some since the town began and were passed down through the generations, father and mother to son and daughter, like Gus McClucken's hardware store and the Brandleys' bookshop. Garozzo's Deli. Lots of towns have family businesses, but Sea Harbor seems to have a monopoly on helping the mom-and-pop places survive. Some people think it's inconvenient not to have a Target close by—and maybe that's true sometimes. But we make up for it with other conveniences you'd be hard-pressed to find everywhere. We actually have a family doctor in town, Alan Hamilton, who still makes house calls just like his father and grandfather before him did."

The snail on its way to Glenn's mouth stopped in midair. His eyes held surprise and his mouth fell open. "What?"

Birdie stepped in. "I know, it's unusual. I hear that having a family practice like that is almost an anachronism—you'd know that better than anyone. But it's true. Alan does exactly what his father did, and his grandfather before him, and another Hamilton before that—keeping the little black medical bag handy and heading out into the night if a call comes in. People are nice about it, though. We try not to take advantage of him. We're good folks; we let him have a life."

Glenn fell silent and seemed to focus intently on the martini Arlene had set before him.

Thoughts of making house calls were clearly not something he'd encountered in his medical school education. Sensing Glenn didn't quite get the concept, Birdie added, "People go to Boston's great medical centers if they have serious problems, but for everything else, most of us go to Alan."

Glenn nodded and drained his martini glass.

Sam noticed. "Another?" He waved Arlene over from another table.

Glenn stabbed an olive and looked back at Sam. "So you'll photograph the businesses?"

"That's the plan. Businesses. Places. People, too, of course. That's what makes the book. We'll highlight the families that go way back, through photos and text." Sam paused, reclaimed the calamari basket from Izzy, and took a drink of water. Then he leaned back in his chair and looked at Glenn, his expression registering a sudden thought. "Hey . . . that gives me an idea."

"Uh-oh. Watch out, Glenn," Izzy said, leaning toward him. "I know that look. Sam's very good at talking people into things. Especially if it makes his life easier."

They all laughed, knowing full well that it was Izzy who was a master at talking people—especially her husband—into things.

Sam tugged lightly on a piece of Izzy's hair and went on. "Ignore my sweet wife. But here's the thing—if you get bored while waiting around Sea Harbor for your car, you're welcome to join me. You might find it fun. You'd get to take some pictures and see the town at the same time."

"See?" Izzy said, her eyebrows lifting into silky streaked bangs, a pleased, smug look on her face. "I've lugged many a tripod around in my day."

This time it was Glenn who laughed. Having the spotlight on him lifted, he settled more readily into the conversation, taking a long drink of the new cocktail Arlene had brought over. "That's quite an offer. Who could turn that down?"

"Oh, lots of people," Izzy assured him.

"Nah, Izzy is teasing. It's just that she's never taken a photograph that didn't look like she'd just had her eyes dilated. My wife is very creative and talented, but give her a camera and she starts to shake."

"Okay, Sam's right—I admit it. And actually it's a great idea. My husband is good—and he can always use extra hands. And eyes, too."

"It will give you a chance to take some shots yourself," Nell said.

"It's a deal, then," Sam said.

He held out a hand and Glenn shook it gladly. "I'm not sure when the car will be fixed, so this'll be great."

"It's nice you don't need to do a lot of rearranging of your life when it's unexpectedly stalled like this," Birdie said. "Some people would be in a tizzy."

"No rearranging necessary at all," Glenn said. He left it at that, talking about other things, like looking forward to learning more about the town.

Nell sat quietly, listening, but mostly watching. Now that Glenn had relaxed—whether it was the company or the martinis Arlene was bringing—he was clearly more comfortable and talkative, even though he was sitting with a tableful of strangers. Maybe it was partially because of Sam, someone he knew remotely, or at least felt he did through Sam's work.

But there was something missing, something she couldn't put her finger on. She found herself looking at Glenn Mackenzie this way and that, hoping to catch a stray glance or word or something that would fill in what seemed like wide cracks. The fact that her thoughts didn't make a whole lot of sense—he was, after all, a stranger—didn't go unheeded, but nor did it assuage the uncomfortable feeling that there was more to Glenn Mackenzie than met the eye. Perhaps it was simply his ease at being stranded in a strange town, but there was something in that very ease that made Nell think Glenn Mackenzie had more of a story to tell than he was revealing.

She knew if she expressed her feelings to Ben later that night, he'd be mildly amused. He'd suggest to her that it had been a quiet, uneventful summer, and perhaps she was building intrigue into the lull, trying to spice it up before fall was upon them. And then he'd wrap an arm around her as he led her out to the deck, where they'd sit close beside each other, heads against the high chaise, looking up at a starry sky. And Ben would explain that at that precise moment, sitting there with her head against his shoulder, he was experiencing all the excitement he needed in his life. His Nell, and a canopy of planets and stars above them, exploding into space.

Soon Nell's wandering thoughts were nicely scattered by the enticing aroma of saffron and garlic, buttery scallops, clams and shrimp and wine. Arlene expertly and without spilling a drop placed a wide bowl of Spanish stew in front of each of the diners. A young waiter helping her added baskets of warm sourdough rolls, bowls of olives, and pots of sweet butter as the waitress uncorked the wine Ben had chosen for the paella—a fine raja.

The perfect meal, the perfect wine, and the conversation was immediately lulled by the need to concentrate completely on the paella.

It was only after bowls were half empty, the basket of rolls refilled, and Don Wooten's shadow fell across the table that anyone looked up for longer than an exclamation of delight at the magical, creative dish created thousands of miles from its proper homeland of Valencia.

The restaurant owner smiled at the looks of pleasure around the table. "I'm guessing you're happy with the meal." He laughed before they could answer. "And the service? You have everything you need?"

He looked over to the next table, where Arlene was serving a couple.

"The paella is amazing, and Arlene is, too," Nell said. She followed Don's look, just in time to see Arlene straightening the collar on the police chief's jacket, finishing it off with a honeyed smile.

"And attentive," she added, coaxing a laugh out of Don.

"Yes, above all, she is that," Don said.

He introduced himself to Glenn, welcomed him to the restaurant and to their town, and was soon called off by a waiter with a question, a hostess with a request, a bartender needing ice.

Sam soaked up the remaining wine-laced broth with a hunk of sourdough and managed to get Glenn talking about his travels. He'd actually been to Valencia, he confessed, and had had his share of paella. And yes, the Ocean's Edge recipe was every bit as delicious, maybe even better.

More wine was poured and the conversation shifted back and forth with ease, from travel to photography to facts about the town. Whether it was the wine or the company, Glenn Mackenzie was soon persuading all of them into sharing stories about Sea Harbor. He seemed genuinely interested in each person at the table, questioning Izzy on her journey from Harvard law to owning a yarn shop; learning from Ben how he'd retired in the vacation home his grandparents had built a century before—and how he had adapted to life in a small seaside town after a successful law and family business career, respectively, in Boston. Birdie rolled out her own family history in delicious and entertaining detail. Nell wasn't left off the hook either, as Glenn wondered about the nonprofit she'd directed in Boston. He treated each path that had brought them to where they were at that moment as a fascinating one.

And in the process, except for a few facts—the kind easily divulged on an application for something or another, such as place of residence, college degree, etc.—they knew little about how Glenn Mackenzie had ended up in New England, his car breaking down on a remote country road.

About the same time as Arlene brought out creamy slices of key lime pie, Birdie issued Glenn an invitation to the Lambswool Farm dinner Sunday night. Dutifully he tapped the date into his phone. "Bring your camera," Birdie said.

But the event was several days away, Nell thought. Surely Shelby Pickard wouldn't take a week to fix a car.

But Glenn Mackenzie didn't seem to mind either way, his schedule stretching as easily as bubble gum. Anything was okay with him. Even missing parts to his car.

And Nell Endicott couldn't shake the uncomfortable feeling that she might not like the reason why.

Chapter 4

Nell pushed Abby's stroller down Harbor Road while mentally checking her to-do list. Fresh rolls from the bakery were in a bag tucked beneath the stroller, right next to a freezer pack that held the chunks of fresh lobster she'd fold into the macaroni and cheese. It was her one cheesy splurge for the month. The kale salad was sitting in her refrigerator, needing only the lemony dressing that had finally convinced Ben that kale wasn't so bad after all. Birdie, Izzy, and Cass loved it, too. It would be a good beginning for Thursday's evening of knitting and sharing life and wine. And most of all of being together with Izzy, Birdie, and Cass.

Glenn Mackenzie was still on her mind, lingering and nudging her as if mentally challenging Nell to go beyond the surface of who he was. Challenging her to try, at least. It was perfect discussion fodder for the intimacy of the yarn shop's back room.

The tradition was as old as Izzy's shop, begun one serendipitous evening when Nell, knowing her niece was working late, had brought her dinner. Birdie had stopped in at that exact moment, too, in desperate need of a needle size she was missing. If Izzy hadn't left the shop door open that night to catch the breeze, Cass might have never joined the knitting group. But the tantalizing odor of

Nell's seafood lasagna had drifted out to Harbor Road, luring the lobsterwoman in.

And so it had begun. Knitting around the fireplace in Izzy's back room, as a friendship that had weathered many storms continued to deepen with each sweater and hat and scarf.

Nell double-checked errands against the list in her pocket, then looked down at Abby. From behind the stroller she could see her little fingers playing with a knitted puppy that Nell had made for her. It had become a favorite, much to Nell's delight, the long lanky ears ragged with love.

She shoved the completed to-do list back in her pocket. Everything accomplished.

Except for one thing—a ritual she and Abby shared at the end of every nice-weather stroll.

As if reading her thoughts, Abby looked back at Nell, her small hands clapping as she began the singsong chant that Ben had taught her recently, one that served both Abby and her great-uncle well when needing their shared favorite treat. "Ice cream, you scream . . . we all scream for ice cream."

"That's what I say, too, my sweet Abby," Nell said, and rolled the stroller to the outside order window that Scoopers Ice Cream Shoppe had recently installed.

Minutes later they were settled at the corner park down the street, a heavily treed postage stamp–sized park that managed to house a gazebo and benches scattered among the bushes and lamplit paths. Built on a V-shaped lot, the park was a favorite place for merchants taking a break, for moms and kids, strolling couples, and sometimes impromptu concerts by amateur musicians. Today it was a perfect spot for Nell and a happy Abby sitting on the grass, her concentration on a vanilla ice-cream cone intense and unflappable, even when a white creamy river rolled down her chin onto her pink T-shirt.

Nell sat back and thought about the calmness of her day, the pleasure of being with her grandniece, the rustle of a breeze tugging leaves free from their branches. Fall was in the air, even as summer fought to hold it back.

On the other side of the park, beyond the small gazebo and a stand of tall pine trees, she heard the high trilling voices of Our Lady of Safe Seas grade school students, the lowered voices of the crossing guards, and straight ahead, the trickle of tourists moving in and out of the historical museum. Just beyond it and up a slight rise, a row of sweet pepperbush shrubs defined the Sea Harbor Medical Center, which housed Dr. Lily Virgilio's ob-gyn clinic on one side, and on the other, Alan Hamilton's family practice.

Architects had done a masterful job with the three-story house—once Captain Delgado's mansion—retaining the flavor of a long-ago era, complete with a widow's walk at the top. And behind it was one of Nell's favorite spots. She sometimes thought of it as a secret garden, although it was actually a lovely landscaped backyard, an almost hidden pocket in what was now Sea Harbor's downtown. Most of the old houses that had been turned into shops and offices had long ago given up their yards to more offices and shops and parking spaces. The Delgado house had remained intact.

The clinic was busy as always, a steady parade of cars and bikes driving into the parking lot and patients walking up the front steps to either of the two offices, Dr. Virgilio's or Dr. Hamilton's. Between the two doctors, there were few Sea Harbor residents who hadn't visited the welcoming clinic.

Nell leaned over and wiped a dribble from Abby's chin, then sat back again, enjoying the soft breeze that lifted her hair from her shoulders, cooling the back of her neck. Her mind tugged on memories of the many visits she had made with Izzy to Lily Virgilio's office, happy visits as Izzy's body grew in magical ways, visits that culminated in the birth of Abigail Kathleen Perry.

She watched a couple making their way toward the doctors' offices. Then, startled, she leaned forward and looked again, her eyes squinting as their features came into focus.

Arlene Arcado was laughing at something her companion said, her wavy hair moving across her narrow shoulders. She stood for a minute at the fan of stairs leading to the entrance of the clinic, one hand on the railing, looking at the man standing a step away. It wasn't until he turned slightly, forking his fingers through his hair, that Nell recognized the man with Arlene.

Glenn Mackenzie.

They spoke for a minute in a comfortable way. Then Glenn waved with a slight bow, turned, and walked away. A gallant departure.

Nell watched him shove his hands in his pockets. He stopped at the curb and seemed to be checking out his surroundings, looking back once or twice at the door to the medical building. Then he crossed the street and walked into the park, crisscrossing toward Harbor Road. His expression was thoughtful, and there was a sense of purpose in his stride. When his gaze shifted around the park, he spotted Nell. He waved, then detoured around the gazebo to where she and Abby sat.

"I thought that was you," he said politely. Then he spotted Abby looking up at him, her eyes round. He bent his knees, crouching low, greeting the toddler and admiring her ice-cream cone, now a mushy blend of grass and thick cream. He declined Abby's offer to take a taste but thanked her. "Is she your grandchild?"

"Grandniece. Izzy and Sam's baby."

"Beautiful kid, just like her mother." He stood and smiled down at the child's cap of curly hair. Then he shoved his hands back into his jeans pockets and looked around again, his gaze settling on the shop across the street, its window filled with baskets of colorful yarn. "I'm guessing that's Izzy's store over there?"

Nell smiled. "The window is a giveaway."

He laughed. "Yeah. I had coffee with Sam and Danny Brandley, the mystery writer, over in Canary Cove this morning. We sat on the restaurant deck, where Danny says he writes some of his books. They were giving me the lay of the land and the scope of this photography project, and they mentioned these great entrepreneurial women around here that have their own businesses—Izzy's shop, the Halloran Lobster Company, Annabelle somebody or other's restaurant over in Canary Cove. There's something in the water, they said. Magic water or not, the town definitely has charm."

Sam had taken him to the museum, too, Glenn said. "His photo history will be a great addition to that place. It's the kind of thing anyone passing through—like me—would enjoy looking at."

"The medical offices next to the museum are in the old captain's house. Some people still call it the Delgado home, but Sam probably filled you in on that, too. It's where our wonderful doctor who makes house calls has his practice."

Glenn nodded, looking back at the mansion turned medical clinic. "It kind of blew my mind. I'm used to enormous glass monsters where doctors save lives or do research and have offices. Sam and I stopped in briefly. It was busy, but I met a few folks. We're going back tomorrow. I'm looking forward to seeing the whole thing. It's a great old home, from what I could see, anyway. It's two separate practices, right?"

"Yes, Lily Virgilio runs the women's clinic and Alan Hamilton has the family practice. It's been in his family as long as anyone can remember. Most all of our medical needs are met in one lovely place."

"So they own it together?" Glenn looked again at the clinic, or more at the building itself, Nell suspected.

"Their practices are owned separately, but they share the building." She realized as she talked that she wasn't really sure about that. She knew that the Hamilton family had owned the mansion for a very long time. Half of it had gone unused. It wasn't until Lily came to town that it had been renovated into two clinics. She wasn't sure if Alan was Lily's landlord or if she owned part of the building.

She waited for Glenn to say more about his visit there, but his attention seemed to be moving on to other things. "So, the deli is down that way?" he asked, pointing away from the park toward Harbor Road. "I'm meeting Angelo, the guy who rescued me when my car broke down, for a hot pastrami sandwich. He says it's the best on Cape Ann and makes for a great midafternoon snack."

"I'm not sure about the midafternoon-snack part—Harry's sandwiches are huge—but you won't be disappointed. And Angelo probably mentioned his brother owns the deli."

"He did. Everyone seems to be related to someone who knows someone or owns something around here. Danny said his parents own a bookstore?"

"They do. It's a great place."

"I'll check it out. It's next to Izzy's shop, right? Maybe they have books about the town."

"Archie himself is a living treasure trove of information. He's like Birdie—he knows all the buried secrets."

"Not so buried, then, right?" A slight grin lifted the corner of his mouth. He knelt down once more beside Abby, taking her tiny hand in his big one and shaking it until she giggled. And then he was gone, across the street and through the heavy doors that opened into the Sea Harbor Bookstore.

Nell turned back toward the clinic, thinking of Arlene. Glenn hadn't mentioned walking her to the door. But then, perhaps they'd just run into each other on the sidewalk and chatted briefly before Arlene went inside the medical building.

When they had left the restaurant the night before, she had noticed Arlene standing in the hallway near the restrooms. Her back was against the wall, her eyebrows pulled together. She was rubbing her temples with her fingertips. Her expression was severe, as if she'd eaten something sour that had disagreed with her. It was a look Nell hadn't seen before on the usually affable waitress. She glanced up, saw Nell looking her way, and quickly replaced the look with a forced smile. A wave. And then she disappeared into the staff lounge.

Now, seeing her go into the clinic, Nell wondered if maybe she had been sick the night before after all. Or perhaps it was a simple checkup. Either way, it certainly wasn't Nell's business. People had doctor's visits every day.

A noise from Abby pulled her attention back to what *was* her business. A butterfly had landed on the tip of Abby's purple tennis shoe, and for an instant the toddler was awash in wonder, her eyes round. And then the butterfly flew away and Abby clapped her hands in utter happiness.

Nell watched this child, who herself was a wonder. She could hardly remember life before Abby. She looked down at the damage created from pairing an innocent Abby with an ice-cream cone. The soggy, nearly empty cone was carefully piled full of pine needles, which Abby now lifted up proudly for Nell to see.

"A true work of art. It's beautiful, Abby. I think you are going to be an artist, or a diplomat, or the president. Or anything in the whole world you want to be." Suddenly Nell's eyes were as full as her heart. She leaned down and removed the cone from her grand-niece's sticky hands before the pine needles were licked along with the remaining trickle of ice cream.

And just like that, thoughts of a woman visiting a medical clinic and curiosity over a stranger in town disappeared, replaced by a child's smile, a butterfly, and a dripping ice-cream cone filled with pine needles.

Chapter 5

Carrots, spinach, plump golden squash. And wonderful felted bowls to hold them?

The ideas flew around the yarn shop's cozy back room faster than knitting needles purling. Claire Russell was expecting their knit centerpieces for the first formal harvest dinner a couple of weeks away. They wouldn't let her down.

Izzy lifted the lid from her aunt's cast-iron roaster and stepped aside as steam, heavy with mouthwatering aromas of cheese, fresh lobster, and wine, filled the room.

Cass stopped dead in her tracks. Her backpack hit the hardwood floor with a thump, and a fistful of patterns Nell had just handed her floated to the floor. She clenched her eyes shut and said in a whisper, "Sweet, buttery lobster, mac and cheese, butter, wine, garlic . . . a dash of heaven, a splash of ecstasy . . ."

Nell laughed at the drama. Cass cooked little beyond fried eggs and canned beans, but she could name every ingredient in Nell's Thursday-night dishes, rarely missing a one.

Birdie set a stack of pasta dishes next to the roaster. "Nell made this as incentive; it's not free. We have work to do tonight."

Cass leaned down and scooped up the fallen patterns as Purl, the shop's calico cat, rubbed against her jeans. "Anything for Nell's food. Should we add a dash of gossip? Things are boringly quiet at the dock. Even the lobster crew is unusually dull. They generally have exaggerated spin on a poacher or lines being tangled or someone hitting on someone's girl. This week? Nada."

"Gossip? I don't know about that," Birdie said. "Things are very quiet on my end of town, too."

"The summer is just about over, that's what's going on," Izzy said. "When the number of tourists and beach people dwindle, the town gets sleepy."

"I like sleepy," Nell said. "Sleepy days are good for knitting."

Birdie uncorked a bottle of pinot grigio and filled four glasses sitting on the coffee table in front of the fireplace. In minutes they were gathered around the table and the wine, patterns neatly stacked in the center and plates filled with Nell's creamy lobster dish taking center stage. Nell passed around the basket of rolls and settled into a worn leather chair that used to be in Ben's den. "These vegetables will be easy to knit. And I love Izzy's idea of felting baskets. Perfect for the outdoor tables," Nell said.

"Laura Danvers wants to help knit the vegetables. She's going to get Gabby and Daisy to help, too," Birdie said. "Gabby is thrilled. She and Laura's sweet daughter are such buddies."

"They came in today to pick out yarn," Izzy said. "Also, Gabby signed up to teach another of her hat classes to the preteens in town. Daisy's helping. Those two are a hoot together. They keep Mae in stitches."

"A pun from our Iz," Cass said. She reached for her glass, then lifted it in a playful toast to Izzy.

They all chuckled, an easier task than talking as they devoured the food.

"So is Mary's B and B guy still here?" Cass asked, forcing the words out around a bite of roll. "I hear talk but haven't seen him around."

"Very much so," Birdie said. "He runs every morning. He has quite a nice physique."

Cass looked over at Birdie and laughed. "He does, does he?"

"One is never too old to look," Birdie said, teasing her right back.

"It's probably a good thing he runs, since he doesn't have a car." Nell had decided not to speculate on Glenn, not to build a mystery around him for no reason. But she felt a sliver of pleasure that someone else had done the deed. Birdie and Izzy had spent time with the man, too. She'd wait and see if they thought there was something mysterious about him.

"Mary gave him an old bike of her husband's," Birdie said. "He likes it. I was out walking this morning and we chatted for a bit. He said he hadn't been on a bike since he was a kid. I suppose it's usually too hot in Arizona."

Nell told Cass about dinner at the Edge and what they'd learned about Glenn Mackenzie. "He's a nice guy, pleasant and easy to talk to. And he's in awe of our Sam."

"Well, as are we all," Cass said, wrinkling up her nose at Izzy. "Awesome Sam. Those words go together like Purl and expensive yarn." She laughed as the small calico cat jumped into a basket of deep blue sea silk yarn.

Izzy gently lifted Purl to the couch. "Sam likes Glenn. He came by yesterday to look at Sam's Canon 1DS. He acted the same way Cass did over the casserole. Practically bowed to it."

Cass laughed. "I get that. Sam has a pretty fancy camera."

"Of course he does," Izzy said. "It's our life insurance policy and will hopefully put Abby through Harvard."

"So, this Glenn is a photographer, too?" Cass asked.

"It's his avocation," Birdie explained. "He mentioned last night that his mother loved photography. Taking photos brings back great memories of her and what she taught him. Maybe that's what he's doing on this little hiatus—remembering his mother as he takes photos of beautiful scenery. Refreshing himself. This is certainly a great place to do those things."

"I thought someone said he was a doctor," Cass said.

"I guess," Izzy said. "He told Sam he's doing a postdoc in medical research or something that sounded hard to understand. He's been in school or doing internships forever."

"But he doesn't seem to be in much of a hurry," Nell said.

"Maybe he's one of those guys who spends his life going to school," Cass said. "Pete has a friend like that. He's afraid to face real life, my brother thinks."

"I don't think Glenn's afraid of much. And I don't blame him for taking his time," Birdie said. She chewed thoughtfully on a roll. "Life is too short not to take time out to enjoy some of the things right in front of us. I don't imagine there's much time for that once you plunge into a postdoctoral research program."

"I don't buy it," Cass said. She got up and refilled her bowl, then returned to curious faces. She looked around. "What? It seems weird to me, that's all. But what do I know?"

Nell waited to see if Cass's "weird" matched her own.

"What's weird?" Izzy asked, spearing her last piece of lobster on her fork.

"That he showed up the way he did, doesn't really care if his car gets fixed in a hurry. Most of us would be pounding on Shelby Pickard's garage door. And why did he detour over to Cape Ann and not head up to Vermont or Maine? It's not like we're right off the highway."

Birdie *tsk*ed at her. "Because, Catherine, lots and lots of artists have detoured over Cape Ann's way to have our great land and sea inspire their art. Well-known artists. Winslow Homer, Fitz Hugh Lane, Edward Hopper . . ."

"Okay, okay," Cass held up her hands in defeat. "You're right. I think it's my own impatient streak coming out. Pickard kept my truck for four days once, and I was ready to kick in his garage door."

Izzy laughed and poked her lightly on the arm. "You're just grumpy that you missed out on the paella last night."

Cass acknowledged that was true. Danny had had a book signing for his latest mystery over in Brookline, and she'd gone along, settling for cheese and crackers and supermarket sheet cake at the signing. "I'm being a good fiancée," she said. "But I do want to meet this guy."

Nell felt sure Cass and Glenn would meet eventually. She didn't get the feeling Glenn Mackenzie was in a hurry to go anywhere, postdoctoral fellowship or not—a thought that mystified her, just as it did Cass.

But before she could think of a subtle way to insert it into the conversation, the subject of Glenn Mackenzie had been dropped. They quickly moved on to second helpings of lobster mac and cheese until only a river on the bottom of the Le Creuset casserole dish hinted it had once been filled to the brim.

When Nell got up to collect the plates, she caught Cass looking at her, and she knew Cass had read a bit of agreement in her eyes about Glenn Mackenzie. One that certainly had no rationale behind it. Just a fleeting feeling was all, the kind that was easily shrugged off—and that's what Nell would try to do.

The plates were rinsed and stacked in the galley kitchen at the top of the short stairway, hands washed, and knitting needles pulled out as the easy allure of Patti Smith's voice moved them back to the fireplace and comfortable chairs.

Izzy piled a stack of yarn on the table. Colorful skeins of orange and red and plum, bright spring green and deep gray, all waiting to be stitched into carrots and eggplants and turnips. A glorious puddle of yarn.

In minutes they'd dug their fingers deep into warm wool fibers, soft cotton and baby alpaca and mulberry silk. "Some of these are so luxurious, Iz," Nell said, hesitating as she fingered a ball of emerald green ultraluxe, something she could envision for a fine, lacy scarf. "Are you sure you want to use them for vegetables?"

"These are incomplete skeins that I balled up. There isn't enough of one kind for sweaters or even scarves. So we'll have the most luxurious vegetables imaginable. Let's just hope no one takes a bite out of one." She pointed to a wicker basket filled with more yarn. "We can use those chunky and worsted balls for the baskets, maybe keep them monochromatic so the fruits and vegetables will stand out more."

Izzy set to work, lining up the colors for her first basket—navy and gray, soft and lovely. Cass pulled together bright orange and green for a bunch of carrots.

Birdie began casting on, the dark and plummy yarn looping easily on her needle. "I'm making an *aubergine*," she said with French flair. "It's my housekeeper's favorite vegetable. I'll add a filmy touch of light green leafing over the top." She looked at the pattern photo in front of her, then pushed it aside, and the others knew she'd knit away without looking at the pattern ever again, her small bent fingers working the needles, adding stitches here and there, then decreasing them along the way, until the plump eggplant had shape and structure, a work of art to grace the harvest table, a standout in a felted basket.

Izzy watched Birdie, smiled, then leaned over and gave her a quick hug. They thought alike, knit alike.

Birdie smiled back, reading clearly what the hug was all about.

Once the knitting began in earnest, talk came in starts and stops, with attention floating from the yarn falling through fingers to Birdie's excitement over the chefs who were lining up to host the harvest dinners they'd be offering at Lambswool Farm.

A rattle at the door startled all of them. Izzy's eyebrows shot up.

Then she shrugged and headed up the three steps into the semi-dark main room of the shop. Mae, her manager, always locked the front door after the knitters were settled, leaving on a few security lights. Izzy peered through the pane of glass, then quickly turned the lock.

"Claire, come in. What a nice surprise. We're all in the back."

"Birdie said you'd be working on the vegetables tonight, and, well, I was wandering by with a few unplanned minutes on my hands, so I decided to stop in and see how it's going. I hope I'm not interrupting."

"Of course you're not. Come see what we're up to." She ushered her quickly down to the knitting room.

Cass sprang up and grabbed an extra wineglass while Nell cleaned off a chair for Claire. Purl provided the ultimate welcome as she effortlessly curled up on Claire's lap, her tail gently brushing the glass of wine.

Claire picked up a ball of pale yellow silk, shiny and filmy and perfect for the tassels on a stalk of corn. She brushed it against her cheek. "You're amazing artists, every single one of you," she said.

Cass laughed hard enough that Purl sat up, looking over at her curiously. Cass apologized to the cat and explained that she'd been called lots of things, but never an artist. "But I'm going to claim it and dangle it out in front of my very talented writer fiancé when I get home."

They all laughed. Calling Cass an artist was a bit like calling her a chef, although her knitting was coming along, and most all of her mistakes could easily be fixed by one of the others.

"Your place won't be big enough to house your head, Cass," Izzy said. "It's ballooning before our eyes. No more compliments, Claire, thank you very much."

Nell brought over a plate of cookies, then pointed out pictures of the array of vegetables they'd be knitting up, while Claire exclaimed nicely over each.

Nell noticed for the first time that Claire was dressed up—a silky blue dress matching her eyes, a lacy shawl draped across her arms, and her curves discreet and noticeable all at once. Her soft brown hair was brushed to a sheen, the waves just touching her shoulders. She was quietly stunning, something that sometimes got buried in Claire's normal attire of late—jeans, boots, and plaid shirts. "You look amazing, Claire. Are you going somewhere?"

"Well, I was," she said lightly, setting the yarn back down on the table and picking up the thick wool Izzy was going to use for a bowl. She seemed to be concentrating on the yarn, imagining it felted into a round table bowl for the brightly colored vegetables. Finally she looked up. "I was stood up, do you believe it?" The dimples in her cheek deepened as she smiled at her own words. "Here I am, fifty-one years old, and abandoned on the steps of the Ocean's Edge Restaurant for all the world to see."

She was poking fun at herself, not angry, but Nell noticed concern in her eyes. "Were you meeting Alan?" she asked.

Claire nodded.

Nothing much was secret in Sea Harbor, including the fact that Alan Hamilton and Claire Russell were seeing each other. The well-liked doctor had been "in demand," as Izzy put it, ever since his wife had died several years before. But for some time now it had been the quiet, lovely Claire Russell who was always seen at his side—and very happily so.

"What happened?" Birdie asked with a *tsk* and slight shake of her head. "My second husband was a doctor. Doctors have to be among the least dependable dates. Alan is probably involved in some piddly little thing, like saving a life somewhere."

Claire half smiled. "He might be. He's good at that." She looked at her hands, rubbing one knuckle with her thumb, and then she added, "He's good at a lot of things."

Nell smiled, and Izzy held up her phone. "Did you . . . ?"

"Yes," Claire said. "I texted him a couple of times. I think Birdie's probably right. He stood me up to save someone's life. Can you believe it? The gall of that man." She held her palms up and drew smiles.

Birdie topped off Claire's wine and settled back into the couch, picking up her glass. "Here's to saving lives."

Claire smiled, her shoulders relaxing as she stretched her neck, easing away the tension. "So, let's have a look at what's going on here." She looked down at the basket of yarn and the pile of patterns scattered across the table awaiting her opinion and she dug right in, explaining that some food critic somewhere was going to be writing about these amazing Lambswool Farm centerpieces in the very near future.

It was an hour or so later, after going through colors and fiber weights and plans for the Lambswool Farm decorations—and plenty of time spent fingering the soft, sensual yarns Izzy had picked out for them—that Claire finally checked her watch. She stood and slipped her purse over her shoulder. "I will most definitely let Alan know he can disappear any time he chooses. I have options—and ones that come with very fine wine. Thank you all for the lovely evening."

"You're always welcome. Next time bring your needles," Izzy said.

Claire looked over at Birdie. "I'm headed home to catch up on some paperwork for the dinners, but will I still see you out at the farm tomorrow?"

Birdie assured her she'd be by with several others who wanted a sneak preview of the finished kitchen. They could probably sell tickets to it, so many people were asking about it, she said. Her only worry was whether they'd ever get Nell to go home, once she set her eyes on those shiny new appliances.

Nell followed Claire up the stairs to the front door. "Am I misreading something, Claire? You don't look miffed, but you do look worried."

Claire shifted her shoulder bag as if it were suddenly carrying bowling balls. "You see through me. It's all those hours we spent together getting your yard ready for Izzy's wedding, sharing memories and wearing our emotions on our sleeves."

"I guess that's it. We did a lot of that, didn't we?"

"I'm not angry with being stood up, at least I don't think I am. But Alan has been on edge lately, so tired-looking. And I can tell he genuinely hurts sometimes. I asked if he thought he was getting the flu, but he brushed it off. Doctors don't get sick, I guess. I know he's under some stress at the clinic, too. I worry about him."

"Do you think that has anything to do with why he didn't show up tonight?"

"I don't know. Probably not, though he's been distracted. He most likely had a call, some kind of emergency. You know him: if a child's fever is high, he'll be off to the house so the mom or dad won't have to take the sick child out." She pulled her car keys from her pocket. "The thing is, when you pile things on top of one another and start to make connections that probably aren't there, everything seems worse, don't you think? Muddled." She took a deep breath, then let it out with a shake of her head. But in the next breath she assured Nell things were fine. And if they weren't this minute, they would get better; she was sure of it. And most important, she was sure of Alan.

The emotion in her voice spoke volumes to Nell, and she knew in that moment that Claire and Alan's relationship was about more than just having dinner together.

Nell waved her off, then stood on the step for a few minutes while Claire climbed inside her car and started the engine. She wasn't at all sure what Claire meant about things getting better, but suspected it was the pressure of getting Lambswool Farm ready for business, coupled with a partner not feeling well—a combination that would certainly throw someone off-kilter. But a pressure that would ease up soon.

Claire glanced in the rearview mirror and caught Nell looking after her. She gave a high sign, a royal wave of her fingers. Then she pulled away from the curb and drove up Harbor Road, turning east toward the sound of the pounding sea and to her small cottage at its edge.

Claire had come so far, rebuilding her life. Returning to Sea Harbor after being away for decades had been difficult. She'd fled the town when her teenage daughter had drowned in a quarry, then returned all those years later to finally grieve her daughter's death. For that first summer, she had lived in Nell's guesthouse, gardening in the backyard and transforming it into Izzy's wedding paradise. Those days of spreading mulch and planting flowers together had nurtured a rich friendship right along with the hydrangeas and roses and irises.

A sound behind her pulled her from her thoughts and she looked into Izzy's puzzled face.

"You okay, Aunt Nell? We thought maybe you'd walked out on us."

"I'm fine, sweetie. Just lost in thought, that's all."

"We're calling it a night."

Nell agreed and followed Izzy back inside. She was suddenly tired, ready to get home to Ben.

The knitting-night routine was as familiar to them as breathing, and in minutes they'd stashed the glasses, packed up their knitting and skeins of yarn, and turned out the lights.

"I'll pick up my dishes tomorrow," Nell said. She waved Birdie and Cass off and waited on the step while Izzy locked the front door.

It was a strange night: huge and dark, with unexpected gusts of warm wind snapping branches on the trees and sending scraps of paper and coffee cups skidding into the curbs. A moonless sky was bright with a million stars flung against a pitch-black blanket.

Izzy shivered. "It feels like Halloween, but it's warm. Spooky."

Nell felt it, too. The strange howling of the wind, the sound of the sea as it crashed against the massive boulders guarding the shore.

Spooky, yes. She wrapped her arms around herself.

They stood in the shadows of the shop awning, listening to the night sounds. Far down the road Jake Risso was indulging in his Elvis fantasies. Hound dog music rolled out of his Gull Tavern onto the nearly vacant sidewalks. The ocean roared, and gulls swooped down to the sidewalk for late-evening snacks.

Moments later the ocean lulled into a split-second hush and voices were picked up and carried on the wind.

"Where is that coming from?" Izzy asked, then looked across the street and spotted the source. Two figures stood on a narrow path in the shadows of the corner park. Their voices rose to be heard above the wind. Angry sounds. Shrill and swooping like the gulls.

Their shadows were a blur, blending into the trees and park shadows, until one of the people stepped into the soft glow of the old-fashioned lamp lights dotting Harbor Road. The words continued, tumbling over one another, angry and fierce, tossed back and forth like weapons.

Shadows weaving beneath the lamplight and then, finally, turning into people. People Nell and Izzy knew.

The two women held their breath and took a step backward beneath the awning.

Across the street, Alan Hamilton lowered his head, shaking it. Then his shoulders slumped and he abruptly turned back in the direction from which they'd come. After what sounded like a curse that flew over his shoulder and landed at his companion's feet, he walked quickly and resolutely back through the park to the darkened building that was once a sea captain's mansion.

Lily Virgilio stood unmoving, watching him walk away. Then she turned in the opposite direction, away from the park, toward Harbor Road. Light from the gas lamp bounced off a large white sheet of paper in her hands, illuminating it. Lily stared at it for a brief moment, then folded it and shoved it in her purse. She started to walk slowly, seemingly unsure of where she was going, but with her eyes directed straight ahead, as if whatever she saw in the distance was far better than what she had left behind.

If she had looked to the left, even for a minute, if she had focused her eyes across the street, she would have seen two friends standing in front of a yarn shop, wishing they were somewhere else.

Chapter 6

Claire Russell thumbed through the messages on her phone. Caterers, painters, deliverymen. A reporter wanting to do an interview.

And then the one she'd been watching for, the one that caused a quick flip-flop in her chest.

There was no explanation, no story about rushing to a sick patient's house, spending hours at his or her side.

Dinner tonight? he typed, almost as if he'd forgotten that he'd missed one the night before. Brief, to the point, but that was how Alan always was.

For a moment Claire wondered whether she was the one at fault, mixing up her days. But she wasn't. Alan must have had a terribly busy day and forgotten. Plain and simple.

Claire answered the text with a smiley face.

Too corny? she wondered as her answer flew off into cyberspace. Maybe that's what happens when one gets involved in a relationship at her age. Yet maybe for the first time in her life she felt . . . what? Attractive? Desirable? She'd often been told she was pretty—but a youthful and ugly marriage had ripped the meaning of the word from her psyche. Finally, returning to Sea Harbor, a feeling of self-worth had gradually come back. And for the first time in a long time, stood up or not, she felt loved.

She shoved her phone into the pocket of her jeans and walked through the open doors into the converted barn. As she often did these days, she stopped in awe. Sometimes she felt like it was almost too much to take in.

She looked into the spacious kitchen. Instead of stalls and rusty equipment, it was fit for a five-star chef. Or two or three of them. Light from the skylights poured down onto stainless-steel countertops and islands, then bounced off them onto the stone floor. Ceiling fans spun the smell of freshly oiled wood around the room. It was beyond anyone's dreams. Certainly beyond hers.

The kitchen brought it all together. It was the link between the abundance of heirloom tomato vines and thick beds of lettuce and kale, spinach and root vegetables that were growing fat beneath the earth's crust just beyond the barns—and the harvest dinners that would fill the old, lovingly finished wooden tables, groaning beneath the fruit of the earth.

Claire tugged a rag free from the back pocket of her jeans and rubbed an imaginary spot from the stainless-steel island, then stood back and imagined the space bustling with food preparation, smells of roasted vegetables, basil and tarragon, chervil and wine and cream sauces filling the heated air. Outside, beyond the rolling barn doors, a flagstone patio fanned out from the barn, a place for diners to gather and enjoy cocktails, appetizers, and magnificent sunsets. She could almost see it playing out in front of her: laughter and music, fine food cooked over grills and boiling up in giant pots.

She had confessed to Birdie and the contractors that her vision for Lambswool Farm was stolen from a Barefoot Contessa cookbook. The contractors and kitchen designers knew and loved the same books, and they had masterfully transformed the once-dilapidated building. A barn that had previously housed feral cats and random animals and lord knows what kinds of vermin was painted white, filled with open shelves, stocked with herbs and spices, foodstuffs and supplies, dinner plates glazed in colors of the land, the harvest, the sky. A smooth stone fireplace at one end of the room held plain candles on a narrow mantel, a seascape canvas above it. Copper pots and pans hung from chains. Outside, beyond the patio and the long rough-hewn tables, were pastures and vegetable gardens. And beyond that, what had brought Claire back to Sea Harbor a few years before—the ocean itself. Home.

Home . . . Lambswool Farm.

It was a dream, but when Claire blinked herself awake, it didn't disappear in the cold light of day. All one needed was a guardian angel.

Claire looked through the open barn doors at the small woman across the way, her hair cut as short as a man's, with silvery wisps across her forehead. She was standing near a fence that bordered a pasture. Across from the gravel drive was a second barn—this one also freshly painted but holding hay and pitchforks, tools and a tractor and gardening supplies. Stalls for lambing and for a horse they hoped to get. It had stood vacant, like the other, for decades, until the silver-haired angel had wrought miracles.

Claire knew that Birdie Favazza would cringe if she heard anyone call her that, but it's what she was. A guardian angel.

Nell and Izzy were there, too, their heads thrown back in laughter. This was her Friday show-and-tell, Birdie had told Claire earlier.

A columbine vine, heavy with blue and white flowers, climbed up the fence beside them. From where Claire stood in the cool shadows of the barn, the scene was a watercolor come alive.

A whoop of laughter rolled across the gravel drive, and Claire watched Birdie's granddaughter racing across the field toward the women, her legs as agile and long as a young deer's. She'd been out in the pasture, visiting the sheep she had claimed as her favorite: Charlotte, a lovely ewe that the youngster had named the day she had met her. A ewe that was about to give birth, causing great drama in Gabby Marietti's life. There were days Claire wondered if the ewe had gotten pregnant on purpose, simply to bring such unabashed joy to this young girl. Claire swore Charlotte related to Gabby, and Gabby had concurred, explaining that sheep could remember up to fifty faces for two years.

The ewe's birthing stall was ready, clean and well equipped. Gabby had watched over the process, carefully doing everything but bringing in stuffed animals for the unborn lamb.

Charlotte and I know each other from another life, Gabby had explained to Claire. And she found herself believing it.

Deep down, Claire knew exactly what Gabby felt. She felt that way herself, though not about lambs or sheep.

Across the gravel drive, Nell fought the sea breeze, pushing strands of flying hair behind her ears. "Sonny would love what you've done here, Birdie," she said.

"Not what I've done, not at all. But you're right. Sonny loved a party, loved the outdoors, and loved to eat. Turning this ramshackle mess into a place that grows healthy food and building a kitchen to lure chefs to cook in it would be right up his alley, provided there was plenty of fine whiskey at a side bar."

"Did you and Grandpa Sonny ever come out here?" Gabby asked, hoisting herself up onto the table. Wild strands of black hair pulled loose from a lazy ponytail that hung down her back, but Gabby seemed not to notice. She haphazardly brushed flecks of straw from her grass-stained shorts, then cupped one hand over her eyes to block out the sunlight.

"Yes, we did. We were newly married, driving off to some party or another—we were quite the gadabouts—and Sonny pointed out the place to me. The weeds were as tall as the barn, which seemed to lean to one side. His grandparents leased the land out to farmers for a while. But eventually no one wanted to bother with it and it simply fell into disrepair." She looked around at the wide pastures, the small flock of sheep, the carefully nurtured gardens. Even the small house, now used as an office, was presentable again, gray shingled and with bright blue shutters.

A blend of nostalgia and amusement deepened the lines in her face. "None of the Favazzas would ever have imagined the farm as it is today, not in a million years. Maybe they are rolling over in their graves at what that crazy woman Sonny married is doing with all their money." Birdie's gray-green eyes lit with laughter at the thought. "What fun it all is. You're right, Nell: Sonny would absolutely have loved it. He'd be right out there with Angelo, pitching hay bales, figuring out how to drive a tractor. And he'd love the vegetables and the dinners we have planned. Most of all he'd love the sunsets. '*Sunsets were made for us,*' he used to tell me . . ."

Nell looked over Birdie's shoulder and spotted Ben in the distance, talking to Angelo and one of the farmworkers. She waved, but he turned away before the wave reached him. He was carrying a plank of wood and walking toward the other barn on the property, the working barn that Gabby had unofficially named Wilbur's Place.

Gabby noticed Ben, too, and jumped off the table in a flying leap. "Oops, gotta go. Uncle Ben had one of the guys make a sign for the barn. We want it up for Sunday night. He needs me to help." She ran after him, a cloud of gravel dust rising up behind her.

Nell watched her disappear into the barn. Although she wasn't a blood relative, both Ben and Nell had fallen in love with Birdie's granddaughter, and each time she called them *Aunt* or *Uncle*, the affection seemed to deepen.

Birdie read Nell's expression. Her voice was soft. "She's a breath of life. And she loves it out here—the sheep, the open air, the pounding of the sea. You'd never know she lives in a New York penthouse half the year."

"She's turning into Abby's favorite daytime babysitter. Gabby has more imagination in one fingertip than all our older sitters combined."

Birdie laughed. "She certainly does. She's teaching Harold how to knit."

The thought of Birdie's groundskeeper using a knitting needle for anything other than staking a small plant made them all laugh.

But the laughter died instantly at a sudden noise coming from the barn—a loud, indistinguishable crash.

And then another one.

It wasn't a tractor gearing up or the bleating of Charlotte or the other sheep. It was a sound that shattered the pastoral air into millions of tiny exploding molecules.

It was the sound of Gabby Marietti screaming for help.

Chapter 7

"It's the smaller of the two bones that's broken," Dr. Alan Hamilton said, his long fingers carefully probing Ben's forearm.

Ben winced. "That's what I've been telling Nell, Doc. Small. Unimportant. No reason to call out the National Guard." He shifted uncomfortably on the padded table. A broken bone carried little significance, and it didn't merit the Indy 500–style ride Nell had delivered over rutted, narrow roads.

"Big or small, it's broken, Ben," Nell said, the tone in her voice tense and leaving no room for argument.

Gabby Marietti stood quietly at the window for as long as she could stand it. At the *click* of the radiograph light, she loped across the room and wedged herself between Nell and the doctor. She stared at Ben's arm, then up at the image on the fluorescent screen, just visible behind Alan Hamilton's head. "It's the ulna," she said.

Alan Hamilton looked over his rimless glasses at the preteen and nodded. "Yes, it is," he said.

Gabby leaned in closer, squinting at the black-and-white image and offering details of the accident to the doctor. "I tried to climb up in the loft to get the wire and hammer for our sign, but Uncle Ben stopped me. He was afraid there'd be shearing equipment up there or rotted wood or whatever. He always says that Aunt Nell worries too much, but he does, too."

She bit down on her bottom lip, re-creating the scene in her head, and then went on. "So, anyway, I went over to the cupboard and was digging out some treats for Charlotte when it all happened. Hay and dust and pieces of wood flew like a tornado had hit—right into Charlotte's bed. My back was turned, so at first I didn't know what happened, but I ran over, and sure enough, right in the middle of the mess was Uncle Ben."

"Looks like Uncle Ben was right not to let you do the climbing," the doctor said, looking back at Ben's arm. Then he frowned as if they'd forgotten an important detail. He looked at Gabby again. "Is Charlotte all right? Should you have brought her in, too?"

Gabby giggled and Ben explained. "Charlotte is a ewe out at Lambswool Farm." He winced again as the family doctor maneuvered his forearm. "But she's fine."

"Charlotte is amazing; she's pregnant," Gabby said. "And she might not be so fine if it weren't for Uncle Ben. He grabbed hold of something and pushed himself away so he wouldn't land on her. That would have been just really awful. He probably saved her life and the baby's, too."

Nell shook her head, wondering how large the story would grow by the time it had run its course.

"Gabby and Charlotte are great pals," Ben said, changing the subject. "Gabrielle is great with sheep. She's good with people, too."

The preteen had refused to stay behind with Izzy and her grandmother. She had been the only eyewitness, she insisted. She might have information that would be helpful to the doctor. Also, she'd taken a first aid course in school and was going to be a veterinarian. She'd climbed into the backseat of the Endicott C-RV before anyone had a chance to argue with her, leaving a very reluctant

Birdie and Izzy behind to handle Mary Pisano and the others Birdie had invited to tour the farm.

Gabby wasn't finished and edged her way closer to Dr. Hamilton now. "Our cook back in New York has a golden retriever who broke her ulna last year. It was painful, but we splinted it, and she was as good as new."

"You sound well-informed, young lady. I think Ben and the dog share a diagnosis." Alan wiped some perspiration off his forehead with one sleeve, winced as if the broken bone were his own, and turned to Ben. "I think we can get by with a splint if you behave yourself. The bones are aligned correctly, and it's a small fracture. You'll be good as new in a few weeks, but I'll want to keep an eye on it."

Ben opened his mouth to say something, but Alan spoke first, reading his mind. "Yeah, you can sail. They make great waterproof protectors these days. Let your body tell you what to do. If it hurts, stop."

Nell watched Alan's face carefully as he talked, in case there were messages there, a hidden concern about Ben. But all she saw was Alan's professional face, though thinner and paler than usual, with another slight wince that made her think the good doctor was working too hard and probably had a headache. "So he'll be good as new in no time," she said out loud, and Alan nodded agreement.

"In the meantime, I can be your left arm whenever you need one," Gabby assured Ben. She moved away from the table while Doc Hamilton pressed an intercom button and asked for supplies.

"This doesn't look like my doctor's office in New York," Gabby said, walking over to the open window where white gauzy curtains flapped in the breeze. "I think people must feel less sick here."

In one corner an old oak glass-fronted cabinet housed bandages, blood pressure cuffs, an assortment of bottles. Two cracked leather chairs, a wheeled stool, and the examining table filled the rest of the space.

Although the Hamilton family practice shared the old mansion, the lab, and the library with the women's clinic, the family practice had kept some of its own office decor from decades earlier. High-tech equipment shared space with flowered wallpaper, old wooden chairs with embroidered seat cushions, and hardwood floors that creaked comfortably underfoot. And Sea Harbor patients liked it.

Gabby was probably right—people felt less sick there.

A light knock on the door was followed by a nurse pushing a small cart that carried the materials that would soon decorate Ben's arm. Her eyes lit up when she saw the others gathered in the room.

"Hey, guys," she said, "what's going on in here? Looks like a party."

"Hi, Carly," Nell said, looking into the bright and familiar face. She embraced the short-haired nurse, finding a sense of relief in having friends care for Ben, no matter how insignificant her husband seemed to think falling out of a barn loft was.

"Carly is going to show you two ladies to my office while I start decorating Ben's arm," Alan said, raising his eyebrows in a way that prohibited Nell and Gabby from arguing. Beneath the brows, his eyes were weary.

And that was when Nell remembered the evening before. Worry over Ben had effectively blocked out concern for anything else—her friend being stood up, arguments overheard, tiredness in a man's eyes.

But now, with the burden of worry over Ben lessening, she remembered it all clearly, and she looked at the doctor more closely. A sailor like Ben, Alan had an outdoor complexion—smooth and tan with just a shadow of a beard. But today he was drained, washed-out-looking. Nell wondered whether he'd slept at all. Clearly the altercation with Lily had affected him.

Alan caught her look and put his own interpretation on it. "Ben's going to be okay, Nell," he said. "He's going to be hoisting sails with that arm in no time."

Nell nodded.

Carly looked over. "Shall I send Arle—"

Alan cut off her sentence with a shake of his head and immediately turned his attention back to Ben and the packages of gauze and folded sling material on the table. "I'll manage fine," he said.

Carly shrugged and headed for the door, lowering her head toward Gabby and whispering, "Doc Hamilton likes to work alone. He's kind of like an artist. But only the elite get to wait in his office." She looked up at Nell. "You two must be special to him."

"We've known each other a long time," Nell said. "He's a good man. I was surprised to hear you'd left your nursing job at the retirement home, Carly—but you picked a good place to be. You probably have already met nearly every family in Sea Harbor—and soon you'll know all their secrets."

"That's for sure." Carly laughed and motioned for them to follow her down the hallway. Her short blond bob bounced as she talked. "I finally finished my nurse practitioner's degree—it took me years—and Doc Alan was looking for one on his staff. As much as I loved the people at Ocean View, I needed a change, a fresh start—and they didn't really have a need over there for a nurse practitioner." She grinned then. "Besides, the hours are better here and I get to catch some of Andy's gigs with the Fractured Fish."

"The Fractured Fish are the best. And Andy Risso is way cool," Gabby said. She lifted her eyebrows knowingly, letting both Nell and Carly know she was up on Sea Harbor gossip. She knew that Andy and Carly were "together."

"Yep, he sure is." Carly stopped at the end of the hall at a partially opened door. She pushed it wide and was about to say something to Nell when a sound startled her.

A woman was leaning over a large desk near the window. She looked up, smiled, and immediately set down a small plant. "Hi, Carly. I didn't hear you knock," she said.

"Is there something I can help you with in here?" Carly's tone carried the answer to the rhetorical question: *Of course there isn't.*

The woman waved one hand in the air. "It's okay. Alan can be messy, right? I was straightening things up, refreshing this poor little plant." She fingered the furry, don't-touch leaves on an African violet. As she stepped out from behind the desk, she spotted the others standing in the doorway.

"Look who's here. Hi, Nell. Hey, Gabs."

"Well, good grief," Nell said, walking in. "What are you doing here?"

Arlene Arcado laughed. "Yeah, I know. I surprise people. One patient ordered calamari when he saw me."

"So you work here?"

Arlene looked less like Arlene the waitress. More like a serious professional. Her white slacks and tailored blouse were still a testament to the curves beneath them, but her hair was pulled back in a bun, and she wore less makeup than usual.

She nodded. "Yes. Three days a week. The Ocean's Edge is part-time, and I needed more income. So here I am, doing whatever they need me to do. It's a decent place to work. I'm getting the job done." Her smile was satisfied and matter-of-fact.

Carly stood quietly at the edge of the desk. She picked up the assaulted plant and put it on the windowsill.

"That's great, Arlene," Nell said, her mind putting pieces of a puzzle together. Arlene wasn't sick yesterday; she was coming in to work. A definite lesson in avoiding quick judgments.

"I know a little about medicine," Arlene said. "I spent a lot of time around it when my mother was sick." Her voice had dropped, along with her smile.

"That was a difficult time for you." Arlene's aunt owned the local beauty salon, and M.J. had kept Birdie and Nell in the loop when Arlene's mother became ill. The mother and daughter were thick as thieves, M.J. said, and the mother's prolonged and painful illness had affected Arlene greatly. For months after her mother died she wrapped herself in a cocoon so dense no one could penetrate it. M.J. had tried to get her to a therapist, but she'd cut her off short; Arlene was angry at the world. A part of her seemed to have died right along with her mother.

M.J. wasn't sure what had turned the girl around, but in the past few months she'd rejoined the living; things seemed to be better and she was even speaking to M.J. again, though in a limited way.

It was unpredictable, the unique path that grieving took, Birdie had said; Arlene's journey was hers and hers alone, and no one should judge it.

Nell knew from watching her at the restaurant that Arlene had many faces. She could handle herself. She suspected the waitress was a strong young woman who hid her pain and her emotions well, pulling them out only when it suited her.

"I've seen you in action in a packed restaurant with waitstaff calling in sick. You work hard," she said out loud. "Alan is lucky to have you."

Arlene shrugged. "I suppose. I like working at the Edge—Don's a decent boss. But bills pile up, you know—this helps me out, at least for now."

She looked over at Carly, but the nurse was intently watching a hummingbird suck up sugar water from a feeder outside the window.

"I didn't mean to take up your space in here," she said to Nell. "You must be here to see the doc. I'll leave you in peace." She glanced once more at Carly, then wiggled her fingers at Gabby and walked away, her heels echoing on the wooden hallway floor.

Carly walked over and closed the door. She pushed a smile into place, took a breath, and the ebullient nurse was back.

"How long has Arlene worked here?" Nell asked.

"A few weeks," Carly said, then changed the subject and motioned toward an old love seat and several upholstered wing chairs near the back windows. "Make yourselves comfortable, and I want to know every last detail about what is going on out at Lambswool Farm." She grinned at Gabby. "And most of all, I want to know how your superman uncle Ben was injured. I want the whole scoop. Leave nothing out."

She handed Gabby and Nell each a bottle of water from a small refrigerator, twisted off the lid on her own, and settled onto the arm of one of the chairs.

"Well, as you know, Ben took a tumble," Nell began.

Carly took a swig of her water, nodding slowly. "I see that worried look on your face, Nell. He's going to be fine. And he couldn't be in better hands. Most fractures like his are easily fixed. You don't have anything to worry about." Carly slipped down into the chair. She leaned forward, her elbows on her knees.

Nell smiled, feeling for the first time in the last hour that everything was shifting back into place. Carly was absolutely right. Ben was in excellent hands. Whatever Alan's disagreement was with the doctor who occupied the other side of the building, it wouldn't affect his medical prowess—and the tiredness she had seen in his eyes was probably a result of the packed waiting room they'd worked their way through a short while earlier.

When she had arrived home the night before, she'd told Ben about the argument she and Izzy had witnessed. He dismissed any concern in a second, and Nell knew that's exactly what should be done with it. She was slightly embarrassed they'd even been privy to a private encounter. Two thriving practices in the same old building were bound to generate some disagreements, Ben said. And he had heard some complaints at the yacht club about the long wait for appointments. Maybe Lily thought it was reflecting on her practice as well. "It's like a marriage—people argue when they're together that much. And then they make up. And that's the good part." Then he had given her a hug before following her up the back steps to a warm, waiting bed.

It seemed years ago, not just last night. Worry, accidents, trauma—and especially a husband's broken bone—had a way of slicing up time, tossing it in a blender, and rendering it useless and ineffectual.

Today was the only real thing. Sitting in a doctor's office. Being sure Ben was all right. And she knew beyond the edge of her worry that he was. This wasn't serious as injuries go. Ben's heart attack several years ago had been serious—and though Ben was doing fine, it had left a permanent scar in Nell—a twinge that twisted and turned at the slightest provocation—a cough, the flu, a sailboat mishap, or unusual tiredness in Ben. She always managed to tap down the ragged slice of fear when it arose, all the while knowing it would never go away completely.

"So, I'll tell you exactly what happened," Gabby began, picking up the story. "I was there; I saw it all. We were all at the farm when Uncle Ben and I—"

The farm. It had already assumed that kind of prominence in Birdie's granddaughter's mind. *The* farm. There was no other. Nell smiled and leaned her head against the wing chair. Carly was now in capable hands, too. Gabby was a masterful storyteller. Nell half closed her eyes and listened to Gabby's light voice dramatically embellishing the story for the nurse.

As the vivid images floated around the room, Nell suspected that by the end of the weekend, the story would have rolled up and down Harbor Road, gathering rich nuances as it traveled from Coffee's to Izzy's yarn studio to Gus McClucken's hardware store. And as the tale gathered moss, Ben might emerge as a superhero, one who had single-handedly saved a prized ewe and Gabby herself from a falling, rotted loft. And in the process Ben had broken a bone—inconsequential for a superhero. Superheroes healed quickly, or simply grew new limbs.

Let the stories spin as wildly as Gabby liked, as long as Ben was whole, with nothing but a temporarily immobile arm to show for it.

Chapter 8

Nell nearly fell asleep in the office, wrapped in a hazy cloud of comfort as Gabby's sweet voice and Carly's attentive replies and questions lulled her mind into a peaceful state.

It was another voice that brought her to sharp attention a short while later.

"It's Sam," Gabby yelled, immediately popping out of the chair.

Carly was the first one to the door. She pulled it open to find a large camera pointed at her.

Behind it, Sam grinned. "Hey, Nurse Carly, what's up? Arlene tells us you've sequestered Nell and Gabby in here." He lowered the camera. "A kidnapping, I presume?"

"Hey back," Carly said, grinning. "And yes, we're here, all three of us, away from Arlene's watchful eye." She looked at the camera, then beyond it to a shadowy form leaning against the back wall. An unfamiliar one. She straightened up.

Sam moved aside and introduced Carly to Glenn Mackenzie. "Glenn, Carly Schultz. Carly is Andy Risso's girlfriend—for which we give her great sympathy and understanding. She's also a nurse practitioner extraordinaire."

Carly shook her head and rolled her eyes.

Sam next introduced Gabby, who took an immediate liking to Glenn when she noticed the Patriots hat on his floppy hair.

"When in Rome," he said to her, touching the brim, and Gabby laughed.

"So, you heard about Ben?" Nell asked.

"Are you kidding?" Sam walked into the room with Glenn close behind him. "Mary Pisano was out at the farm today, for starters."

Nell sighed. *Of course.* She'd forgotten about Mary—one of the reasons Birdie had had to stay behind.

"But actually, it was Izzy. She texted me right away. Mary is how the rest of Cape Ann, maybe Boston and New York, will find out."

"Of course Izzy called you. Where's my head today?"

"Worrying about that man in the examining room, would be my guess," Sam said, and gave Nell a warm hug.

"But Uncle Ben's going to be fine," Gabby said, then stared at the camera hanging from Sam's neck. "You came to photograph Uncle Ben's arm? What's with that?"

Sam laughed. "Nope, that's not why we're here, though I'm sure his arm is handsome and photo-worthy. I'm taking Glenn on a tour of some places we're going to use in that photo series." He looked at Nell. "Glenn here wasn't convinced there's a doctor alive that still does house calls." He looked over at Carly and added, "We'll stay out of your way, I promise."

"You'd better, bud," Carly said with fake sternness. "Doc Alan told us you might be coming by sometime, but he added that if you bothered us at all, we had his permission to kick you out."

Sam saluted. "Yes, ma'am. We're not doing much today. Just checking things out."

"And I'm just kidding. The doctor isn't crazy about having his picture taken, but I think he's pleased that his family's legacy will be preserved in photos. It's really busy around this place, so you might have to step over some patients in the process." She checked her watch, then glanced over at Gabby, who was looking slightly bored. "And speaking of patients, I need to check some specimens in the lab. Why don't you tag along, Gabby? Things might be more lively down the hall. And there's some lemon cake in the break room. You can help finish it off."

Gabby was across the room in an instant. "Call if you need me," she said, and gave Nell a quick hug before flying out the door behind Carly.

Glenn stood off to the side, looking around the room, while Nell explained to Sam what was going on with Ben, what the radiographs showed, and how you can't keep a good man down. "He has excellent bones," Nell said with pride.

"Sure he does. I knew that the first time I met him. Okay, so the real question here is—"

But before he could ask it, Nell gave the answer she knew Sam was waiting to hear. "Alan says he'll still be able to sail as long as he's careful."

The look of relief on Sam's face brought a quick smile from Nell. Ben and Sam's time sailing the *Dream Weaver* on open water was sacred. It went way beyond the simple joy of sailing; Sam and Ben had a tie that even Nell wasn't privy to. And it was just one of the many reasons she'd be forever grateful to Izzy for bringing Sam Perry into their lives.

They both looked over at Glenn. He was walking around the room, taking in the framed paintings of sailing ships and ocean storms on the walls; then he peered through the glass doors of an old wooden bookcase with a glass front.

"It's an interesting office," Sam said. "I don't think it's been touched much since the original Doc Hamilton sat behind that great old desk." Sam ran a hand along the walnut top, his fingers tracing the leather inlay. Behind it was a ponderous swivel chair, its carved arms worn and polished by generations of arms resting on the wood. "It's a throwback to another era."

"It sure is," Glenn said, his eyes taking in the tiles on the ceiling, the braided rug on the hardwood floor. Along one wall were gold-framed degrees and honors that went back through the years, all Dr. Hamiltons, each one with a different first name, different schools, different generations.

"You're thinking what I am," Sam said. "We can get some great shots in here, for sure."

Glenn pointed to the petit point covering on the wing chair and a framed needlepoint saying hanging on the wall. "This reminds me of a parlor in my grandmother's house—my dad's mom. There were needlepoint things everywhere. She even insisted my dad hang one of her needlepoints in his judge's chamber. He took a lot of good-natured ribbing over the slightly cheesy saying on it."

He looked down at an oval picture frame sitting on a drop-leaf table beneath the window. The woman looking back at him was pretty, middle-aged with a gentle smile. "Who's this?"

Nell walked over and looked at the photo. "That's Emily, Alan's wife. She died a few years ago."

Glenn looked at the picture again. "Kids?"

"No, they didn't have children." Nell looked at the photo again as a memory came back to her, a poignant moment she'd had with Emily Hamilton more than a dozen years before. She'd almost forgotten it. She picked up the frame and looked at it more closely, touching the wavy brown hair behind the glass as if to push a lock from the woman's forehead.

They'd had a conversation that day, the kind shared between two people who didn't know each other well but found themselves together for a while with a shared purpose. They were volunteers at the Sea Harbor Library, paired together to document boxes of old donated photographs. The work had been monotonous, and after a half hour of lighthearted banter, a chance sepia photo of a small child took their conversation to a more intimate place.

She and Alan had tried to have children, Emily had told Nell as she stared at the child's photo. The emotion in her voice added nuance to her words, and Nell could tell it hadn't been by choice. Emily had put the photo aside and looked embarrassed at speaking so intimately to a casual acquaintance. Nell tried to ease her discomfort. *It's difficult,* she had said. *Ben and I wanted children, too. It didn't happen.*

But she and Ben had moved beyond that dream and on to others, building a satisfying and rich life, filled with family they might not have raised, but who were as close to her and Ben as children she might have given birth to.

Those additional thoughts she hadn't shared with Emily because the expression on her face made it clear that she and her husband still had a way to go in handling their dreams.

Sam was checking the light from the window while Glenn flipped through an old history of medicine book. He listened as Nell mentioned Emily's sadness at not having children, then replaced the book on the shelf. He walked over to the big desk, checking the old-fashioned ink pad. "I suppose that will change things, then," he said.

"Change things?" Nell asked.

"When the doctor is gone, the clinic will no longer go from father to son."

Nell was surprised at the comment. It was true, but not what she'd have expected Glenn to pick up on. Something she herself hadn't thought about, even though they'd talked about it in a roundabout way. The family tradition was one of the reasons this clinic was so special.

Sam turned around. "Strange. I hadn't thought about it that way. This place has been in a Hamilton's capable hands forever. Things like that—well, you think they'll never change."

"Enough of such talk," Nell said, brushing away an uncomfortable vibe that had settled on the old-fashioned furniture like dust. "Alan is in his prime—there's no need for talk about who will occupy this office next."

Glenn picked up one of Alan's business cards from the desk while Sam scribbled some notes in a small tablet, jotting down angles and lights. But his mind was still playing with the clinic's history.

"You're right about that," Sam said. "The guy has at least twenty years on me—and I can't touch his tennis serve. Beats the heck out of me. He's tough. Indestructible."

Voices in the hallway were a welcome distraction, and in the next minute Carly and Gabby opened the door. "The doctor and Ben will be here in a minute," Carly said.

Sam and Glenn took the cue and followed Carly out to the public areas, checking out lights and atmosphere as they went.

Ben walked in, his arm neatly wrapped and supported in a splint, a denim sling holding it in place. Nell hurried over and touched his good arm, her eyes on the sling. "It's your favorite color at least."

"I made sure of that," Ben said. He kissed the top of Nell's head.

"It's cool," Gabby said, but her disappointment at not being able to decorate a cast was clear in her voice.

"Well, I guess you could use Magic Markers on the sling," Carly suggested, and Nell sighed.

Gabby wrinkled her nose at her, the freckles bouncing as she mentally mapped out her artwork.

Alan gave Nell a few incidental instructions and a prescription for pain medication in case there was a need. "And call me at any time," he said with a wave as he left the room.

They walked through the winding hall to the crowded reception area, where Arlene was looking at a sheet of paper and calling patients' names, then ushering them into the inner examining rooms.

"Busy place," Nell murmured, glancing around the packed room and feeling a slight bit of guilt at having taken up so much of the doctor's time.

Arlene looked over her shoulder and nodded. "The whole place is a traffic jam. They need another doctor over here, like Dr. Virgilio hired on her side of the fence. When they make it bigger, it'll solve the mess, I guess."

"Bigger?" Nell asked.

"The addition," she said, then shrugged and disappeared toward the door, holding it open for a mom with a reluctant adolescent in tow.

"So people know about it," Ben said softly. He looked over at a man slouched against the wall, eyeing the next empty seat.

"What?" Nell asked.

Ben waited until they were out in the foyer, then said, "After you left the room, Alan told me that Lily Virgilio wants to expand the clinic. He mentioned something about plans she had shown him."

"Physically, you mean? An addition?"

Ben nodded. "It's progress, I guess. But Alan hates the idea. He thinks it'd ruin the integrity of the old Delgado mansion. He's very much against it. Said his father would be, too, and all the Hamiltons before him. They'd never approve of it and neither will he. He loves this building."

Nell looked around at the high ceiling, the paintings on the wall. She tried to imagine pushing the walls out one way or another. And then she thought of the crowded waiting room.

Decisions she was happy she didn't have to think about.

Gabby hurried ahead and held the door for Ben, then chatted all the way to the car. Her mind had quickly moved from slings and doctors back to Lambswool Farm and the fact that Daisy Danvers and she were going to be showing off the sheep at Sunday's event. And her own Charlotte, growing by the minute, would be the center of attention.

Nell walked behind Gabby and Ben, looking across the street at the park. Archie Brandley sat on a bench, taking a quick break from the bookstore. The same spot where her friend Lily Virgilio had stood the night before, her hands on her hips, her voice edgy as she argued fiercely with Alan Hamilton.

She looked back at the captain's home. Everyone in town loved the carefully preserved structure. Lily would need Alan's support to get anywhere with expanding it, of course. But the Lily she had seen last night was not the lovely, calm Lily she knew, the one who in addition to a busy practice had also started a free health clinic in town. The Lily she had seen last night looked like she was determined to get what she wanted, no matter what.

As she reached the car door, a deep, husky voice, a familiar one, called her name from some distant place, and pulled Nell from the uncomfortable feeling that two fine doctors might be at loggerheads with one another. Two good friends of hers.

She looked back toward the building and spotted a beefy hand waving at her from the corner near the back of the clinic. The service door was open, and the light behind in the hallway had turned the man into a silhouette—a tall person holding a broom.

Nell squinted, then smiled and waved back. To someone, though she wasn't sure who.

Next to her, Ben cleared his throat to pull his wife's attention back to him and Gabby and a car that was in need of a driver with two working hands.

"Let's get this show on the road," he said. "I have work to do. It's Friday, after all. Time to mix the martinis and light the grill."

Chapter 9

The grill was lit, the coals a dusty gray, and the spicy shrimp and pineapple chunks skewered on wooden sticks and covered with foil.

Ben sat on a deck chair, his long legs stretched out, feeling only slightly uncomfortable from the afternoon's surprise. Causing him more discomfort was having Sam take over his martini shaking.

"You're a tough man to keep down," Sam said. He was standing next to the outdoor bar, a line of tall bottles and an ice bucket in front of him. He put the lid on the silver shaker. "We could have ordered pizza, you know."

"Friday-night pizza on the deck?" One brow arched. Ben's voice lifted. "Pizza and martinis? I'd be run out of town."

Cass plopped down in an Adirondack chair next to Ben and pulled her legs up beneath her chin. "Yes, you would." She leaned forward and ran a finger lightly over the clean white bandaging around his arm. "I wish you had a real cast. Think of the damage we could do with a handful of permanent markers."

"You and Gabby," Ben said.

Danny Brandley pulled her hand away. "Look, but don't touch. Those fingers have probably been inside a lobster today."

"Ew," Izzy said, putting a bowl of chips on the side table.

Cass wrinkled her nose at Danny and whispered an irreverent comment into his ear, but she didn't turn away when he turned his head and kissed her soundly.

Across the deck, Nell was arranging napkins and silverware on the old picnic table, listening to the banter as it mixed with the sound of Ellie Goulding's fresh voice filling the night air. Danny and Cass's engagement was still fresh, and had brought about a shift in their relationship that was unfolding in new and unexpected ways. There was a pleasant looseness in Cass, one that allowed her emotions to flow more freely, be less tangled.

Birdie walked over carrying salt and pepper grinders and candles. She looked at Nell and in her eyes, read her thoughts. She looked back at Cass. "It's nice to see, isn't it? Who knows, your backyard may have another wedding in its future."

"I wouldn't mind that at all." She looked across the deck and down the deep yard that ended at the edge of a small wooded area separating the yard from the beach beyond. Winding through the thick trees was a well-beaten path cushioned by pine needles, a favorite shortcut for family and neighborhood kids to get to the beach.

At the beginning of the woods, tucked into the far corner, was a small guest cottage shielded by knockout rosebushes and pine trees, a *Hansel and Gretel* touch that was packed with many memories, and probably an equal number of secrets. The list of people who had at one time or another—and for as many reasons—called the cottage home was memorable. From Claire to Izzy's brother Charlie, to Pete's girlfriend, Willow. Not to mention overnight guests, family and friends, and an occasional stranger who simply needed a place to rest his head. Dozens and dozens of people, all made to feel at home.

Across the way Sam was straining a martini into a glass. He handed his first try to Ben. "If it's bad, I'll blame it on my teacher," he said.

With exaggerated scrutiny, Ben checked out the thin layer of ice floating on top. He squinted, scowled, held the glass up in the glow of a patio candle, then raised it to his lips. He sipped. "You're going to put me out of business, Perry," he said finally, a wry smile lifting the corner of his mouth.

"My goal, completely." Sam went back to pouring and shaking. He called over to Nell. "So how'd you think Doc Hamilton was today? I spotted him as we were leaving, introduced him briefly to Glenn. We spoke a couple of words, but he was in a hurry, so we didn't dawdle. There had to be a dozen patients in that waiting room." He took a sip of the next martini before handing it over to Birdie, declaring it amazing.

"Well, he was a knight in a shining doctor's coat," Nell said. "But he looked tired, maybe. I did notice that. He winced a few times. At first I thought he was reflecting Ben's discomfort." She pushed the Alan she had seen the night before as far out of her mind as possible.

"I hope snooping around his place with our cameras won't be a problem for him," Sam said. "Arlene Arcado offered to be our in-office guide, though I think it was Glenn she was wanting to guide more than showing us where the light was good."

Cass uncurled herself from the chair and headed over to Sam for the next drink out of the shaker. "You have our place on your list, too, right? You better not forget us."

"Are you kidding? There'd be no proper history of Sea Harbor's finest without the Halloran Lobster Company. Your ma would stop lighting church candles for me if Mary Halloran and her clan weren't included."

"Course she would. And you need them," Cass said.

"I can see why it might distract Alan, though," Izzy said. "He's not raucous and noisy like the lobster crews. And that clinic is so busy."

"Glenn is pretty good at making himself invisible," Sam said. "I watched him today. He sees all the right things, pays attention to little details. And he seems to value the small things, finding them interesting. Some people miss that. He showed me some of his photos online and he's good. I may just let him loose to do that one himself. He offered to hang out there and make a list of possible shots."

Ben leaned over to check the coals, then checked his watch. "Speaking of the clinic, I invited Alan to come by for dinner. He looked like he could use a martini."

"The cure for many ills," Birdie declared, taking a sip of her drink.

"I hope he comes," Nell said. And not just because the poor man looked like he could use a little laughter to end his week—but also on the small chance that the slight discoloration of Ben's fingers needed attention. It wouldn't hurt to have it looked at.

Ben gave her a look across people's heads that said he had read her thoughts. The message he sent back, traveling through the smoke and tantalizing aroma of spices, was clear. He was fine. Fingers and all.

Nell nodded, her face in agreement but her heart still burdened by the image of her tall sixty-plus husband falling from a barn loft.

Footsteps in the family room announced the Brewsters' arrival, Jane appearing through the deck doors in a long flowery skirt, loopy earrings nearly touching her shoulders, and Ham in his usual jeans and Canary Cove T-shirt, and a hint of orange paint in his full white beard. The founders of the artists' colony had enticed Ben and Nell to begin the Friday-night dinner tradition years before, and they rarely missed it, Ham declaring it a necessity of life. *The fuel of friendships,* he would often say. *It's all right here on this deck.*

"Look who we found on the front steps," Jane announced,

turning halfway around and sweeping one hand back to announce Alan, with Claire Russell at his side.

"Hey," Ben said, getting up from his chair. "Much better than finding a UPS package out there. So happy you two came." He walked over and gave Claire a hug with his good arm.

"We wouldn't miss it." Claire handed an arrangement of wildflowers and plants to Nell—plump hydrangea and spiky summersweet blooms, cattails and leafy fronds. "A taste of Lambswool Farm," she said. "We have fields of wildflowers right now. They're beautiful."

Nell breathed in the sweet and spicy fragrance. "This is gorgeous. It was the only thing we were missing—along with you two, of course."

Alan looked over at Ben's arm. "How's it feel?"

Ben wiggled his fingers. "Everything works."

Alan noticed the slight swelling in several fingers that Nell had seen earlier. She leaned in as Alan looked.

"Nothing to worry about," Alan said, but suggested Nell stop by the office in the morning so he could give her something to reduce the fluid.

"Otherwise, everything looks good," he said to Ben and followed him over to the deck chaise, sitting down beside him. His body seemed to sink into the cushions with great relief, as if he'd been standing for days.

Sam handed him a drink. "You look like you could use this, Alan. Rough day?"

Alan leaned his head back and nodded in a noncommittal way.

Night shadows fell across the wood deck floor, and hurricane candles flickered in the breeze. Far off, gulls screeched, and the sound of the ocean, just beyond a thick stand of trees, spoke of the outgoing tide.

"This is nice," Alan said to Ben. "Your invitation came at the perfect time. I would have been awful company for Claire had we gone for a quiet dinner in some restaurant. She'd have been reading the menu for entertainment." He looked over at his date, standing with Birdie, her head lowered as she listened to the small silver-haired woman. "She'll have a livelier group to talk to here."

"We try for lively. Sometimes we make it, sometimes not so much," Ben said. "It's not a necessity."

Tonight's gathering was smaller than usual, a Fractured Fish gig in Rockport keeping Pete Halloran and some other regulars away. "Don't mean to ruin the mood, Alan, but when I was in today, you mentioned wanting to talk to me? Someone came up and we never came back to it."

Alan's forehead wrinkled in concentration. "Oh," he said finally, some memory coming back that eased the lines in his face. "I remember now. Not sure why I thought of it today, but you suggested to me a while back that I do something about my will. Seeing you today reminded me of it, I guess."

Ben nodded, unsure of where Alan was going.

"With everything that's going on at the clinic," Alan said, "I suppose I should update it."

"I'm here to help," Ben said.

Alan drained his martini. "When you have time," he said and turned his attention to Sam, who was wondering if Alan needed a refill.

He said he did.

Nell watched the conversation and saw concern shadowing Alan's face. The pallor she'd noticed earlier was intensified tonight, and even the cool ocean breeze wasn't drying away the thin sheen of perspiration on his forehead.

She filled a glass of water and took it over to him, leaning in to set it on a low table within his reach. "Are you all right, Alan?" she asked quietly.

Alan looked up. He held his martini glass up. "Another one of Sam's drinks and I'll be a new man."

"We're here if we can help," Nell said.

"It's been a long week, that's all. Patients, some staff complications, issues here and there . . ." The last words trailed off, but he managed to finish. "Sometimes the best of intentions can fall flat. Fail you. But it's good to forget it all for a few hours, thanks to that Endicott hospitality. So, you see, you are helping."

He ended his words with a tired grin, and Nell was certainly empathetic. Weekends were important. She felt that need to separate her days that way, even though she no longer held a full-time job. Her days were still filled with plenty of responsibilities and it was important to shrug them off for two days. Weekends were for reenergizing, recreating—and it must be especially important when people's health, even their lives, were in your hands in very real ways.

Alan turned away from her, easing himself into a discussion with Sam and Ben, something about the aerodynamics of sailing, a topic she couldn't imagine him focusing on in his weary state. She watched him for a few minutes more, a sliver of silver in his dark hair catching the evening light. He leaned forward, his elbows on his knees, the stem of the martini glass rolling between his fingers and the tight coil of tension in his shoulders lessening some beneath Sam's first foray into martini making. Helped, she hoped, by the magic of friends and the night air.

Nell walked over to the grill, checked the coals, and motioned to Ben that they were ten minutes away from putting the shrimp on. Then she headed across to the deck doors.

Inside, everyone was scurrying around the kitchen as if in a well-rehearsed play. Birdie was taking butter and condiments from the refrigerator, while Jane stood at the island, tossing a salad. Izzy counted heads out loud as she pulled out napkins from a drawer and rolled them around flatware. Cass was helping herself to a fistful of cashews from a bowl on the island.

Claire was standing at the kitchen window, looking out on the backyard. The same one that only a few years before she had spent a summer transforming into a wedding garden for Izzy and Sam.

Nell watched the wave of emotions play across her face, imagining how it had looked that day—a graceful curve of white chairs, fresh flowers spilling from vases along the aisle. Flowering bushes and stately pines. "I can still see it, too," Nell said, coming up beside her. "It was a magical day."

"Me, too," Izzy said, coming up on Claire's other side and giving her a quick hug. "That day will always be right here inside me." She tapped her chest.

"Yes," Claire said, a slight choke in her voice. "Me, too." She turned back to the island, reaching for a knife to slice up an avocado for Jane's salad.

Nell looked from the yard to the deck, where Alan sat in the same place sipping a martini. She wondered if Claire's memories of Izzy's wedding were in any way connected to the man sitting out there with Sam, Danny, and Ben. Claire was her good friend, but she had an intensely private side and she kept even good friends at a distance when it came to certain things. Nell knew instinctively Claire wouldn't talk to her about her relationship with Alan until she was ready. And that could be never.

Cass had no compunctions about such subtleties. "So," she began, looking at no one in particular as she arranged warm rolls in a basket. "Are all of you aware that Alan Hamilton has seen me naked?"

Izzy choked, a spray of wine flying from her mouth. She set her glass down, grabbed a napkin, and wiped it away. "Geesh, Cass," she finally managed as the others brought their laughter down to a manageable level. "I anoint you queen of the segues."

Claire was laughing, too.

Birdie nodded calmly. "I'm sure that was an enjoyable moment for him, Catherine," she said.

"It was." Cass pulled a corner off one of the rolls and popped it into her mouth. "He's a handsome dude now—can you imagine him all those years ago when he was just a newbie working alongside his father and taking the easy cases? My mother said he gave me one swift swat to my bottom to get the machinery going and all hell broke loose. My cry was so loud they heard it out in the waiting room, and Da's whole fishing crew began singing an old sea shanty—bolstered, of course, by the bottle of Irish whiskey they'd discreetly snuck in for my da."

"Certainly a memorable day," Nell said, taking the cheesy potato casserole out of the oven.

"He loved delivering babies. I think he misses it," Claire said. "Family practice isn't quite the same as it used to be."

"Well, we're doing our best to keep him busy," Nell said. "Maybe not with babies, but we're good with bones."

"That you are," Claire said. "Poor Ben."

"I guess Lily Virgilio has pretty much taken over baby deliveries," Izzy said.

Nell watched Claire's face, but it registered nothing. She just nodded and commented on Alan's being plenty busy without adding babies to the mix, whether he misses it or not. "He wants to be all things to all men, just like his father was. And his grandfather before him. What he finds difficult to admit is that Sea Harbor has a few more people than it did in those days. He can't do it all. But it's working out,

I think. Between him and Lily, most things are covered—births and deaths and the routine health issues that happen in between."

Claire seemed fine, as if whatever might have happened the night before that prevented Alan from seeing how lovely she looked in that beautiful dress—whatever happened to leave her stranded on the restaurant steps—had been explained away or at least resolved. Forgiven. Or maybe simply forgotten. Claire could do that; Nell wasn't sure she could.

The shrimp, pepper, and pineapple kebabs took only a few minutes to cook, the sweet smell of peppers and honey and wine wafting up and mixing with the smoke from the hot coals. Ben insisted he could do it with one arm.

Sam and Danny hovered close—lest he set the whole place on fire, Sam said—but Ben proved his point, wielding the grill brush and tongs expertly. In short order several bottles of wine had been uncorked, candles lit, and the old picnic table Ben's father had found at a farm sale many years before was surrounded by friends filling plates and talking over one another.

Ben tapped his wineglass with the tines of his fork. "I'd like to make a toast," he said, his eyes resting on Claire, then moving to Birdie. "To a brilliant new adventure—Lambswool Farm. May it thrive and bear abundant harvest."

"And to family, to friends, to peace," Birdie added, just like she did every Friday night, her clear gray-green eyes moving from one person to the next, circling the table, pulling them together in a silky web.

"Here, here," Sam said as glasses were raised, sips taken, and happy chatter resumed around the table.

"What's the schedule?" Danny asked Birdie. "Lambswool Farm is the talk of the town."

Birdie looked over at Claire. "Sunday supper?"

"Supper? Well, I think the meal will be more substantial," Claire said gently. "Dinner, perhaps?"

"Well, that's another way of putting it, I suppose," Birdie admitted. Then she laughed at herself. "In my head I am thinking about Sunday as a dress rehearsal, and maybe that's why *supper* came to mind. Dinner seems more . . . well, more like the real thing."

"So this one won't be real? Artificial lobster? Count me out," Ben said, and Birdie laughed.

"It will be real and delicious and wonderful, I promise you," Claire said. "Thanks to Birdie, the guest list keeps growing, but it will be great friends who will understand completely if the new stove doesn't work or dinner is late or it gets too cold outside or the wind blows over glasses of red wine onto white slacks."

"So this is a dry run?" Sam said.

"Well, not exactly dry, but yes."

"A dress rehearsal," Nell said.

"Exactly," Birdie nodded, the lantern light hallowing around her silvery hair.

"People can look around," Claire filled in. "Angelo hired a couple more farmhands, and we'll have a tractor available if people want a ride around the pastures. It will give us time to figure out the glitches before the first official harvest dinners begin—the ones people are actually paying for. This will be our own private party."

"It's a great idea, Claire. You have a good handle on all this," Sam said.

"Oh, yes," Birdie said with a vigorous shake of her head. "Lambswool Farm couldn't be in better hands. Claire is amazing."

"I certainly will second that," Nell said. And murmurs of agreement spread around the table, causing a slight blush to Claire's cheeks. She was handling Lambswool Farm the same way she'd nurtured gardens for years—with remarkable care and skill and emotion. Nell glanced over at Alan to catch his look of pride, but he seemed to be somewhere else tonight, on another planet and not reacting to the praise being heaped on Claire.

Claire noticed his lack of response, too, but artfully hid it behind a glass of Cabernet.

Nell moved to a new topic, trying to pull Alan back into the conversation. "I was surprised to see Arlene working your front desk, Alan."

Alan looked over, a furrow developing in his brow. "Arlene . . ."

"Arcado. I didn't know she was working in the clinic."

"Aha," Jane said, raising her class with an impish smile on her face. "So she succeeded."

At first Alan looked confused, and then he managed a smile. "Oh, you mean her job interview," he said finally. "I forgot you and Ham were with us at the restaurant that night. Yeah, she came on board a couple of weeks ago."

The others waited for Alan to unpack the mystery of her hiring, but Jane filled in for him.

"Arlene was waiting on the four of us, and she did a masterful job of convincing Alan that he needed her in the clinic—and she needed another part-time job."

Alan took a drink of water. "She was determined, I suppose. Much to my surprise."

"A *lot* determined," Jane said.

"Some of the nursing school interns were leaving, so it worked out. I knew she was smart, and she works hard as far as I can tell."

"Don's going to have a beef with you soon if you keep stealing his employees," Jane joked.

"There are more Arlenes?" Birdie asked, looking from Jane to Alan.

Nell put her fork down, realization settling in. "Garrett Barros," she said suddenly. "That's who waved at me today. I couldn't put a name to him until now. He works at the clinic?"

Izzy said, "My Garrett? The guy I used to live next door to?"

"He used to do dishes or something at Ocean's Edge," Danny said.

"Yes," Jane said. "That's the one. He's a bit slow, but a good fellow. He takes an art class from Ham at the gallery. He paints birds."

"Of course he does," Nell said softly, remembering Garrett's bird-watching interest and the binoculars that always hung from his neck. She hadn't seen him for while. "The quiet giant. He's misunderstood sometimes. It was nice of you to take him on, Alan."

Alan didn't answer. He was thinking of something else, or at the least, of separating himself from the conversation. But when Nell looked at him, she knew he had heard them.

"You'd think Garrett was doing heart surgery, the way he talks about the new job," Ham said. He was soaking up shrimp marinade with a crust of bread. It dribbled onto his beard. "He loves it."

Jane took her napkin and wiped the mess from her husband's beard.

Alan took another drink of wine and concentrated on the mound of cheesy potatoes left on his plate—along with the uneaten shrimp and salad.

"Don Wooten recommended him," Jane said. "Garrett still lives with his folks and I think he helps them out. When he saw the ad for the clinic job at a higher salary than what he was getting at the restaurant, he applied. He says he cleans the lab, stocks equipment, records things. I think he helps out Lily Virgilio now and then, too."

Nell wasn't sure why, and afterward, Ben couldn't put his finger on it either, but a sprinkling of tension had settled on the table, noticeable enough that Birdie made an effort to dispel it with distraction.

She reminded everyone again that they were all invited to

Lambswool Farm Sunday evening, and she'd be personally offended if they didn't come. Then she got up and busied herself clearing plates, taking coffee orders, and describing the most amazing dessert that her housekeeper, Ella, had made. Jane and Izzy followed her back to the kitchen to help scoop up the bread pudding.

Sam got up and moved around the table, topping off wineglasses and refilling water glasses. "Hey, all this talk reminds me of something, Alan. I hope we haven't added to your office workload with our cameras. We'll be like flies on the wall—I promise."

Alan looked at Sam and seemed to perk up some. "No, not at all. You're a pro and making something pretty special." He wiped his forehead with a napkin. "My great-grandfather will be dancing a jig wherever he is. He'd love having his family clinic recorded this way, honored for serving Sea Harbor's families. That was his whole goal in starting the Hamilton clinic. My dad was a humble guy, more humble than his ancestors, but he loved the clinic and would feel the same way. So it's fine with me."

"So all's good. That's great."

"And this is great, too," Birdie said, walking back to the table balancing a large tray. "Bread pudding with hot spiced rum sauce. It will help everyone sleep well tonight."

It was more than an hour later that Nell finally turned out the kitchen lights and walked up the back stairs to the bedroom.

"The evening went well, Nellie," Ben called out from the bed. He was already settled, his glasses on the end of his nose, his arm resting on a pillow, and Danny's most recent mystery propped up on his chest. A soft breeze blew through the window, ruffling the curtains.

"Hmm," Nell said. She retreated to the bathroom to wash up, Ben's words trailing after her. She stared into the mirror, wondering about the face looking back at her. Friday evenings usually filled her with well-being—the sharing, mixing, blending of their lives together like a potpourri. The laughter and music and conversations, Ben's sacred martinis, and the smoky warmth of the grill that mellowed out the week, no matter what had happened before or what lay ahead.

But the face looking back at her didn't reflect mellowness.

It reflected the tight worry Alan Hamilton had tried to brush off with a second martini, a second glass of wine. A faraway look that took him away from the magic of Friday night on the Endicott deck and put him somewhere else—somewhere Nell hoped Claire Russell could rescue him from.

Chapter 10

"Ella is experimenting with root vegetables," Birdie explained to Cass and Nell. She hefted a bulging canvas shopping bag into the backseat of Nell's CR-V and climbed in after it. "She's convinced we will all live to be two hundred and fifty if we eat them frequently."

"I'd prefer to eat cheese and wine and butter and ice cream—and shorten the time a few decades," Cass said. She helped Nell stash her bags in the trunk, then squeezed between Nell's car and the one parked next to it, opening the CR-V door a scant few inches and climbing in. "Jeez. Now I know how sardines feel. Could that car have hugged us any tighter?"

Nell looked over. The truck was just inches away from her CR-V. Fortunately the car on her side had pulled out just minutes before.

They'd had good luck parking when they arrived, landing a spot right near the water, but getting out was not so easy. The packed parking lot stretched from the Ocean's Edge Restaurant on one side to Harbor Park, with its paths winding down to the edge of the sea. The large grassy area was the site of everything from concerts and Fourth of July fireworks to the annual arrival of Santa in a lobster boat.

Today it was filled with white tents; tables groaning beneath piles of fruit and vegetables; hot dog stands and cotton candy vendors; and bright balloon bouquets whipping up a frenzy. "Crazy crowd," Cass said, one arm on the car window ledge as she looked out over the people milling around.

Birdie nodded, her face reflecting the profound comfort she felt in the quiet confines of Nell's backseat. She rested her head back against the soft leather and sighed. Jostling crowd or not, she and Nell had been going to the Saturday market for so many years that missing a week seemed almost traitorous.

Having Cass along today was a bonus. When Danny had abandoned her to put in a few hours of writing and Birdie mentioned that she and Nell were ending the morning with lunch somewhere, she'd volunteered to tag along and help squeeze melons or carry bags or be a stimulating conversationalist, whichever they preferred.

Nell turned the key in the ignition, looking back over her shoulder at the continuous string of cars pulling out of the tight parking spaces. The line looked like it had no end.

A sudden, insistent tapping on the driver's window brought her attention back around, and she stared into oversized sunglasses filling Mary Pisano's small face.

The fingers continued their beat until Nell rolled the window.

"Your car, Nell. What's happened to your car?" Her voice was insistent.

Birdie leaned toward the window. "Nell's car is right here, Mary."

"We're sitting in it," Cass added, then checked around her to be sure she was right.

"Oh, sillies, of course you are. But look at this." She looked down at something they couldn't see, running her hand along the side of the back car door. Then she pulled open the driver's door and insisted Nell step out.

They all tumbled out, gathering around Mary and staring at the door. What was once a lovely metallic gray now had a brilliant red streak slashing through it like Zorro's sword.

Nell had missed seeing it when they'd come back to the car, distracted by the imminent challenge of getting out of the parking lot and the line of people walking by. She sighed, knowing immediately what had happened. She recognized the color. The cherry red pickup that had been squeezed in right next to her CR-V. The one that she had watched back out as they made their way into the parking lot, grateful she wouldn't have to worry about nicking it. She knew the new crease and color on her door would be the exact same height and color as the Chevy's passenger mirror.

"Oh, dear," Birdie said.

"Things happen," Nell said, running her fingertips over the paint.

"Not my choice of words," Cass said.

"The driver probably didn't even know he'd done it," Nell said, trying for good-heartedness.

"Nell, you live in a fantasy world sometimes," Mary Pisano said.

And Nell knew right then what Mary's next "About Town" column would be about: *Gracious Parking Lot Protocol,* or some such thing. And she'd somehow manage to find a comic drawing of a bright red pickup to draw attention to her words.

"Hey there, what's up?"

Glenn Mackenzie trudged up the slight incline from the market area, carrying several bags and looking as weary as a grocery store sacker. He looked at Mary. "I couldn't find you in that crowd, but I think I got all your bags."

Mary apologized. "I saw Nell over here and wanted to say hello, only to find her car vandalized."

"It wasn't vandalized," Nell said quickly. "It was an accident."

Glenn surveyed the damage. "That's a bummer, though. I'm surprised there's not more of it around here. This place is packed." He looked back at the crowds, then over the water to the sailboats heading out to open sea, as if that might have been a better option for his morning activity.

Cass made herself known with a pronounced clearing of her throat. They all turned toward her, but it was Birdie who immediately caught the reason for the interruption. "You two haven't met," she said to Cass and Glenn, and offered quick introductions.

"I figured you must be Cass," Glenn said, and stuck out a hand. "Danny told me about your lobster company. He suggested I hitch a ride on one of your boats while I'm here."

"My brother Pete'd make that work, I'm sure. Be forewarned: it's not the *Queen Mary*. Lobsters have their own perfume."

Glenn laughed.

"This fellow has already put in a day's work," Birdie said, explaining that she'd run into Glenn hours earlier on Ravenswood Road, heading to the Hamilton clinic with his camera equipment.

"You were taking your camera on that old bike?" Nell asked. She looked over at Mary. "No offense, Mary, but it is old."

"Of course it's old. My husband is fifty-two, and I think he bought it with his paperboy money. But no, Nell, Glenn had a driver."

"Sam?" Nell asked, surprised. Sam usually took Abby out on some adventure on Saturday mornings while Izzy worked in the shop.

Glenn seemed relieved to have Mary doing the talking, explaining things. He looked distracted, as if he had been interrupted from something in his head that needed attention.

"No," Mary said. Then she looked over at Glenn, nodding at him like a schoolteacher would, encouraging the shy kid in class to talk.

"Sam had something else to do this morning." he said, "but we both thought early morning would be a good time to check things out over there. Arlene Arcado offered me a ride."

"He's learning that it's not true what they say about New Englanders—we are *very* friendly," Mary said.

Glenn shifted one of his bags on his hip and nodded. "For sure. You've all been really hospitable."

"Have you met the doctor yet?" Nell asked.

Glenn nodded. "For a minute yesterday. And again today, but it was brief. He looked like he had things he needed to do. Most of the staff was there, getting ready for the day. Maybe they had a meeting, I don't know. But I got to see the library. Albums, records. Things that go back a hundred years and more. Family history—at least family clinic history. I saw the doc with some patients. I got to observe. That suits me fine. I got some good photo ideas for Sam."

"Alan's grandfather was my first husband's doctor," Birdie said. "That family goes way, way back."

"Speaking of which," Nell said. She glanced at her watch. "I think they close at noon on Saturdays, and I need to scoot over there before they lock up to pick up Ben's medicine."

Mary looked at Glenn. "And I should let this man be about his own business, too. He was kind to give me an hour of his time, but I am sure he has better things to do."

Glenn didn't seem to hear Mary. He had set down the market bags and put on sunglasses, and was looking out over the water again, as if drowning himself in the sound, transfixed by the waves crashing against the long granite pier, foam exploding into the air, then folding back on itself and sliding away.

Until it struck again.

Chapter 11

"You've been wanting to meet our mysterious stranger," Nell said. "Now you have. What do you think?" She spotted a lull in the exodus of cars and slowly backed out of the parking space, easing into the line exiting onto Harbor Road.

"I'm thinking about it," Cass said.

"He seemed preoccupied," Birdie said. "But he's a nice enough fellow. Not very talkative today, maybe. But that's not necessarily a bad thing, now, is it?"

Nell nodded out of habit. But she wasn't sure. As Birdie said, he was nice enough. Friendly. But he wasn't even a true visitor to town. He was simply someone there because his car broke down, and yet he was inserting himself in their lives in a way that baffled her. She shook it off, then barely missed a riderless skateboard that flew into the street near Harry Garozzo's deli. She took a deep breath, slowed down, and turned at the small corner park. The medical building parking lot was emptying out. She found a shady spot in the back near a large maple tree, its low leafy branches spreading out over the lot.

"Lily Virgilio has new paintings up," Birdie said as the ignition died. She opened the car door and climbed out. "Come, Cass, let's tag along and take a look."

The front door opened up to a spacious hallway that had once been Captain Delgado's lavish foyer. Nell liked to imagine a half dozen children racing through it. A recent renovation had turned the space into a mini gallery, showcasing work of Canary Cove artists. Today it was filled with seascapes—beautiful watercolors and acrylics, some with SOLD tags already taped to the edges of the frames.

"Now tell me," Nell said, "where but in Sea Harbor will you find doctors' offices hosting art shows?"

"Nowhere." Lily Virgilio walked through the open door of her office and greeted them. "I hope you're here for the art show and not a medical emergency," she said, concern in her eyes. "Ben is all right, isn't he?"

Nell assured her she was there simply to pick up medicine for him. Lily motioned toward one of the winding hallways off the lobby. "Good. You can go on back to the lab that way to avoid the waiting room. I'm sure Alan has it waiting for you."

Nell left the others with Lily and made her way through the hallway labyrinth that she'd finally mastered, knowing which ones led to Lily's domain and where to turn to find Alan's. Parlors, bedrooms, sunrooms—transformed into examining rooms and offices and waiting rooms. The shared lab, pharmacy, and library were on the back side of the building, close to Alan's office. Nell walked into the dispensary, feeling the immediate assault of medicinal odors. She looked around at the neat rows of bottles filling the shelves, the high counter.

Carly walked by the door and spotted Nell. She stopped and stepped inside. "I think Julie—she handles the prescriptions—has already gone. May I help you, Nell?"

Nell explained why she was there, and Carly looked out the door, then back to Nell. "The doctor is still here. I'm not sure where he is. He might have stepped outside for some air—I don't think he's feeling great. Why don't you wait in his office? He'll be back in a minute."

In the distance a phone rang and Carly hurried off.

Alan's office door was open, the room empty. Nell stepped inside, breathing in the sweet smell of late-blooming roses wafting through an open window, goldfinches and sparrows singing in the giant pines at the back of the property. She walked over and looked out at the birds, fluttering in protest at the darkening sky. The secret garden was as beautiful as always, with its flagstone paths, lovely garden beds, benches and birdfeeders, and tall hedges shielding it from the commerce all around it. An enchanting yard where the long-ago Delgado children played and frolicked. Alan had told her often it was what he loved most about the old mansion.

The peaceful scene was interrupted by the sound of voices, pulling her attention back to the row of pine trees at the very edge of the yard, separating it from the parking lot.

She recognized one of the voices. Carly's guess was right: Alan had gone outside. But he wasn't alone. And from the emotion in his voice, Nell suspected he hadn't gone out to get fresh air.

The usually mild-mannered doctor's words were tight, controlled, and angry. At first Nell wondered if he was arguing with Lily Virgilio again. From where she stood, she could see only his shadow, spread long and narrow as a barren tree across the yard. His body was still, his hands moving slightly, clenching, loosening, then balling into fists.

The silence that followed was marred by a muffled, animal-like sound, one Nell couldn't identify, but she knew instantly it wasn't Lily's. And then she heard the sound of footsteps, slow and methodical, and a heavy door opening and banging closed.

Nell moved away from the window and over to the desk. A moment later Alan Hamilton appeared in the doorframe, his face drawn and flushed.

Nell forced a smile.

"Carly said you were here for Ben's medication," he said immediately, one hand pressed against his forehead. "I'm sorry. It's right here, Nell. Just give me a minute—"

He walked over to a cabinet beside the window and briefly rummaged around, then strode to his desk carrying a small pill bottle. He handed it to her, then leaned against the wall, his hands holding on to the back of the heavy desk chair. He took a deep breath, then put on a pair of glasses and a professional face. "Ben has a little fluid retention," he said. "It's not serious, and this will take care of it. He'll be fine by tomorrow."

"But will you?" Nell said. The words slipped out. For a minute, Nell thought Alan was going to slide right down the wall onto the braided rug beneath the chair.

Alan brushed off her question and pushed himself upright. "I'm tired, that's all. Maybe I need a vacation. The office manager told me I hadn't taken one in three years. And that was a med school reunion back in Cleveland. Not much of a vacation."

"I'd say it's time, then," Nell said. "A nice sailing trip in the Bahamas would suit you fine. You need some sun."

She wasn't totally believing his words, nor her own. Alan looked down at his desk, shuffling some papers. Nell looked at the bottle he had given her and dropped it into her purse. It was time to leave.

Alan sat down at the desk, still shuffling, not looking up, not even when he said good-bye or when Nell thanked him. Or when she quietly walked out of the office and down the hall.

Birdie and Cass were waiting on the front steps, talking with Arlene Arcado. Nell overheard Birdie inviting her to the following day's dinner at the farm. She wondered whether Claire's staff was kept apprised of the growing number of people Birdie was inviting. In the beginning it was close friends, a forgiving group to test the mechanics of serving dinners at the farm. But Birdie's gregarious nature was ballooning the number.

"That's nice of you," Arlene said. "I'll be there, but in a different role. I volunteered to organize the waitstaff for the dinner." Her tone was cordial but businesslike. "You want the best, don't you, Miss Birdie?"

Arlene looked tired, too, or at least preoccupied. Nell wondered briefly if some bug might be rampaging through the clinic.

Birdie smiled and patted Arlene's hand. "Of course. And you are certainly the best. We'll see you tomorrow, then."

Arlene nodded and pushed up her sleeve, checking her watch. "I'd better be off. Busy day." In the next second she was on her way, across the street and crisscrossing through the park at a steady clip.

They watched her for a few moments until she disappeared around the corner.

"That one is a workhorse, though a bit unpredictable," Birdie said as they headed around the building to the parking lot. "She looked a bit out of step. You know what I think? I think that the stars and planets are somehow misaligned today, or the moon must be full and gravity is doing more than holding us to the ground. Think about it. The boisterous climate at the market—people jostling their way about. The damage to your car, Nell. Even people in a place of healing are acting peculiar today."

The last item on Birdie's list was certainly true, and she hadn't even been privy to Alan Hamilton's anger. Nor his uncharacteristic behavior with Nell. How would astrologers explain that?

Cass looked up at the sky. "Birdie's right."

The crisp morning sky had turned darker in the last hour. Restless clouds skittered across the horizon as if late for something important.

Nell shook off the ominous sky and looked around the parking lot.

At first she thought her car was missing—affirmation of Birdie's feelings about the day. Then Cass pointed to the back of the small lot and Nell remembered she'd parked beneath one of the trees not far from the old mansion's service door.

They walked that way, waving to Carly Schultz, who was hurrying to her car to begin the weekend away from work.

Nell clicked her key to unlock the car, glancing again at the dent and paint repair job she'd be bringing to Pickard's Auto Shop on Monday. She grimaced at the gash as she pulled opened the driver's door, then stopped suddenly. She put one hand on the roof of the car and looked toward the clinic building.

An unusual sound rose from behind a thick stand of trees not far from the car. At first it wasn't much more than the beat of a drum. Perhaps a car radio somewhere playing a song with a deep bass.

Nell took off her sunglasses, straining to bring the sound into context. It grew louder, rising above the sounds of the town in the distance, the cry of the gulls. A crashing crescendo that pulled Birdie and Cass from the car.

"What is that noise?" Birdie asked, looking around the nearly empty parking lot, then toward the building.

Just visible through the stand of trees was a wooden fence that hid garbage cans from sight, and just behind that, a bench, and the pathway that led to the clinic's back entrance. A shady private spot for a lunch-break sandwich or where a smoker might retreat to furtively light up.

But it wasn't a smoker who was standing in the shade of the trees, his shoulders leaning forward, his sturdy frame just visible in the shadows of a giant tree.

It was Garrett Barros, his large hands curved into massive fists pounding against the wooden fence. Once, and again and again and again—until the pine boards splintered and broke apart, the shards falling to the ground.

Chapter 12

Birdie's and Cass's predictions of bad weather had blown off to Nova Scotia, and Sunday dawned bright and sunny and windy. By late afternoon the sky was deepening, the wind was settling into a soft breeze, and the forecast for the dinner at Lambswool Farm was about as perfect as it could get.

It was an evening to celebrate the farm's new life, Ben reminded Nell. Good friends, food, and flawless weather. He was sitting on the end of their bed, admiring the way Nell's silky gray dress flowed over her curves—and trying to ease the look of worry that furrowed her brow.

"The day you had yesterday was crazy," he said. "Birdie's probably right. The universe was playing with you, having a good laugh. But let it go, Nell. The car can be fixed."

"That's the easy one," she said. "It's the other things."

The gentle giant.

The man Alan had been with outside the window was Garrett Barros; she was positive of that now. The man who had Alan raising his voice in a frightening way, who remained beyond the window when Alan came inside, perspiring and spent.

The same Garrett Barros who had completely pummeled a fence a short time later.

"Staff problems come up in any office. Things go wrong on the job. It's not unusual and definitely not worth the worry on your face. It's just too bad you had to hear it, and I'm sure Alan would feel the same way." Ben fought with his shirt, trying to button it with one hand.

Nell picked out a scarf Izzy had knit for her, lacy with a half dozen bright colors striping through it and long enough to loop several times around her neck. "Maybe. The fence episode happened less than fifteen minutes after Alan talked to him, though. He was so angry—and he took it all out on that poor fence."

"Better the fence than internalizing it . . . or worse."

"I saw Don Wooten or sometimes the hostess or manager remind Garrett of things at the restaurant, a dirty dish left on a table, leaving a tray in the dining room. He always handled those things well, with a certain grace, almost. This was different. Whatever Alan said brought out the absolute worst in him. Maybe it seemed especially bad because I've always considered Garrett mild-mannered."

"Did you talk to Garrett after he did it?"

Nell shook her head. "It was clearly a private moment. The office was emptying out for the weekend, and he thought he was alone. Whatever had gone on between him and Alan earlier was clearly private, too. To step in would have been an invasion of that privacy, I think. All three of us did. So we got in the car and left."

"Did he see you?"

Nell took a white jacket from her closet and slipped it on over the silky gray dress. She folded back the jacket sleeves and added a silver cuff. "He must have heard me start up the car—there was no way around that. And he might have recognized my car. He saw us leave on Friday, too."

Ben rubbed his chin. "Alan was troubled about something when he set my arm. Something he needed to talk about, but the time didn't seem right. And he mentioned something about staff problems Friday when he was here but didn't go into detail. I get that. I'm a friend, but a patient, too. And Alan is above all a professional. He's come to me for legal advice a couple of times, and he brought up his will on Friday, too—but that's different. Whatever staff problems he was having apparently didn't involve legalities. I think he only mentioned them because I questioned the fact that he didn't look well. You did, too. He offered that as the reason."

Nell looked into the mirror, absently giving her hair a final brush, her lips and cheeks a quick sweep of color. Several of them had noticed Alan hadn't looked well. And he hadn't been quite himself on Friday night. Staff problems. That made sense, especially in light of the run-in with Garrett, and maybe it accounted for it. Running a medical practice and sharing space with another doctor, sick patients, emergencies—it could explain lots of things.

But somehow it didn't seem to fill in the picture completely.

"It will work out," Ben said, walking over to her and wrapping his good arm around her shoulders. He nuzzled her hair, watching their reflection in the mirror. "You're a mighty pretty lady, Mrs. Endicott, and that's exactly what is going to get all my attention tonight."

"It's like something out of a movie set," Nell said. They were walking away from the "parking pasture," as Angelo was calling it. A bevy of farmhands were there, directing cars and people.

"Yes, it is." Birdie stopped at the edge of the drive and looked around. She held her arms out wide, embracing every inch of the lovely scene spread out before her. She was beaming.

Ben had said Lambswool Farm had shaved ten years off Birdie's life, giving her small body a bounce and lift that no miracle age drug could have done.

Birdie had completely agreed, then suggested it was fifteen years, not ten.

"So, who made the final cut on the invitation list?" Ben asked. He took her arm as they crossed the uneven gravel drive. "You're the talk of the town, m'lady."

"Oh, no, dear Ben. Not me. It's this place."

The flagstone patio near the open kitchen barn doors was already filled with friends milling about. Tiny lights were wound through ancient trees and new fences. And off to the side, set up in the mowed grass, was one long harvest table winding off into the sunset like a giant caterpillar. Jane Brewster's ceramic plates highlighted each place setting, with napkins in every color of nature fluted on top. Old pots cleaned and rescued from the barns held bunches of wildflowers, and thick candles in hurricane glass centered the table as if the setting itself were celebrating something new and lovely and exciting.

"Claire had the final list," Birdie said. "But it's just friends and family—"

"And a few strays Birdie happened to run into in the past few days," Nell added.

"Oh, well, you know . . ." Birdie said, her voice drifting away on the pleasure of it all. She waved to Elizabeth Hartley and Jerry Thompson, the police chief, who were being cornered by Beatrice Scaglia. They stood near a tall bar Angelo Garozzo had built from rescued barn wood, the rough boards smoothed and a curved polished slab of granite placed on top.

Ben spotted Jerry's dilemma, too. The talkative mayor took city issues with her everywhere she went. He quickly excused himself to rescue his friend, telling Birdie that Perle Mesta had nothing on her.

Birdie simply chuckled, an excited sound that bubbled up. With Nell close behind, she hugged her way through groups of friends to where Claire Russell stood, just outside the remodeled barn, her eyes scanning the scene, looking for anything that had been missed, anyone who needed help.

When she spotted Birdie, her arms went wide, embracing her tightly until only strands of flyaway silver hair were visible. "We did it," she whispered to her friend.

Birdie stepped away. "You did it, Claire. It's magnificent. Every last detail."

Behind Claire, the side barn doors were rolled open, the kitchen spread out in all its gleaming glory and an array of Sea Harbor chefs scurrying around, cooking and chatting and carefully checking appetizers sizzling on a hot grill. In days to come, chefs from all over the north shore would take turns highlighting their skills to paid guests at Lambswool Farm, but for tonight, it was Birdie and Claire's party. Family and friends, a cooperative affair, with local chefs joining forces to provide a genuine Sea Harbor flair to the meal.

"The truth is," Claire confided to Nell and Birdie, "each one of our chef friends was dying to get his or her hands on all the newfangled equipment in that kitchen. This seemed the right night to do it."

They were all there: Kevin Sullivan from the Ocean's Edge, Annabelle from Sweet Petunia, and Cass's childhood friend Gracie Santos, whose lobster café on the pier offered the best lobster rolls on the East Coast. Tonight she was putting together dozens of tiny ones, piling them on plates and sending them out on waiters' trays to whet appetites.

Nell looked longingly at the brand-new Wolf stoves and ovens. "Someday," she said, envy in her voice.

"I'll get Ben right on it." Claire laughed. "But until then, you're welcome to come out and play anytime you like, Nell."

They were soon joined by Cass and Izzy, who had abandoned a heated discussion at the bar. "Did you know that Lily Virgilio is looking into building permits?" Izzy asked. She pointed back to Beatrice Scaglia, who was pointing a finger in the air, her voice animated as she talked with the obstetrician and Rachel Wooten, the city's attorney. "The mayor seems to have an opinion about it."

"Beatrice has an opinion about everything," Birdie said.

Nell looked over. She couldn't tell from the finger wagging whether Beatrice was for or against. But either way, the topic had come up again. Apparently Lily was moving ahead. She looked around to see whether Alan Hamilton was anywhere near the flow of words, but he didn't seem to be close.

"Speaking of doctors, I haven't seen Alan yet," she said. "He's here, isn't he?"

The Brewsters and Mary Pisano, Laura Danvers and her husband, and a handful of others were listening to a string quartet playing a movement from *The Four Seasons.* Others milled around a table exhibiting before and after pictures of the farm that Sam and Glenn Mackenzie had put together. The younger set was gathered around a table groaning with miniature tacos stuffed with mint, feta, and chunks of lobster; tomato hand pies; and an overflowing plate of Gracie's lobster rolls. The group was greedily relieving the table of its bounty.

But Alan Hamilton wasn't with any of them.

"He's here somewhere," Claire said. She looked around, too, waving and greeting people as she pivoted in place. "He was wandering around with Sam. I think he's avoiding crowds. He's not feeling one hundred percent."

That wasn't a surprise, but having Claire confirm it brought a sliver of relief to Nell. She didn't want Alan to be sick, but if he was under the weather, it might explain his argument with Lily Virgilio—and his anger at Garrett Barros, too. And perhaps the situation might not seem so dire when he felt better. There was something fragile about Garrett, something that made her want to wrap a protective shield around him.

"There was another man with them, too," Claire said. "Glenn—that nice fellow who fixed our tractor."

"Mackenzie?" Birdie asked.

"That's it. He's a doctor, I hear. Maybe he can give Alan something. He doesn't do a great job of doctoring himself."

"Maybe." Nell spotted them then. Sam and Alan were over on the drive that led to the barn and pastures. They stood there looking around as evening began to descend on the land. Sam swung a bottle of beer in one hand, his fingers steadying the camera looped around his neck in the other. And then Glenn Mackenzie walked up carrying two glasses of wine. He handed one to Alan, and the threesome continued on down the road, their stride lazy as they made their way toward the working barn in the distance. Sam seemed to be pointing things out—maybe those special things a photographer notices but others miss, Nell surmised. As she watched, Sam's head went up suddenly and he pointed to a spot over the fence, something in the field, and he was off, abandoning his companions, climbing over the fence. He lifted his camera, ready to immortalize a sheep or shadows in a field or the way the fading light reflected off a post.

Nell smiled, watching, loving Sam's gift to see as much beauty in a blade of grass as in a snowcapped mountain.

Claire was looking after them, too, watching Sam disappear, and Alan and Glenn continue on, walking into the barn. "Alan has been checking on Charlotte now and then, trying to help me figure out when that lamb is going to drop. First-time moms can be unpredictable. The vet says it will happen when Charlotte decides it will happen."

"He's probably taking Glenn to see her. He'd be interested in that, I would think," Birdie said.

"I hear Glenn seems to have an interest in the Hamilton clinic, too. I suppose it's the medical connection, the fact that he's starting out himself," Claire said.

"Well, maybe," Nell began, but before she could explain that Glenn was heading toward a research emphasis, not a practice, Arlene walked up, a bundle of efficiency in her head-waitress role. She asked politely for a few minutes of Claire's time to check on serving details.

Nell watched the methodical, careful way Arlene approached her job, half listening as the two talked a few steps away. She felt an unexpected rush of gratitude to the young woman for helping to ensure that the very first Lambswool Farm dinner—even if it was just a trial run—went off without a hitch. It would certainly help Claire and her staff gain the confidence they would need to handle a pasture filled with paying guests in the future. And it would please Birdie, though her friend considered any gathering of their dear friends pretty close to perfect, no matter what the food or quality of wine.

Claire was back in a minute. They'd be eating soon, she said, before the air turned chilly and while people could still enjoy the magnificent beauty all around them. Later there'd be time to wander, to have Daisy and Gabby take them out to meet the sheep, or to enjoy a moonlit stroll around Lambswool Farm. She motioned toward the table and suggested they sit down, with Birdie at the end. "Save a place for me. And for Alan, too," she added with a shrug, looking over Nell's shoulder. "Wherever he is."

Nell and Birdie looked around, too. Sam had come back from the pasture and was helping himself to another beer and some of Gracie's lobster rolls. Nell walked over and took one off his plate. "Claire was looking for Alan. Weren't you with him?"

Sam shrugged and looked back toward the pasture. "He's around here somewhere. He and Glenn were out near the fence, watching sheep or something. I'm sure they'll come back once they smell the food—though Alan looked two sheets to the wind."

The cast-iron dinner bell—a hundred-year-old monster that Angelo had brushed and scoured until his fingers bled—hung from a pole near the kitchen, and when it clanged minutes later, appetites were ready, teased and prepped by the kitchen's tantalizing odors of grilled salmon, roasted vegetables, and unique casseroles made from the farm's freshest produce and herbs.

Nell and Ben sat across from each other, saving chairs for Alan and Claire. Birdie was at the end, waiting until everyone was seated and wineglasses were filled. She stood and smiled down the long table. "To family and to friends," she said, her voice catching slightly in her throat, *"and to the health and long life of Lambswool Farm."*

A rumble of cheers and clinking glasses assured Birdie it would have exactly that.

Nell looked around and finally spotted Alan and Glenn Mackenzie walking back from the barn. She pointed to the empty chair next to her and mouthed to Alan that it was reserved for him. He seemed to be in a kind of daze, and happy to sit.

Farther down the table, Sam was motioning to a chair saved for Glenn.

"How is Charlotte doing?" Nell asked Alan when he'd settled in.

"Charlotte?"

"The pregnant ewe."

"Ah, Charlotte." He seemed to give the question more serious thought than Nell intended, and then he said, "I'd say she's looking forward to having a family."

"Did Glenn Mackenzie check her out, too?"

"Glenn, yes," Alan said. A soft smile lifted the edges of his mouth.

Then he took a deep breath, followed by a long drink of water, and sat back, content to listen to Birdie, Ben, and the Brewsters engage in a detailed and lively conversation about the art history of Cape Ann, of the early days of Canary Cove, of the historic Rocky Neck art colony down the road in Gloucester.

At least he seemed to be listening, but Nell couldn't be sure. His face was still pale, but his eyes held something that Nell hadn't seen there before. Something she couldn't put a word to. Pleasure? Surprise, or a new awareness of something? It reminded her of the look in Izzy's eyes when she found out she was expecting a baby.

What Alan was seeing or feeling or thinking seemed so private that Nell felt she had no right to be seeing it, too. Perhaps it had something to do with Claire, watching her in this place, *her* place—but whatever it was, Nell felt compelled to look away.

She turned her attention to her surroundings, the music, the attentive waiters making sure wine was poured, water glasses refilled. And most of all the gathering of people who filled the harvest table from one end to the other. She would be happy spending the whole evening doing exactly that: observing, absorbing, not speaking a word. The voices that rose up were all warm and familiar. Each face, one after another, full of meaning, each person significant to her in some way. An unusual gathering and a night she'd remember for a long time.

The string quartet was gone now, and music was being pumped through speakers that were above the barn door and attached to tall posts all around the grounds. Soft jazz—comfortable and nonintrusive—accompanied the bevy of waiters bringing out trays that carried bowls and platters of the farm's finest produce. Roasted vegetables with a dozen sauces—aioli and chimichurri and hollandaise—filled colorful platters, and individual flaky pies of fresh spinach, Gruyère cheese, and pine nuts were set on each plate.

Nell looked down the table again, her gaze moving from one face to the next, each one filling her with its own unique kind of joy. Glenn Mackenzie sat halfway down the table with Sam and Izzy,

Pete Halloran and his girlfriend, Willow. Cass and Danny, Carly Schultz, Andy Risso, and a few others were a part of the group. Glenn wasn't talking much, seeming content to leave the others to their jokes and banter. His chair was pushed back, his hands folded behind his head. Now and then a question came his way and he'd say a few words, smile, then settle back again, as if completely comfortable in his own world.

Nell guessed in that talkative group there was probably no need for him to say much, maybe not much opportunity, either. He was on the edge of it, not really a part of friendships that had been nurtured through the years. But he seemed perfectly content in whatever his role was, happy to do what Nell was doing, observing and checking out everything around him. She attempted a smile when their eyes met, but Glenn didn't respond.

Slightly embarrassed, Nell looked away, then took a quick glance back, only to find him still focused her way. His look was thoughtful, as if he was playing something out in his head. She fidgeted and took a drink of her wine.

"Nellie, come back to us," Ben said, breaking into the moment. "Where've you been?"

Claire had finally had the chance to sit down and she joined them, sitting next to Ben. She smiled at Nell, nodding. "I get it, Nell. It's almost sensory overload, isn't it? All these people we love, gathered in this incredible place. I find myself doing the same thing, looking around and then pinching myself to see if it's real." She looked over at Alan, sitting next to Nell. Claire's look pulled him into the conversation. "It's quite wonderful, yes?"

Alan looked at her carefully, weighing her words. His eyes were locked onto hers. "Wonderful . . ." he said. His voice had an unusual tone, the words coming from the back of his throat. Perhaps all the way from his heart. "Yes. Could you have imagined it . . ." His voice dropped off, but not before they all heard the unexpected emotion coming from a man who usually held his feelings in check.

Claire smiled at him and looked surprised when Alan moved his hand across the table, nearly toppling a glass of water as he reached for her fingers, touching them lightly. His hand shook slightly, but his eyes held steady on her face. "Amazing," he said, but it was clear he meant more, wanted to say more, but maybe it wasn't the place. He pulled his hand back and the corners of his mouth lifted in a smile.

Yes, Nell thought, sending up a silent thank-you that Alan had filled in the one thing missing in Claire's special night. He had seemed strangely out of touch the past few days, his mind wandering and his conversation not always on target, but in that moment, he'd come through. A new kind of happiness brightened his eyes, blocking out the pained look they had all seen there of late. And she suspected whatever he had to talk over with Claire Russell might even surpass the evening's successful dinner.

A while later—after empty plates had been taken away and a million stars appeared in the night sky—Arlene announced to everyone that the dessert bar was open for business on the kitchen patio. Coffee and tea. After-dinner drinks. Time to stretch and wander and enjoy Lambswool Farm in the light of the moon and the millions of tiny lights strung in trees all over the property.

Gabby and Daisy, dressed in farmer overalls and red checkered scarves, led a steady stream of people through the old barn to visit Charlotte from a distance, to wish her well as she settled down in her clean, fresh-smelling stall. Others lingered near the bar, enjoying the pie and the music, until finally the reluctant gathering began to thin out as people headed toward their cars, bodies full and thoughts moving on to the workweek ahead.

Claire was everywhere, seeing the guests off, praising the staff.

Nell hadn't moved from her chair except to push it back from the table so she could comfortably stretch her legs. Ben brought his around and sat next to her.

Nor had Alan moved, and Claire had happily entrusted him to their care while she played her hostess role.

Nell glanced at Alan's tired-looking eyes. He looked as if sleep was just a few minutes away.

"You look like you're feeling better—though not one hundred percent," Nell said, leaning toward him. He'd done little with his dinner other than push the food around the plate. And she had noticed a wince now and then, one hand gripping his abdomen. But whatever discomfort he was feeling seemed shadowed by something bringing him pleasure.

"Better?" He seemed to have trouble understanding her question.

He managed a smile but didn't pursue Nell's observation, choosing instead to sit quietly, his eyes settling on the movement of guests in the distance.

"Sitting is good," Birdie said, walking over to their group. She put her coffee mug on the table and welcomed the chair Ben pulled over for her. "Daisy's mother has finally pried the girls away from the sheep," she said. "They're on their way home to bed."

"Which is probably where we should be headed soon," Ben said, looking around for approval.

Birdie nodded in wholehearted agreement and thanked her kind chauffeur for staying so late. They'd outlasted Izzy and Cass and the younger set, a rare happening. But Birdie had wanted to stay on to support Claire—and Ben and Nell agreed.

Sitting beneath the moon, eating slices of pie, wasn't all that difficult, was Ben's take on it, but even he was fading.

Arlene appeared with a few brandy snifters and a small square bottle. "Any takers?" she asked. She left the glasses and bottle without waiting for an answer and headed back to the kitchen to help close it down.

"Alan?" Ben asked, picking up the bottle.

The doctor's face was gray now, his eyes nearly closed. Beads of perspiration dotted his forehead.

Nell turned to look at him. In less than a few minutes his face had changed. He looked terrible. She reached for a glass of water and tried to hand it to him.

Alan sucked in some air and reached out a shaking hand for the water. But his fingers refused to curve around the glass and it slid straight through, falling to the soft grass. Water splashed across his slacks and shoes, puddling around them.

Nell reached for another glass, while Birdie grabbed a handful of napkins.

Alan's head lolled to the side and he looked at Nell, pulling his eyes open with difficulty. He started to speak. "It's Sun . . ." But the words were garbled, the sentence falling off.

"It's Sunday, yes," Nell finished for him.

"Family," he managed to say. "Tell Claire—"

Ben saw the movement almost before it happened and was up out of his chair in seconds, his good hand reaching toward his friend.

But it was too late to stop his slide.

Before anyone could do anything, Alan's head dropped onto his chest, and his body—as fluid as water—slid silently off the chair and onto the ground.

Chapter 13

The moon was indeed full that Sunday night. Perhaps Birdie's prediction was spot-on, a harbinger, coming the day before the planets threw their Earth off-kilter.

Claire had gone off in the ambulance with Alan, while Arlene Arcado corralled the waitstaff to finish up in the kitchen, channeling her shock at the unexpected event into efficiency. Angelo Garozzo and his farm staff took care of everything else.

Angelo insisted that Nell, Ben, and Birdie go home. Everyone needed their sleep, he said, and there was nothing they could do at Lambswool Farm. Alan was in good hands, and he'd check in on Claire after he left the farm.

It was a logical plan. So they assured one another several times over that Alan had a nasty bug, just as they'd suspected over the last couple of days. That he was dehydrated. That the hospital staff would pump him full of fluids and he'd get a good night's sleep. He'd be fine in the morning.

In the morning.

But in the morning, Alan Hamilton was dead.

It was Angelo who broke the news, calling Birdie before most of Sea Harbor had plugged in their coffeepots.

He knew Birdie would be up; her daily constitutional, as she called it, was a ritual that began as the sun started its climb to the sky. The police chief had told Birdie once that she was more effective than a whole neighborhood watch patrol. Most robberies in high-end neighborhoods occurred just after dawn. With Birdie walking Ravenswood Road at a steady clip early every morning, a sturdy walking stick in hand, her neighborhood hadn't had a robbery in years.

Birdie admitted to her friends that she'd come across a tryst or two—a young man sneaking out of his girlfriend's bedroom window at dawn, shoes in hand, that sort of thing—but no burglars, not a one.

So Angelo knew Birdie would be up. And he knew she should be the first person to hear the news because his thoughts were with Claire Russell. How many times had Claire told him that Birdie was her guardian angel? She'd need someone. Just like Doc Hamilton, Claire had no family left, but guardian angels sure counted for something in Angelo's mind.

An hour later, Birdie sat at the island in Nell and Ben's kitchen, drinking Ben's dark Colombian roast. She was still in her gray sweatpants and hoodie with the bright yellow reflective band on front and back, looking a little bit like a gentle, silver-haired Hobbit.

"Angelo went by the hospital after he locked up the farm to check on Alan and to give Claire a ride home," Birdie said. Her voice was in disbelief mode—ordinary, matter-of-fact, as if she were giving a weather report. The way someone got through relating bad news.

"He found Claire sitting on a stone bench outside the hospital. She was in a daze. Angelo took her back inside, where they talked with the attending physician, a young woman who knew Alan

Hamilton well. He had privileges at the hospital and was liked and respected there, she told Angelo. The whole ER staff was stunned and saddened. All his systems were shutting down when he was brought in, she explained. There was nothing they could do."

Ben took a deep breath. Alan's death was an enormous loss for the town. But a personal one for many of them, especially Claire Russell.

Nell looked at Ben, then checked the time. "Is it too early to call Claire?"

Birdie didn't think so. "Ever since she got involved with Lambswool Farm she's been on a farmer's schedule. I'll call."

Claire picked up on the first ring. She was walking the shore, she said. Walking barefoot in the wet sand as the morning tide swirled around her ankles and sucked away her footsteps. "Just like that," she said to Birdie. "I look down and my footprints are gone." And then her voice cracked, but she fought the tears and answered Birdie's question.

Yes, she was just a few blocks away, and yes, a cup of Ben's coffee would be very much appreciated.

She walked up Ben and Nell's well-worn beach path, through the "Endicott woods," past the guesthouse she had lived in for months and the gardens she had nurtured, and into the waiting arms of her friends.

Instead of asking questions no one had answers to, they sat and drank coffee and picked at day-old scones, and mourned a man who had taken care of nearly the entire town. And slowly, the little Claire knew came out, but it shed little light on how a fit man like Alan Hamilton could succumb to something as common as the stomach flu.

"They don't know anything for sure," Claire said. "They took blood when they thought they could stop whatever it was that was destroying his body. So they'll know more soon. But it doesn't really matter, does it?"

Nell pushed the box of tissues across the island, but Claire was composed, her eyes dry, yet the puffiness below them was an indication that hadn't been the case earlier.

"It will matter in a clinical way, that's all," Birdie said kindly. "If whatever Alan had is contagious, steps will need to be taken."

Alan had probably been with hundreds of people that week. Lambswool Farm attendees, patients, and office staff. And everyone on the Endicotts' own deck.

Ben put his coffee down and looked out the window. "It doesn't feel right to me. Alan was a doctor. He'd never intentionally expose people to an illness."

"Yes," Birdie said. "He was a healer. But sometimes even doctors . . ." Her words drifted off and her brow furrowed as she thought about what she intended to say. Finally she said, "Alan was also human. And proud. Something was definitely going on with him this week; that much we know. We'll have to wait."

Ben walked around the island and refilled coffee cups. "I've spent a lot of time with Alan over the years," he said. "I know he has no immediate family, but I never even heard him mention cousins, aunts, uncles."

"I don't think he has any," Claire said. "At least that's what he thought."

Birdie agreed. "I talked with his wife about that one day, about what happens when a lineage—at least one you know of—ends. Alan said his mother had spent a lot of time doing genealogy, and there really wasn't anyone she could find who was still alive."

"I wonder if Carly Schultz needs help canceling patients," Claire said suddenly. "She's been filling in as office manager while Alan looked for a new one." Her voice was strong and deliberate, belying the profound sadness in her eyes.

Taking action was better than sitting around; they all knew that. Bringing food, making phone calls, giving rides—it's what one did for the family when people died. But there was no family, so one moved on: Alan's patients. His staff. His friends.

"It won't be an easy day for Lily Virgilio," Nell said. She reached for her phone.

Lily was distraught—Nell could hear it in her voice—but she couldn't think about the personal side of Alan's death right now, the loss of a friend. She and Carly were getting things under control, doubling their staffs together to cancel Alan's routine appointments. The young ER doctor who had admitted Alan had offered her assistance and would see patients needing immediate help.

Claire slipped off the stool. She needed a shower. And she was going to go out to the farm, she said. Angelo would be there. It was better than walking in circles and feeding her sadness. She needed to be out in the open air with the sheep and the green pastures and the dirt.

A knock on the door, followed by heavy footsteps, brought Father Northcutt into the room, his face long and his gait slow.

Claire's face crumbled slightly when she saw the priest. She walked to him. "Father Larry," she started, her other words smothered in the warmth of his embrace. He kept his arm around her as they walked back to the kitchen.

"A good friend, a good man, a huge loss," the Irish priest said, settling his wide bottom on a kitchen stool. He pushed blunt fingers through the few strands of white hair remaining on his head.

The pings on Nell's phone indicated the news was spreading around town with lightning speed. She glanced at her phone, then away.

"It doesn't take long," Father Larry said, nodding. "Not when everyone in town knew the man."

"I don't suppose there's been talk of a funeral?" Birdie asked.

"Not just yet, Birdie. But soon."

The priest looked at Claire. "Claire, my darlin', you were Alan's closest companion, his confidante, his best friend. He told me as much himself not but a few days ago. So together you and I will come up with a service and a way to help Alan's good friends, to help the town, celebrate his fine life." He lifted Claire's hand from the island and sandwiched her slender fingers between his large palms, holding them still.

Nell felt the same relief that she saw soften Claire's face at Father Larry's words. Someone to take charge, to do the right thing. Someone to lean on and somehow see them through the days ahead.

"There are things that need to be done first," Father Larry went on. "The hospital is working to find out the cause of his death. They're speeding up the reports out of deference to all of us who care about Alan. And then we can bury him in a manner he deserves."

"And there will probably be an autopsy," Ben said. "When a fit guy like Alan dies suddenly, they'll want to know why, too. It's routine." Ben passed a blueberry scone across the island to Father Larry and freshened cups of coffee all around. In between bites, the priest talked gently about the good things Alan Hamilton had done for the town, for Our Lady of Safe Seas Church, with some humorous anecdotes thrown in.

Nell felt the calm he'd brought into her kitchen. Priests—at least Father Northcutt—seemed to absorb the concept of death in a unique way, maybe seeing more clearly the next chapter. Or maybe they were simply more grounded in the ways of life and death. The grand cycle. Whatever the reason, his presence was slowly driving the awful shock of Alan's dying from the room.

Chapter 14

By the time Nell and Birdie made their way to Coffee's patio to meet Cass, it was nearly noon and the buzz about the doctor's death was in full bloom, with people expressing sadness, acknowledging his importance to the town, remembering the last time they had seen him, the cough he'd lessened, the compassion he'd shown. But in addition to the sincere sadness, a current of unrest ran beneath the talk. He'd been sick, some said. And a fear that some contagious disease might be taking over Sea Harbor hovered in the air.

Nell went inside the coffee shop to order while Birdie sat down at a small table just inside the patio gate. She didn't want to walk by all the faces and well-intentioned folks who already knew that the doctor had fatally collapsed at Lambswool Farm—*her* farm—and were filling that fact with their own conjectures.

"You know, that farm that Birdie Favazza owns," Nell heard as she wound her way back to the table with lattes and an Americano for Cass.

Cass was already there, with her bike leaning against the railing. Birdie had filled her in on what they knew.

"We went to the Gull Tavern after leaving the farm," Cass said. "Izzy and Sam, Danny. Andy Risso and Carly were there, and Pete and Willow showed up with Glenn Mackenzie in tow." She took a sip of her coffee and then went on.

"Tommy Porter came in and told us an ambulance had been sent to Lambswool Farm. His poor girlfriend, Janie, never gets a break—he keeps his police radio on even when they're on a date."

Nell was crazy about the young policeman—now detective—as were most of Sea Harbor's residents. No one even resented, at least not too much, the many parking tickets he'd given them before he'd been promoted. Tommy was Tommy, and lovable.

"So Tommy knew who it was?"

"No, and we were all a little crazed—we knew you were still out there—Izzy called you right away, Nell, but when you didn't answer, we really freaked. So Tommy's girl, Janie, being a nurse and knowing how to get around people at the hospital, called and found out who it was. They told her he had a crew of doctors treating him. That's all Janie knew."

Nell looked around the patio. She could feel a charge in the air, heavier than usual, filled with emotion and speculation and curiosity and questions—all those things that surround unexpected death. And when it's the town doctor, it becomes even more personal, more acute.

"So Carly Schultz was with you? She must have been upset," Birdie said.

Cass nodded. "She'd been worried about Alan for days. She knew he hadn't been feeling well, even though he denied it. But nurses know pain, and she'd seen him doubled over a couple times the past few days. He claimed it was nothing. Tension, lack of sleep. And he insisted on keeping to his schedule, coming into work. I think Carly was kind of relieved hearing he was taken to the hospital—she thought at least he'd be treated and get better. Danny and Sam said the same thing. They'd been over at the clinic a few times because of the photo shoot and didn't think he looked great."

Nell thought back to the night before. "Alan was walking around the farm last night with Glenn and Sam. Did Sam say anything about it? Did Alan talk about his health?"

"All he said was that Alan was quiet—that's about it. And guys walking at dusk through a farmyard are probably not going to notice each other's health. Nor talk about it."

"Did Glenn say anything?" Birdie asked. "He and Alan walked off alone for a while. Angelo saw them, too. At first he thought there was something wrong, but he was too far away to see. And next thing he knew they were sitting side by side on a bale of hay, talking. Serious talk, Angelo thought. He likes Glenn, you know. Glenn fixes tractors." She gave Cass a small smile.

Cass shrugged. "Maybe he fixed a tractor, but last night at the bar, all he did was listen. Like an eavesdropper, in my humble opinion. Intently, as if he actually knew all of us well and belonged in the conversation about someone we knew who had just been rushed to the hospital. Don't you think he should have excused himself, left us alone to worry together? But in answer to your question, no, he didn't say much at all."

"You don't like him, do you?" Nell asked.

"No," Cass said. Then she shrugged away her own abruptness and chewed a bite of bagel, washed it down with coffee, and lightened up a little. "Danny likes him, though. He says I need to give him a chance. *Why?* I asked him. He'll be long gone as soon as his car is fixed and I'll never see him again."

The mention of Glenn's car reminded Nell that getting a car repair estimate for her insurance company was on her list for today. Ben had called ahead for her; Shelby Pickard said he'd be there waiting. She mentioned the errand to Cass and Birdie.

"I'm off, too," Cass said. She got up and slung her bag over her shoulder and tossed the empty coffee cup in a nearby trash can. She was off to meet Mary Halloran for lunch at Sweet Petunia, she said.

For once she was the one who had initiated the mother-daughter lunch, she told Birdie and Nell. Her ma was sure to be all caught up in the funeral preparations for Alan at Our Lady of Safe Seas, and she wanted to be sure she didn't take on the whole burden of it herself.

"Cass is getting thoughtful in her old age." Nell picked up her bag and followed Birdie through the patio gate.

"Catherine has always been thoughtful," Birdie answered. "But I think sometimes her concern for her mother isn't the whole story. Sometimes I think, though she'd never admit it, Cass needs a hug from her ma."

"Don't we all?"

The ride to Pickard's Auto took less than ten minutes. The small repair shop was just across the train tracks, on the edge of the town. Nell drove past a few prefab buildings and into the small parking lot. She pulled up near the garage door.

Shelby spotted them through the smudged window fronting his shop and came outside as Birdie and Nell got out of the car.

Instead of a hello he waved a greasy rag in their direction and walked to the side of the car. "So this is the damage?" he asked, running his fingers over the red paint and feeling the dent beneath. "Least the fella who did this could have picked a color that looked good. This red isn't you, Nellie. Not by a long shot."

"Maybe a deep emerald green?" Nell said.

"That'd be better." Shelby walked slowly around the car, checking for dents and dings. Then he probed the damaged panel, testing it for looseness. "Looks like this is it, then. Okay." He took out his cell phone and snapped some pictures of the dent, then pulled a pencil stub from his pocket and scratched the model number and other details onto a dog-eared pocket tablet. "I got what I need. I'll get out my books and send an estimate off to the insurance company.

We'll take care of it. And if I see a junk heap painted this color come in here, you bet I'll give 'em a piece of my mind."

Shelby turned to go inside, then turned back and said, "So, I heard about Doc Hamilton. Damn shame. He took care of us."

Birdie and Nell agreed—it was something they knew they'd hear again and again in the coming days. A good man. They talked for a few minutes about what they knew about a memorial, a Mass.

Shelby added a few words here and there, listened and nodded and cursed the vagaries of fate. Then he headed back toward the shop door.

Nell was about to get in the car when the thought stopped her, her hand on the handle. "Shelby," she called out, her voice neutral, "what's the situation with Glenn Mackenzie's car? Do you think mine will take that long to fix?"

She knew she was really asking about Glenn's car, not her own; Shelby knew it, too. And afterward she would wonder why she had even asked the question—it was none of her business. Birdie suspected it was Cass's skeptical attitude toward Glenn Mackenzie that had put the thought in her head and pushed it out her mouth.

"What are you talking about?" Shelby asked, his bushy brows raising clear up to his thinning hairline and Sox cap. Then he frowned and pointed over to a chain-link fence surrounding a gravel lot with several cars sitting in it. "There it is—that little green Mazda. Been sitting there for days now. Fit as a fiddle." He took off his baseball cap and scratched his head.

"What do you mean? It's repaired?"

"Course it is. Piston rings were shot to you know where and the engine was in cardiac arrest. But I got it in time. Didn't take much."

"Have you told Glenn Mackenzie?" Birdie asked.

"Told him? Sure. I called the guy three times, left messages. I'll be charging him rent if he doesn't get over here and pick it up soon." Shelby chuckled at his humor, shook his head, and walked into his shop.

Chapter 15

It seemed irreverent somehow, and no one was in a festive mood, but they'd promised Jane and Ham they'd stop in at the Canary Cove art show Monday night.

"It's all so weird," Izzy said. She was walking down Canary Cove Road from the parking lot, her arm linked through Sam's. "Dying without a family messes up the traditions. We are all sad—and we have nowhere to put it, nothing to assuage the feeling, like taking food or sending flowers or cards." She looked sideways at Sam.

He looked down at her, smiled, and said, "What?" knowing exactly what was on Izzy's mind.

She wanted more kids, a huge family. He pulled her close.

Nell and Ben walked just behind them. They'd talked about the same thing, that Alan had no family. *Next of kin* was such a familiar term when someone died. Family was where your thoughts went, and only afterward, in a peripheral way, to friends and neighbors. Nell thought about Claire, who was on that periphery. And how societal rules were sometimes so inbred they bordered on unintentional cruelness. Claire wasn't married to Alan. They weren't even engaged. But she was as close to him as family could be.

The saving grace was Father Northcutt. He knew relationships mattered—sometimes even more than family. And he wouldn't let Claire be in the last row.

"Sam, have you seen Glenn today?" Nell asked, taking a step closer so he could hear.

She'd told Ben about her visit to Shelby Pickard's shop and seeing Glenn's repaired car, sitting there, waiting for him. Sitting there for a few days.

"Strange," was Ben's response, but it didn't seem to hold much more importance to him beyond that.

Birdie and Nell thought it was more than strange. Deceptive? They weren't sure. And if it were, what possible reason could he have had for saying his car wasn't ready? Who would have cared if he'd simply fallen in love with Sea Harbor and decided to prolong his stay? They would certainly have understood.

"Yeah," Sam said. "I had coffee with him this morning. He seemed a little out of sorts. Actually, a lot out of sorts. I think the fact that we'd been over at the Hamilton clinic a few times, photographing the old offices, picking through the history—it made Alan's death more personal in a way. He was doing some of the history research for Danny and me, making sure we got the facts right and didn't miss important family events. There was a connection, and I get that."

"You spent time with Alan at the farm last night, too," Nell said.

"Sure, Glenn and I both did. Alan seemed to want to escape the crowd, so we walked around, talking about the photo shoots at his clinic, the Hamilton history, his late wife, Emily. Glenn wanted to get to know him better, I could tell. He was asking nice questions, coaxing Alan on. It helps sometimes to make the photo shoot as personal as you can."

"Is Glenn a good photographer?" Ben asked.

"He is. Medicine is his real love, though—that's clear to me. He's not going to chuck it because I took him on some photo shoots.

But he likes cameras. I could turn chunks of this project over to him if he were interested."

"Is he?" Nell asked.

"Nah, I don't think so," Sam said. "He's got that other life waiting for him."

"And a car," Nell said.

Sam looked at her, puzzled.

"Car?" Izzy asked.

Nell told them about the trip to Pickard's Auto Shop and the little green car, which had been ready to go for days.

"That's weird," Izzy said. She looked at Sam. "Didn't he tell someone last night he was waiting for it to be repaired? I thought that was the reason he was still here?"

Sam wrinkled his forehead, thinking back to snippets of conversation. They'd all had a beer or two, and it'd been noisy in the tavern. "I think he just said he was waiting for his car. Or waiting to pick it up, or something." He shrugged it off as unimportant.

Picky points, Nell thought. And maybe Ben was right: it didn't make any difference in the long run. Maybe Glenn was simply enjoying the break. Who wouldn't enjoy extra days in Sea Harbor?

The only thing that was truly strange was why he didn't just say so.

They had reached the beginning of the Canary Cove galleries, and farther up the narrow street, light poured out to the sidewalk from the Brewsters' gallery. A steady stream of people moved in and out.

Thoughts of Glenn's car were left on the curb—or at least pushed aside—as they jaywalked across the street and moved toward the gallery and the lights and friends and neighbors.

"Jane and Ham were smart not to postpone the exhibit tonight," Ben said. "It's good to see people out."

He looked across the street at the bustling Artist's Palate Bar & Grill, its big attraction being a large old deck that wrapped around the small building and, with the help of giant heaters, stayed open year-round. "There's good business going on over there, too. Merry Jackson has done a great job with that place, making it welcoming. It's a better place to be than sitting at home tonight."

The Artist's Palate deck was packed and noisy with waiters bustling around, the smell of beer and burgers heavy in the air. They could see the keyboardist from the Fractured Fish scurrying about, waving at customers, her long braid flying in the breeze. She had woven hundreds of tiny lights into a canopy that lit the tables and her diminutive form as she greeted customers warmly, some with hugs, but all with a smile that made them feel Merry's deck was their own back porch.

"Hopefully it'll clear out a little in an hour or two," Nell said. They'd encouraged Claire to join them for a burger later if she was up to it. She might, she said. Her house had shrunk in the past twenty-four hours. The walls close and confining and stifling. She knew she needed to be with friends. But she would have to see, she had said, and Nell understood. The waves of sorrow and grief were unpredictable. There was no telling when they would strike.

They walked through the open door of the gallery and were greeted by Ham's broad smile and a beefy hand waving them in. Nell gave him a warm hug. It always intrigued her that Ham's big fingers and hands could paint with such beautiful, artful strokes, fine lines that captured the coast in all its magnificent beauty.

"Good crowd," Ben said, looking over the tops of heads to the exhibit on the other side of the room.

"It's a student exhibit," Ham said. "Many of the artists around here are teaching classes on the side, and we decided to showcase some of their students, see how it goes."

Nell and Izzy moved away from the men, over toward the long exhibit wall. It was a mix of watercolors and acrylics, some charcoal drawings tossed in. A painting with bright crimson lines at one end of the wall caught Nell's eye, and she moved toward it, intrigued. Most of the acrylics were muted, the moody atmosphere of the sea created by an artist's broad stroke and a blend of pastels.

This one was a dazzling red cardinal, sitting on a branch with a sea green background. The painting was different from the others, not only in subject matter but in style. At first Nell thought some of it must have been done in colored pencil, but a closer look showed the fine lines of the bird's wings, layer over layer, wing over wing, all done with a brush.

"Fascinating, right?" Jane Brewster said, coming up beside her. "Ham was flabbergasted. The student used a fine sable brush and has the steadiest hand I've ever seen. Every line is purposeful, perfect."

"It's beautiful," Nell said softly. She looked down in the corner and saw a swoosh of indistinguishable initials.

Jane laughed. "He isn't quite ready to claim his paintings yet—but he should. They're good." She looked around the room and waved the artist over.

Nell looked up into the proud face of Garrett Barros. Surprised, she took a step back and studied him. "Garrett, you painted this?"

He couldn't quite manage to keep the blush away, and he looked down, shifting from one foot to the other.

"It's beautiful. I remember you bird-watching when you lived near Izzy's old house. I can see that your hobby has led to something quite lovely."

Izzy walked up on Garrett's other side. "Your art is impressive, Garrett. I like it very much."

"Thanks," he said, smiling shyly at Izzy. Nell suspected he'd had a slight crush on her those years before when she lived next door. He'd shoveled her walk, mowed the lawn, fixed things for her.

"So," Izzy began, breaking the awkward silence. "How are your folks doing?"

"They're fine," Garrett said, then looked away, around the room, as if seeking out someone.

"Well, say hi," Izzy said. "I hope they've seen your paintings. They're beautiful."

Garrett walked off with a look of pure pleasure on his face, matched only by his embarrassed shuffle.

"He's talented," Jane said. "And definitely not used to being the center of attention. But I can tell he appreciates the praise."

"He's so incredibly precise," Nell said. "Apparently that's the way he is in his job, too. Careful. Exact." She had wanted to say something to Garrett about his employer's death—express some kind of sympathy—but she wasn't sure what, especially since they'd argued so recently. And then the moment passed.

Jane nodded, her eyes following Garrett until he was out of earshot. She turned back to Nell and Izzy. "It's because he's so exact, so careful about things, that Ham hired him."

"What do you mean? Hired him for what?"

"To work for us—for the whole Canary Cove Artists Association. We always need someone in the association office, and Garrett seems unusually good at keeping track of things, Ham says. He's excellent at recording paintings, equipment, sales, and dates. And besides that, Ham likes him and is a pushover for people who need a break."

"But—" Nell began.

Jane nodded, indicating she knew what was going through Nell's mind. She answered her question before she could ask it.

"Alan let him go."

The crowd at the Artist's Palate restaurant had thinned out some, just as Ben had predicted it would. The crowd came in waves, and the late-nighters would be coming to grab tables soon, but for now it was almost peaceful.

Ben nabbed the empty table near the edge of the deck in the back. It was out of the mainstream, a place where they could sit in quiet and then go home to bed. It was the same table Danny Brandley often sat at to write his novels—slightly hidden behind a gnarled old tree that grew up out of a hole in the deck.

Nell had texted Claire where they were, but she hadn't shown up. A brief text came back. *Tired,* it read.

Nell knew Claire had been at the farm all day—probably the best place for her to be, walking through the fields, feeling the soft rich earth beneath her feet, grounding her. Weeding the garden and feeding sheep were maybe the grieving assistance she needed today. Hopefully she'd sleep tonight.

"Did you see Garrett Barros in the gallery?" Ben asked, settling down as the waitress set a pitcher of beer on the table. She took their orders and disappeared.

Nell and Izzy nodded, and Izzy filled them in on Garrett's new job.

"Ham is a good man," Nell said.

"So was Alan Hamilton," Ben replied.

Certainly true. He wouldn't have fired Garrett without cause. And yet Garrett had been misjudged before. Second chances were not a bad thing—and Alan certainly seemed like a second-chance kind of employer. Clearly they didn't know the whole story. "Maybe I shouldn't have been surprised that he lost his job," Nell said. "Alan was visibly upset Saturday when he was talking to him. But I am surprised. It doesn't sound like something Alan would have done."

"It must have unglued Garrett, poor guy," Izzy said. She cupped her hands around a beer stein, her fingers playing over the textured glass. "But I'd rather work in a gallery than a doctor's office—maybe this will work out okay for him."

"Even if it does, getting fired is always a bummer," Sam said, "And from everything we've heard, Garrett liked the job at the clinic. I think he felt important."

Nell thought back over what she'd overheard when Alan and Garrett were outside the window. Not much, really. What she'd been left with was more of an impression. Alan was angry. As for Garrett, it was what happened later that she remembered—the frustration he had taken out on the fence. Or maybe it was anger, not frustration at all. She hadn't seen his face; only the crackling sound of splintered wood.

"Did Jane say why he was fired?" Izzy asked Nell.

"No. Is there a difference between 'let go' and 'fired' these days? She said he was let go, and I'm not sure she knew why. She just knew he needed a job."

Four plates with sweet potato fries and thick steak burgers smothered in caramelized onions arrived about the same time that Cass and Danny did.

"Where've you guys been?" Izzy asked, using both hands to pick up the crusty bun.

Cass sat down next to her and helped herself to a handful of fries.

"We were late getting to the exhibit," Danny said. "Jane said you'd probably be over here." He slipped one leg over the bench next to Nell and flagged a waitress, ordering burgers for Cass and himself.

"We were more than late," Cass said. "No one was there except the artists and their proud relatives."

"Was Garrett Barros still there?" Izzy asked. "His painting was beautiful."

"He was. And it was," Cass said, pouring beers and passing a mug to Danny. "He seemed animated, a word I'd never have used on that guy."

"Was anything said about Alan's death while you were there? I wonder if he knows about it," Nell said.

"How could he not know?" Cass asked.

That was true. Even someone who wasn't very sociable and usually stayed out of the mainstream would have heard the news. And especially someone who had worked for Alan.

Of course he knew. But it was also understandable that it might not have been the most important thing on his mind tonight at the gallery.

"Has there been any news from the hospital?" Danny asked.

"I saw Jerry Thompson today," Ben said. "They're expecting toxicology results any minute. Alan's body had already been moved. They're speeding everything up, probably at Father Larry's urging. He wants the funeral held this week."

"Ma is already in deep funeral-planning mode," Cass said. "She got ahold of Claire and told her that together they'd make it a celebration of his life."

"Your mother will be good support for Claire," Nell said. Mary Halloran was good support for everyone, having lost her own husband when Pete and Cass were still young.

"Alan wanted to be cremated, Claire told my ma, so at least they know that much."

Nell looked beyond the wide deck railing and into the black sky. A stand of crooked pines separated the old deck from the sea. Below the back of the deck, waves crashed against the narrow Canary Cove shoreline, somehow a fitting background for the night. She thought about Alan sitting next to her at Lambswool Farm. He had tried to say something that second before she handed him the water. Something that brought a fleeting light to his eyes. As if he were happy. Or surprised. Or maybe both—a happy surprise.

But now, shadowed by death and funeral planning and the loss of a friend, she wondered if she'd imagined it.

"Looky," Cass said, holding a hamburger in one hand and pointing across the deck with the other.

Nell and Izzy strained their necks to see what she was looking at.

Garrett Barros had just walked up the few steps from the street and stood there looking around for a place to sit. Nell was about to lift her hand and wave him over to their table so he wouldn't be out there alone.

But he never saw her hand, or if he did, it didn't register that it was meant for him. And he wasn't alone.

"Is that Arlene Arcado?" Cass said, craning her neck to get a better look.

Wearing spike heels, Arlene Arcado was a good match for Garrett, in height, at least. She held a program from the gallery show, waving it at a few people she knew, and then she followed Garrett to a table near the outdoor bar.

"Good for Arlene," Izzy said. "That's thoughtful. Things had to have been sad and hectic at the clinic today. But she showed up for the exhibit even though Garrett wasn't on their staff anymore."

Nell agreed. "I wonder if any others came." She looked back toward the stairs, half expecting to see Carly Schultz or other clinic staff.

But the person who came into view, one hand on the railing, standing tall and scanning the restaurant patio, wasn't clinic staff.

Jerry Thompson stood alone on the top step, then moved over to the side as others made their way to the bar. He stood beneath a deck light, out of uniform, the sleeves of his plaid shirt rolled up, his jeans slightly baggy. At first glance, he looked like he'd just pulled himself up from a Barcalounger and was headed to the fridge for a seventh-inning beer. But when Nell looked closer, all thoughts of a comfortable night in front of the television disappeared. His eyes were dark, intense. His strong face was all business, his jaw set and the fingers of one hand absently forking through his hair. In that moment, it looked as if the few strands of silver in his dark hair had multiplied.

Ben spotted Jerry and half stood, his eyes on the chief's face. "Something's up," he said. He lifted one hand.

Jerry spotted it immediately and nodded. In a few strides he was at their table, pulling a chair over from an empty spot and taking the beer that Ben handed him. He looked around, greeting each of them with a nod, a dip of his chin. "I've just come from Claire Russell's," he said.

Nell's heart leapt into her throat. She didn't know what she had expected him to say, but it wasn't that. "Is she all right?" Her voice demanded that the answer be *yes*.

Jerry nodded. "She'll be fine in time. She told me you were all here, which is why I came. It seemed easier somehow than the phone. I wanted to get to you before anyone else did." He turned and looked behind at the milling crowd. In the center of the deck some artists from the Cove had pushed a table aside, turned up the music, and were dancing in a haphazard way, working out the day's tension. No one gave the chief a second glance.

"It's the hidden table," Danny said, pulling a slight smile from the chief. "Tried and tested. When I sit out here to write, I become invisible."

"Good," Jerry said. "For now, anyway. By morning it won't matter. The news will be all over town." He rested his forearms on the table.

A deadly silence fell over the table for seconds, though it seemed to go on forever. In a way, they all wished it would go on forever. No one wanted Jerry to say anything more.

But eventually he took a deep breath and gathered them all in one encompassing, don't-look-away look.

"Alan didn't die from a contagious bug or the flu or from being overworked," he said. He cleared his throat, releasing them from his stare, and looked down at the keys still hanging from his finger. Then he took a quick breath and went on.

"Alan Hamilton was murdered."

Chapter 16

No one moved. Jerry's words disappeared, swallowed up in the music. All but the one, the word that now hung in the air as if dropped from some deadly drone, dangling there, an awful presence that had no place on the Artist's Palate deck.

Murdered.

Jerry explained that he and Elizabeth Hartley had ordered carryout Chinese and were at home eating it when the call came in. It was from the lab, reporting that the tests revealed significant traces of arsenic in Alan's system. The pathologist in charge of the autopsy confirmed it.

"He said once they look at the stomach contents, they will know much more. The suspicion is that the poisoning happened gradually, over days. I'd call it a clear case of murder except there's nothing very clear about it. Not when a well-respected doctor, a good man like Alan Hamilton, is intentionally poisoned to death. There's nothing clear about that, nothing at all."

There was sadness in Jerry's voice, but it was nearly drowned out by the anger and frustration that coated each word.

"You've told Claire?" Nell asked. A whole new layer of emotion was about to wrap itself around her friend, and for that brief moment she hoped Jerry's answer would be *no*, he hadn't told her.

And that somehow, by some miracle, it would all go away before it could stampede across her life.

"Yes, when I visited with her just now," Jerry said. "Elizabeth came with me. She stayed on with Claire, not wanting to leave her alone, trying to make sense of the news—which of course neither of them will be able to do because it doesn't make sense."

Elizabeth Hartley and Claire had become friends when Claire taught an organic gardening class at the headmistress's Sea Harbor Community Day School. They were kindred spirits in a way, Nell thought; both knew firsthand about lives being upended, about cruel things shaking innocent people. And they both seemed to have whatever it was that enabled one to handle bad things.

"Could the poisoning have been environmental?" Danny asked. "Something in the clinic, like that decades-old wallpaper still up in a couple of rooms, maybe?"

Cass looked at him sideways. "Wallpaper?"

"Arsenic is a chemical. It's in a lot of things."

Everyone got quiet. The thought was an awful one. Hundreds of people passed through the clinic, some of whose health was already compromised.

They looked at Jerry.

He shook his head. "Not likely, almost impossible. But we'll have the technicians check all that. His house, too. But that's routine, just to make sure all the *t*s are crossed. There was enough arsenic to kill him in a relatively short period of time. It was intentional and probably put in his food or drink. That's all in a report, and a reporter somehow got ahold of it from someone at the hospital."

"Is there anything else the lab reports revealed, anything that'll help figure this out?" Ben asked.

"The poison was cumulative. Had it been caught earlier and had he been treated, Alan most likely wouldn't have died. But the last dose raised his levels so high it caused the coma and his death."

A million questions surfaced as their minds went off in a half dozen directions, dissecting lives and conversations, the hours and minutes and seconds of the past days.

"I know, it's a lot to take in. And pretty damn terrible. But we'll get through it. We'll find the person who did it. It's what we do."

He picked up the beer Ben had poured for him. Then set it down again with a *thud* that caused a layer of foam to dribble down the outside of the thick glass. He pushed it aside and stood up from the hard chair, rotating his shoulders, trying to work out the tension.

He looked at the stein. "I don't know what I was thinking about that beer, except that it sounded awfully good. I'll take a rain check." He checked the large clock above the bar. "I'm off to work," he said and walked off, working his way around the dancing bodies on the deck, his head down, avoiding eye contact with anyone who might wonder why the chief of police was walking alone across the Palate deck.

Chapter 17

Harold Sampson dropped Birdie off at the Endicotts' home early Tuesday morning. She was dressed in her gray sweats and ready to walk the beach in bright green sneakers.

But coffee came first.

Because Birdie was the only one of them missing when the police chief showed up the previous night, Ben had delayed a Tuesday-morning meeting so he and Nell could fill her in. The fact that Alan had died shortly after having dinner at Lambswool Farm had been troubling but it didn't compare to the possibility of its being a place that factored into his murder.

But Birdie surprised them both.

"Jerry Thompson wouldn't let a reporter or the television tell me the awful news," she said, walking across the family room and dropping her backpack on a bench. "It wasn't the way news got to people who mattered to him, he told me, and though he knew you would be in touch, he thought a phone call from him would work, too."

Birdie sighed as she hoisted herself up on one of the island stools. "When he got back to the station last night he closed his door, put his big old feet up on the desk, and called me. At least that's how I imagined him, with his feet up. So I poured myself a sherry, put my own feet up on my Sonny's cracked leather couch, and spent an hour talking to a dear friend about good people and evil acts, about loss—and how we live with it. And a few other things thrown in between."

"He's a good friend," Nell said, the image of Jerry and Birdie on their phones taking some of the chill off the day.

"He's sad and disturbed and confused and angry, all of those things—and not just because his life for the near future is going to be hellish and difficult. Alan was a good friend. And we can't pretend the murderer was some bad person who slipped in and out of town. A monster with a blank face. Alan's death wasn't random and it didn't happen in a single moment. The murderer had to be someone we know. Maybe a friend. For sure, a neighbor."

Birdie finally stopped talking. She took the cup of coffee Ben handed her and stirred a spoonful of sugar into it slowly, waiting for Ben or Nell to speak.

"It's a mess," Ben said.

"I can't imagine where the police will even begin looking for suspects," Nell said, glancing around the counter for her cell phone. She slipped it in her pocket.

They hadn't had time to fully process the fact that Alan had died. None of them had. Nell picked up her mug and turned toward the window, watching a lone gull swoop down into the yard. She had yet to feel the fact of his absence, that he wouldn't be there to take off Ben's splint or remind them to get flu shots. Or pick Ben up to go for a sail.

Blanketing his death with murder had changed everything. The time to grieve would have to be put aside while neighbors looked at neighbors oddly, while Alan's days were dissected endlessly, while stories were spun like kids playing telephone. It would go on and on while the police worked late nights and the whole town looked for a needle buried somewhere on the sandy shores of Sea Harbor—or even in the haystacks of Lambswool Farm.

Nell sighed and turned back to the others, trying to rearrange her head to allow for the new information to find a place.

"Beatrice Scaglia is probably already at Jerry's door, wanting the murderer found yesterday," Ben said. "She'll insist it be handled as quickly and quietly as possible." He was moving around the kitchen, on edge.

Nell nodded, watching him. "I suppose that's a good thing. A mayor wants to keep her town safe. It's why people voted for her." Nell was defending Beatrice, a woman who often drove her crazy. But when push came to shove, in Nell's mind at least, she was a public official who loved Sea Harbor even more than she loved her elegant outfits, her uncomfortably high heels, and being the center of everyone's attention.

"Sure, you're right, Nellie," Ben said, clumsily pulling on a light jacket with his one good hand. He breathed deeply, then topped it off with a sigh. "But it's one more thing Jerry has to handle."

"So you're off?"

He nodded. "I have a guy coming out to fix something on the sailboat and a library board meeting. I have to file some papers at the courthouse later. I'll stop in at the station and ask Jerry if there's anything we ordinary folks can do."

Of course he would. Nell sometimes teased Jerry and Ben that they were brothers from different mothers. Even their names sounded like some astute women knew that someday these two boys would have ice cream named after them. They thought alike, had great respect for the same kinds of issues, and though Ben didn't talk about it, they had sometimes eased each other's burdens, just by listening. The way brothers did.

He kissed the top of Nell's head.

Her smile dimmed when she stepped back and closely examined his sling and wrapped arm.

"It's fine, Nellie," he assured her. "Lily Virgilio is already on top of it. She's sent e-mails to all patients with instructions on what to do."

"How can she physically manage all that?" Birdie asked Ben as headed to the door.

"With good help," Ben said. "Carly Schultz, Arlene Arcado—and some of the others from Alan's staff, an MD friend of Lily's, the ER doctor—they're all rising to the occasion, or so I hear. No one knows quite what will happen down the road, but for now it's under control, at least as far as patients who need to be seen are concerned." He found his keys and reminded Nell that he and Sam had a late meeting at the yacht club to interview a new sailing instructor. He said he'd be in touch about dinner.

And just in case either of them was wondering—*no,* he wasn't looking forward to the day and encountering dozens of friends and neighbors. And he knew they weren't, either.

Nell and Birdie left the house soon after Ben, heading away from the town proper. Their motivation was clear: to stay away from the tidal wave rushing down Harbor Road, the wave that poor Ben would face at least a half dozen times with each new meeting he walked into. Once the morning paper hit Coffee's patio—or maybe before that, when people plugged in their coffeepots and picked up the paper from the steps, eyes still bleary from sleep, or when they turned on the morning news and they saw and heard the word *murder*—it would begin, gaining momentum until it had touched nearly all Sea Harbor lives, leaving people buried in questions, in sadness, and in fear.

They walked across the backyard and down the wooded path to the beach. Izzy would meet up with them there—a place where they could escape, at least for an hour or two.

"Izzy has her annual checkup later this morning with Lily Virgilio, so she took off work," Nell explained.

"Her appointment wasn't canceled?" Birdie asked, surprised.

"Not so far. Izzy was surprised, too. It's just routine and she thought Lily would have more pressing things on her plate just keeping things moving and making Alan's patients feel they had nothing to worry about. Maybe she's trying to keep everything as normal as possible."

The tangy smell of pine needles rose up and cleared their heads as they walked along the spongy path, trying to get their thoughts around the word *normal*. And then the trees fell back and the ocean appeared before them, the air crisp and clean. They headed toward the beach and spotted Izzy coming from the opposite direction when they reached the sand.

Izzy waved a hand in the air, the other clutching her golden retriever's leash. When she realized she was losing the battle, she dropped the leash to the sand and Red ran free, racing toward Nell and Birdie in giant retriever leaps. His tail flapped in the air in welcome and sand flew from beneath his paws in all directions.

Nell dropped to her knees, waiting for the dog in a safer position, one that wouldn't lay her flat. She dug her fingers into his long silky coat, rubbing his neck and head. "That's what this day needs," she murmured to the gentle beast. "It needs a Red."

"This is great timing," Izzy said. She looked up at the sky. Fat clouds gathered on the horizon, moving across the sky quickly. "Those look like rain clouds, but I'm sure they'll wait."

The wind had picked up, too, but between the clouds, there was plenty of blue sky for now. Izzy grabbed a handful of flying hair and wound a band around it. She turned and pointed toward a runner heading in the same direction as the clouds and suggested they do the same, skirting the yacht club and walking over toward the breakwater. "Less traffic," she said.

And fewer sunbathers buried beneath the sandstorms Red generated.

"Perfect," said Nell, pushing herself up and brushing the sand from her tights. She loved the solitude of the breakwater—even when fishermen hunkered over on its ledge or walkers wandered out. To Nell it was a pathway to the sea—and no matter how many people were there, she felt alone.

They headed down a narrow stretch of beach around a bend, a private path, according to the sign, raising their walk to a slow and gentle jog. Not much, Birdie directed—*gentle, gentle, gentle.* Just enough so she could feel her heart beating nicely against her chest, to know it was there, alive and happy.

The sign read PRIVATE, but most walkers or runners ignored it. It was simply to keep tourists out, was what most residents decided. Surely not the rest of them. Owners of the magnificent homes that lined the rocky shore wouldn't—or shouldn't—mind seeing familiar faces on their beach.

When they came to the beginning of the yacht club property, the beach grew wide and perfect, the sand raked and tended. The shadow of the breakwater lay ahead, beyond the sailboat slips and freshly painted dock, beyond flagstone patios and green lawns and stone benches facing the sea, to where the sea grasses grew tall and wild on one side, the beach cobbled and rough on the other.

They slowed their pace to a walk, feeling the sun hot on their arms as the rays slanted down through the clouds and reflected off the faceted rock, shining and turning into hundreds of tiny glittering stars, the sea wind cool and fresh on their faces.

The breakwater was nearly empty, save for a few people here and there, sitting along its flat bridge. A fisherman, a bird-watcher, a sunbather.

A man wearing sunglasses sat not far from the beginning of the breakwater, where it began its path out to sea. Long legs hung over the side, boots resting against the granite wall. The man sat still, his palms flat on the stone behind him as he leaned slightly back, looking out to sea. The bill of a cap shielded his gaze.

They might not have paid any attention to him, but Red, who rarely met a stranger, had plans of his own.

As if being called into the wild, Red wagged his tail and made a dash for the breakwater, up along the granite slabs, then flew onto the smooth surface to where the man sat.

"Doesn't Red know he's too old to run like that?" Izzy mumbled, running after the high-flying tail. She focused on the rocks, taking Red's shortcut to the breakwater carefully. Nell and Birdie followed slowly along the longer, intended path.

"I'm so sorry," Izzy began, grabbing Red's collar and pulling him back as he tried to lunge for the figure.

The man looked up, more curious than startled, as if his thoughts had cushioned him from surprises.

"Glenn?" Izzy said, looking down at him. "Hi. It's Izzy Perry."

The man squinted, then pulled off his glasses as recognition registered. "The sun turned you into a silhouette. Hi, Izzy."

He put his glasses back on as Birdie and Nell came up behind her.

"Glenn Mackenzie," Birdie said. "It's nice to see you."

Glenn greeted them both, tipping his head back, his eyes hidden behind the dark sunglasses.

Red settled down next to the man, nuzzling his backpack.

Glenn glanced down at the dog. "I thought at first it was me he was crazy about, but I think he smelled my lunch. Tuna fish sandwich." He reached over and kneaded the dog's ear.

"He likes tuna fish," Izzy said. "But usually prefers it grilled with ginger sauce."

One corner of his mouth lifted in a smile, his eyes still on Red.

Nell looked from the backpack to a camera sitting beside him, a takeout cup from Coffee's next to it. Then she looked at Glenn's face.

It had a hollow look, pale, maybe from lack of sleep. She knew Pete and Andy had gone over to Gloucester the previous night to check out a band. Perhaps Glenn had gone along. "Are you all right, Glenn?"

He swung his legs up from the side of the breakwater and stood. "I was taking a few last photographs of the town," he said. "It's really beautiful out here. Peaceful. I was never big on meditation, but this spot seems to pull you into it, willing or not."

"It does that, yes," Nell said. "I love it out here."

Glenn looked out to sea again. "My car's fixed. Ready to go, Shelby Pickard tells me. I'm leaving town, getting out of everyone's hair."

"Leaving?" Birdie repeated.

It surprised them all, although Nell thought about the irony of it later. For days they'd been surprised and curious that Glenn was still in Sea Harbor. And now . . .

"Yeah," he began, "I need to be moving on." But his words stuck, as if the nearby gulls had swooped down and snatched them away.

"Are you leaving today?" Nell asked.

"Later today. Maybe tomorrow. I need to settle up with Mary Pisano at the Ravenswood bed-and-breakfast and give Sam a flash drive with some photos on it. Say thanks to you nice folks who've been so welcoming to me."

For a moment, Nell wondered whether he had heard the news about Alan's murder. In the next second she shook away the ridiculous thought. *Of course he knows.* He couldn't have taken twenty steps through town without being assaulted with the news somewhere along the way. She glanced again at the empty cup from Coffee's. He certainly knew.

He saw Nell's expression and read it head-on. "It's an awful thing about Alan Hamilton. You—all of you who were his friends—you must be having a hard time with it. It's difficult to imagine."

An awful *thing*. Glenn was like all of them, using ordinary, nonthreatening words to try to explain what happened. *Murder* wouldn't be one of those words. *Murder* was for back-alley crimes and strangers prowling needle-strewn streets. Murder wasn't for Sea Harbor. And it definitely wasn't for people you knew.

"Yes, it's difficult for everyone," Birdie said. "You met him, too, even though it was brief. You talked with him. You knew his clinic, and you were learning about the Hamilton history here in Sea Harbor. I know you're a sensitive man, Glenn. His murder must have touched you, too."

Glenn listened to Birdie and seemed to give her words careful attention. He shoved his hands in the pockets of his jeans, kicking a stone into the water with the toe of his boot. Finally he said, "Yeah. Our conversations were brief. But I liked him. He was interesting, his family, all those traditions built around the clinic. I would guess the whole town is shaken by this. I've only been here a few days, but it doesn't take much to know that evil doesn't belong in this place. Not here. And it shouldn't have touched the doctor."

"That's right," Izzy said. "And now that evil has to be weeded out. But it will be."

Glenn rotated his shoulders as if to ease out tension. His head moved slightly from side to side, his face somber. "If, if there's anything I can do . . ." His words fell off.

"We all feel that way, wanting to do something," Birdie said. "Unfortunately, words don't go far, do they? But not doing anything is an awful thing, too. So that's why the three of us and Red are going for a walk along the shore, and maybe that's why you are here, sitting alone on the breakwater, letting the sea's energy help you with your thoughts. Maybe those are the best kinds of things to do right now. It's a start, anyway."

They were all quiet for a minute, and then Nell asked, "Is the fact that there's been a murder the reason you're leaving rather suddenly?" She realized as the words came out they could be interpreted in different ways, but by then it was too late.

Glenn took a sideways look at her and took off the sunglasses. His expression hadn't changed, but his eyes were wary. "Well, it's not sudden, not really. I never intended to stay long. I was just hanging out, waiting for my car to be fixed—"

No one said anything. Not the fact that his car had been ready for days. Not that he had been planning several photo shoots with Sam that might take days more.

Glenn went on. "I really like it here. It's a great place to be stranded. I enjoyed working with Sam. Getting to know all of you. But now . . . It's different now. You need to be grieving your friend. And I need to be moving along, getting back to my life."

His words were hollow, Nell thought. Just like his face. "I understand. Things have changed, certainly. But here's a thought. Why don't you come over to the house tonight? Sam and Ben have something going on tonight and will probably bring over pizza and beer after it's over. If you'd like to join us, it will give you a chance to say good-bye to whoever might show up."

Glenn nodded, thanked her, but said his plans were uncertain. He'd see.

They left Glenn a short while later, once he had torn off a piece of his sandwich and passed it along to Red.

Just before they rounded a curve that would take Glenn Mackenzie out of their sight, Nell stopped and looked back. He had gone back to sitting on the cool rock, his legs hanging over the side, his back to the land, blocking them out. Blocking out the town. He seemed to be off somewhere, over the ocean, thinking thoughts that Nell suspected were as far removed from Sea Harbor as the land beyond the sea.

"He is in a peculiar place today," she said.

"Peculiar, yes," Birdie said. "But I understand his coming out here, away from people. He's an outsider, an uncomfortable position to be in when the whole town is pulling together, trying to work out a world without their doctor and friend, and now this awful twist, this huddling together to protect one another against some kind of evil. Glenn isn't a part of it. He doesn't fit in this picture and what the town is going through."

"I think he looks sad," Izzy said. "But his leaving so suddenly is surprising. What is that about?"

"It's probably just as he said—and what Birdie described. I suppose it's understandable," Nell said, thinking it through as she listened to her own words. "A few days ago Sea Harbor was a pleasant place in which to hang out. Today it's a town with places cordoned off with yellow police tape—a murder scene. A town muddied. If you were a stranger here, would you want to stay?"

They walked quietly, their thoughts tangled, moving away from a stranger who had dropped into their lives and onto a more pressing present. The loss of a friend and a murder so close they may have rubbed shoulders with the person who did it.

Izzy hung on to Red's leash, following him along a path that wandered away from the sea. Birdie and Nell followed, up into a hilly neighborhood of nice houses with kids kicking soccer balls in the street and moms sitting on front steps. A place millions of miles away from the dire picture Nell's words had painted in the air—and one Glenn Mackenzie was escaping from.

Chapter 18

Nell considered canceling her appointment. Being held captive in M.J.'s salon while someone fussed over her hair and constant chatter floated above the *whir* of hair dryers wasn't appealing, not today.

"But you'll go—I know you," Birdie had said when Nell dropped her off at her home. "Last-minute cancellations are the bane of M.J.'s business."

Of course she would go; they both knew that. Canceling wasn't a serious thought, only an emotional one. Leaving gaping holes in a salon's schedule was bad for business, no matter what was happening in the outside world. But she had a while before she had to go, and at the rate their great world was spinning, who knew what would happen between now and then. Perhaps the murder would be solved, just like that, in a heartbeat. It was a terrible, fatal mistake. A food product contaminated. Nothing anyone could have predicted. And like the gentle aftermath following a storm, Sea Harbor would settle back into a lazy seaside haven.

She shook off the crazy dream and opened her computer to a list of things she needed to do. She was grateful to have a little time alone. She'd catch up on bills and a few household tasks that she would put off doing on a normal day. Today they were strangely appealing. Simple, mundane, predictable tasks.

For a brief time, the world would seem normal.

But once she had scheduled a few household repairs and laid out the bills on the kitchen island, shuffling them around needlessly, the numbers in front of her began to blur into images of Alan Hamilton. Alan preoccupied at the clinic. Alan slipping off the chair at Lambswool Farm. Alan murmuring words to her. *"Tell Claire . . ."* he had said. *Tell Claire.*

And then slipping to his death. She closed her eyes, her elbows on the island and her chin resting on her hands, and she went back over the entire night in her mind. Walking into the magical evening from the parking lot, the *baa*s and bleats of the sheep coming from the pasture, the sweet sounds of jazz floating on the air. Friends and family milling around, cheerfully walking in and out of the barns and touring the barn-turned-kitchen in happy disbelief. And the amazing meal. Prepared to perfection, served beautifully. Wine.

Arsenic poisoning.

She stared at her computer as if surely there'd be an answer there.

Alan's collapse at the farm had been frightening. Jarring. But with the implications of murder layered over it, it was almost impossible to comprehend.

A sound at the door pulled her out of her thoughts.

"Hey," Danny said, coming toward her. He crossed the family room in a few long strides. His hair was windblown, his worn backpack strapped across his shoulders, and his eyes gentle.

Nell welcomed him as if she hadn't seen him in weeks. He was headed to the library, he said, to get some chapters written, but when he spotted her car, he stopped in. It was impulse.

Nell smiled and put on the coffee. Danny knew and she knew

that there was no way he'd be passing by her house on his way to the library. People drove up Sandswept Lane only to visit the people who lived there. It didn't take you anywhere else.

"I've been reading up on arsenic," he said, shifting his body up on one of the island stools.

Nell looked over. "The curse of the Borgias," she said.

Danny gave a short laugh, but there was little humor in it. "You've checked it out, too. Those Borgias dispatched people right and left. Beware of fancy dinner parties." He helped himself to a cold bagel left on the island. "But the fact is it doesn't make much sense now. If you want to really kill someone, there are much easier and faster ways to do it."

Nell thought again of Lambswool Farm, the image of Alan sitting next to her. Was he drinking coffee? Wine? She couldn't remember.

"Alan had been feeling bad for a few days," Danny said, inching his way into her thoughts. "We had a tennis match scheduled a couple of days before—Alan, Sam, and another guy. He tried his best to get out on the court but ended up in the men's room feeling pretty awful. That night at Lambswool Farm might have been the last straw—but I'd be willing to bet there's more to it."

"Have you heard that?"

"No. It's just been a day, but now that they've determined it's arsenic poisoning, they'll look at other things. I heard from Carly Schultz—it was her doctor friend in the ER who alerted the supervisor to some odd bumps on Alan's hands, some discoloring. Things that didn't go along with having a bad flu."

"Bumps?"

"Small things that wouldn't mean anything if Alan had had a bad case of the flu. Doctors don't know a whole lot about poison unless they specialize in toxicology. Carly said her friend had just read a book about it, purely out of interest. It was about the history of poisons—nothing she had learned when she was in med school."

"So it was chance?"

Danny shrugged. "It was chance, maybe, that they determined it as soon as they did. But unlike the old days, when arsenic was difficult to detect, it can show up easily now in labs and autopsies."

Nell thought about that. The idea that things were discovered by chance was uncomfortable to her. In the world of medicine, there should be more certainty—at least that was her hope, as unrealistic as it might be.

"What does Ben say?" Danny asked, chewing on his bagel.

"He had a zillion things going on today. He hoped he'd see Jerry at some point. Maybe he'll have some more information later."

"Yeah, maybe. I got a text from him before I came over here. He said it's a rough day to be out in public. People are still trying to get their heads around Alan's death, and then they hear he's been murdered. It's personal to people. Alan was *their* doctor, not just some guy walking the street." He looked over at her computer, still open on the island, the bills strewn all over.

"It looks like we're in the same boat," he said. "Good intentions going down the tubes. It's hard to make headway on a fictitious murder, trying to come up with intriguing, clever ways to have the protagonist bring it to its careful, surprising conclusion, when there's a real live one spinning around us. One that has a whole lot more at stake than selling books." He finished the last bite of bagel and washed it down with black coffee.

Nell felt Danny's emotion as it walked alongside her own. She finished her coffee and rinsed the cup in the sink just as her cell phone calendar *ping*ed and she realized it was time to brave the outside world. Time to hit the salon.

Danny heard it, too. He stood and wiped his bagel crumbs into his hand, walking them over to the sink. "You know why I'm really here?"

He turned toward Nell and grinned, the boyish grin that Nell suspected had served him well when he was a kid in school. Today it made him look twenty, not nearly forty. It had been one of the first things that endeared him to Nell those years ago when he'd come back home to Sea Harbor.

"You don't need a reason, Danny."

"But I have one. I needed a dose of Nell, that's it. And it worked. My day's already better." He picked up his backpack and slung it over one shoulder. "Maybe I'll see you tonight, someplace or another. Ben talked about pizza and beer."

"That's what I hear." Maybe that's what they needed. A diversion. Being together—yes, certainly that. Even the thought of a ball game droning on in the background would be welcome.

She got up and walked with Danny to the door, one arm looped around his waist. She looked sideways at him. Alan's death was more than the effect it would have on a town, on a police force, on parents worrying about their children and evil lurking in the quietest of corners. She could see it in Danny's face, feel it in the hollow space inside herself.

It was *personal*. Alan was a good man. A friend. A person without enemies.

A healer.

Who on this good earth murdered healers?

The receptionist ushered Nell right back to the hair-washing room, as if she'd been warned not to make her wait. Something M.J. might well have done, Nell thought. The waiting room in the salon was lovely—a coffee and wine bar, tall glasses of water with lemon and cucumber slices. A gift nook with handmade jewelry and colorful scarves. Nell had fallen asleep in one of the leather chairs one day. But it was also a place filled with ladies who most often preferred talking to reading the stack of current magazines the staff spread out on the round coffee tables.

Nell was grateful to walk quickly through it today, waving briefly to acquaintances and not allowing anyone the chance to get up and stop her with talk and questions and conjectures. She welcomed the dark, soothing room in the back where hair was washed, heads and shoulders gently massaged, and the only sounds were the swish of warm water sprays and soft, sleepy music.

By the time she had a towel wrapped around her shoulders and moved to the sunny corner of the salon where M.J. liked to work, she felt almost human.

M.J. had reduced her client base to a few favorites, giving the salon owner the time she needed to shuffle papers around the desk in her office. *Boring* was how she described that job. What M.J. loved was the activity on the salon floor, the voices lilting and laughing as they poured out of the stylists' stations, the smell of eucalyptus shampoo, and the gentle heat of hair dryers. What M.J. loved was people.

And knowing what's going on, was Birdie's wise assessment.

The salon owner was waiting with hot coffee for Nell. She gave her a quick hug, then pulled away, a concerned look in her eyes as she searched Nell's face. She leaned her head to one side, her brows pulling together. "Maybe you'd prefer wine, Nell?"

Nell managed a chuckle and a shake of her head. She slipped her bag into the cubby beside the mirror and shifted in the swivel chair. "I suppose we could all use that today," she said. "But four is a little early for me."

"Well, it's just plain awful. Awful, awful, awful. The news is all over town, as you'd expect." M.J. ran a comb through Nell's wet hair as she talked, looking at it in the mirror. She slipped a strand of silvery hair between her fingers and switched briefly into stylist mode.

"You know, Nell, people pay for this kind of highlighting. These silver streaks in your thick dark hair? Incredible. I should be so lucky. My gray will appear one day and swallow me in one huge gulp."

Nell smiled into the mirror. She wondered sometimes if it was the mirror that encouraged personal talk in salons. Often intimate conversations. Two people speaking to each other in a mirror, removed from their real selves, one sitting in the chair and the other standing behind it. But always between them was the mirrored glass.

"You will always look wonderful," Nell assured her as she watched M.J. fingering shoulder-length plaits of her hair, her head leaning this way and that as she gauged the length.

M.J. took a small scissors from the tray and got into the meat of the conversation. "It's a difficult time over there at the Hamilton clinic, that's for sure," she said. "You know my niece—well, Ralph's niece, really. His brother's daughter. She works over there. But I guess I told you that. You and Birdie. You both were so nice to care about Arlene's mom when she was in that awful, slow process of dying."

"Arlene is being a big help to Dr. Virgilio, from what we hear."

"She's a worker, for sure. Smart as a whip. A genius, that one. Gets what she wants. We keep wondering, Ralph and I, why she doesn't go off and finish her college degree or make something of herself, but she tells Ralph that boat has left the dock. It's never too late, Ralph says to her. But she doesn't listen to him."

The familiar sound of M.J.'s voice floated around the chair. Her touch was gentle, sliding strands of hair through her fingers, holding it taut, trimming, cutting. Nell closed her eyes.

". . . so when we saw her with that Garrett fellow, we wondered what was up. Arlene's a pretty girl."

Nell opened her eyes. "Garrett?"

"Oh, you know. The Barros boy. Well, *man*, I suppose, is more accurate. His mother Dorothy comes in here. She's a little on the cranky side, but we all have our moments, right? I think Arlene vouched for him when he applied for the clinic job."

"I didn't know that." This added a new and nice dimension to Arlene. Her heart was in the right place.

"We didn't know it either. Garrett's mother told Maureen, the girl working the desk. She said Garrett loves working in the clinic. Happy as a clam and doing so well. Dorothy and her husband are as proud of him as if he were a brain surgeon. She went on and on and then some about her son. She claimed it was the best thing Garrett had ever done. The whole family are patients over there, and to have Garrett employed by Doc Hamilton was definitely a feather in his cap—or maybe in Dorothy's cap, the way she went on about it. Garrett's job had put Dorothy Barros in a much better mood, though, which Maureen likes because it makes her job at the desk much easier. A win-win, Maureen called it."

Nell listened, waiting for more. She wasn't that interested in Maureen's comfort level with Dorothy Barros, but she did want to know if Garrett had told Dorothy about her son's problems at the clinic.

But M.J. dropped the subject. She seemed more focused now on whipping Nell's bangs into shape. There was no mention of anyone losing a job.

"When was Dorothy Barros in?" Nell asked.

"In here? Oh." She stopped for a moment to think, her scissors held in the air, her eyes on Nell's reflection in the mirror, until she remembered and began cutting again. "Saturday, that's it. She's here every Saturday morning, rain or shine, getting her curls set. Beth does her hair."

Nell waited to hear more, although she wasn't sure what that would be. But M.J. had moved on to talking about a new play that recently opened at the Gloucester Stage Company, the topic of the Barros family seemingly over.

The thought of Garrett losing the job he had loved lingered in her head, crawling around in it uncomfortably.

She thought of Dorothy and Robert Barros—proud of their only offspring, maybe for the first time. Nell remembered conversations with them years ago when Izzy was their neighbor and she and Ben would see them out in the yard. After high school, Garrett had spent a decade holding down ordinary jobs. *Menial,* she remembered Dorothy saying about his job at Ocean's Edge. Maybe to some people, Ben had said to her that day, but he was a hard worker at the Edge, and the people who got to know him liked him.

His parents' pride in his new job was understandable, Nell supposed—working with the town's respected family doctor might have been considered a step up. Something they'd happily talk about to their friends. But the importance of it held a certain sadness. Garrett was a nice fellow, and what he did wasn't that important, not really.

And now . . . now he was a nice guy who no longer held the job his parents were inordinately proud of.

From M.J.'s silence, Nell knew the news of Alan Hamilton's relieving Garrett of the job he loved hadn't hit the salon yet.

And perhaps not even Garrett Barros's own home.

Chapter 19

Ben was beat.

He walked through the garage door into the family room, bringing with him a whiff of the rain that hovered above and a cloud of his own. His khaki pants were wrinkled and his blue checkered shirt was a little worse for wear. With his one good hand he carried a six-pack.

"A long day?" Nell met him halfway across the family room.

He nodded. "Sam's gang is close behind with food." He set the six-pack on the floor and wrapped Nell in a full-blown embrace, pulling her close and ignoring the sling between them.

Her breast pressed against his chest, her ear against the strong beat of his heart. Nell's breath caught in her throat. "Hi, you," she whispered, her words barely reaching open air.

Ben released her slowly. He smiled at her. "I needed that."

"Me, too," Nell said.

She had hoped for a few minutes to decompress quietly with Ben, to hear what was behind his words, but the sound of a car in the drive interrupted, and reluctantly she moved away from Ben and toward the front door.

It was the Chamberses, and once Abigail Kathleen toddled in, the need for private time with Ben was put on hold. The light that Izzy and Sam's child brought in with her swallowed up the need for private moments, at least for now. Abby was the perfect antidote for emotional ills. Nell scooped up her grandniece and waltzed her through the family room to the corner play area. Abby giggled and planted a wet kiss on Nell's cheek before disengaging and tumbling into the pile of stuffed bears waiting for her on the floor.

"I hope it's okay that we brought Abby," Izzy said, following them through the room. "Our usual sitter canceled. Her mom is uncomfortable with her being out. It's irrational, I know, but mothers, including me, tend to be that way—totally and completely irrational." She looked over at Abby, hugging her toddler with her eyes.

Abby was happily lining up her bears in a row, her world perfect.

Maybe such fears were irrational, especially when analyzed against logical criteria. The fact that a doctor had been poisoned didn't really hold a threat to others. There was nothing random about it; it was clearly planned. But Nell understood Izzy's emotion. Someone *was* murdered. No matter how. And that act had opened up a crack in the safe and invisible wall they had built around the town and its children. Something evil had wormed its way through the crack, something that didn't belong in Sea Harbor. Something bad.

"I'm glad you brought her. The crib is always ready. And if the rest of you want to go over to the Gull to watch the game later, I'm happy staying with my sweet Abby. I love stuffed bears, too."

"I'm with you, Aunt Nell. I even brought my knitting. Why is it that knitting and bears calm us, make us feel warm and safe?"

Nell glanced out the patio doors. A brisk breeze slapped branches against the glass and picked up fallen leaves, tossing them against the gray sky. "The rain is close," she said. "Knitting and rainy nights—and bears, of course—go together."

Sam and Ben walked into the family room from the entryway, Sam with an armful of pizza boxes. "I might have overdone it," he said. "I wasn't sure who would be here. Danny just texted that he and Cass are holing up at home." He followed Ben into the kitchen.

"If no one else comes, there's more for us." Izzy stuck her phone into the Bose dock and soon Adele's smoky voice floated in the background while pizza boxes were opened and glasses pulled from the cupboard. Sam uncorked a bottle of wine.

Nell checked her watch and looked at Ben. "I invited Glenn Mackenzie to stop by. I'm kind of surprised he's not here yet."

Ben turned around quickly, dropping a bottle opener onto the island. He looked at Nell. "When did you see him?"

"This morning. We ran into him out on the breakwater."

"He told us he's leaving town tonight or tomorrow," Izzy asked. She was leaning into the refrigerator, checking its contents, pulling out cheese and fruit. "Aunt Nell thought he might want to come over to say good-bye to people. He didn't really commit to coming. It was a *maybe*. I think being on the fringes of a murder has spooked him."

"He's not leaving town tomorrow," Ben said.

They all looked at him.

"How do you know? Have you talked to him?" Nell asked.

Sam took the opener from Ben and flipped the cap off a bottle of beer. He handed it back to Ben.

"No. But I saw him this afternoon when I dropped by the station."

"The police station?" Nell asked.

Ben nodded. "I was dropping off Sox tickets for Jerry. He was busy, but I ran into Tommy Porter. He said they were moving full steam on the investigation, starting to bring people in, as you'd expect. I'm sure we'll have our turn, all of us. They're trying to get their arms around all of Alan's movements that week and make some kind of sense out of them. That's no surprise.

"The surprise was seeing Glenn Mackenzie in one of the rooms, sitting across from Jerry, being questioned."

"Why would—" Nell's question was cut off by the doorbell. They all looked toward the front of the house, startled by the ring. It couldn't be Birdie or the Brewsters or Cass and Danny. They didn't know the Endicotts had a doorbell. And those who knew there was a button to press rarely used it, since the door was never locked.

It must be Glenn. He'd come after all. Nell moved toward the door, hoping she was right, but knowing, somehow, that she wasn't.

Jerry Thompson stood beneath the porch light alone, a badge peeking out beneath his jacket. He looked like he'd been up for three days. Rivers of rain ran off his nylon jacket and onto the porch step.

"Hey, Nell, sorry to bother you."

Nell opened the door and tugged on his arm. "Jerry, come in here; get out of this rain."

By the time he had brushed off his jacket and stepped onto the inside mat, Ben was there, concern shadowing his face. "You okay, Jerry? What's up?"

"Fine, fine. Everything's okay. I just wondered if Glenn was here?"

"Glenn Mackenzie?" Nell asked, though no other Glenns came to mind at that moment.

"Yeah. I had a question for him, and when I stopped by the B and B where he's staying, Mary said he wasn't there. She hadn't seen him since around noontime, when he mentioned maybe coming over here tonight to say good-bye to people. Mary had the impression he was leaving town."

"Well, yes," Nell said. "He mentioned that to us, too. But Ben said he's probably going to stick around."

Jerry turned to Ben. "Tommy said you saw him at the station?"

"Right. I did."

"It was just routine. I hope he got that. We're talking to lots of people who came in contact with Alan."

"Of course," Nell said.

"We're working our way through a list as heavy as Cass's lobster traps." He managed a smile.

"Sure," Ben said. "It's difficult. Not to mention that Alan was one of the best-liked guys in town."

"To put it mildly," Jerry said with a half smile.

"Alan was anything but a recluse," Nell said. "He probably saw half the town in the last few weeks—and we saw more of him than we usually do." She gave Ben's sling a nod. "Surely someone will know something that will help." Although she couldn't imagine who or how or what. She knew Alan well; she'd seen him several times in the last week. And she couldn't fathom anyone in Sea Harbor wanting Alan Hamilton dead.

"We'll help however we can," Ben said. "You know that. You got yourself a job there, Jerry."

"Yep, sure do. Anyway, this Mackenzie fellow was around Alan at Lambswool Farm the night he died. He was at the clinic, too, taking pictures with Sam, I hear, and he's someone I hadn't met—so I wanted to meet him, introduce myself, just in case he knew anything that could help us out. So I called him in. He seems like a nice guy, cooperative. Told me a little about his time at the clinic, his background in medicine."

Nell was impressed that Jerry already had information she might have thought insignificant. "We've spent time with Glenn," she said. "Danny, and Sam, too. We've all come to like him."

Jerry listened, nodding as if adding that to a mental list of things to remember. Then he said, "Along with what we'll be telling everyone else, I asked Glenn not to leave town for a couple of days, until we had gathered all the information. That's routine—but it seemed especially worth mentioning to someone who doesn't live here. He told us that he was planning on leaving—but plans can be changed."

"Well, then I'm sure he will st—" Nell began. And then she

stopped. What was it she was sure of? Glenn Mackenzie was pretty much a stranger to all of them; she had no idea what he would do or not do.

Jerry picked up her sentence, reassuring her. "I'm sure, too, Nell. I just thought while I was in the neighborhood, I'd see if he was here. A couple of questions popped up. Better to ask them while they're fresh. If he stops by, would you please have him give me a call?"

"Tonight? Or tomorrow?"

Jerry looked back through the glass storm door at the rain, heavier now, small rapid drops that bounced off the front step, flashed bright as diamonds in the door light. He looked back, his jaw set, his brows pulled together in a way that brought a sternness to his usually affable face.

Nell watched his body language, the professional stance obscuring friendship for the moment.

The police chief took a deep breath. Then he said, "Tonight would be good, if it's no trouble. Thanks."

Just routine, his voice said, but his body sent another message.

Ben and Nell watched Jerry's shoulders hunch up around his ears as he headed into the rain. He walked fast down the front walkway to his squad car as if fighting the world. He climbed in and slammed the door, then sat there for a minute or two, his hands on the wheel, rain pelting the windshield. He stared straight ahead as if planning his next move.

And then he was gone.

Chapter 20

Nell woke up early Wednesday morning.

Her eyes still closed, she reached out one arm, her fingers crawling over the space next to her, searching for Ben's warm body. Instead her fingers flattened out on a cold sheet.

Pulling her eyes open, she sat up and disentangled herself from the sheets. Her bare feet hit the floor. Cold. The rain had chilled the air, then moved on and left a hazy sun in its place.

She listened for the familiar morning sounds—the coffeemaker, Ben shuffling around in the kitchen pulling cups from the cupboard, opening and closing the refrigerator door.

It took just minutes to take a quick shower and to pull on a clean pair of jeans and a cotton blouse. Nell checked the mirror, ran her fingers through her wet hair, and headed down the back stairs.

Ben looked up. "Did I wake you?" He was sitting on a stool, the *Sea Harbor Gazette* spread out on the island in front of him.

"No. But it's early." Nell poured herself a cup of coffee and pulled out the stool next to Ben. "Couldn't sleep?"

"About as well as you did. I felt you tossing a few times." He picked up his phone and checked through his messages.

"Anything from Jerry?"

Ben shook his head *no* and continued thumbing through the screen to be sure, then checked voice messages. He listened, frowned, then looked at Nell with a curious countenance. "Here's a voice message I wasn't expecting. It's from Dorothy Barros."

"Garrett's mother? What does she want? Is Garrett all right?"

"She doesn't say. Only that she needs to talk to me. *Soon*, she says."

"Why would she be calling you?"

Ben shrugged. "Who knows? I helped her husband once with some disability forms for Dorothy. She was a nurse's aide and hurt her back on the job, but that was years ago. Other than that, I barely know the woman. I can't imagine why she'd be calling me." He looked at his phone again. "But there's nothing from Jerry."

Nell poured a thick stream of half-and-half into the strong roast and took a drink, then cupped her chin in her hands. "I worried about Glenn during the night. No, make that *wondered* about him. I don't know him well enough to worry about him. Where do you suppose he went?"

Ben shrugged. "I texted Jerry to let him know Glenn hadn't stopped by here last night."

They had ended up having a quiet night, almost normal. The cold rain—and a general weariness—had kept most people at home. Safe and dry.

So it had been just the five of them sitting in the family room eating pizza, with Abby falling asleep on the couch and the Sox game muted on the television in the background.

Glenn Mackenzie had been on their minds, so they'd talked about him—until they quickly realized that they had little to say. It wasn't that he was mysterious, not exactly. But there was something about the way he had dropped into their lives that didn't ring true, at least in Nell's mind. Not those first couple of days.

And not now.

Sam didn't quite climb on that bandwagon—there wasn't much mysterious about a guy loving photography; that was his take on it. Glenn enjoyed the art and probably wouldn't have much opportunity to play around with his camera once he started his postdoc work. His sticking around Sea Harbor made sense to Sam.

So the conversation had ended without getting started, and when the baseball game ended, too, the Perrys had packed up Abby and a couple of extra pizzas and headed home. But in the bright light of morning, the earth washed clean and a cool breeze wafting through the open windows, Glenn Mackenzie was still on their minds, like a fly that refuses to leave.

"Why do you suppose Jerry wanted to see him again?" Nell asked Ben, refilling her coffee.

"I guess he could have come up with another question, something to help with the investigation."

That was logical. But it didn't explain the urgency in the chief's voice. Nor the fact that most questions could wait until morning, couldn't they?

Unless . . .

Nell slipped off the stool and put one hand on Ben's shoulder, glancing down at the sports page, then at Ben's face.

He was thinking the same thing.

Most questions could wait until morning—unless Jerry Thompson thought Glenn Mackenzie was going to skip town.

And there was some very good reason the chief didn't want that to happen.

A call from Birdie a short while later was the distraction Nell needed.

Gabby wanted to check on the sheep at the farm. Especially Charlotte. She was as big as a house, close to having her lamb, and Gabby was worried she might have gotten wet.

Birdie had done her best to convince the preteen that rain probably wouldn't hurt a sheep, even a pregnant one.

Gabby was adamant. Didn't her *nonna* know that every year over a million lambs died of exposure?

Birdie didn't know that, but she knew Gabby wouldn't give up until she was able to spend some time with her sheep and to see firsthand that Charlotte was fine and the rain had not resulted in hypothermia or pneumonia or something else she had Googled that morning.

She also guessed that Nell would love the chance to get some fresh air.

She was right. Nell welcomed the diversion, and it took her less than a half hour to check her calendar for the rest of the day, cancel a few nonessential things, text Ben where she'd be, and make the short drive to Birdie's house.

Gabby Marietti and Birdie were waiting on the step when she pulled into the long drive leading up to Birdie's house. Gabby jumped up, a fat braid flying between her shoulder blades and a halo of long loose strands flying around her face. She helped Birdie up from the step and raced toward the car, waving a bulging white bag.

"Ella made blueberry muffins. It's Charlotte's favorite treat."

"Mine, too." Nell laughed and leaned across the front seat to open the passenger door for Birdie.

"Charlotte and I are good at sharing," Gabby said, climbing into the back and snapping her shoulder strap in place. "There's one for you. Besides, you know Ella. There are enough for all of us and any hungry farmhands hanging around. Ella's awesomesauce."

Already Nell felt better. *Gabby magic,* Birdie called it. If they could bottle it and sprinkle it over the world, it would solve all kinds of problems.

Gabby thanked Nell for coming with them—*Did you know that over one million lambs die each year from exposure?*—she asked. And then she settled back into the seat and plugged white buds in her ears, smiling and bopping her head as she tuned out the front seat chatter and tuned in to Taylor Swift.

"Have you talked to Mary Pisano this morning?" Birdie asked.

"No, why?"

"She met me on the road when I went out for my walk to tell me that Glenn Mackenzie didn't come back to the B and B last night. I didn't know Mary was keeping track of her guests' nocturnal habits, but it seems she was concerned about Glenn. You know how Mary gets attached to people."

They glanced across the street as Nell pulled onto Ravenswood Road, as if maybe they'd spot Glenn's car, or see him driving onto the bed-and-breakfast property. But all was quiet at Ravenswood-by-the-Sea B&B.

Birdie went on.

"I told Mary he was probably enjoying his last night here. Maybe he went to the Gull, had a few beers, and didn't want to drive back, so he camped out on Pete's floor or some such thing."

Nell held back a smile at Birdie's solution. It was neat and tidy and made perfect sense. There was that logic again. Perhaps Birdie and Ben had had the same philosophy professor.

Birdie sat up straighter in the seat and looked over at Nell. "But then Mary said that Tommy Porter had come by the house this morning. Very early, she said, before she had even put the coffee on for her guests. Much too early for any policeman to be coming up her drive. He was looking for Glenn, too."

"Did Mary say why they were looking for him? I'm sure she asked."

"Of course she did. But all Tommy told her was that they were talking to everyone who had had contact with Alan, collecting every conversation that people could remember, observations on how Alan looked and when he looked that way, anything unusual that they may have noticed in his daily routine in the days before he died. Or disruptions in the practice. All those things."

Nell listened and calmed the thoughts vying for attention in her head. She and Birdie could certainly address some of those out-of-the-ordinary things the police were asking about—Ben and the others could, too. But it had been a mere forty-eight hours since they had learned that Alan Hamilton had been murdered. Two short days. There hadn't been time to process any of it. Nor the effects of his murder on the people around them. Casting suspicion on anyone they knew wasn't something any of them would rush into.

"What is your take on all of this, Nell?" Birdie asked, pulling Nell from her thoughts.

"I don't know. I can't imagine how Glenn Mackenzie could provide any useful information about Alan Hamilton's death. They barely knew each other."

"My thoughts, too. Why are the police so interested in him? I'm thinking Jerry might be going out on a limb, grasping for straws."

Nell made a left turn onto the hilly drive that would take them out to Lambswool Farm. To fresh air and green grass, a hazy sun drying up the night's rain, to something that would clear their minds of cobwebs.

Birdie rubbed her cheek with her index finger, a habit that accompanied her thinking. "I think the police interest is confusing because Glenn is confusing," she finally said.

Nell nodded, admitting as much. Her opinion of the man had flipped back and forth a half dozen times since that first night when they had dined at the Ocean's Edge. He was difficult to read, that was true enough.

They felt Gabby's body moving to the beat of her music in the backseat. "Perhaps the police know something about Glenn that we don't," Nell said. "I hope for his sake he shows up soon. If he did leave town after Jerry asked him not to, it won't bode well for him."

They fell into silence, their thoughts and emotions getting all mixed up as they faced the fact that grieving their friend Alan wasn't a luxury they could afford right now. Not until things were put back in order. Nell opened the moonroof and the smell of plowed pastures and salty sea breezes began to work its magic. At least being out here was a break, a step back from things they didn't want to think about and a stranger who suddenly wasn't a stranger anymore.

It wasn't until they were driving along the white fence that bordered Lambswool Farm, its posts perfectly contouring the roll of the land, that Gabby pulled the buds from her ears and rejoined them. She opened her window and breathed in the fresh air in gulps. "Listen, I hear them," she said loudly.

She pressed against the seat restraint, leaning out the window frame. "They're talking to one another. They do that, you know. I think I hear Charlotte. Maybe she knows I'm coming. She recognizes me. Sheep do that. They can recognize faces for a whole two years. I know she knows me. She does."

Neither woman in the front seat would have questioned Gabby. She was probably right. She'd been filling them with lamb and sheep facts for days; if she said Charlotte's bleat was distinctive and she was calling to her, that was good enough for them.

Nell pulled into the drive and parked near the big barn adjacent to the pasture. Several trucks were parked nearby. Ranch hands, they supposed.

"It looks like Claire is here," Birdie said, pointing beyond the barn to the farmhouse at the end of the gravel drive. They had remodeled that building, too, at least enough for Claire to have a nice office suite on the first floor, and a separate bunk room and bath on the second floor where farmhands could crash if they needed to. Claire's blue Kia was parked next to a slightly rusty truck. "Angelo is here, too. That's good. He's become Claire's right-hand man out here—those two have the same nice chemistry between them that

Angelo has with Elizabeth over at the day school. He's good moral support. He'll probably miss being out here when school starts and he has to go back to helping Elizabeth run Sea Harbor Community Day School."

"Me, too," Gabby said sadly, climbing out of the car.

"You still have days of freedom left, young lady. How about you find your favorite sheep and make sure she's dry while we let Claire know we're here," Birdie said as she and Nell headed up the driveway to the house.

Gabby was gone before Birdie finished speaking, the bag of muffins in one hand and her long legs moving as fast as bicycle wheels.

Claire was coming out the front door as they approached.

She looked tired and sad, but pleased at the company. "Where's Gabby?" were the first words out of her mouth.

"Looking for her Charlotte."

"Great. That's where she needs to be. I'm so glad you're both here. It's the best place to get away. It gives me the space I need right now."

"It's hard to find that in town, at least right now," Nell agreed.

"It's not that I don't care what's going on," Claire said. And then she stopped and the corners of her mouth lifted in a sad smile. "Well, maybe it *is* that I don't care. At least not in the sense of it mattering to my life. Alan is gone and nothing will change that."

Claire pushed a handful of brown hair back behind her ear, then looped her arms through Birdie's and Nell's. Her voice brightened slightly. "But for right this moment, let's find joy. Come walk with me."

When Birdie explained that Gabby was afraid Charlotte might get wet in last night's rainstorm, Claire didn't laugh. "Gabby's right. It was a cold rain, which can be hard on an expectant ewe. But come, today's a new day: no rain, only sun."

Nell looked sideways at her friend, surprised but pleased at the lift to Claire's voice. She wondered if they should all move to a farm.

They neared one end of the large working barn, walking around the new tractor and into the shadows and sweet, pungent smells of hay and straw and oiled tools.

"Is Charlotte inside today?" Birdie asked, her eyes adjusting to the shadowy indoor light, but before Claire could answer, Gabby's voice filtered out of one of the stalls at the end of the barn.

"Ah, Gabby found her friend," Claire said and hurried toward the sound with Nell and Birdie in tow.

"Is Charlotte all right?" Birdie asked.

"Absolutely. Better than all right," Claire said.

Gabby stuck her head out from the stall at the sound of the familiar voices. "Hurry," she called out, trying to keep her voice a few decibels lower and softer than normal.

They quickened their step as Birdie murmured that her stepson Christopher would never forgive her. The thought of Gabby trying to fit back into her father's New York penthouse lifestyle was about as difficult to imagine as sending her to a finishing school.

Gabby's arm was still waving at them, pulling them down to Charlotte's stall.

Inside the stall they found Charlotte lying down on the fresh bed of straw Gabby had been checking every day. Her head was lifted and a strange and melodious sound was coming from deep in her throat. A low, whispered bleat.

And responding in a higher pitch were two small lambs, standing on wobbly legs, welcoming their mother's touch, the sweep of her tongue cleaning them, her head touching theirs before they nestled down in the curve of her body to happily suckle their morning snack.

"Ohhh," Nell said, her breath coming out slowly, her eyes widening. One hand lifted to her mouth as tears sprang to her eyes. She touched Birdie's shoulder.

Behind them, Claire stood as proud as if she'd given birth herself.

"And look here, the godfathers," Gabby said excitedly, her voice holding pure joy as she pointed into the shadows of the stall where two figures crouched low, their jeans and jackets dirty.

In spite of his weary face, the short squat figure looked up as if he'd just come back from the moon. His voice was raspy and weary and filled with wonder. "Hey, whattaya think? Not bad for a night's work."

"Angelo has missed his calling," Claire said.

"Me, yah, maybe so, but not this big guy here." Angelo reached out and clamped Glenn Mackenzie on the back. "Little did Charlotte know she'd need a doc around for this gig. We got it all here at Lambswool Farm—full-service delivery."

Glenn could barely muster a hello, his eyes still checking out Charlotte's newborns, the leakage around Charlotte's rump, the lambs' breathing.

Beside him was a box with bloodstained rubber gloves, iodine, lubricant, and cords. Things Birdie and Claire had insisted the farmhands stock in the barn cupboard in preparation for Charlotte's big day. Just in case they'd be needed, knowing that the laws of life dictated that if they had them on hand, then they wouldn't need them.

Lambs were born every day; a ewe as smart as Charlotte would know how to handle it just fine.

Except that Charlotte had some problems.

And instead of leaving town against the chief's orders, Glenn Mackenzie had saved two lives.

Chapter 21

"The second lamb was breech," Claire explained a short while later. They left Glenn—with Gabby sticking like glue to his side—to do some final checking and headed up to the big barn kitchen, where Claire had put coffee on and was keeping an egg casserole warm for Angelo and Glenn.

"He had to pull 'em out," Angelo said. "First he cupped the little guy's tail and rump, got him tucked back in right, and then—with those big hands as careful as you wouldn't believe, he helped the little guy into the light of day."

They walked into the big, shiny kitchen, pulling out tall chairs at one end of the long stainless steel island. Sunlight poured in through the skylights and the smell of cheese and eggs and coffee filled the air.

"I'm still confused. When were they born? Why are all of you here?" Birdie asked.

Claire explained that she hadn't been there. She'd come out to the farm only a few hours ago to work in the office and check on the farmhands—and just get away. "I spotted Angelo's car and went looking for him." She looked at him now, sitting next to Birdie, his elbows a reflection in the stainless steel countertop. His shirt was a mess, his jeans rumpled and soiled—and he had a glow about him as if he'd just had the time of his life. "Angelo is the man who should be telling the story. It's his and Glenn's to tell. I'm not even sure of all of it."

Angelo was happy to take over while Claire got coffee and mugs. "Here's what happened. I ran into Mackenzie in the Gull Tavern real late last night, right in the middle of all that nasty rain. He was alone, nursing a beer and looking like a man with the sins of the world weighing him clear down to hell or thereabouts.

"We got to talking and I asked him if I should be worried about Charlotte because of all the rain, knowing she was bulging out all over. He's a doc, you know. I figured he should have a few smarts rolling around up there.

"He said maybe, and that it would be worth checking. Jake Risso was about to close up the bar anyhow, so off we went. It was darker than Hades out here, and we finally found Charlotte pacing around near the old pond, restless. She'd somehow lost her bearings, moved away from the rest of the flock. We finally got her back to the barn, and Glenn checked her over. He could see the straining and thought we should stick around, so we camped out in the bunkhouse briefly, taking turns to check on her, and then lo and behold, shortly after the sun came up, she decided it was time."

Angelo took a long swig of his coffee, then put it back down. "The first little guy came out like he was on a playground slide. Whoosh. There he was. But the other little monkey had his head and feet all mixed up and wasn't about to budge. And that's when Glenn came in and saved the day."

And that was also when Glenn walked into the kitchen with Gabby at his side, the dark shadows of sleeplessness beneath each eye. But when he said that Charlotte was settled, bonding happily with her twins, his voice was more robust, satisfied, and sleep seemed not to matter much.

They were starving, Gabby said. It was almost past lunch.

Over eggs and coffee and bagels, the story was twisted and turned, revisited and embellished and chuckled about, until finally Nell and Birdie could tell it themselves, from start to finish.

Birdie checked the clock above the stove with a look of surprise. The day was melting away, she said.

Nell agreed that it was time to get back to real life. Claire had a pile of things on her desk, too.

Glenn was quiet as they all shuffled about, carrying dishes and mugs to the sink, rinsing and stacking and filling the shiny new commercial dishwasher.

When they were almost finished, Nell suggested she walk back to the barn with Glenn to check on Charlotte and her lambs. The others said they'd follow shortly.

They headed down the gravel drive without saying much. Glenn kept his eyes straight ahead, focusing on something Nell couldn't see.

She felt his weariness and wondered if either man had gotten any sleep at all the night before. But beneath the weariness she sensed a wariness, too, and the reason Glenn didn't meet her eyes.

Nell was the first to speak. "It's a gift to all of us that you and Angelo came out here last night." Her words were tentative. Glenn's quietness had put a barrier between them. She was uncomfortable, unsure of what to say to him—of what she wanted to ask. *Were you on your way out of town last night? Why does Jerry Thompson want to talk with you again? What are you up to, Glenn Mackenzie . . . and why did you come here?*

The questions lay there between them, and she wondered if Glenn even knew he was being looked for, almost—but not quite—like a common criminal.

Finally Glenn spoke. "Yeah. I'm glad we came out, too. It was crappy weather for a pregnant sheep to be out in, and I'd seen Charlotte's distended belly last Sunday. Alan and I looked at her together. Her belly had an odd shape—possibly a problem, we both thought.

I love animals. We had cows on my family's ranch, horses. Never sheep, though."

"Angelo picked the right person to bring with him."

He shrugged. "Maybe. We just ran into each other, is what happened. I was glad I could help." He looked off toward the pastures, the wind whipping his hair around his cheeks. Nell looked sideways and saw a flicker of happiness flit across his face.

"The truth is, last night was the bright spot in my week. I could see Charlotte was in trouble. Once that first lamb came out, her pushing seemed to do nothing. She was struggling. When I got that little troublemaker back in the right position and he came out, I held my breath, and then he sneezed life right into that scrawny little body. He breathed cleanly; that's when I knew he'd be okay. That sweet bleat coming out of him. It was one of those high points. The kind of thing that made me fall in love with medicine and healing."

The images of Angelo and Glenn saving the animals' lives were vivid for Nell, playing across her mind. She could picture Glenn, spattered with blood and fluid, helping the lamb into the world.

It made it difficult to say the other things that were on her mind.

They walked a little farther, and finally she was able to compose her thoughts. She needed to talk to him, to say something that would keep him safe—or not, but that would be his choice. If Glenn was running away, he'd better run fast. And if he wasn't, he should call Jerry Thompson before the image of someone running away took hold. She had no idea why the police thought Glenn might know something more about Alan's murder, but they did. *That* she knew to be a fact, and Glenn should know it, too.

"I don't mean to interfere with your life," she finally began. "I know we hardly know each other."

Glenn kept walking, his jaw set, as if preparing himself.

"The chief has been trying to get in touch with you."

"I was in the station yesterday," Glenn said. "I talked to him."

"Yes, but since then. Apparently he thought of something else, something he had forgotten to ask you. He came by our house last night. And then Tommy Porter dropped by the Ravenswood B and B today, wondering if you were there. Concerned, you might say."

When Nell finished, Glenn took a deep breath. He let it out slowly. "You're saying the police are afraid I left town when they asked me to stick around. I suppose it's tough to trust a stranger, and I know that's what I am here. But I don't run away from things. I never have. And I do what I say I'm going to do." He shuffled the gravel around with the toe of his boot. "My dad was a pretty amazing guy, a wise, fair judge who held me to the same standards he lived by."

He didn't look at Nell while he was talking, his eyes focused instead on the barn down the road, the flock of sheep beyond it.

Finally he looked at Nell directly. "I don't mean to sound self-serving, like I'm this good guy and how could they doubt it? I understand that the police have to talk to everyone, and they don't know me from Adam, so maybe I get special attention. I get it."

Nell listened to what he wasn't saying. He was a suspect, not trusted. And that must be difficult. But Glenn Mackenzie was smart—and he understood what the police and the whole town were dealing with.

Glenn shoved his hands into his pockets and started to walk again. His voice had lost some of its edge when he spoke. "Here's the thing, Nell. I just want to go back to Arizona and get on with my life. That was my plan when I saw you yesterday. Leave you good people to mourn your doctor. Leave the police to figure out why someone would want him . . ." His voice fell off and he grimaced. For a minute he seemed like one of them, caring about this man in a way that made talking about it painful. Finally he left the thought dangling and went on. "I shouldn't have come to Sea Harbor—I knew that before I came. But sometimes you do what others ask.

Even if you know you shouldn't. And as that good man would say, it's how you deal with what life throws you that's important. Don't waste time wondering how you could have avoided it." A soft laugh came from the back of his throat.

"Good man?" Nell said.

"The good judge. My father. He was full of pithy sayings and advice. And he was usually right."

He quickened his pace and Nell followed him through the barn doors, watching him move slowly, without sound, toward the stall. His whole body seemed to loosen as he listened to the gentle bleating of a mother communicating with her lambs.

She stayed just outside the lambing jug, watching the slight movement of Charlotte's head as Glenn entered and crouched down in the straw. He checked the lambs' suckling strength as they nursed and looked closely at Charlotte's teats.

As gentle as a lamb, Nell thought, watching his hands touch the ewe with great carefulness.

Glenn was dealing masterfully with what life had thrown him in the middle of a cold, rainy night. His father would have been proud.

But how would he handle what life had thrown him outside the innocent lambing stall? How would he handle being caught up in a man's murder?

Chapter 22

Gabby stayed on at the farm without objections from anyone. The mystery and glory of new life were far healthier than the mystery Sea Harbor had to offer.

Angelo said they had sheep to tend. He'd bring her home later.

Mae Anderson had texted that the merino cashmere blend Nell had ordered was in. It was a sweater for Gabby, and Izzy had picked out the pattern. She was sure Gabby would wear it all winter with the skinny jeans Izzy was buying her for her birthday. The raglan sweater was wide and loose and had long sleeves with thumbholes in them.

Nell admitted to Birdie that the thumbholes had seemed peculiar to her at first, and then had intrigued her. As someone whose hands were always cold—but who texted more than she was willing to admit and needed free fingers and thumbs to do so—she was thinking of knitting up one for herself. The yarn could probably wait until tomorrow. But Nell decided she couldn't. It was the perfect distraction.

Birdie said she'd tag along. She could always find something of interest in Izzy's yarn shop—chatting with Mae or checking up on a friend or neighbor, or discovering a skein of merino wool so soft and intoxicating she couldn't leave the store without it.

Nell welcomed the company. On the ride back from the farm with Birdie, she had shared her conversation with Glenn, and only in the retelling did she realize how little Glenn had actually told her. She still didn't know if he had planned to leave, or "skip town," as it might be thought of. Or why he had been one of the first names on the chief's list to question in the first place. Or . . . or why he had come to Sea Harbor at all.

All she really knew was that he was tender and caring and successful in delivering healthy twin lambs to Charlotte and Lambswool Farm.

And that mattered enormously to her.

Birdie had readily agreed.

Harbor Road was buzzing with activity, but Nell managed to find a parking place around the corner from Izzy's shop, adjacent to the small park on the corner. She looked across the street at the Delgado home as they walked along one of the park's crisscross paths. Then she quickly turned away. The thought of business as usual in the medical clinic without Alan was sad. She remembered when her own father had died. In that single moment her family's life had changed forever, yet all around her the rest of the world had swung back into its familiar rhythm, moving on to jobs, to school, to grocery shopping and baseball games and meeting with friends for lunch. She was grateful Claire Russell had Lambswool Farm and the birth of twin lambs to soften the aftermath of Alan's death for her. Nell hoped it would help.

"It's the most amazing yarn," Mae said, calling to Nell as she walked through the door of the yarn shop. "I'm thinking of keeping it for myself."

Mae Anderson was standing straight and tall and as skinny as a cornstalk behind the checkout counter, her rimless glasses covering kind, soft eyes that defied her stern stance. A line of customers stood in front of her. She wiggled her fingers at Birdie.

"We can share, Mae. Is Izzy here?"

"She's in the back room, teaching some unbelievers about the magic loop. Something we need around here."

"Loops?"

"Magic," Mae said, dismissing Nell as she moved on to extolling the merits of a yarn the next customer was cradling in her hands.

Purl appeared from nowhere, rubbing against Birdie's legs. She leaned over and scooped her up. Izzy's voice filtered up the short staircase as they approached.

Nell spotted a few friends—some neighbors and a group of young moms.

Izzy's shop had become a gathering place. She had created a safe and cozy environment in which to hang out, to sit and chat with people whether you knew them or not. Or sometimes to just sit alone in the middle of happy movement and voices and life.

She spotted Rachel Wooten and waved at her longtime friend, happy to see her sitting up front with Izzy. She'd nearly forced Rachel to take up knitting, sensing that it would help ease away the City Hall tensions that were tied to being the town's attorney. And it was working. Rachel was becoming addicted.

Beatrice Scaglia sat at the end of the old library table, a skein of hand-dyed alpaca yarn in front of her and her needles still as she listened to the conversations spinning around her, mentally recording things she deemed worth noting.

Birdie sidled up to her with Purl still in her arms. "Dear Bea, one of these days I shall teach you the fine art of knitting."

Harriet Brandley, sitting next to the mayor, guffawed at Birdie's comment. They all knew Beatrice would never learn to knit. Izzy knew it, too, but she also knew that Beatrice was one of her best customers. Having access to the backroom conversations gave the mayor insight into what was going on in her town, and she showed her appreciation by stockpiling some of Izzy's finest yarns. *Someday,* she told anyone who asked.

At the sound of Birdie's voice, Beatrice looked up. Then immediately got up from her chair as if she'd been expecting the two women. She slipped her yarn and needles into an oversized tote, and motioned them over to the window seat.

"Your dinner at Lambswool Farm was wonderful, Birdie," she began, pulling a chair over and sitting down. Her face was somber. "Was the food contaminated? E. coli? I'm getting calls and I can't get through to Jerry Thompson. I understand that the man is busy, but he needs to be responsive to me. I have a town to take care of."

Nell looked at the mayor with some surprise. Beatrice was smart and not usually an alarmist, especially after she became mayor and was charged with keeping order in her small town. She knew that Alan hadn't died from E. coli. "Beatrice, Alan's death was days in coming. It was not from anything he ate at the Lambswool Farm dinner."

Birdie leaned forward on the window seat and smiled her soothing, wise smile. "I hadn't considered that people would think E. coli was involved with Alan's death. I do understand how someone might worry about that. But no, Bea, there wasn't anything but calories and marvelous tastes in what was served Sunday night."

It was true. Leftovers had filled the double refrigerator in the big barn kitchen, and they had been taken in for testing almost immediately, even before the report indicated Alan had been murdered. Alan had been very ill that night, and accidental food poisoning had to be considered.

Beatrice admitted she knew better. "But there's no information coming out, and that's frustrating and has people on edge. I've never seen Jerry so tight-lipped."

"He doesn't want the town worrying about this. The police will find out who did it," Birdie said, stroking Purl's fur.

"They're questioning that man who's been hanging around town."

Birdie and Nell sat quietly, wondering what hypothesis Beatrice would be gathering from Glenn being questioned. The mayor didn't like being on the fringes of anything, and the fact that she hadn't met Glenn Mackenzie in the days he'd been in town would not work in his favor. He was a stranger to Beatrice, something that left her free to form her own opinions.

"You must know who I mean," Beatrice said. "He's been staying at the Ravenswood and has been taking photographs with Sam. He was at Lambswool Farm for the dinner, although I couldn't figure out why."

"I invited him," Birdie said.

Beatrice went on as if Birdie hadn't spoken. "At least the chief knows that some stranger coming into town, making inroads and asking questions the way he did, is certainly suspicious."

Getting no reaction, Beatrice changed topics. She glanced over at Rachel Wooten, then lowered her voice. "I wouldn't bring this up to anyone but the two of you, but has Ben mentioned anything about Alan's will? He has no family, you know."

Nell wondered where Beatrice was going with the question about Alan's will. It was such a personal thing, though she supposed the fact that it involved the future of the Hamilton clinic made Beatrice feel it might be her business. The clinic had become the *town's*, at least in their minds. In fact, Ben *had* mentioned Alan's will. He'd been planning on helping him write a new one, since the old one left everything to his now-deceased wife. But such personal matters had nothing to do with Beatrice, and it puzzled her that Beatrice had even brought it up.

Something else was on her mind.

"Ben is on the development advisory committee. He is open-minded and fair, and he cares about Sea Harbor." Beatrice kept her voice low, and Birdie and Nell had to lean in to hear her over the voices in the background and Purl's purring.

Nell nodded. Those things were all true, but somewhere along the way Beatrice's words had lost the feeling of being a compliment and were turning into a favor. "Yes," she said. She liked the mayor—but she didn't like being put in awkward positions. And Beatrice had mastered that art a long time ago. She had no doubt that's exactly where she was headed.

"Lily Virgilio has a wonderful plan to expand the Delgado building and the two clinics it houses. It will be good for the entire town."

"What are you saying, Bea?" Birdie asked. "Out with it, dear. Speak your mind."

"Changes like that have to be discussed at the advisory meetings," Beatrice said. She paused, and then she added, "And, of course, be approved."

"Ben hasn't mentioned it being discussed," Nell said, her voice neutral.

"It hasn't been discussed; that's correct. It hasn't even been presented to the committee."

Birdie and Nell waited patiently. Beatrice Scaglia was bright and calculating. Whatever she was about to say was planned, and there was some reason behind it.

"It hasn't been discussed because Alan Hamilton, as good a man as he is—as he *was*—was blocking Lily Virgilio every step of the way, but now the plan can be discussed in a thoughtful way. Alan was too emotional about it. He was adamant that as long as he had a say in it, he'd never allow the Delgado mansion to be changed in any way. As good a doctor as he was, Alan was a roadblock to progress, to Doctor Virgilio's plan."

And now, in Beatrice Scaglia's mind, plans should finally move forward.

Chapter 23

Nell went to dinner with Jane and Ham Brewster at the Ocean's Edge that night. When she finally got home, it was late and the house felt empty. Ben was in Boston for an Endicott family board meeting, and he wouldn't be back until morning. It wasn't an unusual occurrence, but somehow she found his absence that night discomforting.

It was the long day, she supposed. She was tired. But mostly it was because she wanted to talk to him, to her soul mate. She wanted to share the conversation she had had with Glenn and the odd one with Beatrice.

Even to share the wondrous birth of Charlotte's lambs.

That was what they did beneath the stars or in front of the fire when they were alone, just the two of them. They shared the day, their lives, their love.

But Ben wasn't there. So instead Nell poured herself a glass of wine and settled on the deck, watching the darkness fill the sky and feeling the deep night sounds surround her.

She knew Glenn had gotten in touch with Jerry Thompson—Mary Pisano had said as much to her when she had seen the B and B's owner at the Ocean's Edge earlier that evening. And that was good—at least Jerry knew Glenn wasn't planning on being some kind of fugitive.

Although Mary was happy to have Glenn stay around, she wasn't at all pleased with the reason for it and the shadow it cast over her guest. Glenn was a fine person, which she would tell anyone who would listen. And if they didn't listen, she would work it subtly into her "About Town" newspaper column, setting the record straight on someone she cared about.

Nell had considered offering the guest cottage to Glenn, but for reasons she couldn't put her finger on, she had held back. Mary liked having him at the Ravenswood, and he was already settled in, so moving might be an unnecessary hassle; at least that's what Nell told herself. Affording the steep weekly rates at the luxury bed-and-breakfast didn't seem to concern him either. So she'd left well enough alone.

She leaned back into the Adirondack chair, looking at the darkened guesthouse, a collection of shadows in the far recesses of the yard, and wondered now if she was having doubts about Glenn. Was that why she hadn't offered him the cottage?

And that was when she heard the noise.

At first she thought it was an animal, the neighbor's cat or a raccoon. There'd been a rash of them in the neighborhood recently, raiding garbage cans and causing minor disturbances.

It was a dark night, and with only dots of illumination from a line of low solar lights in the back garden, the woods beyond it looked deep and black and menacing.

So silly, Nell told herself. How many times had she walked through those very woods for a nocturnal stroll on the beach? And it wasn't even a woods, not really. It was a thick patch of pines and shrubs that separated the Endicott backyard from the beach road. And the only reason one couldn't see from the beginning of the path to the other end was because it wound its way through the trees, a well-worn path, a safe path. But not a straight one.

Nell sat up. She set her wineglass on the table and leaned forward, straining to see if it might be a neighbor's dog thrashing around in the brush.

A shuffle. Not the frisky gait of the Aussie who lived next door. And louder certainly than a cat mousing in the dark.

And then she spotted the figure. Hunched shoulders appeared out of the woods, at first disembodied, then followed by limbs and torso and head. It was shadowy and foreboding, like something out of a horror film where scene after scene is so dark you can barely make out the figures.

Nell shot out of the chair, her hand on her phone.

Later she would try to explain to Ben why she hadn't run inside and locked the door. Her heart was slamming against the wall of her chest, but she stood stone still, one hand gripping the deck railing and her eyes peering into the darkness as she watched a tall, lumbering body walk up the side path. The neighborhood children called it the Beach Path—a shortcut from the street to and from the beach.

But it wasn't a child making his way toward the deck. Nell took in a huge lungful of air, then released it slowly, her whole body relaxing as the intruder's features came into focus.

"Garrett Barros, is that you?"

Garrett stopped dead in his tracks, his head lifting as he stared at the figure on the deck.

"Mrs. Endicott," he choked out.

"Yes," she said.

He coughed, covering his mouth, then mumbled, "I'm looking for Mr. Endicott."

Nell frowned. Garrett was standing still now, one hand fiddling with a cord on his hooded sweatshirt.

"Please call me Nell, Garrett. And why don't you come into the light so I can see you while we talk."

He moved obediently to the foot of the deck steps, then stopped short, his head bowed.

"Would you like some tea?" Nell asked.

He shook his head and lifted his chin. "Just your husband, is all. I didn't . . . I didn't mean to bother you. I gotta see him, though."

"Might I help? He's . . ." She hesitated to say more. Then looked more closely at the frightened, desperate face staring up at her. "Garrett, Ben can't see you right now. But I'm here. Please tell me what I can help you with. Would you like to come up to the deck and sit?"

He shook his head no and stuffed both hands into the pockets of the hoodie. His muffled voice made Nell wonder whether he had had a beer or two. "Would you give him a message?" he asked.

"Of course I will."

"Mother said he has influence; people listen to him. He's got friends. He helped my dad get a job at the plant, and she knows he can do this. She says he has to get me my job back at the clinic. He . . ." His head lifted up and he stared at Nell as if forcing her to understand what he was saying, to read between the words and fill it all in. And then do what he was asking.

"But, Garrett . . ." she began. She paused, not really sure what she was going to say next. Remind him that Alan Hamilton was dead? That his request made little sense? That . . . ?

She looked into his eyes, black and piercing—and begging her for help.

But before Nell could process the rest of her sentence, to try to come up with something that would assuage his distress, Garrett Barros turned around, and with his back to Nell and his head lowered into his chest, he walked down the path the way he'd come, across the long yard, and disappeared into the safety of the dark Endicott woods.

Chapter 24

Nell picked Ben up at the train the next morning, and they headed directly over to the Hamilton clinic, realizing as they pulled into the parking lot that although it looked the same, the Delgado mansion was forever changed. It no longer had a Hamilton at the helm.

Ben was concerned when Nell told him about Garrett Barros's sudden appearance in their backyard the night before, although as they talked it through, turning it this way and that, he agreed that Garrett's coming up through the woods was a natural thing for him to do, not sneaky or nefarious. He'd made that trek hundreds of times as a child, shortcutting to Harbor Road or back to the beach. Nell had even encouraged him one day to bird-watch on their property. Ben's grandfather had installed a stone bench at the end of the path, a place to sit with binoculars and look out over the ocean. She and Ben had recently seen a beautiful red-necked phalarope at the water's edge, she'd told him.

But his odd request last night had surprised her.

"Especially," Nell told Ben, "because Jane and Ham told me at dinner that he is doing a great job at the gallery. And he seems to love it. The other artists who come in and out like him, he's helpful, and he gets a chance to paint. He finally seems to have found his niche."

Ben was puzzled. "I suppose I could talk to his dad, see if he knows what's up. The thing is, the man is thirty years old. Talking to his dad seems a bit inappropriate. And it's interesting that he even knows about my helping Robert get a job. That was several years ago, and it wasn't a big deal. I knew a foreman at the fish processing plant who needed someone. I ran into Robert at the Gull one night and knew he needed a job. And that was about it. I didn't perform miracles—not a single one."

"Maybe you should talk directly to Garrett," Nell suggested, pulling into a parking place. "Find out what is bothering him. I think it's about more than needing a job."

Ben was silent for a moment, and then he said, "Garrett may like working at the gallery, but we know he wasn't happy about losing that job. You saw that firsthand. You saw that mild-mannered fellow let loose with an angry streak strong enough to smash a fence."

He was also someone who had been around Alan Hamilton often in the weeks before he'd died.

Ben was all for being cautious. And he preached his message to Nell eloquently.

The office was active, but Carly Schultz and the office manager seemed to have things under control. Carly ushered Nell and Ben into an examination room.

"You're amazing—you know that, don't you?" Nell said as Carly motioned her toward a chair. "You're making a difficult situation bearable."

Carly mustered a smile. "Everyone is helping, trying to keep it normal." She looked around. It was clear that in Carly's mind, things were far from normal. And the profound sadness in her eyes showed how much she missed her boss.

"Lily Virgilio is making sure our needs on this side of the clinic are met," she said. "She's calling in favors from both her and Doc Alan's doctor friends to make sure things are covered. There's a doctor scheduled for each day this week so no one will fall through the cracks."

But they all knew that it was only a temporary fix, and the fate of the Hamilton clinic hung ominously "out there" in what wasn't said.

"So, Ben," Carly said, switching into nurse practitioner mode. "Let me see what's going on here."

Ben sat on the edge of the table while Nell watched Carly unwrap Ben's arm and probe gently, all the while asking Ben questions and nodding at the answers. The swelling was gone, the pain so minor a simple ibuprofen at night took care of it. He felt fine, he told her.

"Everything looks good," Carly said when Ben had answered all her questions and the examination was finished. She rewrapped the injured limb and made some notes on an iPad. "We'll do an X-ray in a week or two, but you're healing fine. You have strong bones. Doc Alan thought so, too." She smiled wistfully and held up the notebook. "He wrote in his notes here that you can't keep a good man down, and Ben Endicott is definitely a good man. It says that, right here." She shook her head, her eyes scanning the device. "He did that, put personal things in his notes sometimes. He sure loved his patients. Not all doctors do, you know."

Nell felt an urge to wrap Carly in a hug, but instead she nodded, agreeing, knowing instinctively that the hug would have instantly caused tears, and it wasn't a good time for the busy nurse to be crying.

"Alan was a good friend, a good doc," Ben said, pushing himself up from the edge of the table. He looked down at the sling and wiggled his fingers at Carly to coax a smile. "And he sure knew how to hire the best nurse practitioners."

Carly smiled.

Nell picked up her purse and stood. "Carly, I have a question for you. I don't want to put you on the spot, so stop me if this is a private matter and I should simply mind my own business."

Carly leaned against the table and waited.

"Do you know why Alan fired Garrett Barros?"

"I don't know, Nell—none of us do." Carly shook her head as she talked, clearly holding nothing back. "I wish I did know. It surprised everyone—except maybe Arlene. Garrett was a big help around here. He had no ego about doing little things like some people do; he'd just do whatever anyone asked—sometimes even if they didn't ask. Doc Alan had him keeping inventory, making sure the dispensary was neat, bottles clean, counters wiped, even cleaning up the snack room and making sure the bathrooms were equipped. I thought Doc Alan trusted him. And then, boom, last week he was gone."

Carly paused, her face pinched as she tried to think back over the days. "It's all kind of a blur in my head. The doctor wasn't himself last week. I wondered if maybe that was the problem. He must have been feeling terrible. Maybe Garrett made some little mistake and it seemed bigger—you know what I mean?"

Nell knew. She'd considered that, too. But somehow it didn't fall as neatly into place as she wished it did. They knew now that Alan really had been experiencing physical pain. But ill or not, Alan Hamilton was anything but impulsive.

Carly walked them back down the hall toward the waiting room and they stood there for a minute in the open door. Carly talked a little about the Fractured Fish and how well they were doing. "I don't know how they do it, with Andy managing his dad's bar, Pete working at the Halloran Lobster Company, and Merry running the Artist's Palate. But they do. They're amazing. And they even find time to practice." Nell caught the blush to her cheeks. It wasn't just Andy's hard work at the Gull or his drumming ability that was causing it. She suspected Andy Risso had a large role in helping Carly through this difficult time.

"So," Carly said, switching back into nursing mode again and motioning toward the receptionist's desk, "Bridget will set you up for another checkup, Ben. Take care and . . ." Her words trailed off as the outer lobby door opened with a whoosh, sending a magazine flying to the floor. A big-boned woman walked in, her hair mussed and her eyes fiery. Carly's eyes opened wide.

At first the woman didn't see Carly or the Endicotts. Dorothy Barros headed straight to the desk and placed both hands flat on the surface, startling the receptionist.

"Who's in charge?" she demanded, staring daggers directly through the innocent girl behind the desk.

Behind the receptionist, Arlene Arcado was pulling a file from a cabinet. She shut the drawer and moved toward the desk. "You're Garrett's mother, aren't you?" she asked. "What can we do for you?"

"Plenty." The woman's voice rose. A man sitting nearby glared at her.

Dorothy took a deep breath, realizing she was gathering the wrong kind of attention, and attempted to force some order to her hair, pushing curls haphazardly behind her ears. She assessed Arlene, then said, "I certainly hope somebody can help me. Are you in charge? There's been an awful misunderstanding that needs to be straightened out. My son works here, but he thinks he no longer has a job. It is a mistake. He's a hard worker."

Arlene looked over Dorothy's shoulder and spotted Carly. She made a motion with her head. *Help,* it said.

Carly was already moving toward the desk.

The movement caused Dorothy to turn sideways, and it was then that she spotted Ben.

She brushed Carly aside and walked toward him. "Ben, you're the person I need to see," she said.

"Good morning, Dorothy," Ben said calmly. "What can I do for you?"

He nodded to Carly that it'd be okay. He knew Dorothy Barros.

Dorothy's face softened, but only a little. She acknowledged Nell with a nod, then took a deep breath and said, "My son Garrett worked in this clinic. He said he was told not to come back, that they didn't want him here. But he's wrong. Of course they want him. This is where he works; this is his job." Her face was flushed and her voice fluctuated, rising and falling, as if difficult to control.

Ben nodded, listening. He took Dorothy's arm, bending his head as if trying not miss a single word, and began walking her slowly toward the door.

"He needs to be here," she said. "They need him here."

Nell opened the door to the lobby.

"It's quieter out here," Ben explained. "We'll be able to talk better."

Dorothy nodded and followed.

Sitting on a bench in the lobby beneath a majestic seascape painting was Robert Barros. He stood when they came through the door, his long face reminding Nell of Wood's *American Gothic* painting—somber and sincere and looking at them evenly. She could easily imagine his long fingers wrapped around a pitchfork.

"Sorry, folks. I didn't know you were here," he said solemnly. "Dorothy is upset about our son losing his job."

"*Garrett*," Dorothy said, her voice rising. "Garrett is upset. This job meant everything to him. He needs it back."

"Robert, do you know what happened?" Nell asked.

Robert looked at his wife, and then he shook his head.

"It was that doctor who did it," Dorothy said to Nell and Ben. "He didn't like Garrett. Well, now," she said, pausing to catch a breath. "Well, now he can come back."

She forked her nervous fingers through a tangle of curls and looked back at the sign on the door. THE HAMILTON CLINIC. She read it out loud, and then her voice dropped so low they could barely hear her words. "He's a good boy. Garrett is a good boy."

Robert nodded and held out his arm to his wife. "Yes, he is, Dorothy. Yes, he is. Now let's go home. It's time for lunch."

To Ben and Nell's complete surprise, Dorothy Barros put her hand through her husband's arm and, without another word, quietly followed him out the front door and into the morning sun.

Chapter 25

Birdie was perplexed when Nell related the incident. "I've known Dorothy Barros for a long time. She's always been a bit gruff, but why on earth would she barge into the clinic and make a scene like that?"

"That's the question." Nell peeled back the foil from a farfalle salad she'd thrown together quickly for the Thursday-night knitting session. It was still warm—with chunks of shrimp, snow peas, and red peppers forming a rainbow of color against the creamy pasta. The lemon, fresh mint, and olive oil sauce filled the room with enticing odors.

"I didn't see Dorothy much when I lived next door to them—she was kind of a recluse—but Garrett and his dad were always nice, mowing my lawn and cleaning out my gutters every fall," Izzy said. She fanned out four napkins on the table.

Birdie sprinkled some vinaigrette on a lettuce salad and tossed it lightly. "What doesn't make sense to me is that Garrett is truly enjoying his time at the gallery. I saw it for myself this morning when I went in to talk to Jane. He talked more than I've heard him talk in a lifetime, explaining the techniques used in the different paintings Jane and Ham had on display, even showing me one of his own. I would almost say he was charming."

Nell tried to juxtapose that young man with the frightened one who'd stood at the foot of her steps the night before. She wondered what went on behind the closed doors of the Barros house. "Where's Cass?" she asked, looking around the room when she realized they were one knitter short.

"On her way. Something about Danny needing a ride."

"I'm here, I'm here," Cass called from the front of the store, taking the three steps in a single leap. She walked over to the table and took a cracker from the cheese board, inhaling the aromas. "What have I missed?"

Nell filled her in on her nocturnal visit from Garrett and his mother's odd appearance at the clinic.

Cass listened, not interrupting, and slicing the sharp cheddar into neat slivers. When Nell was finished, she said, "I don't know Dorothy well, except to know that when I rented Izzy's cottage for a while she rarely came outside. She had hurt her back or something. Her behavior at the clinic is very odd, though. Even my ma wouldn't get that involved in making sure my life was perfect. But . . ."

"But?" Birdie asked.

"But putting his mother's goofy behavior aside, I can't stop thinking about Garrett and how he figures into this mess."

Mess, Nell thought. Another of those acceptable words, gentle words that in the end simply mean *murder.*

Cass took another cracker and nibbled on it. "The thing is, Garrett was around that clinic every day."

The thought certainly hadn't escaped any of them; it loomed large and uninvited and was one they would just as soon get rid of.

"And if three of us heard him destroying a fence in anger, others must have heard it, too," Birdie added. "The two together aren't a good thing."

"Especially to the police," Cass said, her voice taking on a tone of certainty. "They aren't as inclined as we are to remember the mild-mannered Garrett or the sweet guy who cleaned Izzy's gutters."

Nell looked across the table at her. "You're telling us something. What is it?"

Cass picked up a plate and began spooning pasta onto it. "Danny was working on his book in the library today and his bike tire blew when he tried to leave, so I went to pick him up."

They waited while she added a roll and a giant pat of butter to her plate. "I had parked across the street in the City Hall lot, and as we were carrying the bike to the truck, who walked out of the police station but Garrett Barros?"

"The police station?"

"Yep. Garrett was never crazy about me, but he likes Danny, so when Danny waved to him, he came over to us. He looked like someone who had just had his life ripped away from him. I guess that's a bad way to put it, but he was one sad dude. He'd been in there a couple of hours, he said."

"That distresses me," Birdie said, walking a bottle of wine and her full plate over to the fireplace corner. She set them down on the round coffee table. "Garrett is a decent fellow. Life hasn't always been easy for him, but he's made it work. I like him, and being questioned by the police must have been a terrible ordeal for him to go through—much worse than it would be for most people. It's taken Garrett years to feel good about himself."

Nell moved to the fireplace area, sitting down in an old leather chair of Ben's that Izzy had confiscated for the shop's sitting corner. "It bothers me, too, yet we knew they'd want to talk to Garrett. Two hours seems excessive, but it was going to happen. As Cass said, he was at the clinic every day. He had access. And he did something, whatever it was, that caused Alan to fire him."

"And Alan is dead," Izzy finished softly. She pushed Purl

gently to the side of the couch and sat down, curling her legs up beneath her. "Means and motive."

"Did Garrett say what kinds of questions they asked him?" Birdie asked. "Maybe they were just trying to find out things about the clinic. Things that might lead them in new directions."

"He mentioned a few things, but not much. Honestly? I thought he was going to cry. He said Tommy Porter had done the questioning. Danny said later that that was probably a kindness on the chief's part. Sitting across from Jerry Thompson would have been awful for Garrett—the ultimate authority kind of fear. But Tommy is closer in age, and he and Garrett have known each other from growing up here. And Tommy's nice. He asked him things about Alan: What kind of boss was he? Did Garrett like him? Did other staff like him? Did Garrett like his job there? That kind of thing."

"Did he talk about his answers?" Birdie asked.

"He was probably being selective, but he said he told Tommy that he *loved* Doc Alan. He talked about how wonderful and kind he was and that he'd never hurt him, not for anything in the world."

"That's interesting. He *loved* him? He was certainly angry at him that day we were there," Nell said.

"Or mad at something, anyway," Birdie said. "We're assuming it was Alan, which I guess is a valid assumption, since Nell had heard the altercation earlier." She leaned toward the table and poured four glasses of wine.

Cass swabbed up the last of her sauce with a hunk of bread. "I probably should have kept out of it, but I mentioned the fence, that we'd been in the parking lot that day and heard him."

"Oh, Cass," Nell said. She wasn't sure why that saddened her, but it had been such a private moment. It seemed like an intrusion to let him know he'd been observed.

"I know, I know. It just came out. Danny had told me they'd

talked to the whole office staff, so I figured someone had to have mentioned it. A destroyed fence is going to be noticed."

"What did Garrett say when you mentioned it?" Izzy asked.

"Well, that's the thing. He didn't say anything. He didn't get mad; he just closed up, like his whole body was folding in on himself. And then he shuffled off across the lot and climbed into that old Chevy he drives, and off he went."

Cass got up and helped herself to seconds while they thought about a sad Garrett Barros.

Nell wondered whether his parents knew that he'd been questioned by the police. She guessed they probably didn't know.

Cass picked up Purl and scratched her chin. "Can you make any sense of Dorothy Barros trying to force the clinic to give Garrett his job back?"

Nell didn't have any idea. "After seeing Dorothy today, it makes me think that Garrett's trip to our house last night was something she told him to do. I'm not at all sure he wanted to be there. I think he's happy at the Brewster Gallery."

"But he was upset about losing his job that day," Birdie said.

That was true. They all played around with it until Nell pulled their thoughts into words. "Maybe he was upset because he knew how his mother would react."

Izzy began piling plates up, while Nell wiped the table off.

They all mulled over the comment, giving it credence, but had no idea where to go with it. Yet.

Soon they all settled back down for chapter two, as Cass called it. The first chapter was food, without which she would never have been a part of the group. The second was knitting.

They pulled out their yarn and needles, and soon the table was littered with skeins of colorful yarn, half-knit carrots and pea pods, along with a leafy head of cauliflower that Birdie had begun knitting, bulky white yarn forming its body and lacy green leaves hugging it all around. She passed around her finished eggplant for approval.

Izzy brought to the table the rest of the wine and a carafe of fresh coffee, and they settled back in, relieved to have something to do with their fingers—but unable to let go of the prospect of a young man they all knew possibly being suspected of something as awful as murder. They found their emotions and the actual facts were at war with one another, tugging uncomfortably as they knit.

Nell mentioned Dorothy's bragging at the hair salon about Garrett's job. "He had already been fired, but apparently Dorothy didn't know it yet. The staff thought her pride excessive," she said. "There's something not lining up about any of this. It's true Alan fired Garrett. And we know his mother wanted him to get that job back. And it's also true that Garrett had opportunity. If someone was poisoning Alan over a number of days—"

"Every day?" Izzy asked.

Cass shook her head *no.* "Not necessarily. Danny is an expert on this. He used it in a mystery. He said it wouldn't have to have been every single day. And the amount could have been different from one day to the next. People don't always die from arsenic poisoning. The person can be treated if it's discovered soon enough."

Nell thought back to the first indications that Alan wasn't feeling well. They had noticed it the day Ben broke his arm, but that was the first time they'd seen him in a week or so. Had someone noticed it sooner? Claire had. She'd mentioned it that night in the shop, the night that Alan hadn't shown up for their dinner date.

Izzy pulled out a skein of soft gray wool, beginning the second color on her bowl. Blues and gray would wrap around it, and if she had time, she'd knit some sheep to stand beside it, guarding the felted bowl when it sat on the harvest table. "When I did that stint as an assistant prosecutor, one of my first trial cases involved a man who was poisoning his wife with arsenic. He was putting it in her wine every night. She actually thought he was buying special wine and considered it a romantic gesture. Apparently the arsenic improved the taste of the wine, which accounted for her confusion."

"Did she die?" Cass asked.

"No. Her wise sister had never trusted the husband and forced her to see a doctor. She was treated, ended up fine. But the husband didn't. He got twenty years."

Nell thought about the wine that had been served at Lambswool Farm that night. Poured at the bar, passed around on trays. Could someone have served Alan a glass? Dissolved some arsenic in it first? He was drinking water when he sat with them. But she remembered him walking across the yard with Sam and Glenn. Sam had a bottle of beer, but the other two were carrying wineglasses.

Suddenly even wonderful parties were taking on a sinister feel.

"Alan was our friend for a long time," Nell said. "I can't imagine anyone wanting to harm him; that's what throws this all off-kilter. All doctors have disgruntled patients from time to time—people expect their doctors to perform miracles, so there will always be some of those. But I don't know of anyone who didn't like him."

"He's broken some hearts," Birdie said. "After Emily died and before Claire came along he was rather sought after as an eligible bachelor."

Izzy chuckled. "Tell me about it. There's a group of single middle-aged women who meet in the yarn shop once a month, and Alan was a frequent topic of conversation. They called him the Silver Fox, but it was all in good spirits. And everyone likes Claire. They applauded her victory."

"I remember Arlene doing a little flirting with him, too," Nell said.

"But that was just to get a job, I think," Cass said. "At least in Carly Schultz's opinion."

"Well, it worked," Izzy added, passing around a plate of cookies.

They all laughed.

"Speaking of dear Carly," Birdie said, "she and Andy stopped by yesterday with Pete. They wanted to see an old guitar that my Sonny had. Pete and Andy are fascinated by old instruments. While they fiddled, Carly and I talked some. Carly said the entire office staff—and even Lily's staff—have been questioned already, and the police seem mystified that no one had anything to offer. Carly said they all feel like they're suspects somehow, since they had such ready access to Alan."

"It is odd they don't know more," Izzy said. "Office staff usually know a lot, especially in a case like this."

"Apparently Tommy Porter was especially upset that no one, not a single person, knew why Alan fired Garrett Barros. Carly admitted that it was odd that they didn't know, but it was the truth. Usually there's scuttlebutt, gossip, but not this time. They checked his employment file and there are no notes from Alan, nothing. And Garrett won't talk about it. Not to anyone—not even the police."

"I wonder if Alan talked to Lily Virgilio about it," Nell mused. But remembering the argument she and Izzy had overheard, she suspected they weren't asking each other for staff advice, at least not in recent weeks.

"Back to legitimate motives," Cass said. "None of us want to say it, but if we're lining people up, Garrett has to be on the list. He had a motive. And this secrecy about why he was fired only adds to it."

Birdie frowned, not liking the list, but admitting Cass was right. "I suppose Dorothy fits on the list, too, then, since Garrett's employment at the clinic seems to have been so important to her. With Alan gone, maybe her son would have a chance to get his job back when a new doctor takes over. But I can't imagine either of them taking such awful action over a job. It doesn't make any sense."

"Murder doesn't make sense," Nell said. "Especially the murder of a good man, a good friend. And another friend who has been left floundering. Working at the farm is helping Claire through this, but her life is on hold until Alan can be put to rest. She went through this once with her daughter years ago. She shouldn't have to go through it again."

They were silent for a few minutes, their fingers looping yarn around needles in a way that calmed them.

Finally Cass said, "We are carefully not mentioning Glenn Mackenzie. I think he's getting to all of you. You're drinking the Kool-Aid."

There was silence, and then Cass went on. "I know you think I don't like him. But it's not that. I don't know him well enough to not like him. And I trust Danny's instincts enough to give the guy a chance. But on paper, he's guilty as sin."

Birdie frowned. "Because he's a stranger here?"

They all knew that the entire town would much prefer a stranger to be the bad guy. Always. Even folks who argued with neighbors or didn't like something the mayor said or disagreed with Harry Garozzo's politics would back anyone in the town if push came to shove. That's what Sea Harbor people did. And that's what they would always do. They would never hang one of their own out there to dry if there was a stranger they could pin it on.

Which left Glenn in a very bad situation.

Cass put her knitting down and took a drink of wine. "No, it's not just that he's a stranger here. Danny had a drink with him, to talk about the photographs they were planning, and Glenn pummeled him with questions about the Hamilton history. He had even brought along a family album that he'd 'borrowed' from the clinic. He was really interested in the place. He had access—he was at the clinic several times with Sam."

Izzy looked up. "And none of us quite bought his 'passing through' reason for coming here in the first place."

"Not to mention that he wasn't honest about why he stayed here. The car was ready to go long before Glenn was." Nell's voice dropped off, as if she were betraying someone. She liked him, but *like* didn't always factor into judging people's actions. She said, "I think Cass is right. Glenn hasn't been completely forthcoming about things. He's a bit mysterious. And he was anxious to get out of town as soon as it was made known that Alan was murdered. But even so, I think he was genuinely saddened by everything that happened. That's difficult to hide or to fake."

"The police have questioned him," Izzy said. "I suppose they think there's something there—"

"But what could there be?" Nell said. "Other than the facts that he was at the clinic a few times and at the Lambswool Farm dinner—and that he doesn't live here—I can't imagine why the police called him in. What possible motive could a man from Arizona have in coming all the way to Sea Harbor to poison the town doctor—a man he readily admits he had never met before? Why?"

Birdie poured more wine and they sat back, knitting in silence, relying on the rhythmic sound of needles in the night to clarify and settle their thoughts. Glenn Mackenzie seemed to be the biggest mystery of all.

And as often happened on knitting nights, before the evening ended, their thoughts merged as one. Why would Glenn Mackenzie want Alan Hamilton dead?

Why indeed?

Chapter 26

A possible Glenn Mackenzie motive was revealed sooner than anyone expected it to be. But it didn't happen until another disturbing piece of information fell into their lives.

Ben walked into the family room and dropped his briefcase on the closest table. He sank into the couch and lifted his feet onto the heavy coffee table.

Nell looked up from stirring the sauce for that night's chicken. Ben brought his own twist to being retired, rarely saying no when asked to help with thorny business or legal issues that cropped up in friends' and neighbors' lives. "It's Friday. You know that, right? Time to relax."

Friday, almost four thirty in the afternoon. In two or three hours the house would be filled with friends. Hungry friends.

The dinner wouldn't be a problem. Most people brought something, and the chicken breasts were ready to put on the grill. A salad washed and crisped. The bar stocked.

But a hot shower would be nice.

She had watched Abby all day—a true pleasure, but somehow

more exhausting than cooking or going to board meetings or writing grants. It was because Izzy and Sam's absolutely amazing toddler demanded every ounce of intellectual and emotional energy Nell possessed. And she loved every second of it. Abby had the power to make her forget everything else in her life for those few hours. She pulled Nell into the present moment, totally and completely, and to whatever magic it brought her way.

Nell carried a mug of coffee and a bottle of wine across the room. She couldn't tell from looking at Ben which of the two would be more welcome.

"I've just come from a meeting at the courthouse," Ben said. "It was last-minute." Ben had almost skipped it, he told Nell, slightly irritated at its being unplanned, and wanting to fix a broken window in the guest cottage. But he hadn't. He had gone to the meeting.

And now the expression on his face told Nell he wished he hadn't.

Ben thanked Nell for the coffee and glanced at his watch. "I hate to do this, Nell, but Father Larry asked if he could drop by. He won't stay long. Something's come up that he wants to run by me. It will be brief—he promised."

Nell poured herself a glass of wine, then sat down beside him and sighed. It wasn't that she needed the Cabernet to bolster her for a visit with Larry Northcutt—he was a dear friend. It was that an impromptu visit from the silvery-haired priest late on a Friday afternoon wasn't likely to be social.

"Well, sure, of course," Nell said. "But what's up?"

"It's about Alan Hamilton's will. Why is it that people go to priests with these things?" he added rhetorically.

"Alan talked to you about his will just last week, right?"

"He mentioned it. In retrospect, I'm wondering if he thought about it because physically he felt awful. Sometimes that makes people think of things like wills. He had done one a long time ago.

It was simple, with a behest to Our Lady of Safe Seas, which may be why Larry wants to talk about it. I guess we'll find out. I hear his car." Ben took his feet off the table.

Nell welcomed the priest with a hug and ushered him in, where Ben already had a cup of coffee poured for him.

Father Larry set his battered briefcase on the floor with a thud and settled himself into a large overstuffed chair. He looked at the coffee mug, then at Nell. "As fine a barista as you are, Nellie, I'm thinking a shot of that whiskey that Ben keeps beneath the kitchen counter would serve me nicely. It's been quite a week, now, don't you know."

On her way to the kitchen, Nell nodded, agreeing it had been quite a week for everyone. In minutes she was back with two glasses, a small square bottle, and a basket of pretzels.

Father Northcutt pulled open the briefcase and brought out a yellow pad.

"My notes," the priest said, pointing to indecipherable scrawls on the long piece of paper. "I know what you're thinking; Mary Halloran is after me day after day. *Get yourself an iPad*, or a tablet or laptop or whatever it is she calls them, but a pencil and yellow pad have always served me well." He chuckled, deep wrinkles spreading out from his eyes. "A Luddite, that's me, and proud of it."

Nell glanced at the iPhone he had set down next to the tablet. "Well, not entirely, Larry. There's hope for you yet."

Ben looked over at the scribbling on the pad and made out Alan Hamilton's name.

"You want to talk about Alan's will?"

"Yes, I do. Alan and Emily were regulars at church, her more than him, but after she died, he took it a little more seriously and we had some nice talks. He came to me one day after she died and showed the will to me. He asked me to be his executor. Somehow I'm getting a reputation for that." The priest rolled his eyes as he rummaged around in the briefcase and pulled out a few pieces of paper stapled together.

"That's good," Ben said. "He mentioned it to me, too, and I wondered where the copy would be found. He wanted me to help him revise it, but we never got around to it. But at least having the original may make it a lot easier to straighten out the mess at the clinic."

"Mess?" Father Larry said.

"Yes, figuring out what will happen to it. Lily hired an architect to add a wing to the clinic, a place where they could do more outpatient emergency kinds of things."

Father Larry's eyebrows lifted and he nodded his head slowly. "Ah, yes, *that* mess."

"You knew about it?" Ben asked.

"Yes. Alan was quite upset when Lily proposed it. He came to talk it over with me. I think he considered our talk a kind of confession because he leveled some serious words at poor Lily." He swirled the liquid in his glass.

"Where would they expand?" Nell asked.

"Out the back," Ben said. "Lily wants to get rid of that back garden and yard area. She had the plans at the meeting today."

"Oh, no," Nell said.

"That was Alan's reaction exactly," the priest said. "He loved that yard and was completely against her plans. It caused some friction between them. Alan talked to me about it as recently as the week before he died. He said when he was a kid his dad put a play set out there for him, so when he came in on Saturdays to see a patient, Alan and his friends would be just outside the window, swinging away. Alan's mother, and then his wife, Emily, loved it, too. Emily planted that beautiful garden. It was a magical place in Alan's mind, and he said it would be a cold day in hell before he would let Lily ruin it."

Nell understood. It was a beautiful spot. The argument she and

Izzy had overheard was probably mild compared to the tension that had built up between the two doctors over such a decision.

Ben fiddled with a loose end on his sling. "It makes Lily sound like the bad guy, but she isn't. She's a compassionate person—but she's practical, too. The point she made at the meeting today is that it would serve the people of Sea Harbor far better to turn the unused land into an outpatient clinic. There's green space right across the street from the clinic—the corner park—land everyone has access to. That backyard is rarely used by anyone, and certainly not the public. I'm all for green space, but Lily makes a strong point."

"And Alan, sadly, was equally as adamant. Without his approval, it could never be done, even if the city council approved it," Father Northcutt said.

"That's right," Ben said. "Apparently Lily invested in half the building when she opened her clinic; Alan kept half. I worked up those papers myself. They were dependent on each other's approval for everything from painting to new windows."

They fell silent, putting the pieces together in their heads and not wanting to think about any of the ramifications of the conversation. Nor the fact that one of the decision makers was now dead.

"According to what was said at the meeting today, nothing can be done until Alan's estate is determined," Ben said. He looked at the last will and testament that Father Larry held in his hand. Some law firm in Boston had handled it. "I suppose that will tell us what we need to know, or, at the least, to whom Alan was willing his half of the clinic."

"Not exactly," Father Northcutt said. He put the will down on the table. "This will is the one he probably told you about, the one that needed to be updated. He'd gotten copies back from the firm that wrote it up for him. It leaves a large sum to the church, a few other beneficiaries, and everything else to Emily."

Nell and Ben looked down at the top piece of paper and saw

what they'd missed when the priest had pulled it out of his briefcase. The word VOID was written in large black letters across the width of the paper and initialed at the bottom. *AGH.* Alan George Hamilton.

"He voided it?"

"Yes."

"Why?" Nell asked.

The priest looked at Ben. "He said he needed a new one and that you were going to help him. For one thing, he was giving more to the church. He laughed about that and joked that he had seen the light. He had plans for the rest of it that he didn't go into—the clinic, in particular, but also his house and all the rest."

"But he never got around to writing the new one," Ben said, talking more to himself than to Nell and the priest.

"What does that mean?" Nell asked.

Father Northcutt leaned in to listen, not sure himself.

"It means he died intestate. It's not that complicated when there's a wife or close relative. It takes longer because of probate, but the beneficiary is the closest relative, usually a spouse."

"Alan had no relatives," Father Larry said. "Not even a third cousin, not anyone. An only son of an only son of an only son, and so on. I think it bothered him because of the practice more than anything. He felt he'd failed all those before him who had built the Hamilton clinic, served the town, and it would end with him. He joked that he'd work until they buried him."

"If he hadn't voided that will, Emily's share would go to the few relatives she had," Ben said.

"But now?"

"Now it will be dictated by the intestate code, but the existence of this earlier one will help some. Knowing how Alan felt about the church will help make sure that bequest is honored. But it's more complicated, for sure. Except for one part."

"What part is that?" Father Northcutt asked, slipping the papers back into his satchel. He took off his reading glasses and slipped them into his pocket.

"The Delgado mansion. I helped with a similar case. If there is no stated beneficiary for the deceased's half of a structure, and someone owns the other half, that person—the owner of the other half—is granted ownership of the whole thing upon the death of the other."

They sat in silence, but the single thought in each of their heads was ringing as loud as a church bell.

With Alan dead, Lily Virgilio's dream *could* become reality.

Chapter 27

After Father Larry left, Nell and Ben carried the glasses and mugs to the kitchen sink and rinsed them out, putting them in the dishwasher. Rote, easy movements.

Neither of them said much as they moved about the kitchen, replaying the conversation with Father Larry in their heads, trying to put the pieces together. And most of all, trying to poke holes in the facts that suddenly appeared in neon lights. Facts that on the surface turned two people they knew well into murder suspects.

"We know Lily Virgilio isn't a murderer," Nell finally said. "We know that with absolute certainty. *I* know that with certainty." And she did—if emotion and instinct and her heart could lead to certainty.

She didn't expect Ben to answer, and he didn't. Instead he used his good hand to line up glasses on a tray, to take lemons and olives out of the refrigerator, to pull cocktail napkins from the drawer.

Nell checked her text messages to see who'd be coming. Although she never knew for sure, the usual crowd had taken to texting a *yay* or *nay*. Sometimes it could be four or six of them, sometimes fourteen or more.

She looked over at Ben. "Pete and Andy are coming," she said. "That means Carly will be here."

"And Willow, I suspect. Pete doesn't go far without her these days."

Nell nodded absently. She loved the fiber artist, but it was Carly she wanted to talk to. She must know something about Garrett's firing. Even if she didn't know she knew it. Some little thing that she'd noticed or that had been said. And maybe it would be something that had nothing to do with Alan, nothing that could possibly turn Garrett Barros into a murderer.

As much respect as Nell had for Tommy Porter and the chief and the rest of the Sea Harbor Police Department, she knew that sometimes police weren't allowed to ask questions that might get the answers they needed. Sometimes protocol interfered. But she didn't need to abide by such rules. And neither did Birdie, Izzy, and Cass.

An hour later the deck was alive with conversation, *clink*ing of bottles, and the steady sound of Sara Bareilles's vocals attempting to keep people upbeat. The dark shadow of the week was there, hovering over the deck, but everyone was working at keeping it at bay—and succeeding well enough that Jane Brewster's heaping plate of mushroom puffs was rapidly disappearing and Sam was once again declaring himself an excellent martini shaker/maker.

Carly had come with Andy, and she waved to Nell from across the deck. She mouthed that they would talk later, then waved to Pete and Willow as they came up the deck stairs from the backyard. Pete had brought Glenn Mackenzie with them. Nell swallowed her surprise, feeling a twinge of guilt that she hadn't thought to invite him herself. The week had to have been an awful one for him. The thought that people might be looking at you every time you walked down the street was surely not a pleasant one.

She was happy he had come, and relieved when she saw Izzy and Birdie immediately pull him into the group and make sure he had one of Sam's martinis.

For a moment Nell was filled with déjà vu. The scene one week to the day, when Alan had been the one pulled into the group. When Sam had handed him a drink. When he had settled down on the chaise next to Ben.

One week.

"You're far too serious for the night," Rachel Wooten whispered beside her. "Come, let's get a glass of wine." The city attorney walked with Nell to the bar and then to a quiet corner of the deck, carrying their wine with them. They sat side by side on an old farm bench Nell had picked up at a garage sale. "Are you all right?" Rachel asked her.

"You caught me at a weak moment, Rachel," Nell said. "I'm fine. Sometimes things flash before my eyes as if they are happening right now, and it takes me a minute to get rid of them."

Rachel nodded. "I get it." She shifted on the bench and changed the subject. "Your Ben was a master of diplomacy at the advisory meeting today. He's a careful listener."

"You were there?"

"Sometimes when an issue might involve legal issues, or need that kind of opinion, I get called in. Lily Virgilio was presenting plans for expanding the clinic."

"Ben told me."

"Alan had come to me a while ago to stop her. He was determined and angry, and I understood why. He had such attachment to that property. He felt as if she was trying to destroy a memory, I think."

Nell sipped her wine. "What did you think of the plan?"

"The decision isn't up to me. But of course I always have an opinion," she smiled. "I think Lily's plan would be wonderful for the town. It would allow for more services and increase the care Lily is already providing for those who can't get the medical services they need. Lily's heart is as big as this town, and includes everyone in it—and that's her only motivation. It's certainly not to make money."

Nell smiled, feeling a welcome wave of affirmation. It's what she felt about Lily Virgilio, the doctor who had delivered Abigail and taken such good care of Izzy. At that moment she was able to block out the deep, angry voice she had heard lashing out at Alan Hamilton on Harbor Road.

"I'm glad you came tonight," she said to Rachel. "You have a great knack for putting just the right spin on things. You get to the heart of it."

Rachel laughed, tossing her head back and looking sideways at Nell. "You do the same, Nell Endicott. Don't ever doubt it."

Nell didn't have time to catch up with Glenn Mackenzie until the grilled chicken with chimichurri sauce had all but disappeared and just before Carly Schultz, perhaps stimulated by a second glass of wine, had stood at the table and reminded everyone that Andy—oh, and the rest of the absolutely amazing Fractured Fish—would be performing the next night in Canary Cove. "It will benefit all of our cherished starving artists," she said with some drama, and everyone clapped, promising her that of course they would be there.

Gradually people got up from the table and moved around, letting the food settle before diving into Danny Brandley's famous lemon bars. *It's the quarter cup of whiskey,* he had confided to Nell one day and made her promise to hold the secret close. He added that it went a long way in garnering favors from Father Northcutt.

Nell spotted Glenn standing near the deck stairs talking to Izzy. Nearby Pete strummed lightly on his guitar and Willow hummed along. Glenn looked slightly subdued, but Izzy was putting him at ease.

She walked over to them, and Izzy welcomed her with a quick hug. "Just for nothin'," she said.

Glenn smiled at Izzy's warm gesture and thanked Nell for the dinner. "I almost didn't come when Pete called—I thought about everything going on, and I wondered if it would be an intrusion. But, truth is, I wanted to be with all of you."

"It's never an intrusion to come to this house, Glenn Mackenzie," Izzy said. "Never, ever. This is where we all come when we need to feel better. And after the damnable week you've had, you need to be here."

Leave it to Izzy to not beat around the bush and pretend that the day was a normal one, just like any other. Nell wondered if she could love her more.

Glenn managed a laugh. Nell looped an arm around Izzy's waist. "Izzy is right, of course."

Izzy nodded happily. "Why are the police badgering you, Glenn?" she asked. "We can't figure it out."

Glenn took a deep breath and let it out slowly. He leaned back against the crooked trunk of the maple tree, his hands in his pockets. "The obvious, I guess. I'm a stranger here. But they found my phone number on a card in Alan's pocket. My address in Arizona was on it, too."

"Oh?" Nell said.

"Not a big deal. We talked that night and he offered to show me some things at the clinic, the Hamilton family history, so I gave him my contact information—that's it. We discovered we had a few things in common and it was kind of nice—medicine, for sure—"

"What else?" Izzy asked.

"Just things. It pleased him, I think, to know there was someone else in the same profession who loved medicine but did other crazy things on the side. Astronomy. Hiking, skydiving . . ."

"Skydiving?" Izzy said. "Are you serious? The thought of that ties my stomach into tiny knots."

"Yeah. I know it's crazy. Doctors shouldn't skydive, right? Too dangerous. Bad example. But, hey, it's the greatest high. We thought it was a coincidence that we both liked it. Anyway, we exchanged information so we could, well, you know, talk more, maybe." His voice broke a little, but he coughed it away and went on. "It's just crappy that . . ."

The sentence didn't need finishing, but the expression of profound regret that Nell saw on Glenn's face was enough for her. Izzy would be more circumspect—she would try to see it through her lawyerly eyes, how the police might look at it, but Nell wasn't hindered by any of that, and in her mind, Glenn was innocent. Plain and simple.

When Sam walked over carrying Ben's telescope, Glenn's eyes lit up, and he and Izzy followed Sam into the backyard, where he showed Glenn just one more thing that made Sea Harbor a magical place: a special piece of the sky that was even more spectacular when seen from a spot in the Endicotts' backyard. And, Izzy added, the very same spot that she and Sam had stood on and married each other.

Nell saw Birdie through the kitchen window, chatting with some unseen person, her arms elbow-deep in suds, and went back inside to help.

The unseen person was Carly Schultz, leaning against the counter with a towel in her hand. Her wineglass was nearby, and she was grinning at Birdie, her short hair glossy and swinging with the movement of her head as she listened to Birdie and the music at the same time. Other than the two of them, the kitchen was empty.

"Come into our little private club," Carly said, her voice as animated as her face. "Here." She picked up a wineglass she'd just wiped dry, filled it, and handed it to Nell. "Birdie is cheering me up and convincing me that the police won't be permanently camped out in our clinic asking two zillion questions that have no good answers."

She smiled in spite of the police talk.

Carly brought light into a room. No wonder she was such a successful nurse, Nell thought.

"We're also watching activity on the deck, seeing people shake off the gloom," Birdie said. "Looking at the heavens will certainly do that."

Nell looked out and watched several others joining Sam and his telescope in the backyard.

"Doc Alan would hate all the sadness and awfulness," Carly said. "He'd want us to live life. Oh, sure, he'd want us to find the evil, horrible beast who did this, but he wouldn't want us to cloak ourselves in gloom and doom along the way. That's one of the reasons he was so great at Ocean View—lots of the people there knew they were dying, their relatives knew it, too, and in spite of all that, Doc Alan brought joy into that place."

"I had almost forgotten you and Alan worked together out at the nursing home. You've known him awhile."

"Ocean View. Yes. We worked closely together. Remember? That's where I first met all of you."

"I do remember; I just hadn't connected the dots." Nell hadn't thought about those days for a while, nor made the connection. But she remembered it now vividly: the sweet, generous nurse who had been instrumental in helping them figure out that one of her patients at Ocean View hadn't died as peacefully as everyone thought.

"That's where I first met Doc Alan and where we became friends. We shared a philosophy about patient care, I guess you'd say. I appreciated how he was with everyone. I had a crush on him for a while—I think half the nursing staff did, no matter the age difference. He was simply a good man—a handsome one, too—and we all respected and fell in love with him."

Carly's smile stayed in place, but as she talked about her mentor, her voice thickened with emotion. "Patients really liked him," she said. She took a sip of wine. "Sometimes relatives get cranky—that happened now and then at Ocean View. They always want miracles, and I suppose you can't blame them, even when there aren't any miracles to be found. But patients never got cranky with him. But you know that. You knew him. You knew how he was."

"Yes, dear, we do—and we did," Birdie said. "But it's so nice to hear it coming from you, someone on the front lines." Birdie patted Carly's hand, spreading soapsuds across her knuckles.

Carly laughed and lifted her hand, blowing the bubbles back at Birdie.

"So that's how you got the job at the Hamilton Family Clinic, I guess?" Nell asked.

"That's how I knew about it. They teased Doc Alan at Ocean View. They said he stole me away." Carly half sang the last words, clearly pleased at the teasing—and at being stolen.

"Speaking of the clinic, are you managing all right?" Birdie asked. "What a burden this is on all of you. And the police presence can't help."

"Like I told you guys yesterday, it's all thanks to Lily Virgilio and Janie Levin—Janie is a great nurse. I admire Dr. Virgilio a lot. She didn't have to cover Doc Alan's clinic the way she has done. She doesn't want his patients to have to move somewhere else. And you know how it is around here: everyone is connected to everyone else. Her pregnant moms take their kids to Doc Alan for strep tests and flu shots. It's all back and forth." She took a glass from Birdie and dried it, pulling together her thoughts. "No one is a replacement for Doc Alan, that's for sure, but patients are being treated really well until this is all worked out."

Nell took a sip of wine. "M.J. at the salon says that her niece—well, her husband's niece—is working extra hours, too." Though she sensed Arlene wasn't Carly's favorite person, she had been nice to Garrett, and maybe, she hoped, Carly knew more about that, about anything Arlene might have confided in her about his firing.

"You mean Arlene. Yes, she works hard," Carly said.

"That doesn't surprise me," Birdie said, drying her hands on a towel. "She's a good waitress, too. And very organized. She kept the whole staff on their toes at the Lambswool dinner."

"That's Arlene," Carly said. "Organized. Keeps everyone in line. She'd have been a good army sergeant. It was smart to hire her, I suppose, although you could have knocked me over with a feather when I found out she was going to work with us at the clinic."

"She said the pay is good," Nell said.

"Oh, sure, that's true—Doc Alan was generous. But there are other places she could have worked. She's smart. And I thought we'd be the last place she'd ever want to work."

"Why is that?" Birdie asked.

"I knew her from when I worked at Ocean View. She—how shall I say it—she hated—no, no, my mom never let us use that word except for hominy, which I really did hate. Arlene couldn't stand me—really. So I was shocked when she showed up to interview for the job. Doc Alan was as surprised as I was. Maybe even more. But anyway, he hired her. And somehow it's working out okay. It's really no big deal and not worth talking about. She actually does a decent job in the clinic and we stay away from each other."

"You said she was nice to Garrett when he was there?" Birdie said.

"Yes. And I liked that. One of the staff members was a little rude to him, just because he kind of marches to his own drummer, but he's a nice guy and Arlene was nice to him." She moved over to the island and pulled out a stool, sliding onto it. "We were surprised when Garrett lost his job."

"His mother certainly was shocked," Nell said. "I think he liked that job, but he found another one quickly." She thought about the visit from Garrett, the look in his eyes. "Carly, I know I've asked you about this before, but I'm wondering if maybe anything has come back to you, a stray conversation, something Alan might have said or done, anything that would explain Alan's letting Garrett go? Garrett won't talk about it."

Carly played with the stem of her wineglass, rolling it between her hands. "Like I said, it's a mystery. I actually asked Doc Alan about it because I was upset, and it didn't seem like the kind of thing he would do. I know it wasn't my place to ask, but some of us were concerned—most of the staff, in fact. It was such a surprise, you know? Usually you can figure things like that out, like when someone isn't doing her job, or is missing work, leaving early, or being rude to a patient, whatever. But in Garrett's case there wasn't any obvious reason. He came early, left late, and did just about anything anyone asked him to do."

"What did Alan say when you asked?" Birdie asked.

Carly shook her short bob. "Nothing, at least not about the reason why it happened. He made it clear that it was between him and Garrett, a private matter, which I should have known he would do. And I appreciated that, I really did. That's how Doc Alan was, respecting each person. And he was trying to make it as easy as possible on Garrett—he didn't want anyone to think poorly of him, being fired and all, though I could tell it upset the doctor a lot. Like I said, Doc Alan was a good man. And he liked Garrett. But for whatever reason, he thought it was the right thing to do to fire him."

"It was hard on Garrett," Birdie said. "Even if you don't like a job, being fired is an insult to who you are."

"Hard on Garrett? Oh, Birdie. He went ballistic." Carly's voice trailed off, the memory still fresh. She looked into her wineglass, her face sad. "And that was something the police have questioned every staff member about again and again. What did Garrett do?

How mad was he? Were they afraid of him? Was Doc Alan afraid of him? Did he hate Doc Alan? They won't let up on it, no matter that no one has an answer for them. Silly questions, at least that's what some people thought."

"What do you think, Carly?"

Carly didn't pause long. It was clear she knew exactly what she thought. "I think Garrett Barros thought Doc Alan hung the moon."

She looked up, her eyes filled with emotion and disbelief. "So why would he kill him?"

The evening ended a short while later, and Ben and Nell both thought it had been good therapy for everyone.

"Friends, food, music," Ben said. "They have their own healing powers."

The evening had some sad moments and some happy ones. Some poignant ones, too.

They turned out the kitchen lights and climbed slowly up the back stairs. Ben followed Nell with one hand playing on her back. When they reached the darkened bedroom, he wrapped her in his arms and held her close.

"It will be better soon, Nellie," he whispered into her hair. "I promise it will."

Nell nestled there in his arms, unwilling to move away as Ben worked to ease her fears and frustrations.

And for that moment, his heartbeat strong against her breasts, she believed him.

Chapter 28

"Ella is teaching Gabby how to make *poffertjes,* and I am in great need of friends who will eat them," Birdie said, her voice far stronger than usual for the early-morning hour. "I've already frozen enough to supply Father Larry's soup kitchen for several months, but they are better fresh, and they're perfect for breakfast. Ella claims they are called brain food in Holland, though she may have made that up." Birdie didn't wait for Nell to say she'd be right over.

The thought of anything coming out of Ella's kitchen made Nell's mouth water. While she considered herself a good cook, she couldn't compete with Birdie's housekeeper in the baking department. And when Ella took to mastering her grandmother's Dutch specialties, it was dizzying.

"I think Cass smelled them all the way over at her house in Canary Cove," Birdie went on. "She's on her way here right now. Besides, while dinner last night was delicious, I think we all need some time to talk. And don't forget to bring your knitting."

Izzy had called Nell that morning, too.

She couldn't sleep, she said. Things kept tumbling around in her head. She needed to bring some order to it—and better sooner than later.

Nell picked Izzy up at the yarn studio. She had gone in early to do some paperwork, and then she had put the overly capable Mae in charge, and her manager had happily ushered Izzy out the door. She got more done with Izzy gone, she said.

Nell pulled into a parking spot in front of Coffee's and asked Izzy to run in for a cardboard carafe of coffee. As wonderful as Mae was at baking, she considered tea the drink of choice, and her attempts at brewing coffee bore testimony to her preference.

The smell of the tiny Dutch pancakes greeted them as they walked in the door closest to the kitchen. The main house of Birdie's estate had several entrances, but the one closest to the kitchen was used the most.

They looked into the heated room where Gabby stood near the butcher-block island covered in snow.

"Powdered sugar," she said, then blew on her sleeve and giggled as it flew through the air. A fat black braid, now sprinkled with white, hung down her back.

Ella stood at the stove, beaming at her prodigy and nodding proudly toward a special cast-iron frying pan with small dimpled indentations, each just big enough to hold a dollop of the special yeasty dough she'd made the night before. On the island sat dozens of already cooked *poffertjes* waiting to be dusted.

Birdie ushered them past the kitchen, down the tiled hallway, past the sunroom that was filled with blooming tropical plants, and through the mullioned doors to the stone patio that overlooked the harbor. And where on good days, Birdie claimed, she could see all the way to Nova Scotia.

Nell set the coffee carafe on the table next to the mugs.

They settled in a semicircle around the old teak table, which was weathered to a gray sheen. Some thought the Favazza patio had the best view in all of Sea Harbor. Birdie once said that the Favazzas had built the whole house around it. It circled around, high above the water, and from the ancient telescope mounted near its edge, the harbor, the community center, Canary Cove, and even the yacht club came into ready view.

The estate itself was built on high, forested land off Ravenswood Road. One of many such houses, Birdie's was nearly hidden from the road, except for the low stone wall that defined the land and the always-open wrought-iron gates that stood tall at the driveway entrance. No one was sure how she did it, but for all its elegance, Birdie's home was as cozy and relaxed as any of her friends' more modest residences.

And on good-weather days, the patio was one of the favorite spots on the whole magnificent estate.

Nell took a sip of coffee, then set the mug down and sat back in an old ocean-liner chair. She pulled her knitting onto her lap. "A perfect day," she said. "We won't have many more of these."

Cass sat down next to her, scratching at a paint spot on her jeans—the color of the Halloran buoys. "Except it's not really perfect at all, is it?" She took the mug Izzy handed her and poured in a generous serving of cream.

Instead of answering, they busied themselves pulling balls of yarn and wooden needles from their bags, prolonging a discussion of why it wasn't a perfect day as long as they could.

Cass stirred her coffee, watching the black liquid turn the color of Izzy's hair, warm shades of tan and taupe and gold. Finally she started in. "I got home last night and it finally hit me—what had been niggling at me as we left your house last night, Nell. We all had a great time on the deck like we always do, no matter what. Wining and dining, even laughing, maybe for the first time all week. It was a great place to be. A perfect place. We wrapped ourselves in a warm, cozy blanket and we took it home with us. Like we were protected somehow, living in our private world.

"Danny and I weren't tired, so we grabbed a couple of beers and went out on the porch to get sleepy. We sat there for a while on the swing, looking out over the water, feeling strange but not really sure why—but the warm, fuzzy feeling was wearing off bit by bit. We spotted some stray lightning way, way out above the sea. Maybe that's what got to us, the unexpected electric sparks in that perfect, inky, soft sky.

"I looked over at Danny and I squeezed his hand tight, knowing at that moment what was bothering me. I said, *Danny, we could have been sharing our chicken wings tonight with a murderer. We don't know. We could have. He might have been right there looking through the telescope with us or listening to Pete play, or—*"

Startled, Nell said, "Cass, that's just not . . ." But she stopped short when she saw Gabby and Ella coming out on the patio, carrying a large platter of small, perfectly puffed Dutch pancakes, a bowl of strawberries and blueberries, and a stack of small plates.

Ella was explaining to Gabby about carnivals in Holland where the pancakes were always sold and how it was impossible to eat a *poffertje* without smiling. The two cooks barely paid attention to the quiet group as they set the breakfast goodies down on the table and disappeared back inside, never breaking their conversation.

The knitters watched them come and go, marveling as they did each time they saw Ella and Gabby together. Birdie's housekeeper usually spoke less than a few dozen words a day, but she never stopped talking when Gabby was in town.

Birdie passed around plates and surveyed the pancakes, the fruit, the small pots of warm butter and dish of strawberry sauce. "I wonder if Ella is right about the smiles. I hope so." Her face was sad as she talked, the laugh lines that fanned from her eyes noticeably absent. "But what I do know is that Cass is right about the possibility of a murderer in our midst. Maybe he wasn't with us last night, but maybe so. Maybe he was at Lambswool Farm, eating that marvelous dinner the night that Alan's body couldn't take any more poison and finally gave up. Maybe it was someone visiting the clinic. We may have talked to the murderer at one of those places. Maybe at all of them."

It was a sobering thought. For days they had toyed with Alan's murder, picking it apart—following in the police's footsteps. Wanting to prove that the friends and acquaintances who had been targeted couldn't possibly have done it. But no one had yet come up with a sure way of eliminating suspects—of finding a murderer. No one had figured out how to pull the evil presence out of their town—and leave it whole again.

Birdie put her needles and yarn back down and passed around the pancakes, not saying a word. No one else did, either.

Izzy popped a pancake into her mouth and chewed it whole, then licked the remains of the powdered sugar from her fingertips.

She smiled.

That brought smiles all around. The power of a Dutch pancake.

But the conversation returned in seconds to topics without a hint of sweetness.

Nell filled them in on Father Northcutt's visit, what the lack of a will meant, and the fact that Lily Virgilio had gained more than anyone suspected from Alan Hamilton's unexpected death.

"I hadn't known the legalities of the two practices sharing the Delgado mansion, nor did I really care, I suppose. Ben knew. Alan sold her her half of the building when she started her practice. Ben said it was important to her not to be a tenant. Alan agreed because he needed someone to occupy the other half of the building. Now that he's dead and there are no beneficiaries for his half, Lily owns it all. That's the intestacy ruling. Alan's death has benefited her maybe more than anyone."

"That's a mind-boggling thought," Cass said. "Lily Virgilio is almost as saintly as Birdie with all the good things she does, and now she'd going to be up front and center in a murder investigation?"

"Probably," Nell said. "The police will have to consider it. It's not a secret that Alan was blocking her efforts to build onto the clinic. Nor that she was furious about his resistance. She didn't try to hide it."

"And now that resistance is gone," Izzy said, passing the bowl of fruit to Birdie. "She can do whatever she wants as long as the city approves it."

"So we have these decent people—Lily, Garrett, Glenn Mackenzie—all considered possible murderers. It's like a horrible stain on our town, a disease that's tainting all these good people."

"Danny mentioned something else last night that got us both thinking," Cass said. "We all agree that Mackenzie is kind of a mystery man. Danny likes the guy a lot, but even he thinks Glenn holds back things. The police must have thought that, too. And if they did, they probably have checked out his background."

Nell spoke up. "They did," she said. "Ben had breakfast with Jerry Thompson and did a little probing. Glenn was very cooperative with the police, apparently, and gave them everything they asked for—all his personal information and contact information. He answered every question they asked him about his life. They looked into everything—his school, his home in Arizona. It all checked out perfectly. He was an only child, came from a very good home. His mother died right before he went off to college—cancer, I think. He was very close to his father. He's almost too perfect, Ben said. One speeding ticket when he was sixteen. That was about as nasty as it got."

"But sometimes the police only look at things like facts," Birdie said. "You can look into someone's driving record and college grades—or you can look into how they came to be who they are. Those kinds of personal things."

They all knew what Birdie was saying. It was the basic difference in getting to know *about* someone, and getting to really know someone. The difference in the police's approach. And in theirs.

Nell thought back over early conversations with Glenn. "He mentioned his dad to me a couple of times," she said. "He died just a short while ago." She thought about the other day at the farm. They'd been walking toward the barn, just the two of them. His voice was full of emotion. "We talked the day he delivered those lambs. He and Angelo had barely slept and they were both exhausted. Maybe that's why Glenn was a little more forthcoming. He talked about how he'd loved his dad, what he'd learned from him, the strong ethic his dad had instilled in him. He was missing his father that day, I think. And he was sad about Alan's death. And then mixed up in it all was an anger that he'd come here with good intentions—whatever those might be—and ended up being a suspect in a murder. His integrity was being questioned, and that was terribly hard for him."

"I suppose most suspects feel that way," Izzy said, bringing a practical slant to the conversation. "Even the ones who really did it."

"Even if the sentiments are sincere," Cass said, "and if he's been completely up-front about records and phone numbers, the fact is, Glenn isn't being truthful with us. I hate to sound like a broken record, but the more I say it, the more sure I am that I'm right. If he's worried about his integrity, maybe he should come clean."

"Was the reason he came here, then, to kill Alan Hamilton?" Nell asked. It wasn't a serious question. It was to point out what she thought was a flying leap from one set of facts to another. From not telling them why he came to Sea Harbor—to killing the town's doctor. "I think there's a missing middle in here somewhere," she said.

"Well, then let's find out what's missing," Birdie said.

Cass took another heap of the miniature pancakes and added dribbles of butter and strawberries. "Yes. Let's. The police haven't dug up a motive for murder for Glenn. Maybe digging a little deeper would help us figure it out. At the least, it might clear him of suspicion. That would be a good thing, right?"

Nell nodded. "You have a point. If we can figure out some of the things that don't add up—not only for Glenn, but for Garrett, too—we can make their lives a little easier and concentrate on finding out who really did this."

"And for Lily Virgilio," Nell said. But to all of them, bringing Lily's name into any talk of murder was almost like accusing Father Northcutt of stealing from the collection basket.

"I do worry about Garrett," Izzy said. "His mother came into the shop yesterday, but she wasn't in a talkative mood. Mae tried. She asked about Garrett, but Dorothy was so irritable at the question that Mae backed off. I wonder if Garrett has even told his mother the reason he lost his job. Someone has to know what went on in that clinic."

But no one seemed to, Nell said. She and Birdie had poked and prodded Carly Schultz the night before and gotten nowhere. "She doesn't know anything—and Carly seems unable to tell a lie."

On a side note, Nell went on to tell them about Arlene Arcado and Carly's feud. "Well, not so much a feud. Apparently Arlene dislikes Carly. Carly didn't say if it was reciprocal."

"Now I ask you, how could anyone dislike that sweet Carly?" Birdie said. "It rather puts Arlene in a bad light, if you ask me."

"Did Carly say why Arlene doesn't like her?" Izzy asked.

Nell realized suddenly that she hadn't asked her why. Somehow it hadn't seemed relevant, but now . . . now she wished she had. Anything that went on at the Hamilton clinic now seemed important. "No, she didn't say why. They knew each other when they worked at Ocean View. Something happened there that caused the rift. Carly made Arlene's feelings sound serious, and said that her coming to work at the clinic was completely unexpected. She said even Alan was surprised." Nell thought back over the conversation and it was only in the repeating that she wondered more about it. Why would Alan have been surprised? Carly hadn't given details, and she wondered now if she and Birdie had made some assumptions. She made a mental note to ask Carly about it.

Birdie must have been thinking the same thing.

"This brings up another point. We've limited our thoughts about Alan's murder to the small circle the police have painted around it. That's a mistake—and not like us at all. We need to move outside that circle. Maybe that's where we'll find the answers we need."

"People like Garrett's mom," Cass said.

"And that whole clinic staff," Izzy said. "They saw Alan every day. Also patients that were regulars."

They all agreed. Every workplace has secrets. Why should the Hamilton Family Clinic be exempt?

As they plowed through names, Lily Virgilio was the only one who seemed not to be hiding things. She'd made it clear she wanted to expand the clinic. And many people knew that Alan Hamilton had been blocking her way.

Everyone else, from Garrett and Glenn to sweet Carly Schultz—who somehow had incurred the wrath of a coworker—were shadowed by something that hadn't been explained.

"Lily's motive is out there for everyone to see. With Alan alive, she couldn't achieve her goal. With him dead, it's full speed ahead," Cass said.

"Do you think she knew that Alan didn't have a valid will and the building would go to her?" Birdie asked.

"Ben said Father Larry wondered about that, too. She may have. Until this whole expansion plan came up, they were good friends and may have talked about things like that," Nell said. "But it might not make a difference if she knew or not. The problem was all Alan. Someone else taking over that practice wouldn't have Alan's attachment to the building's history and might have been fine with Lily's plans. Alan was the one standing in her way, will or not."

"Well, here's what I know," Birdie said, picking up a spoon. "We have one week to figure it all out." She added a dollop of strawberry sauce to her pile of pancakes.

They all looked at her. *One week?*

"What are you talking about?" Izzy asked.

Birdie looked up. Powdered sugar dotted her lips, creating a ghostly image, but she ignored it and went on. "In one week we are having the first dinner for the public at Lambswool Farm, and I refuse to allow even a faint smell of evil anywhere within a hundred miles of here.

"And so, you see—we need to get to work, for better or worse." She licked the powdered sugar off her lips and smiled.

Chapter 29

It was Cass's idea to go to the library. Personal computers probably had all the information they needed, but Cass liked library research, the smell of the old books, the quiet buzz. It was Danny's influence, she said with a shrug.

Izzy had to get back to the shop, but asked that Birdie, Cass, and Nell bring her a sandwich when they were finished at the library. But what she really wanted, they all knew, was to be kept in the loop.

After devouring a half dozen more of Gabby and Ella's *poffertjes* and cleaning up, they climbed into Nell's car, dropped Izzy at work, and circled back to the library. The old stone building was just off Harbor Road, across the street from the Sea Harbor City Hall and the police station.

Nell stopped at the curb and looked back at the courthouse. It was quiet, the offices closed for the weekend, its facade imposing. Next door to it, the police station looked equally quiet, but behind its heavy double doors she knew there was plenty of activity. She imagined Garrett walking down those steps a few days earlier, confused at the barrage of questions, trying to process the unfathomable turns his life had taken. And terribly frightened at what would happen next.

And yet he refused to tell the police what they needed to know.

Why? she wondered. His reticence to talk about his firing looked so bad for him, and revealing the reason why might be the only way he could clear himself. But he didn't seem to be in any hurry to do so.

When she had said as much to Ben, he had patiently listened, but she read the message in his eyes: Nell didn't want to believe Garrett could have hurt Alan Hamilton. She felt deep down that he was innocent. But her emotional certainty wouldn't stand up in court or on paper or just about anywhere.

Ben wasn't often wrong; Nell would give him that.

But this time he was.

"Let's go," Birdie said, taking Nell's arm and walking up the wide fan of steps to the heavy double doors of the Sea Harbor Public Library.

They found a table in the back of the reference room, right next to a line of library computers and monitors and away from the line of study carrels. A place where quiet talk wouldn't be frowned upon.

"Glenn Mackenzie," Cass said with some drama.

"Let's try to be objective about this," Nell said.

Cass tugged on her dark ponytail, thinking about her response. "Actually, Nell, he's growing on me. I'm beginning to like him. Maybe if we can learn more about him, I'll like him even more. I know the guy is holding something back from us, and that puts me off. I think Jerry Thompson feels the same way. He hasn't been very up-front with us. So if we can clear that up, I can more easily decide if I like him."

"Not everyone wants to be an open book, Catherine," Birdie said.

"Sure, I know that. But his secrecy is different. It's like he's hiding something we *deserve* to know about. I think he came here for something very specific. He moved into our lives and everyone has been nice to him, but he won't tell us something as basic as why he's here."

Nell thought about that, playing back through the days, trying to pair up Cass's observations with what she had seen or heard. But Cass wasn't through.

"And he lied to us, you both know that. Waiting for his car to be fixed when he knew it was ready all that time—what was that about? It's as if he was using it as an excuse to hang around. But why did he think he needed an excuse? Let's figure out what's going on with him, and then we can cross him off our list and move on. He can be our best friend and come back to visit us every summer. I'll even take him out on a lobster boat."

She flicked the switch on the desktop computer and it hummed to life. Birdie sat on one side with a yellow pad in front of her, just in case. Birdie liked notes. Nell sat on the other side, drumming her fingers on the tabletop.

A needle in a haystack. That's what they were looking for. And they had no idea what the needle looked like.

The search began with what they already knew. Basic facts about Glenn—schools he had attended, awards he'd won, sports he had played. His birthday, graduation dates, and some family photos that focused more on his father and mother.

"It's called job application information," Cass said, but she printed it out anyway.

"His father was a judge," Nell said. "Glenn admired and loved him. Maybe we'll find more information about the son by looking at the father."

They were picking at little things that might not have any bearing on anything. But sometimes in little things there were surprises.

Judge Mackenzie, Cass typed into the computer.

It took one search for Arizona judges to find Glenn's dad's first name. Maxwell. Judge Maxwell Mackenzie.

And a search on the judge's full name brought up nearly five thousand results.

Pictures and articles that spanned years and went from highly professional pieces in law journals to human interest articles on the judge's family life and his service to the community.

The most recent articles were tributes that appeared after Judge Mackenzie died just a few months before.

"There's Glenn," Birdie said, pointing to a photo on the screen of father and son standing in the judge's chamber. His father was medium height, a distinguished-looking man with a full face, gray hair, and a nicely trimmed beard to match. Even in the fuzzy computer photo, his eyes appeared to be warm and smiling, set deep in a kind face. And from the many tributes they skimmed through, he was all that and more.

"Is there anything about his mother?" Nell asked.

Cass added key search words and a long article in a popular Arizona magazine popped up. It was headlined "Arizona's foremost family"—and proved it in the colorful fourteen pages that followed. There were pictures of their home, of their ranch, and a folksy telling of Ann and Maxwell's romance—after attending college in Ohio, the beautiful Ann Wallingford had come home to her Arizona roots. There, Maxwell Mackenzie, nearly twenty years her senior and already a distinguished lawyer, was waiting to sweep her off her feet. He had first met "Annie," he told the reporter, when she was on the summer tennis team he coached and he was on his way to college—but he'd never forgotten her. He had waited for her to grow up.

And before the print on her college diploma was dry, they were married.

Photos of their wedding were few—a small summer wedding in a chapel—but their home and the family ranch outside Tucson were featured in a big way, along with a beautiful baby boy who was born soon after. There was even an interview with Glenn's godfather and his father's best friend and personal lawyer, Brady Sorge, along with a photo of him with Glenn, fishing off the end of a pier. Brady was a guy with a friendly face who reminded Nell of comedian Martin Short. She wondered if he was aware of the trouble his godson was in. Her intuition said no—Glenn Mackenzie wouldn't burden loved ones with his troubles if he didn't have to. Besides, so far the police had found no motive and no real evidence, unless a scrap of paper with his name on it in Alan's pocket pointed to evidence.

Nell looked at the new screen Cass had pulled up. More articles about the Mackenzies of Arizona and the good things they did for the city, for the environment, and for each other.

"Geesh," Cass said. "I'm surprised they haven't made a movie about these guys."

They might not be uncovering the kinds of secrets they were looking for, but they were certainly discovering what a blessed life Glenn Mackenzie had—and the certain knowledge that he was well loved.

Nell leaned in to look at a photo of Glenn's mother. She was lovely. There was a photo taken in a church—Glenn's baptism, Nell guessed. Brady Sorge held a baby boy over the baptismal font while the adoring parents looked on, the priest holding up his hand in a blessing, a lit Christmas tree in the background. She squinted at the screen text, looking for details, dates, anything that might bring Glenn into focus. "Let's print this out," Nell said. "There's a ton of information in it about Glenn's mother and his growing-up years. Maybe they visited this area at some point?"

But Glenn had denied that. He'd never been to the North

Shore—he had told them that. Cass's question rang in her head. *So why now?*

Nell sat back, her eyes wide.

Cass and Birdie looked over.

"What?" Cass asked.

"I remembered something Glenn said to me. It was out at the farm, the day he helped Charlotte deliver her lambs."

"When we thought he had skipped town," Cass said.

"Right. He was clearly disturbed by Alan's death. And he said something strange, with unusual feeling. He said he shouldn't have come here. At the time I thought he meant because of everything that had happened, but I think it was more than that. I think Cass is right that he planned to come to Sea Harbor. And for a reason. He wasn't just passing through."

"Did he say anything else?" Birdie asked.

"Yes." Nell forced her mind back a few days, to standing outside the barn and feeling Glenn's sadness like a heavy rain. To hearing the bleat of the sheep in the background.

"He said he had come to Sea Harbor because someone had asked him to come."

Someone had wanted him to come to a little town halfway across the country from his home.

They stopped at Harry Garozzo's on their way back from the library. They had missed the lunch crowd and hoped to get in and out quickly. Although Cass had declared that she'd probably never eat again after their Dutch breakfast, that was several hours ago and she could hear her stomach working up to a grumble.

Harry stood behind the counter, wiping his hands on his smudged apron. His ruddy face lit up when he saw Birdie, Nell, and Cass.

"M'ladies, where've you been? It's been days," the deli owner bellowed. Margaret threw him a quieting frown from the stove.

With a quick nod to his wife, he lowered his voice. "Sorry, ladies. But it's just pure happiness seeing all of you. I cannot contain it." He grinned and beat his chest with stubby fingers.

"All right, you crazy Italian," Birdie said, laughing. "Just calm down and tell us what's your best sandwich today."

Harry lifted his palm like a salute. He'd take care of it.

Then he looked off into the restaurant area of the deli, nearly empty now except for a few diners, and leaned over the glass case. He said, "Jerry Thompson was in for lunch today. He and that pretty Elizabeth came in with Claire Russell. Nice to see. And I think it was friendship they were sharing, not business. They sat off in the corner hoping no one would bother them, but you could just see the world pushing down on that poor man's shoulders. He's a bothered man for sure. Margaret watched me like a hawk, worried I might go over and ask him something I shouldn't, like why in the you-know-what hadn't they taken the scumbag off the street. But I wouldn't have done it, not with Claire sitting right there and missing Alan the way she does. So I didn't get too close to say much. I just gave Claire a hug when they left and slapped the chief on the back nice and hard."

"We have a fine police department, Harry," Nell said. "They're doing their best."

"Sure we do, sure we do, and sure they are. But it's time to put the city back on its feet, Nellie. At my mother's Sunday dinner I asked Angelo what he knew about the case. I asked him about the Mackenzie fellow. Not much, he said, except that Mackenzie's a good guy. He likes him."

"I do, too," Birdie says. "Your brother has discriminating taste."

The fact that Harry didn't have more to say about Glenn was probably a good sign, Nell thought. The gossip may have slowed down.

Harry put his beefy arms on top of the counter and leaned even closer to them, the garlicky smell of marinara floating from his apron to the women just inches away. "I'm thinking there was something going on at that clinic, something not so good."

"What makes you think that, Harry?" Birdie asked sweetly.

"Arlene Arcado comes in here a lot. She used to come in for my chicken piccata to take to her mother when she was so sick. Never saw a more devoted daughter. Got so she'd fight with me or Margaret if we didn't get the spice just right. Feisty, mad. Make us do it over. A real protector of her ma, that one. Anyway, she was in today—she had a salami on rye and was just about to leave when that one came in." Harry nodded toward a diner in the far corner.

Dorothy Barros sat alone, finishing a slice of Harry's lasagna and staring out the window between bites.

"Arlene was getting up from her chair, getting ready to leave, and Dorothy went clear up to her, stopped her dead in her tracks. Dorothy put her hands on her hips, her face just inches from Arlene's. I couldn't tell from here what she was saying, but she was talking fierce-like."

"What did Arlene do?" Cass asked.

"Nothing. That was the weird thing. I've seen Arlene in action. She could control an army to get what she wanted. But she didn't say a word to Dorothy, not that I could tell, anyway. She just picked up her bag and smiled at her—a hard smile, you know what I mean? The kind someone gives you when they're telling you to back off."

"And did she back off?" Nell asked.

"Yep. That was the crazy thing," Harry whispered. "She did; she backed off, and the lady doesn't do that easily."

Out of the corner of her eye, Nell saw Dorothy Barros get up. She slipped a large flowered bag over her shoulder and began walking in their direction, her eyes scanning her check and her lips moving as she checked the numbers.

"How was the lasagna, Dorothy?" Harry asked loudly as she approached.

Dorothy's head shot up. "Lasagna?" she said, as if she had no idea what he was talking about. At the same time she spotted the other women and forgot about Harry, managing a surprised hello. She had a wary look on her face, as if they might be there with bad news or to arrest her.

For a moment Nell was afraid Dorothy might be about to make another scene, demanding again that Ben get Garrett's job back, even though his employer was dead. Demanding help. Disturbing the few customers still in Harry's shop.

But she didn't. Instead, Dorothy acted as if she was in a hurry. She rummaged around in her purse for something. Finally she found what she was looking for and pulled out a large key chain filled with keys and trinkets and plastic grocery store cards. As she tugged, one of the metal trinket loops caught on the shoulder strap of her purse.

Cass said later Dorothy had the strength of a horse to snap the purse shoulder strap the way she did—*crack!* Like she'd sliced it with a knife.

The strap fell from her shoulder, the purse broke loose, and in the next instant, it fell to the tile floor—the contents spilling around their feet, coins rolling beneath the deli counter, paper receipts fluttering everywhere. The clatter and *clink*s were as noisy as a video arcade.

Dorothy gasped.

In an instant Cass was on the floor, scooping up brushes and change, lipstick and T passes, pens and tissues and eyeglasses, boxes of mints, rolls of stamps, aspirin and candy bar wrappers. In what seemed like seconds she was upright again, handing Dorothy her bag. Full and intact. "You're going to get curvature of the spine if you don't lighten that thing up a bit," she joked.

Dorothy's face was beet red and dots of perspiration covered her forehead. She mumbled what might have passed for a thank-you—or something else. Then she turned and rushed out of Garozzo's Deli without a backward glance, her unpaid check still clutched in her hand.

They left Harry sweeping up the remains of Dorothy's purse and in no time had walked down the street and into the cozy confines of Izzy's back room, the bag of sandwiches securely in Cass's arms.

Izzy was leaning over the pocked library table, cleaning up a mess of yarn threads and scattered patterns.

"Where is everyone? It's Saturday afternoon," Nell said.

"Jeez, no customers, no class. Are you going out of business?" Cass dropped the bags of warm pastrami sandwiches on the table and looked around the empty room.

"It was Gabby's day to teach preteens how to knit another of her crazy hats. You know, the ones with the huge flowers? This time she's doing winter ones. Thick and woolly—with huge flowers on the side."

Birdie looked worried. "Didn't anyone show up?"

Izzy gave her a squeeze. "Of course they did, you worrying *nonna*, you. A whole happy crowd of giggling girls. But Gabby and her friend Daisy decided the day was way too beautiful to stay inside, so they marched all the girls down to the pier, where they'd be inspired by the fish and boats and lobster traps. I swear if she had a bus and could drive, they'd all be out at Lambswool Farm."

Nell laughed, imagining the line of young girls sitting on the pier with their colorful yarn, knitting and purling to the pulse of boat horns and screeching gulls and wild music pumped through iPods.

"So, *voilà*, the room is ours," Izzy said, hands spread wide. "And

I'm starving; you're just in time." She opened a white bag and began pulling out wrapped sandwiches and bags of chips. "So, what did Harry dish up for us?"

"Plenty," Cass said.

"Oh?" Izzy said, her eyebrows lifting into her bangs. She held a sandwich in midair.

Nell and Birdie looked over, curious at Cass's tone.

Cass took the sandwich out of Izzy's hand and pulled out a chair. She sat down and shook her head, brushing it all off and not completing her thought, mumbling something instead about needing food or fainting.

Nell went over to the small refrigerator and brought back four plastic bottles of water. She opened her bag and pulled out her computer and the copies of the articles and Web pages that they'd printed at the library.

"We found out lots about Glenn's life."

"It was straight out of a Disney movie," Cass said. She licked a river of rich, creamy horseradish dressing running down her finger. "But I think there's something in all this. We waited to read it more carefully with you."

Izzy was speed-reading the article—a trick she had learned in law school, one that Nell had never understood. Why would anyone speed-read when they could read slowly, savoring words and the way they were put together? It was the same thought she had when people devoured in less than an hour a beef Wellington that took all day to fix.

"You said you have a list of dates, too?" Izzy asked, looking up from the article. "I like these people, by the way." She tapped the printouts with a fingertip. "Glenn's no murderer. Not with a family like this. He even had a godfather—the church kind."

Nell handed her the list of dates while Izzy chewed a bite of sandwich, her eyes running down the article, underlining things with her eyes. Strings of sauerkraut fell to her plate, but she didn't seem to notice.

"Apparently Glenn's parents married shortly after she graduated from college," Birdie said. "That hardly happens anymore. Late twenties is more the average, I hear."

"Where did Ann Mackenzie go to college?" Izzy asked.

"It's in one of the articles. A women's college in Cleveland, I think," Nell said.

Izzy found it quickly and pointed to the college name. "I've heard of it. The mother of a friend of mine from Kansas City went there. It's an exclusive women's college—or at least it used to be. My friend's mother said the rules were very strict back then and she told us wild stories about how the women would sneak out on weekends, meeting up with guys from nearby colleges. My dad's closest friend went to Case Western in Cleveland—it was a few blocks away—and he confirmed the stories and said that those nice Catholic girls sure knew how to party."

"That's what happens when you're too strict," Cass said. "Remember that when Abby's sixteen."

"Sam says no boys until she's thirty," Izzy said. "And then only if he can go along."

Speaking of Abby made Nell remember another photo in the article. "Did you see this one, Iz? It's very sweet." She pointed to the family picture of Glenn being baptized, a beautiful Christmas tree in the background.

"Well, now, that's interesting," Birdie said, leaning in.

"He was a handsome baby," Nell agreed.

"No, I mean the Christmas tree."

Izzy looked at the photo and then at Birdie, and then at the list of family dates once more. "Birdie Favazza, you are one giant step ahead of all of us. Very interesting." She sat back in the chair, her smile going from Birdie to the piece of paper.

Birdie smiled back with satisfaction. "I'm wondering if Glenn's sweet mother might have been one of those nice private school girls who snuck out on weekends, who just needed to let loose once in a while," Birdie said. "It's certainly a thought, now, isn't it?"

Izzy looked at the date sheet, grabbed a marker, and circled some items. "It was a big year for Ann Wallingford Mackenzie. A graduation, a marriage, and a beautiful baby boy. All in a few short months."

Chapter 30

The results of their library work had slightly unnerved Nell. As they had said earlier, some personal information should stay that way—personal and private. And she instinctively thought that this might be one of those times.

Both of Glenn's parents seemed to be lovely people—amazing people, in fact. Everything they'd read told them it was true. And an interview video they found of Max Mackenzie only confirmed it. These were good people who did good things. So who cared—or whose business was it to know—exactly when Ann Mackenzie got pregnant with her and Max's cherished son or in what order the important events in her life happened?

Birdie thought there was a chance it *was* their business, and Nell agreed to make a simple phone call that might, at least, calm those thoughts.

There was so much noise in the background that Nell could barely hear Carly Schultz when she answered her cell phone. Carly shouted that she was at Andy Risso's apartment listening to the Fractured Fish practice for their concert that night over in Canary Cove. They were going to pass the hat for the Starving Artists cause. They were all coming, right? The band was counting on it.

Carly then moved into the kitchen so they could hear each

other, and Nell told her the reason she had called. Carly laughed when she heard what Nell asked.

Of course she knew. "Doc Alan told me it was his wife, Emily, who had insisted that all the Hamilton doctors' diplomas were framed and hung," she said. "She was proud of him and didn't want anyone to think he wasn't a real doctor. Doc Alan called it his rogues' gallery. You've probably seen them yourself and paid no attention."

So of course she knew where Alan had gone to medical school and when he graduated, because she saw the lavish, gold-framed diplomas every day at work. He went to a really good school in the Midwest, she added. One of the best.

When Nell hung up, she repeated Carly's reminder about the Fractured Fish concert that night in Canary Cove to all of them.

Only then did she tell them where Alan Hamilton had gone to medical school.

And they agreed that Birdie might be right: Ann Mackenzie's graduation and marriage and little Glenn's birth might well be very much their business.

And other people's, too.

It was the rush of girlish laughter that stopped their serious discussion midstream and sent Nell, Cass, and Birdie to the main room of the yarn shop.

Daisy and Gabby were back, leading the rest of their entourage down to the back room to finish up their knitting session with brownies and soft drinks.

Izzy rejoined her friends once she had settled the girls. "It's late and I have to get home. Mae's going to close up for me. We have a sitter coming tonight for this Starving Artist thing. But jeez, we all need to talk."

They needed to do more than talk. But that was a start.

"I feel we've opened a jigsaw puzzle and tossed it up into the air," Cass said. "Ten pieces landed perfectly—a clear and perfect image. And the rest are scattered to hell and back."

They walked outside, making ordinary plans about meeting up that night, knowing it would be difficult to talk and it wasn't at all where they really wanted to be.

But tomorrow, for sure. Tomorrow they would figure it out.

"Figure it out?" Nell asked, pulling out her keys. "I don't even know what that means right now. We're following Glenn's footsteps, but are we going to like where they take us?"

Cass listened, standing on the sidewalk, looking off into space as if she stood in her own lonely world. Finally she said to the others, "We can't jump to conclusions, for sure. Think of all those pieces scattered out there.

"And there's something else, something I wasn't going to talk about yet—and I'm not at all sure how this fits into the puzzle, but it's at least related." She paused slightly as if she wasn't sure whether to continue. And then she did. "My ma always told Pete and me not to mind other people's business—we had enough to do to pay attention to our own. But, heck, we've already stepped over that line today—"

"So what are you saying Cass?" Izzy said with slight impatience. "I have to get home. Out with it."

Cass looked at Izzy and told her quickly about Dorothy Barros dropping her purse in the deli. She looked at Nell and Birdie. "You saw it all spill out, but you didn't see everything."

And then, in short, clipped sentences, she told them what she had so discreetly scooped up and pushed back into Dorothy Barros's bag before Harry had a chance to see it. Surprises, she said.

Ben was getting ready to leave the house when Nell got home.

He apologized. He'd forgotten to tell Nell that he had an early reception to attend. A command City Hall performance. The mayor was having a reception for some big-time businessman from Boston who might be opening a branch office in Sea Harbor. Ben and Danny had to make an appearance because they were on an advisory committee. Beatrice Scaglia had also talked Sam into coming because he was famous, or at least that's what Sam joked. Apparently the businessman liked his work.

They would come over to Canary Cove afterward, but they'd be late—and much better dressed than anyone else there.

Nell straightened his tie and kissed him. But made him stay just long enough to listen to the information they'd pulled together that day.

Ben was quiet and thoughtful. He didn't know quite what to think about it, or if it was even worth thinking about. His thoughts were not far from Nell's, feeling deep down that Glenn was not a murderer. And that probing into his private life deserved caution.

Did they really want to open that part of a man's life unnecessarily?

Ben's final words before he headed out the door left Nell with a hollow feeling.

"You know if you're right about this," he said, "you might be making Glenn Mackenzie's life very difficult. You may be throwing him under the bus."

Since the men were going to come later, the women decided to go to Canary Cove together. Izzy volunteered to drive.

It was a sweater night, and Nell grabbed a heavier one than usual, feeling a chill she wasn't sure was from the northern breeze.

"Did you get a chance to talk to Ben?" Izzy asked.

Nell shared what Ben had said as they pulled into Birdie's drive.

"Sam had the same mind-set, but with more doubt. He asked if

I had any idea how big Case Western Reserve was. A huge medical school, he said. And then he started talking about statistics, the chances of this person being in that place on that date and on and on. Talk about a needle in a haystack, he said."

"They both like Glenn," Nell said.

"We do, too. That means nothing," the lawyer in Izzy said.

Birdie had already climbed into the backseat, catching the end of the conversation and piecing it together.

But they all knew that it wasn't just the dates, the years. It was all the other things surrounding it that added heft to their theory. It was Glenn Mackenzie coming to Sea Harbor for no apparent reason. It was the sadness they had all seen in his eyes when Alan had died. It was the many snippets of conversation that Nell was piecing together. He loved his father, the judge, there wasn't any doubt about that. Max Mackenzie had been bigger than life.

Cass hadn't seen Danny to talk about it. He had already headed out to the mayor's reception, Cass said. In a way, she was okay with that. She didn't really know what to say about their day. They had nosed into someone else's life with the hope that they'd be able to come closer to who'd killed Alan Hamilton.

But in the process, they may have come closer to incriminating a person they didn't want it to be.

Izzy and Nell drove down the hilly drive from Cass and Danny's house to the art colony's public parking lot. It was mildly crowded, but they knew it would get more so as the night went on. People liked the members of the Fractured Fish as much as they liked their music. And when a good cause was involved, they'd come in droves.

"Where's the band setting up, anyway?" Cass asked. They were walking along Canary Cove Road, toward the center of the art colony, where the street was blocked off to traffic. Gallery doors were open for the evening, and people roamed freely in and out of shops. The spirit seemed good, almost like a normal night.

"I think it's that grassy area at the very end of the road where it splits off toward the water," Nell said. She pointed ahead and they could see a small stage and people unfolding chairs, staking out their space. The band was already there, tuning and strumming and testing equipment. Nell spotted Willow helping Pete with extension cords and waved. She looked to see if Glenn was there. The band members had been good about including him in things while he was still in town.

But more people crowded in, blocking her view, and she followed Izzy, Birdie, and Cass into the Brewster Gallery and out of the fray.

Jane waved from the exhibit area on one side of the shop, and they headed her way.

Nell spotted Garrett Barros standing near the counter. Ham was helping a customer and Garrett was standing alone, looking uncomfortable. She smiled at him, but he had looked away, spotting someone to the side. His face relaxed and a smile eased away the tense look. Nell looked over.

Arlene Arcado was standing at a side door that led to a small sculpture garden. Garrett headed toward her.

Such a strange friendship. Arlene was a loner, according to M.J. And so was Garrett. Maybe that was what made it work. But it still seemed odd to Nell, and she couldn't quite put her finger on why.

Nell let the others go ahead and walked over toward the side door to say hello. Or talk. She wasn't sure. The gallery was crowding up, and by the time she worked her way through, Garrett and Arlene had moved out to the patio.

Just before she reached the door, Arlene's voice stopped her. It was strong, annoyed, louder than usual.

"You need to tell your mother to stay away from me, Garrett," she said. Her words were controlled but edged with anger. "Listen to me clearly. You need to do that for me. She can't come to me to do her favors like you did. And if you don't keep her away from me, you know what will happen." She stopped talking, waiting.

Nell could hear Garrett sigh, and she imagined his thick shoulders slumping, his head hung low. "She needs me," he mumbled, his voice ragged and barely audible.

But in those few words, Nell knew that Garrett hadn't killed Alan Hamilton. Losing his job had been an awful thing, but not for Garrett. Garrett would be fine.

Nell slipped back into the shadows and turned away, moving through the gallery crowd, looking for the others. The welcome sounds of the Fractured Fish warming up filled the gallery and she headed toward the door as they began their concert with a favorite cover. Pete's voice was as melodious as Paul McCartney's as he pulled the crowd up to sing with him, *"All together now!"*

Birdie was standing just outside the door, clapping her hands to the music. Pete had pulled Daisy and Gabby up to the front, and they'd happily joined him, counting, clapping their hands.

Birdie looked over at Nell.

Nell was clapping, too, but her head was turned, and she was looking back inside, where Garrett Barros was standing at the gallery counter again, this time looking as if he had lost his best friend.

They all met up later, Izzy and Cass having wandered around looking for Ben and the others. They found them near Willow Adams's Fishtail Gallery, far enough away from the music to hear one another. Izzy texted Nell and Birdie to join them.

They'd paid their dues, they all decided. They'd stuffed bills in the pot going around for donations to the Starving Artists fund, they'd listened to the music, and they'd clapped—and now they were all ready to call it a day.

Even Izzy and Cass, often the holdouts, were ready to cash it in.

The weary group walked back to the parking lot together, looking as if they'd been doing hard physical labor all day. Their bodies as tired as their spirits. They all stopped when they reached Izzy's car to pair up—Cass riding with Danny and dropping Birdie off, Nell with Ben, Sam taking the keys from Izzy.

"I'm up the road," Ben said to Nell, then turned to Cass as they started to walk away. He stopped, remembering something. "Cass, I want to get this straight. Tell me again what you found in Dorothy Barros's purse," he said. "Are you sure it wasn't Advil or aspirin?"

Nell was hoping the same thing. That Dorothy Barros had an ailment, and along with it, a prescription or something to ease a pain as simple as arthritis.

"Positive. I wouldn't have thought much about it. People have legitimate needs for Percocet," she said. "I had a prescription once when I broke my foot. But not a half dozen packets. And not in sample containers that have HAMILTON FAMILY CLINIC scrawled across them."

Cass lowered her voice. Then she stopped talking completely as a shadow appeared from behind Izzy's car. At first they thought it was someone heading for his car, but when the figure stopped, ducked, and then moved slowly between two cars, Izzy held up her hand to tell the others to stay quiet. She was closest to the car, just a few feet from the noise. Finally, while they looked on in silence, the shadow morphed into a person.

"Hi, Garrett," Izzy said softly. "I didn't see you there at first. You frightened me for a minute."

"I'm sorry, Izzy. I wouldn't want that. I wouldn't want to scare you."

His hands were shoved in the pockets of baggy jeans. Finally he pulled his gaze away from Izzy and looked over at Nell. "I know you saw us talking, Nell. Right? You heard my friend Arlene. She was upset, but it's okay—she's trying to explain, or . . ."

When he didn't complete his sentence, Nell nodded to put him at ease. "It's all right, Garrett. I understand. Arlene was right. She shouldn't do what your mother is asking her to do. What she asked you to do when you worked for Dr. Alan. Arlene can't take medicine from the clinic for your mother."

"My mother needs it so bad," Garrett said. His head was turning back and forth. His eyes squeezed shut, fighting back tears. "Doc Alan wouldn't prescribe it for her. I begged him to, but he said, *No, Garrett, it'd be bad for her.* So I had to wait until he wasn't around and I was cleaning up, and I'd take it myself. Just a few. They're little. Doc Alan was wrong. It wasn't bad for her. She told me it would make her feel better, and it did. It was the only thing that made her feel better."

"I know that's why you did it, Garrett—and I bet it seemed like your mother felt better for a little while. You were trying to be a good son. You were helping your mother, but you can't just help yourself to medicine like that," Izzy said kindly. "Arlene was right."

He shook his head, "No, she doesn't think . . ." And then he stopped and started over, his voice resolute. "I had to help my mother."

"Medicine that a doctor has to prescribe can be dangerous. And you know not to steal," Izzy said.

Garrett's face was in shadows, but they didn't need to see it to know he was in pain. His voice was filled with anguish. "I don't know if you're listening, Izzy. I had to do it—don't you understand? Please don't tell them. It will be better now because my mother says I'll get my job back when a new doctor comes. Arlene'll put in a good word for me."

Suddenly Nell felt chilly. She wrapped her arms around herself. Garrett was so earnest; he sounded so truthful. But she wasn't at all sure of the ramifications of what he was saying—and she wondered if he himself knew.

"Dr. Hamilton didn't want to fire you," Izzy was consoling him.

"But doctors take their medicines very seriously, Garrett. What you were doing was very wrong, and he had to let you go so you would stop. You didn't leave him with any choice." Izzy's voice was steady.

"I loved Doc Alan. He was very nice to me. But I knew . . . I knew it would be so awful for my mother and she would be so mad. She told me she'd kill herself if I didn't help her."

"Did anyone else at the clinic know what you were doing?" Izzy asked.

Nell was happy Izzy was doing most of the talking. Garrett liked her. He seemed to respond with less fear when she was the one talking to him.

"Just Arlene," he said. "But she would never tell on me . . ." He stopped, a sheepish look on his face. "We're friends. We help each other.

"When Doc Alan caught me, he was so mad. So awful mad." He shook his head as if the worst thing he had done were disappoint a doctor he loved.

Garrett looked at Izzy as if she were the only one there. "You won't tell anyone, will you? Promise me, Izzy?"

"Garrett, did you hurt Dr. Hamilton?"

Garrett's whole face collapsed. Fat tears ran down his ruddy cheeks. "No, Izzy, no, no, no. I would never have hurt Doc Alan. How can you even think that?"

He turned abruptly, until his back was to them, his large hands falling to his sides.

And then he walked urgently away, as if they'd all come running after him if he didn't hurry. His lumbering turned into a jog, faster and faster, until all they could see was a dark flurry of sweatshirt racing down Canary Cove Road as if his life depended on it.

Chapter 31

Sam and Izzy stopped over at the Endicotts' for a nightcap on their way home. A half hour earlier they were asleep on their feet, but now, after talking with Garrett Barros, they were too wired to sleep.

"I don't think he even knows exactly what this all means," Sam said. "Garrett is high functioning in some areas, but not this kind of thing. He was doing what his mother told him to do. It was the right thing to do, what he had to do."

What wasn't addressed was how any of it related to the murder of Alan Hamilton.

"He said *now* he'd get his job back," Izzy said. "That sounds ominous, like maybe something had been planned."

"I don't think that's what he meant," Nell said. "I think he means what he says: that he loved the doctor. I don't think Garrett can lie. He didn't lie to the police. No one knew why he was fired—he could easily have made something up. But he didn't. He just kept quiet. *I can't tell you* was all he would say to the police. I think his only crime is taking the opioids from the clinic because his mother told him to, and because he thought if he didn't, his mother might commit suicide."

"And it made her happy," Izzy said sadly.

Nell nodded.

Ben added that one of the things the clinic staff valued about Garrett was that he didn't argue; he'd do whatever anyone asked him to do. He was a helper.

"Which Don Wooten said about him when he worked at the Ocean's Edge," Nell said.

"He became a hero in his mother's eyes," Ben said. "Something I suppose every child wants to be. And I am one hundred percent with Nell on this. I don't think Garrett could have pulled off an arsenic poisoning unless someone else carefully monitored it. From measuring the poison, to dissolving it, to giving it to Alan. And even then, even if it would have helped his mother in some way, I don't think Garrett would have done it. It doesn't seem feasible on many levels."

Hearing Ben describe Alan's murder so methodically was chilling, and for the second time that night, Nell wrapped her sweater tightly around her.

Izzy said, "All right, if not Garrett, then who?"

"Dorothy Barros had a motive," Nell said.

"Motive maybe," Sam said. "But I wonder about access. She's a very noticeable woman, and I think if she'd been prowling around the clinic or restaurants Alan ate in or his neighborhood, trying to get poison into his food or drink, someone would have called the police pretty fast. Probably Alan himself. Dorothy is scary."

The image of Dorothy barging in the office to demand Garrett's job back popped into Nell's head. "Yes, she's noticeable," she said. And excitable, and probably not thinking clearly half the time because she is in an opioid haze.

"Do you think Robert Barros knows what's going on in his family?" Izzy asked.

Ben poured a little more scotch in his glass and passed the bottle to Sam. "I ran into Jason Smith the other day. He's the foreman of the plant where Robert works and he somehow feels he needs to give me reports on Robert because I recommended him for the job."

"What does he say about him?"

"That the guy volunteers for extra shifts every chance he gets. He's a quiet guy, a good worker, and Jason thinks he wants to *not* be home, to put it nicely."

Nell looked at Ben and saw what was running across his mind. Robert Barros needed to check out his insurance policy and find a facility for his wife that would help her with a serious illness, because that's what addiction was.

It was Ben's first day back on the sailboat, and Nell was nervous, but Sam and Danny were both going along. And maybe, if they could wrest him away for a couple of hours, they'd take Jerry Thompson with them and put some color back in his face.

Nell was secretly pleased to have the private time. Izzy was, too. She called her aunt before Sam was barely out the door. "It's a perfect day," she said. "The shop is closed. Abby's babysitter is asking me if she can have her for the afternoon. She's getting some kind of credit toward a babysitting certificate. Who knew? So I'm going on a hike to clear out the cobwebs and make me sane again. It's all getting to me, Aunt Nell. Wanna come?"

Of course she did. Izzy couldn't have suggested anything that would have pleased Nell more—not a trip to Belize, Hawaii, Paris. A hike with Izzy was the perfect way to clear out the dust storm in her head, but even more, spending alone time with her niece was pure luxury.

Murder investigations be damned.

She forgot to ask where they were going, but it didn't matter. After packing a few roast beef sandwiches, water, and apples into her backpack and rummaging into the closet for a windbreaker, she was off.

"I'm thinking Halibut Park," Izzy said, climbing into Nell's car. She flung a fleece into the backseat. "It's easy and beautiful and sure to cure what ails us."

Nell thought it might take more than the state park to do that, but the exquisite coastal park, spread out on a magnificent ancient granite slab, was one of her favorite spots on earth, and she wasn't about to argue.

They arrived around noon to an almost empty parking lot—a few cars and an old bike leaning against a tree, unchained. Nell glanced at it. "That looks familiar."

"It's an old bike, Aunt Nell. You've seen hundreds of them."

Of course she had, like the one in her own garage. "I think someone is watching over us, Izzy. All this silence. It will be like our own little retreat."

They linked arms and walked the short distance to the Babson Quarry. They stood at the edge of the deep silent pool, their eyes focused on the bottomless blue water.

"You don't think Garrett killed Alan, do you, Aunt Nell?" Izzy asked.

Somehow, in this pure beauty, maybe they would find the answers they were looking for. "No. On the outside, Garrett looms large and even scary sometimes, but he's soft and sweet on the inside. And he has an awful crush on you, Izzy."

"Me and Arlene. I think she's winning."

"Do you think?" Nell chuckled. On the other side of the quarry a little boy shouted his name. *Simon . . . Simon . . . Simon . . .* It echoed across the deep pool.

"Arlene is interesting. Maybe she's been good for Garrett."

"And maybe not," Izzy said. "I'd like to talk to her about Garrett. Make sure she isn't playing games with him. He doesn't need that."

No, none of them needed games.

Nell began walking again and Izzy followed. They took to the loopy trails beyond the quarry, listening to the wildlife in the distance. For a long time they walked in silence, finally heading over to Halibut Point to find a spot to sit.

Izzy pointed to a smooth ledge and they climbed over the ridge and settled down on a slice of granite, backpacks off and the sun warming their faces.

"It's hard to imagine anyone having a reason to kill Alan," Izzy said. "That's what makes this so hard. His patients liked him. No one kills without reason, do they? At least not that kind of killing. Not a planned, orchestrated, systematic poisoning."

"It's hard to imagine. Unless they thought the doctor had hurt them in some way."

Nell thought about what she'd said as she opened her backpack. Carly Schultz had said something similar. "Or had hurt someone they love. Maybe that's it, not the patients themselves," she said. She hadn't pursued the thought with Carly when she brought it up. It didn't seem relevant then. Now she wondered, and she tucked the thought away.

"Hmmm . . ." Izzy said, and slipped on her sunglasses, thinking about Nell's comment.

"I remember when my mother—your grandmother—was dying. Your mom and I took turns being with her. We wouldn't leave her alone because we didn't trust the medical staff to be as diligent as we were." Nell laughed a little at their staunch advocacy efforts. "If your grandmother wanted a sip of water, we wanted the nurse to have it there ten minutes ago. I'm sure they were all excellent doctors and nurses, but we wanted a miracle—that was the bottom line—and they weren't giving it to us."

"Do you think Alan Hamilton had patients—families—like that?"

"Probably. I don't know if you can be a doctor or nurse and not have times when patients or families are dissatisfied with you."

"Dissatisfied enough to kill you?"

Nell pulled out two sandwiches and handed one to Izzy. "Well, now, that's a whole new direction. Consider this, your uncle Ben and I are Alan's patients. Can you imagine, if one of us were very sick, you being angry at him if you thought he wasn't doing all he could—even if he were?"

"Of course. In a heartbeat. Probably not enough to kill him, though. At least I hope not."

Nell caught a piece of tomato falling out of her sandwich and tucked it back in. "It's difficult to see someone you love suffer. I think that's partly what made Garrett steal those pills. His mother was in pain, and then once he gave her the pills, she said she felt better."

"But instead of killing Alan for not giving him the pills, he simply took them when Alan wasn't around."

Nell smiled. "Perhaps the better part of valor."

"For sure." Izzy pulled up her knees and wrapped her arms around them, looking off at an endless view. "I think that's Maine," she said, pointing.

Nell pulled a hat from her backpack, putting it on and looking out over the sea. Izzy's observations were interesting—and important. They had all talked about stepping outside the circle that the police had drawn. She was feeling more certain that that was the direction in which they should be moving. "Carly knew Alan for a while. She could give us some insight into him. Into all of this. Unhappy patients—or patients' families."

"His families include most of Sea Harbor."

"He had lots of patients, true."

Izzy took an apple out of Nell's pack and shined it on her jeans. She took a bite, her face in deep thought. "It's good we've released Garrett from that awful secret he was carrying."

"I think so, too. Ben isn't sure what will happen, but Garrett has good support, and the fact that Alan never reported him is helpful. It's not officially a theft, I suppose. Ben talked to Father Northcutt before going off sailing today. He knows the family well. And now maybe Dorothy will get the treatment she needs."

"And Garrett can be crossed off our list."

"I suppose that remains to be seen, at least if we're trying to be objective. The motive is still there no matter what Garrett said."

When they finally left their perch an hour later, Nell felt renewed. She wasn't sure if it was the magic of being with Izzy, the beauty of Halibut Point, or the feeling that they'd finally pushed themselves to look at Alan Hamilton differently. And certainly to look at his death in a different light.

She hoped the new focus would magnify things that had been in front of them all along. Not complicated and fabricated. Human nature at its deepest level.

They packed up their sandwich wrappings and apple cores and walked back along the wildflower-lined path to the parking lot, the smell of bayberry following them.

"What's that?" Izzy asked. She pointed off the worn path to a grassy area. "It looks like a backpack."

They walked over to a bulky canvas pack leaning against a tree. Izzy looked around for an owner.

At first they didn't see anyone, and Izzy crouched down, looking more closely at the bag, checking for a name. "It's a camera bag," she said.

"Izzy," Nell said softly. "Over there."

Izzy stood and followed the point of her aunt's finger.

A few feet away, oblivious of his surroundings or the women standing nearby, Glenn Mackenzie sat on the top of a granite boulder. His feet were pulled up on the rock, his chin on his knees and his arms wrapped tightly around his legs.

His weeping was a mournful sound, as silent as the quarry water.

Chapter 32

Their first thought was to quietly walk away as if they'd not seen him, not to intrude on his privacy.

Nell wasn't sure why they didn't. But without a word between them, she and Izzy walked quietly over to where Glenn sat.

It simply seemed like the right thing to do.

Glenn looked up at the sound of footsteps. He registered little surprise, then wiped his eyes with his sleeve and smiled. He motioned to a small boulder a foot away, a bench at its side. His gesture and expression invited them into his space.

Izzy pulled herself up on the granite rock. Nell sat on the bench.

Finally Nell said quietly, "Grieving takes many forms. It has its own timetable." She let the words be, not sure where Glenn would take them.

For a long time he said nothing. His breathing was even and regular. Finally he looked at them with a slight nod of his head.

"You're grieving your father," Nell said.

Glenn again registered no surprise. But his face had relaxed, the protective mask gone.

"Both of them," she added.

Glenn breathed deeply. His story unfolded in starts and stops, but in the end it wasn't a long story. Izzy, Cass, Birdie, and Nell had put together pieces of it. What had been missing was the emotion that informed it all.

Glenn knew he was adopted almost from day one, he said. Maybe when he was still in utero. There were no secrets in his family. Even the story of how he came to be was told to him when he was old enough for the words to make sense.

It was a wild one-night romp before graduation. His mother knew the med student, but not well—he was one of the good ones, though, she had told him. Smart and handsome and nice. But not a boyfriend, no one she would want to spend her life with. Nor he with her. Their lives were just beginning—and going in totally separate directions. She loved Max Mackenzie, even before he knew it.

She was back home in Arizona and had accepted Max's proposal when she found out she was pregnant. Alan had graduated, too, left Case Western, and Ann had no idea where he'd gone, no interest in finding him.

Max had been overjoyed when she'd told him of her pregnancy. He couldn't have children—and now he had not only the love of his life but a son. From all reports, he was a crazy man when he heard, Glenn said. Crazy with joy.

Nell noticed that whenever he mentioned Max Mackenzie, Glenn's face lit up. Sad and happy, and missing his father profoundly.

When they finally headed to the parking lot, Nell realized the old bike they had spotted when they'd arrived was Mary Pisano's. Glenn had made it all the way to Halibut Park on the ancient vehicle.

"I'm sure that's the longest distance it has ever traveled," Nell said. "You'll never make it back."

They loaded the bike into the back of her CR-V.

The next chapter of Glenn's life came out as they drove out of

Halibut Park and headed back to Sea Harbor. He had never had any interest in finding Alan Hamilton, he said. The opportunity had been offered to him many times, but the fact that someone else had provided sperm seemed somehow inconsequential. No man could be a match for his father.

His dad's friend Brady Sorge had found Alan a few years before, mostly to surreptitiously find out if there were medical issues that might be important for Glenn to know about. "Brady and my dad were quite a pair," Glenn said, laughing. "They had ways of getting information that would surprise even Mark Zuckerberg.

"I'm not sure why, but when I got to be an adult, my dad thought I should at least see for myself the man who had been instrumental in my 'coming to be,' as he put it. He suggested I come here, and when he died, Brady repeated it. They didn't put pressure on me—it was okay if I didn't do it. And I probably wouldn't have if my dad hadn't died. Somehow that put a different spin on it. Like it was something I had to do for him, not so much for me. So I did. And here I am." He looked at Nell. "Like I said to you the other day, I probably shouldn't have come. Look at the mess I've made of things."

They drove along the coast, waves crashing and the sun setting, the car filled with quiet and memories.

And the thought that Glenn Mackenzie wasn't the one who had made a mess. No, not at all.

"I had decided just to come and look," Glenn said a while later. "And then to leave. I didn't tell anyone why I was here because it was private, and I never intended to do anything. I didn't come here to mess up anyone's life. But then I saw this man, a really fine doctor. Running a clinic that had been in his family forever. A man who cared about the people in this town. And I saw how much the town cared about him.

"I liked him. It was unexpected—I never intended to get close enough for any kind of emotion. But it happened. I wanted to learn more about him."

Nell didn't say a word, didn't ask, but the question in her head was so loud she was sure Glenn must be hearing it: *Did you tell Alan Hamilton he had a son?*

Glenn rested his head against the seat back and went on, almost as if talking to himself. "I don't know exactly how it happened," he said. "But that night at the farm, we sat together on a bale of hay and talked, and we discovered that we both loved medicine, tennis, philosophy, skydiving. All sorts of things. It was kind of amazing. And I told him then what I had promised myself I wouldn't."

Izzy was the one who said the words, because Nell's voice was caught somewhere in her throat, unable to find a way out.

"You told him he had a son."

Chapter 33

Nell was up early the next day. She hadn't slept easily the night before, and wandered downstairs to put the coffee on, not knowing exactly what this Monday would have in store for her. The thought was a discomforting one, full of uncertainty, and it wasn't lessened at all by urgent texts from Birdie and Cass.

Cass was off most Mondays, and if Izzy needed to be at the shop, they'd camp out there. Birdie had even added a little homemade emoticon to her text—a circle. With arrows pointing out of it.

She had already answered the texts and had one cup of coffee when she heard Ben coming down the back stairs. She looked over to see him trying to button his shirt collar.

She walked over and quickly tugged the tiny buttons through the holes. "A meeting?" she said, glancing at his creased slacks.

"Sort of. I just got a call from Jerry Thompson. It looks like Glenn was there at the station when the chief came in to work this morning. He told Jerry he needed to talk to him. He needed to get everything out in the open, especially why he'd come to Sea Harbor in the first place. It's great he's being so up-front about it, even though . . ."

Nell's face fell. *Even though in a detective's eyes, Glenn Mackenzie now had a serious motive for coming to Sea Harbor and killing Alan*

Hamilton. The clinic and all Alan's property would be his. The next of kin. An easy inheritance from a man he'd never met.

Was Ben right? Had they indeed thrown Glenn under the bus?

When they'd picked apart Glenn's life and his family, the furthest thing from any of their minds was that Glenn would inherit anything. And they knew with some intuitive certainty that it would be the furthest thing from Glenn's mind, too. It wasn't just that he seemed to have plenty of money and that it wasn't a priority to him. It was that he didn't ever intend to claim the relationship with his father. All he'd wanted was a look . . .

But it was the first thing Ben thought of.

Nell had tossed and turned all night, thinking about Alan and his wife, Emily, and their desire for a son. And Alan finding one the night he had died. Her eyes widened suddenly when she thought back to the last time she'd seen Alan. As sick as he was, there was happiness in his pain. And he'd tried to tell her something. *Sun,* she thought he'd said. Sunday. *Tell Claire.*

But he wanted Claire to know he had a *son.*

Some things that had happened in the last couple of weeks fell into place in a new way, now—the emotional look from Glenn reaching all the way down the table the night of the Lambswool Farm dinner. Nell had thought he was looking at her, though he hadn't reacted when she'd smiled at him.

But he wasn't looking at her at all. He was looking at the man sitting next to her. The man whose life had just become entwined with his own.

And the sadness when he died, the interest in his office and history. There were so many things that became clear in the glaring light of hindsight.

Ben poured a cup of coffee and drank it carefully, keeping it off his shirt. "Jerry asked Father Northcutt and me to come down together, try to figure this all out. What it means and what it doesn't mean."

"Does Lily Virgilio know about what's going on?"

The news that Lily would own the entire Delgado mansion once Alan's estate was settled was already known around town. Probably because Beatrice Scaglia knew.

"I don't think anyone knows, except for the group of us. It hasn't had time to work its way into the grapevine. But you know it will, and not through Glenn. It's those bored cub reporters and groupies that hang around City Hall and the station, I think. They have a sixth sense for this sort of thing."

He left then, not doing a good job of masking his worry, but assuring Nell that everything would be fine.

Izzy had decided to stay home with a coughing, cranky Abigail; Mae was in charge of the shop, so Birdie, Cass, and Nell shifted gears and agreed to meet later at Izzy's home.

Izzy called Nell back with one request. Would she pick up some reports from Mae that she needed to look at? Oh, and maybe a quart of Harry's chicken soup for Abby. Wasn't chicken soup the cure for everything?

Nell smiled to herself, and then stopped, remembering Harry talking about chicken piccata. She frowned until the memory came back, along with the conversation. And the image it painted. One she'd almost cast aside. This time she tucked it closer to the front of her memory.

She'd be happy to pick up the soup, she said. And the reports. She had to pick up a couple of books from the Brandleys' bookstore anyway.

Nell found a parking spot right in front of Izzy's shop. She hurried in and got the reports from Mae, then walked next door to Harriet and Archie's bookstore.

She waved to Archie, who was standing behind the counter

with a customer. And then she spotted Harriet Brandley sitting in one of the old easy chairs near the coffeepot, her knitting in her lap. Nell walked over, smiling before she even got there. She needed a dose of Danny's sweet mother today.

Harriet Brandley brightened up a room, no matter where it was. Even when she'd gone through breast cancer treatments in the middle of the worst winter Sea Harbor had ever had, she kept her spirits up, starting, among other things, a knitting group to make hats for chemo patients.

"Harriet, you are a feast for sore eyes. How are you?"

"Fit as a fiddle, Nellie dear. Had a checkup last week and I'm blessed, is all I can say. But feeling so sad about our dear Alan Hamilton for sure, just like we all are. Such a good man."

"Was Alan your doctor?"

"Is the Pope Catholic?" Harriet laughed, and then she said, "I went to a Boston oncologist for treatment. But dear sweet Alan did everything else, monitoring me, treating the pain. Even stopping by the house in the middle of a snowstorm when Archie'd get worried because I had a slight fever or a tiny ouch somewhere." She *tsk*ed at Archie's silly worry.

Nell laughed. She reminded Harriet of the knitting group she and her friend had started that winter. "Such a good thing."

"Good for us, for sure. Agnes Arcado helped me with that and what a good time we had, giggling and laughing and acting like we had the world at our fingertips. Dorothy Barros helped us, too. She was having that awful back pain and wanted a distraction. We even made *her* smile now and then. Anyway, Agnes and I went to the same oncology practice. Archie would drive us both to Boston for treatments and help us hand out the hats. Agnes had that awful cancer, you know. So painful. Finally she couldn't do the treatments anymore. There comes a time when you know you have to just stop."

"And that's when Doc Hamilton steps in," Archie said, coming over to say hello. "A saint, that man was. Killed me when people said differently."

Harriet *tsk*ed. "Archie," she said.

Archie shook his head. "I know, I know. Don't speak ill."

Harriet smiled at Nell. "It's hard to see people you love in pain, that's all. So hard. Agnes had a lot of pain."

Nell thought, *Of course.* She remembered her father again. It was an awful time.

"I have those books you ordered ready, Nell. Should I put them on your charge?"

"Books? Oh, sure, sure, Archie," she said, distracted. "That'd be great."

She leaned over and gave Harriet a quick hug, took the bag from Archie, and walked down the street to pick up Abby's soup, her head filled with uncomfortable thoughts and a sudden headache threatening behind her eyes. She shook it away.

Cass and Birdie were both ready at their doors when Nell picked them up, as if there was something important about to happen and they needed to be ready. They arrived at Izzy's home in time to see her putting Abby down for a nap.

Izzy ushered them to the back of the bright, open house, to the big old pine table Sam had found somewhere years before and Izzy would never get rid of. She had replaced nearly everything else in Sam's bachelor pad when she'd moved in, but she loved the big old table, and before Abby was even born, she'd imagined her daughter doing homework on it.

Paper and pens were already on the table along with a laptop, and Izzy added coffee mugs and a loaf of banana bread.

"You baked this, Iz?" Cass said, smothering her slice in butter.

Izzy wrinkled her nose at her. "The lady next door bakes. We exchange Abby's smiles for muffins and banana bread. It works."

The night before, Izzy and Sam had gone by Cass's and Izzy had filled Danny and her in on their Halibut Park adventure; Nell had done the same in a phone call to Birdie.

"Being right isn't always nice, though, you know?" Izzy said, thinking of the problems they may have handed Glenn.

"Maybe, maybe not. This might be the shove we needed to find out who murdered Alan so we can end all this trouble for people we care about," Birdie said. "The answer is right there. Right in front of us."

"Was Glenn surprised we knew about his family history?" Cass asked.

Izzy wrapped her fingers around the coffee mug. "I don't think he was, not really. I think it has been on his mind so much and so vividly that he probably thought we saw it there, written across his forehead or something."

Birdie was doodling on her paper, her circle small—just big enough to hold Glenn and Lily and Garrett. Outside the circle was white space. Outer space, with arrows pointing into the vast whiteness.

"But it's not so vast," Birdie said. And somehow, they all thought that to be true. Their world was small. Sea Harbor, the clinic. Patients, friends.

Rather than broadening their search, it was becoming smaller in their minds, and something they felt they could get their arms around now.

They'd been scattered, following Alan all around town, devoting energy to who *didn't* do it. But there was one place where Alan's presence was predictable. Where it would be easy to reach him and find out what he was all about. Who he related to . . . or didn't. His practice staff . . . and his regular patients.

Nell shared dear Harriet's appreciation of what Alan did for his patients. Archie's observations were keen, too. Already a part of the puzzle that was coming together image by image. With the Hamilton clinic right in the center of it.

Cass said she felt silly that they'd skimmed over the clinic as if it were a bit player in the drama. Instead they'd concentrated on those connected only tangentially. But not what was at the heart of the clinic—the people who really cared about it, about Alan, about their medical care.

Birdie tapped on the paper with her pencil. "Alan drank coffee every day, ate at his desk often, paced around in the break room. I saw him do that myself," she said, adding that she had brought him some of Mae's muffins two weeks ago. And probably other patients did the same.

Dorothy Barros could have brought treats to the doctor, and could have come in on some other excuse, too—the clinic was a busy place.

"But the timing bothers me," Nell said. "Although they can't pinpoint exactly when the poison entered Alan's system, he was feeling sick for a few days before Ben broke his arm. Carly mentioned it to me when I said he looked pale. And that was before Garrett was fired."

"So before either he or his mother would have had a motive," Izzy said.

"That's right," Cass said, standing up suddenly as if they had said something of great significance. "So what if . . . what if the motive for killing him wasn't something that happened that week? What if it related to something that happened earlier? But this was the right time for . . . for what? For revenge or payback? For forcing Alan to do something maybe he didn't want to do. For . . ."

They all latched onto Cass's thinking, and their what-ifs continued for a while, with snippets of remembered conversation thrown in from clinic staff, from patients, from family members, even things overheard in places about town—like M.J.'s hair salon. And finally, when the pieces of Cass's virtual puzzle began to form images in front of them, one piece locking into another, they all sat back and looked at one another.

Birdie finished the last piece of banana bread and stood up. "It's not solved. But almost," she said decidedly.

The arrows were pointing in the right way. Out of the circle. And suddenly Dr. Alan Hamilton's doctoring—and his patients—came under the microscope in a brand-new way.

Birdie had to pick up a prescription at the clinic. Perhaps they could have a look around while there.

They left Izzy's, promising to text any developments, and drove out of the neighborhood of small, well-kept houses, slowing down for the Big Wheels and strollers scattered about.

Nell had one stop to make first, she said. M.J. had called to say her hair products had come in.

That was fine with Cass and Birdie, and Nell drove down Harbor Road in search of a parking spot. When she couldn't find one in front of the salon, Birdie offered to go in. "Just double-park right here," she instructed, and she climbed out of the car and went inside.

Through the window Cass and Nell watched M.J. greeting Birdie with a hug, then walking with her to the desk, talking the entire time. "It's why we come here," Nell said. "Where else do you get a hug before your shampoo?"

A few minutes later Birdie was back. She climbed into the car and handed Nell the salon bag.

"What's that smile?" Nell asked, looking at her curiously.

"It's that cat-and-canary look," Cass said from the backseat. "I'd know it anywhere. Out with it, Birdie Favazza."

"Just another piece of grist for the mill. If we're going to keep track of Hamilton clinic staff and patients, we need to keep our facts straight." The smile disappeared. It was a good feeling when their instincts took them in the right direction—and quite awful at the same time.

Someone behind Nell honked, and she started driving slowly up the street.

"So what is it, Birdie?" Cass asked.

"It's Carly Schultz. She misled us," she said. "At least according to M.J., and she certainly should know. She said Carly and Arlene Arcado absolutely did *not* work together at Ocean View. Carly was wrong, she said, and certainly knew better."

"What?" Nell felt a sharp stab of disappointment, partly because she didn't want Carly to be wrong about anything. Also, the thought of Carly lying to them was disturbing.

"That's what I said. M.J. was about to expand on it, but a frantic stylist rushed up, grabbed her arm, and said her client's hair had turned pink. M.J. seemed to think that was of greater importance and rushed off. She didn't even charge me for your bottle of shampoo."

A car came around Nell too fast, impatient with her slowness, and Nell bit down on her lip, concentrating on driving again as she made a right turn.

In front of her, traffic slowed as they neared the post office drop-off lane, and Cass glanced out then rolled down her window, calling out to Garrett Barros.

"Hey, Garrett," she said. "How are you doing?"

Garrett smiled, a welcome sight. They all were concerned about the recent turn of events in his life. Nell pulled over to the curb and he walked up to the window, carrying a parcel. A messenger bag hung from his shoulder.

"Hi." He looked slightly sheepish. "Is Izzy in there?" He peered into the backseat.

"No, she's at home," Cass said.

"I didn't mean to scare her last night. Or any of you guys—you know that, right?"

"Don't you give that a second thought," Birdie said. "You look good today, Garrett. I hope that's how you're feeling."

He nodded and his smile grew. "I have a good job. Jane and Ham Brewster let me do all sorts of things that I like to do—I order all their art materials, and I pick 'em up and keep track of them. I'm good at that." He showed Birdie a tablet and opened it, pointing to his excellent record keeping, the perfect printing, the neat columns. "I like doing it like this. Keeping order. I used to do it for Doc Hamilton, too. Order all his supplies and then pick them up."

At the mention of the doctor's name, his smile faded, but it came back when he explained that the Brewsters were helping his dad figure things out for his mother. She was going to a place where she'd get to feeling better, he told them.

So Robert had already looked into rehab for Dorothy. Jane and Ham were instrumental in making it happen, they all suspected.

While he was talking, Garrett opened his messenger bag and pulled out another lined tablet, just like the one he had shown Birdie. "Here're my records from Doc Hamilton's office. We had lots of things coming in."

"Oh?" Birdie asked. "You still have those? Do you think they might want that for their own accounting?"

Worry shadowed his face. "I shoulda left it. But it was my own tablet. And I was just so, you know, upset." He stared down at his tablet as if it hurt his hand now to hold it.

"Of course you were upset," Birdie said kindly. "I'm going over there right now. Would you like me to return it for you?"

Garrett looked like Birdie had just given him a Christmas present. He thrust it into her hand. "Thanks so much. You guys are great." He checked his watch. "I gotta go now."

"A date?" Cass teased.

Garrett blushed. "Nah. Just meeting a friend from the clinic. We're having a beer at the Gull." He announced it with a note of pride in his voice. Then he touched the brim of his baseball hat, tucked his chin low, and moved off across the parking lot to his beat-up truck, a happy look on his face.

Nell exchanged looks with Cass and Birdie. And then they all watched him walk away.

"He will be fine," Birdie said, but her words didn't carry their usual confidence.

"Can I see that?" Cass said. She leaned over the seat and took the tablet from Birdie. "My cousin is an engineer and he prints like this. So perfect and exact."

Birdie agreed. "It's beautiful. A lost art."

Cass leafed through the pages and shook her head. "I wouldn't have the patience. But this is very cool, what he does. You could do it on the computer, too, but it wouldn't look like this."

"And it seems to bring him pleasure. Like art does." Nell pulled back into traffic, and in a few more turns, she pulled into the clinic parking lot. The lot was half-full, a respectable number of cars, but not as busy as usual.

She turned the engine off, and she and Birdie opened their doors and grabbed their purses, then looked to the backseat and noticed Cass wasn't moving.

"Cass?" Nell said. "Do you want to wait out here?"

"No. It's just . . . Well, this is interesting," Cass said, her voice almost hushed. "It's a record of everything Garrett ordered and picked up for Alan Hamilton and the clinic staff. Look at this." She folded back the page and passed it over the seat. Some of the entries were familiar, some surprising, things you don't think about that an office needs to keep running. Paper and pens, toilet paper, soap, sugar, coffee. A wreath.

Garrett had recorded the information in columns: date, company, item, initials.

Alan had trusted him with a lot—aspirin and syringes, bandages.

And then there were a few orders that Birdie read out loud. A Barbie doll from Amazon. Two romance books. A Halloween mask.

Nell shook her head. "I think that happens in a lot of businesses. Staff sneaking purchases in with supplies. Intending to pay back the postage. Do you suppose Garrett knew that he was ordering a birthday present for some staff member's child?"

Birdie chuckled. "If he was told to do it, he'd do it. No questions asked."

They read through the page, and it wasn't until they got to the bottom that they understood the hushed sound in Cass's voice.

"The office manager probably doesn't even know this exists," Birdie said.

Nell looked at it carefully, then at Birdie. "What do you say we keep Garrett's notebook for a while?"

Birdie tucked it into her purse.

Chapter 34

They ran into Lily Virgilio in the lobby of the building. She was pointing out the paintings in the art exhibit to a patient. When she saw Nell, Birdie, and Cass come in, she excused herself and walked over.

"Is everything all right?"

"We're fine, Lily," Birdie answered. "Just here to pick up a prescription, and we thought we'd check out the new paintings in the process."

"They're lovely, aren't they?" Lily said, her voice normal, but her body showing the tension they were all feeling. "I think our next display will be kids' paintings from the community center. What do you think? And the money from sales can go into the art therapy program we're starting."

"Lily, do you sleep?" Nell asked.

Lily smiled. She looked around the lobby, determined they were alone, and said, "I heard about Glenn Mackenzie and his relationship with Alan."

They waited for a reaction, for disbelief or dismay, but Lily's face was calm, peaceful, even. And then her mouth tightened slightly, her eyes holding back something—moisture or emotion. "The great sadness is that Alan wanted more than anything to have a son. He has one—and not only that, but he's a doctor, too. And he can't experience the joy of sharing his life with him."

Lily nodded at a patient walking toward the entrance. She turned back. "Alan and I were friends for a long time. And a disagreement over the future of the backyard of this building may have caused a lot of sound and fury, as the Bard says, but truly, it signified nothing. We would have worked it out. I'm not sure what the outcome would have been, but it would have been something we both would have lived with—and we would have remained friends."

If Nell could have written a mini speech for Lily, that would have been the one. It was exactly as she would have predicted it would be. She had no idea if Glenn would walk away from whatever was legally his or not, but whatever happened, it would be all right.

Lily's face turned to one of concern, and Nell read it clearly.

No matter what happened with a historic building or a backyard or a medical practice, Alan's murderer had to be found.

"Lily, it will all be over soon," Birdie said.

Everyone looked at Birdie with a touch of surprise. But not really. Birdie might not have known every one of the particulars, but she was always a small step ahead in pulling something down from the heavens—a message, an intuition. No one ever knew for sure.

When they left Lily and walked into the Hamilton clinic, empty chairs brought them back to reality: a first for the busy practice. Nell wondered where the patients were going, or if people were putting off checkups, vaccinations, blood pressure checks.

Nell looked around to see whether Arlene was there, then remembered Garrett's happy face. They would find her later. A sudden sadness gripped her tightly, like a wind that came from nowhere and blew straight through her. Birdie touched her arm lightly, the feelings passing from friend to friend.

As much as they all wanted Alan put to rest, for Claire to find some closure and peace, and for the murderer to be brought to justice, Nell hoped, for that one frozen moment, that their suspicions were wrong. That they had taken a bad turn somewhere, that it was all some kind of a terrible mistake.

Evil couldn't lurk in a place of healing.

Behind the desk a woman with a name tag that read GEORGIA answered the phone and took notes. Nell had seen her before. She wondered absently if she had a little girl who wanted a doll for Christmas.

Birdie was talking with Georgia and the receptionist smiled, then waved her toward the door that led to the dispensary. Birdie motioned to Cass and Nell and they all walked through the door and down the hall to the library and lab, with the dispensary and Alan's office adjacent to them.

Although there were nurses' aides and a lab technician and a few patients headed toward examining rooms, it felt empty. Devoid of its soul, somehow.

How sad, Nell thought. Alan's clinic always had a spirit about it—a kind of hopeful vibe that made being sick not so bad because you knew you'd get better. He'd help you get better. He'd help the pain go away.

Usually.

But what if he couldn't?

"Nell?"

Nell's head shot up. "Carly, hi. I'm sorry, I was daydreaming. We were hoping we'd run into you."

"We?"

"Cass and Birdie are here somewhere. Birdie had some medicine to pick up."

Carly nodded.

"Is everything all right?"

"Yes. No. It will be."

"What's wrong?"

"One of the lab technicians didn't show up. And Arlene quit. It's adding insult to injury."

"Arlene quit?"

Carly nodded. "She's leaving."

"Leaving?"

"Town. She has a job offer in Boston."

Cass and Birdie walked out with Birdie's medicine and looked from one to the other. "What's wrong?"

Carly just shook her head and Nell looked behind them, through the door to the library and file room. "Let's step in here for a minute," she said, and urged Carly inside.

Carly leaned against a bookshelf and forced a smile. "It's just the day. It will be better."

Nell told Birdie and Cass about Arlene's leaving.

"That's okay, though," Carly said. "It's probably a good thing."

"Because you didn't get along?"

"Not that. It's just the awful reminders. Especially now, with Doc Alan not here." She leaned over and picked up a piece of paper that had fallen to the floor, unwilling to say more.

"Carly, there's something we need to ask you," Birdie said gently. "It probably doesn't matter, but it's puzzling because you've always been up-front with us."

Carly frowned. "What do you mean?"

"That night in the kitchen, you told us that you and Arlene worked together at Ocean View, but her aunt said—"

Carly's eyes were huge. "Oh, no. That's not what I said. I said I knew Arlene at Ocean View." She slumped down on the chair then, her hands shaking.

And then the tears came.

Birdie found a box of tissues, and in between the tears, in a quivering voice, Carly told them about her. And Arlene. And Ocean View.

But most of all about Dr. Alan Hamilton.

Chapter 35

The desk sergeant put her right through to the chief.

"Nell," he said, surprised. "Ben is here. Did you need him?"

Nell explained that she was calling from her car, but could he please put Ben on for a minute? It would be easier somehow to lay it out to Ben. He could finish her sentences, read into half meanings, and clarify whatever she managed to mush together.

It took only a few short minutes to tell him about an order for arsenic revealed in Garrett's log, a cancer patient in unbearable pain, and a daughter who didn't get the miracle she asked for. A daughter who wanted to even the score. Who wanted someone to suffer like her mother had suffered. The doctor who hadn't stopped the pain.

Dr. Alan Hamilton.

Nell told Ben that Garrett was heading toward the Gull when she'd seen him earlier. He was meeting a friend from the clinic. His good friend who had exchanged favors with him. She kept his secrets and he kept hers.

For once Garrett's large frame was a blessing. They spotted him right away, straddling a stool in the darkest corner of Jake Risso's nearly empty Gull Tavern. Next to him, Arlene Arcado stood, her hands on her hips, as if giving an order.

Garrett's face was sad, his head bowed. This time Nell suspected he really was losing his best friend. Or at least the person who had pretended to be that.

Garrett spotted them first. He started to stand, to say hi, to make it an ordinary day.

A flash of something that might pass for fear flickered in Arlene's eyes, then disappeared just as quickly. She sat down on the stool next to Garrett.

"What are all of you doing here at this time of day? Shouldn't you be knitting or something?"

Arlene's voice had changed, the tone edgy.

Birdie spoke first, her voice kind. "You never mentioned Dr. Alan cared for your mother at Ocean View, Arlene. I know that must have been an unbearable time for you."

Arlene refused to react, and Birdie went on. "Alan tried to help your—"

At the mention of Alan's name, Arlene snapped, cutting off Birdie's words. Her eyes blazed. "Alan Hamilton was a charlatan. He helped nothing. They were all idiots, but he was supposed to help her. He was her doctor. That's what doctors do. My mother was dying. She was in unbearable pain. And he couldn't—he wouldn't—he didn't make it go away."

"There are laws about narcotics, Arlene—rules. The doctors—"

"Are fools! All of them. Those stupid nurses were worthless. They never helped, but he was the worst because he was her doctor. He was supposed to make her better!" She was screaming now, her voice shrill and shaking. Garrett Barros backed away, as if suddenly he didn't know who she was, this woman who had been his friend. Who had kept his secret when he'd stolen the medicine, and he'd done favors for her in return. Placing orders. Signing his own initials, just in case . . .

Nell looked back and saw Jake Risso move out from behind the bar. He glanced toward the door, and she guessed Jerry Thompson and Tommy Porter were there. Ben and Sam right behind them.

"I wanted him to suffer; that's all I wanted. I wanted him to feel what my mother had felt, to scream like she had screamed. I wanted him to throw up and be dizzy and have his stomach twist in knots. I wanted him to feel like his head was exploding and his body ached and throbbed. I wanted him to know what pain was."

Arlene seemed to deflate then, slowly, the air releasing from her lungs. Afternoon sunlight came through the blinds behind her, slices of dull light slanting across her body. Her shoulders sagged and her voice dropped so low that they all strained to catch her words, the last before she slumped to the floor. She looked up, and for the first time since they had known Arlene, her face registered something that resembled regret.

"I wanted him to suffer. But I didn't mean for him to die."

Chief Thompson and Tommy Porter walked across the barroom floor and stood near Arlene, waiting until two police officers came and read her her rights.

She was no longer the Arlene any of them had known—not the competent waitress or the flirt or the woman who'd managed an entire waitstaff at the Lambswool Farm dinner.

Not the daughter who had screamed at and abused and vilified a nursing home staff.

All the fight and venom that had been fueling her, keeping her alert, waging her war, was gone.

Nell looked at her with great sadness. Arlene was a rag doll.

They stepped aside as the policemen helped her to her feet and watched her leave walking between them, her head lowered and her eyes vacant.

After they left, Birdie pulled Garrett's record book from her purse and handed it to the chief. She smiled at Garrett, assuring him it was all right.

The arsenic had come from a company in China. It had Garrett's initials in the last column.

Garrett stared at his neat writing. "Arlene saw me taking the pills," he said slowly. "But she promised not to tell—that's what friends do for each other. And I could do favors for her, too, and keep it a secret. She needed something for her house, to clean her garage. She had mice or rats or something. So sure, I ordered it from work just that once. And I signed right there." He pointed to the page. "But she paid for it. It was okay. She didn't steal it."

He looked so ashamed that Nell had to stop herself from putting her arms around him.

Arlene had planned it carefully. On the off chance someone figured out what the order was for, it would be blamed on Garrett. His word against hers.

Next to Nell, Birdie was explaining to Jerry that Carly Schultz would have more details. She and Alan had both taken care of Agnes Arcado when she was dying at Ocean View. Arlene had been there every day and every night, her mother's advocate.

And she'd never forgiven any of them for not pulling out a miracle, for not being able to erase all the pain. For not saving her mother.

It was over.

Nell looked back to where Arlene had slumped to the floor. The last words she had uttered rang there, loud and clear—and sad.

"I wanted him to suffer. But I didn't mean for him to die."

Chapter 36

They'd done what Birdie had asked.

By the time the first harvest dinner was scheduled, the lazy peace that marked the end of summer gently rolled down the streets of Sea Harbor, all the way to the green pasture land on the edges of the town.

And true to everyone's prediction, the first ever Lambswool Farm harvest dinner was an outstanding success.

The guests were gone, the restaurant critics off to write eloquently about the mesclun, arugula, and fennel salad; the butternut squash ravioli; the root vegetables; the mushroom pie; the vegetable terrine. The list went on and on, the innovative creations made from ingredients that began as seeds in Claire's garden and were turned into magical dishes by the featured chef.

Magical was the word Birdie heard most. *Amazing* and *fabulous* were Claire's favorites.

But no matter what words were used, no one left hungry—they all agreed on that. And no one left not wanting to come back as soon as they could get reservations for another Lambswool Farm event, which might be a whole season or two away, the way reservations were selling out.

Claire collapsed at a table she and Birdie had reserved for a special group. They called it the "friends" table, although the friends all called themselves staff. Izzy, Cass, and Nell had come early, decorating the tables with Izzy's felted baskets, then filling them with hand-knit vegetables that looked good enough to bite into. They added candles and name tags, folding orange and plum napkins into wineglasses, all up and down the long elegant table.

In spite of the sadness that had surrounded them for weeks, everyone wanted and needed to move on. Arlene would have good lawyers, Jerry Thompson had told them. And hopefully, despite the awfulness of the deed, her lack of intent to kill might generate some leniency in the sentencing. It was over, and now they would rebuild.

And that night, with a hazy moon shining down on them and the spirit of the harvest everywhere, it was time to begin doing just that: ushering in a new spirit and leaving the sadness behind.

The men had come that night, too—Danny, Sam, and Ben. They followed Angelo's directives, smoothing the parking lot and posting signs.

Claire and Birdie had issued a special invitation to Glenn, who was still in town wrapping up some legal matters, and he'd accepted with gratitude. Even Father Northcutt showed up to help string lights. He also offered to provide a blessing, if desired, not realizing at the time that the blessing might be for farm animals.

Despite the late hour, Birdie was refreshed and animated as she ushered off the last of the guests. Her small body almost bounced as she said good-bye to members of the jazz band and waved off Angelo and his crew.

Father Northcutt approached the group, declaring Charlotte's lambs duly baptized, then looked down at Gabby, who had insisted on—and planned—the ceremony.

Claire laughed. "I'm sure Charlotte is relieved," she said, and gave the padre a hug.

Glenn Mackenzie trailed behind the priest. Gabby pointed at him with a grin and announced that he was the lambs' godfather.

"Not my idea," Glenn said quickly.

"It's only right," she said. "And you know that being a godfather brings certain obligations, right?"

"I'm sure you'll let me know," Glenn said, tugging on her ponytail.

"So," Gabby said, looking up at him, "are you going to tell them or what?"

Glenn laughed. He looked around the table. They were all sitting quietly, watching him.

They had all wondered when Glenn would be leaving for Arizona, but no one had asked. They knew his postdoc was waiting, his research, and his return to the world he'd left what seemed like a lifetime ago.

The kitchen noise was diminishing, the parking pasture almost empty except for their own cars. Ben had brought a bottle of scotch to the table and was passing it around.

"Well, sure, Gabby," Glenn said. "I guess this is as good a time as any."

Gabby sat down next to her *nonna*, a pleased look on her face.

Glenn started in, explaining first that he had talked to Brady Sorge, his godfather, the last couple of days. A few times, in fact. Brady was a wise and funny man, a wonderful mentor. "You'll all enjoy him when he comes to town," Glenn said.

"He's coming to Sea Harbor?" Nell asked, surprised. *Will you come with him?* went unspoken.

"Yep," Glenn said. He had run an idea past Brady, he said. Brady had listened to the whole thing, taking it all in, and when Glenn finished, he told his godson that it was about time he had finally gotten some sense into his thick head. "His words were more colorful,"

Glenn said, "and probably appropriate—but anyway, that was the gist of it."

Glenn's father had never liked the idea of his going back to school—and neither had Brady Sorge. He'd been there too long, they both thought. What was he hiding from, anyway?

"Brady has his own idea of what research is—a big glass building with books and papers and no people. *'That's not you, Glenny,'* he told me. *'Life's too damn short. It's time to start living it.'*"

Glenn chuckled as he repeated the conversation. "The man may cuss like a sailor, but if you can weed out the message, he's usually right, just like my dad was."

So he'd decided he'd do what Brady said. He would start living life. For now, taking over the Hamilton clinic seemed the right way to do it. There'd be a few tests to take, licenses to get. But in the end, he'd keep the Hamilton legacy alive.

"The doctor in the clinic might have a different name," he said, "but the tradition will continue. From son to son to son, that sort of thing. It'll be Alan's clinic. Here to stay for a few more years. He'd probably like that."

How he and Lily Virgilio would settle things wasn't discussed. Not then. But Nell suspected it would turn out just fine.

Sometimes things just worked out and life began again, fresh and new.

In the distance, the bleating of a new mother as she settled down with her lambs brought the sentiment full circle.

New life. A new day.

Yes, sometimes things simply worked out.

Izzy's Felted Bowl

Izzy knit and felted this bowl for the Lambswool Farm dinner table.

Materials

- Size 11 circular or double-pointed needles for the beginning
- Double-pointed needles for the end (when the decreases begin)
- One skein of Noro Kureyon or any worsted-weight yarn. I used color #74. (For a firm bowl, use two skeins.)
- Markers
- Tapestry needle

Abbreviations

CO	cast on
BO	bind off
pm	place marker
st (sts)	stitch (stitches)
st st	stockinette stitch
k	knit
p	purl

dpn	double-point needles
ssk	slip, slip, knit
K2tog	knit 2 stitches together

The gauge is not specific, but it should be very loose.

Tips on yarn and felting

For a firmer bowl, use two worsted-weight strands held together or a bulky yarn. Do a test swatch on a new yarn before starting your project to be sure it will felt correctly. Caution: do not use superwash wool. It's treated not to felt in the washing machine. In addition, white or off-white yarns do not felt well, as the bleach has usually destroyed the fibers to some extent.

Instructions

CO 75 sts. PM and join to work in the round, being careful not to twist the stitches.

K in st st until piece measures 5½ inches from CO.

Decrease as follows, changing to dpn as necessary:
Round 1: *ssk, k11, k2tog; rep from * to end of row—65 sts

Round 2: k

Round 3: *ssk, k9, k2tog; rep from * to end—55 sts

Round 4: k

Round 5: *ssk, k7, k2tog; rep from * to end—45 sts

Round 6: k

Round 7: *ssk, k5, k2tog; rep from * to end—35 sts

Round 8: k

Round 9: *ssk, k3, k2tog; rep from * to end—25 sts

Round 10: k

Round 11: *ssk, k1, k2tog; rep from * to end—15 sts

Round 12: *ssk, k2tog; rep from * to last 3 sts, ssk, k1—8 sts remain

Finishing

Cut yarn, leaving an 8-inch tail. Using a tapestry needle, pull the tail through the remaining stitches on the needle. Weave in all loose ends. Remember that felting will make the ends virtually disappear; however, you must eliminate any large holes or gaps by darning them before felting. Felting will not close them up completely.

For a bigger bowl, cast on the number of stitches that will give you the size you want and decrease by ten stitches every other row until the last row. (For example, for a third bigger, start with 100 stitches; 50 percent bigger, about 115.)

Felting

Before you felt, remove anything in the knitting that you don't want there—stray threads or lint, etc., will be felted into the fabric permanently and be virtually impossible to remove.

Put the bowl in a lingerie bag or pillowcase tied at the top. Put in the washing machine with a small amount of soap, at the hottest temperature possible. Add a pair of old jeans that you don't mind shrinking. Agitation is as important as hot water for felting, and if the bowl is by itself, there won't be enough agitation.

Turn on the washer. Check the bowl every few minutes to see how it's doing. There should be virtually no stitch definition left when it's finished. Reset the washing machine if necessary. Don't allow it to go into spin cycle—the spinning can stretch the bowl. When it's finished to your satisfaction, rinse in tepid water, squeeze out the excess, and roll the bowl in a towel. Press out as much of the water as possible. Dry the bowl for a few days. A coffee can or similar object placed inside the bowl will help weigh it down and flatten the bottom.

This pattern is used with the kind permission of Deborah Gray, the designer. Her Web site is deborahgray.org and provides a photo, along with additional tips on knitting and felting this pattern.

The Seaside Knitters thank her for permission to use it.

Nell's Shrimp, Pineapple, and Red Pepper Kebabs

(The Endicotts served this meal the day Ben broke his arm.)

Serves 4

Ingredients

Skewers (if using wooden skewers, be sure to soak in water for an hour before using)

1 pound large shrimp (cleaned, peeled, deveined, with tails on)
1½ cups pineapple chunks, fresh or canned
1 red onion, peeled and cut into chunks
1 red or yellow pepper, seeded and cut into 1-inch squares
⅔ cup pineapple juice
¼ cup lemon juice
¼ cup lime juice
2 tablespoons minced fresh ginger
Sea salt and ground pepper to taste
1 tablespoon red pepper flakes (if desired)
3 tablespoons soy sauce
3 tablespoons honey or maple syrup

2 teaspoons olive or sesame oil
¼ cup chopped cilantro
¼ cup chopped parsley
1 lime cut in thick slices for garnish

Directions

Preheat grill to medium heat.

Thread shrimp, pineapple, red onion, and yellow or red pepper on skewers, alternating ingredients.

In a small saucepan whisk together pineapple juice, lemon, and lime juices; ginger; soy sauce, and honey or maple syrup. Simmer mixture over medium-high heat until the liquid is reduced by half. Brush or drizzle the kebabs with the pineapple glaze. Heat coals.

Oil the grates and grill the kebabs for approximately 2–3 minutes per side. Brush often with the glaze. Grill until just cooked through and nicely charred. Sprinkle with cilantro and parsley; serve with lime slices.

AUTHOR'S NOTE: Printable copies of the pattern and the recipe are available on my Web site, sallygoldenbaum.com.